THE BLOOD OF IUTES

The Song of Octa
Book One

JAMES CALBRAITH

FLYING SQUID

Published December 2020 by Flying Squid

Visit James Calbraith's official website at
jamescalbraith.wordpress.com
for the latest news, book details, and other information

Copyright © James Calbraith, 2020
Cover photo: NataliAlba via Shutterstock

This book is a work of fiction. Names, characters, places and incidents either are products of the author's imagination or are used fictitiously. Any resemblance to actual events or locales or persons, living or dead, is entirely coincidental.

All rights reserved. Except as permitted under the U.S. Copyright Act of 1976, no part of this publication may be reproduced, distributed or transmitted in any form or by any means, or stored in a database or retrieval system, without the prior written permission of the publisher.
Fan fiction and fan art is encouraged.

THE STORY SO FAR

In the year 410 AD, the magistrates of Britannia voted to banish Roman officials and leave the Roman Empire. Years of civil strife and peasant rebellions followed, resulting in the Roman governor, Ambrosius, fleeing to the West, and a man called Wortigern taking over the rule of the eastern part of the island as *Dux* of all Britannia.

In 425 AD, the Iutes, a German tribe from the East, beyond the Narrow Sea, seeking refuge from a war encroaching upon their land, fled to Britannia. *Dux* Wortigern settled them on the small island of Tanet under their warchief, *Drihten* Hengist. One of the Iutes, a child of unknown name, fell overboard during the crossing and was taken in as foster-son by one of *Dux* Wortigern's closest comrades-in-arms, Pascent of Ariminum, who named the child Ash.

Under Master Pascent's care, much like his foster-brother, Fastidius, Ash was taught how to fight, how to read and write Latin, politics, diplomacy, the history and geography of the Empire. A rebellious soul, his first act of mutiny was defying his Master and eloping with the local girl, Eadgith. Though both were forgiven, Eadgith was banished from the *villa*, and Ash was sent to Londin, to prepare for baptism. It was there that he met his fellow Iutes for the first time, and discovered his roots — though not, yet, his true identity.

After playing a crucial role in helping settle the Iutes on the Briton mainland, and defeating an army of forest bandits led by warchief Aelle, Ash was given a seat in the Londin Council, at the right hand of *Dux* Wortigern; at that time, he fell in love with *Drihten* Hengist's niece, Rhedwyn — and earned himself jealous hatred of *Dux* Wortigern's only surviving son, Wortimer.

Now in his twenties, Ash found himself at the centre of events that changed Britannia forever. After helping foil Wortimer's first coup against his father, he supported *Dux* Wortigern in his struggle against Bishop Germanus, who arrived from Gaul ostensibly to stem the last vestiges of Pelagian heresy, but in reality, to undermine *Dux* Wortigern's rule and help his enemies come to power. Faced with excommunication, *Dux* Wortigern called for a Council of Bishops of Britannia; far from bowing to Germanus's power, however, the *Dux* used the Council to announce his turning to the faith of the pagan Iutes and, to cement his alliance with *Drihten* Hengist, the marriage of Rhedwyn and Ash.

None of his plans, however, came to fruition. Ash, recovering from a wound suffered during a hunt, remembered his past: he was Rhedwyn's brother; he was Aeric, son of warchief Eobba, and their union was, unwittingly, an incestuous one. Worse still for Wortigern, Wortimer and the Bishops allied against him and overthrew him for the second time, banishing the *Dux* and his supporters into the West.

Captured by the new *Dux*, Rhedwyn was forced to bear Wortimer's children, while Ash was tortured and nearly killed, before his fellow Iutes helped him escape. Under Wortimer's regime, the Britons waged war on all heathens, and while Ash led a resistance inside Londin, outside the city Briton armies destroyed Iute villages and forced the tribe back onto the island of Tanet. At long last, in 452 AD, Ash and Rhedwyn defeated Wortimer: Rhedwyn poisoned the *Dux*, but died herself giving birth to her daughter, Myrtle. Leaderless, the combined Briton armies were defeated in the great Battle of Eobbasfleot by an alliance of Iutes and Saxons, now led by the same Aelle whom Ash helped defeat many years earlier.

While in Londin, Ash reunited with his first love, Eadgith, and discovered he had a son, Octa, abducted by Wortimer's men. After the victory of Eobbasfleot, Octa returned to his mother and was sent to be tutored by Fastidius, by now the Bishop of Londin. Eadgith was given the rule of a small Iutish colony on the island of Wecta; however, the colony was soon attacked by a rebellious cousin of *Drihten* Hengist, Haesta — secretly allied with Aelle and his Saxons. Ash, sent to investigate, managed to repel Haesta's assaults, but not before Eadgith died in his arms.

Faced with the growing threats to the tribe's future, Ash — now known by his birth name, Aeric — saw no other option but to overthrow *Drihten* Hengist, disband the slow and ineffective gathering of the tribal elders, and declare himself king — *Rex* Aeric I of the Iutes. He also brought his son Octa back from Londin, to prepare him to one day inherit the king's circlet...

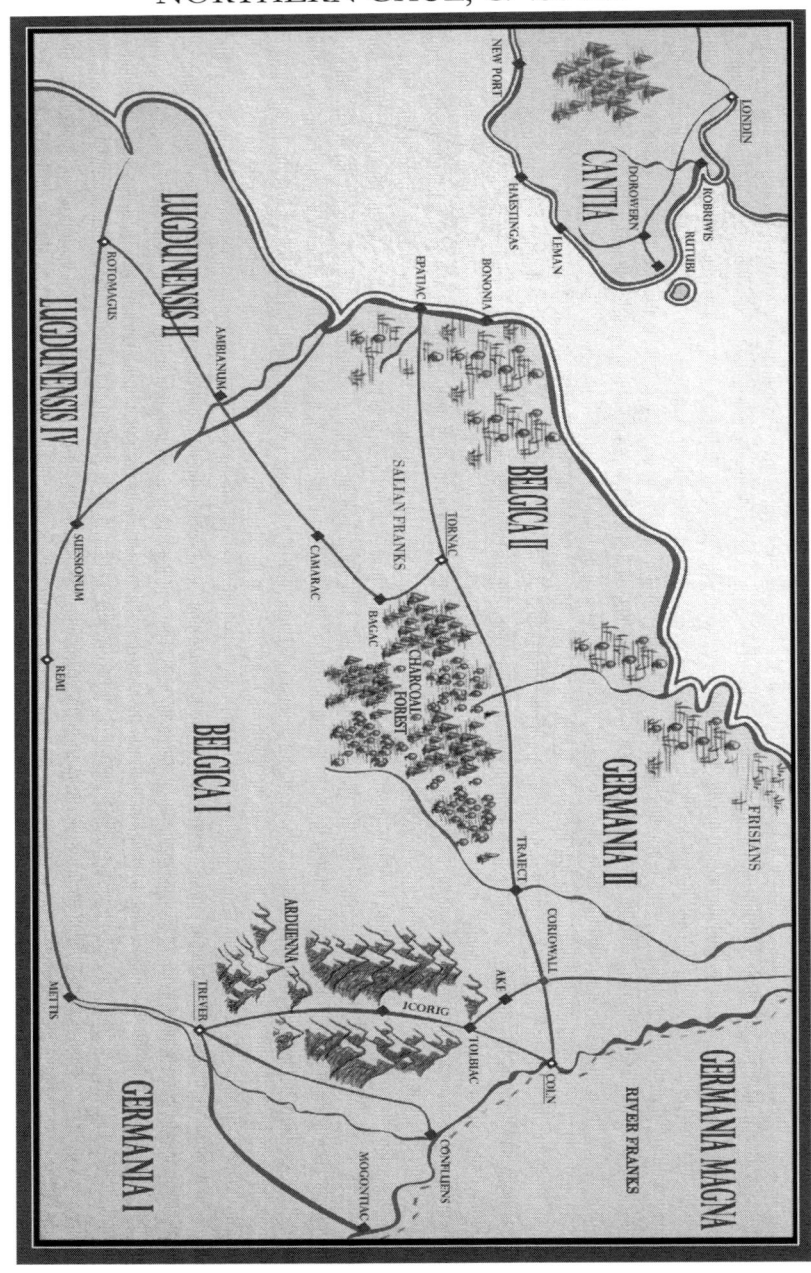

CAST OF CHARACTERS

Britannia:

Aelle: *Rex* of the Saxons
Aeric I: *Rex* of the Iutes
Betula: *Gesith*, commander of King Aeric's household guards
Fastidius: Bishop of Londin, brother of King Aeric
Haesta: rebel chieftain of the Haestingas clan
Octa: *aetheling* of Iutes, son of King Aeric
Hrothwulf: chieftain of the clan settled on the River Limenea
Ursula, Audulf, Gille and Bana: companions of Octa

Frankia:

Basina: Hildrik's betrothed, Thuringian princess
Clodeswinthe: wife of King Meroweg, Queen of the Salian Franks
Hildebert: chieftain of the River Franks tribe
Hildrik: *aetheling* of the Salian Franks, son of Meroweg
Ingomer: Meroweg's brother, chieftain and merchant
Meroweg: *Rex* of the Salian Franks
Sigemer: Meroweg's brother-in-law, chieftain of Camarac
Odo: former cavalry *Decurion*, now a merchant in Bononia
Weldelf: chieftain of a clan of River Franks
Seawine, Odilia, Oxa, Haeth, Nodhbert, Huda: Iutes captured by Frankish pirates

Gaul and Rome:

Aegidius Syagrius: *legatus* of Imperator Maiorianus
Agrippinus: *magister militum* of Gaul under Imperator Avitus
Arbogast: *Dux* of Trever
Asher: Rav, leader of the Iudaeus community in Coln
Avitus: previous Imperator of Rome
Falco: *Praetor* of Icorig
Maiorianus: Imperator of Rome
Odowakr of Skiria: barbarian warlord
Paulus: *Praetor* of Ake
Pinnosa: *Comes* of Coln

GLOSSARY

Caldarium: hot room of the Roman bath
Carcer: a prison
Ceol: narrow, ocean-going Saxon ship
Centuria: troop of (about) hundred infantry
Centurion: officer in Roman infantry
Circus: chariot-racing stadium
Comes, pl. Comites: administrator of a *pagus*, subordinate to the *Dux*
Curia: administrative building in a Roman city
Decurion: officer in Roman cavalry
Domus: the main structure of a *villa*
Drihten: war chief of a Saxon or Iutish tribe. *Drohten* in Frankish.
Dux: overall commander in war times; in peace time — administrator of a province
Equites: Roman cavalry
Fulcum: Roman shield wall formation
Fyrd: army made up of all warriors of the tribe
Gesith: companion of the *Drihten*, chief of the *Hiréd*
Hiréd: band of elite warriors of *Drihten*'s household
Hlaford, Hlaefdige: Lord and Lady in Saxon tongue. *Herr* and *Frua* in Frankish
Insula: a block of streets in a Roman city
Liburna: Roman warship
Mansio: staging post
Pagus, pl. Pagi: administrative unit, smaller than a province
Praefect: Roman military commander
Praetor: high administrative or military official

Praetorium: seat of the *Praetor*
Pugio: small Roman dagger
Rex: king of a barbarian tribe
Seax: Saxon short sword
Scop: Saxon poet and bard
Spatha: Roman long sword
Stofa: Saxon bath hut
Villa: Roman agricultural property
Tengri: chief god of the Huns
Vigiles: town guards and firemen
Villa: Roman agricultural estate
Wealh, pl. *wealas*: "the others", Britons in Saxon tongue. *Walh, walhas* in Frankish
Witan: gathering of the Elders

PLACE NAMES

Ake: Aachen, Germany
Andreda: Weald Forest
Anderitum: Pevensey, East Sussex
Arduenna: Ardennes
Arelate: Arles, France
Ariminum: Wallington, Surrey
Bagac: Bagacum, Bavay, France
Bononia: Boulogne-sur-Mer, France
Camarac: Cambrai, France
Cantiaca/Cantia: Kent
Coln, Britannia: Colchester, Essex
Coln, Germania: Cologne, Germany
Dorowern: Dorovernum, Canterbury, Kent
Dubris: Dover, France
Eobbasfleot: Ebbsfleet, Kent
Epatiac: Portus Aepatiacum, near Etaples, France
Icorig: Icorigium, Junkerath, Germany
Kelb: River Kyll
Leman: Portus Lemanis, Lympne, Kent
Limenea: River Limen, Kent
Londin: Londinium, London
Lugdunum: Lyons, France
Medu: River Medway
Mettis: Metz, France
Mogontiac: Mainz, Germany
Mosa: River Meuse
Mosella: River Moselle
New Port: Novus Portus, Portslade, Sussex
Remi: Reims, France
Rhenum: River Rhine
Robriwis: Dorobrivis, Rochester, Kent
Rutubi: Rutupiae, Richborough, Kent
Saffron Valley: Croydon, London
Tamesa: River Thames

Tanet: Isle of Thanet, Kent
Tolbiac: Zulpich, Germany
Tornac: Tornacum, Tournai, Belgium
Traiect: Maastricht, Netherlands
Trever: Trier, Germany

PART 1: CANTIACA, 458 AD

James Calbraith

CHAPTER I
THE LAY OF BANA

I force myself up the steep, soggy dune slope; the damp, almost oozing sand swallows my feet with every step. When I reach the summit, my thighs are burning, my knees are buckling, my chest feels as if clamped by an ever-tightening chain. A leather satchel bumps at my side, heavy with bread and a flask of ale. A dense lattice of shallow scratches, from the myriad of tiny thorns of gorse and bramble I had to push through to cut the route short, covers my arms. Dark spots dance between my eyes.

I bend down, leaning against my legs, gasping. I hear my pursuers close behind me, running up the dune. My prey is far ahead, but I still have a chance to draw closer before we get to the seashore. I just need to catch my breath first. I have been running for nearly a mile, uphill and downhill, through tall, sharp grass, greasy mud and wet sand. I feel exhausted… and it's only the beginning.

I hear hurried footsteps approaching. I don't need to look; I know that pace. I take a deep breath and brace myself for the inevitable.

Ursula runs up and slaps me on the bottom with full force. I wince. She laughs.

"What's wrong, Octa? Ran out of breath already?"

"I was giving you a chance to catch up!" I reply, and rush downhill while she's still laughing. I leave her behind, but I have to slow down when we're on flat ground again, and by the time we reach the boats, we're running head to head.

I'm quicker to push the boat into the waves of a quickly ebbing tide, but I'm having trouble with the oar, and soon she moves ahead by a boat length. Audulf is nowhere to be seen — has he reached the other side, already?

I'm not too worried. There's plenty of time to race ahead. We've got two miles of the narrow channel to cross until we reach Tanet, and I'm a better rower than she is. I look ahead and see one more boat before us, halfway across the strait. It must be Gille. The small, Frisian boy is the fastest runner of us all, and would have been the first to reach the sea, but he's weak with the oars, and Audulf must have overtaken him in the water. It doesn't look like I can catch up to either of them before the island, but I'm going to give it my damn best try.

I soon reach Ursula, our boats so close I could reach out and grab the long, thin braid of black hair flowing down her back. She grunts and picks up the pace, but it does her no good. With a wave and a grin, I pass her by. She wobbles her boat, trying to push me off course. I pull at the oars and push ahead.

My father would be pleased with us. He insists that anyone who wants to be a Iute warrior needs to be able to swim and row a boat; possibly because he himself was never good at either. He has feared water ever since childhood,

The Blood of the Iutes

when he almost drowned in a sea storm. I don't believe I have the makings of a warrior — I always imagined myself as a priest or a scholar, like my uncle — but I like the thrill of the challenge, especially if I can share it with my friends.

"Damn you, Octa! I'll get you in the swamp!" Ursula cries between gasps.

"Looking forward to it!" I cry back. The burning in my shoulders reminds me it's still a long way to go — we're not even halfway across the channel — so I slow down a bit, to conserve strength for the last stretch of the race.

With the final push of the oars, the boat grinds on the gravel. Audulf's and Gille's boats are already here. There's no chance for me to outrun Audulf now; second place is the best I can hope for. I leap out into the shallow water, wade onto the shingle beach. It's an even worse surface than the sand on the other side. I shuffle more than run, before finally reaching the steps carved into the low, white cliff that bounds the island from the south.

In leaps and pulls, I climb to the top. I drop to my hands and knees and glance back down — Ursula just reached the bottom; I give myself a few seconds to calm the fiery stabbing in my chest before picking myself up again. I see Gille — a few hundred paces ahead, along the remains of the old palisade. He's moving slowly; he must be exhausted after crossing the channel. I launch into one last dash; he hears me, looks back and scowls, but has no strength left to go any faster.

I run past him and reach the opening in the palisade, and finally see the target of our race: a great stone, standing upright, carved with red runes all around the edge, and with magical symbols and weaving figures in the centre. Audulf is already here, of course; he's leaning against the standing stone, chewing on a reed. I reach the stone, tap it with my hand and fall, face-first, into the soft, foul-smelling mud.

It's hard to believe that, not so long ago, this fly-infested, swamp-soaked, mud-pit of an island was home to an entire tribe of Iutes, a few thousand of my kindred, squashed together, waiting, refugees from the land across the sea, threatened by war, at the mercy of their Briton hosts. Nowadays, the island is mostly empty, except for a few fishing villages on the outskirts and some shepherds raising their flock on the seaweed left scattered on the beach by the tides. The palisade marks the spot where the Iutes once had what counted for the capital of their island "kingdom" — a mead hall, surrounded by what must have been a tightly packed village of cottages built from the ships in which they arrived in Britannia, the only timber available on the island. Now all that remains is the rune stone, recently carved — and a fresh grave at its foot: the last resting place of Hengist, the first and last *Drihten*, all-chieftain of the Iutes in Britannia.

I sense a stomping in the mud and open my eyes to see Ursula's bare feet next to my face. I lift myself on my elbow. Gille is the fourth to reach the rune stone — he must have given up as soon as I overtook him. Now, there's only one of us left still in the race.

"Has anyone seen Bana?" I ask.

The Blood of the Iutes

Ursula, wincing with ache from strained muscles, hobbles up to the opening of the palisade and looks out.

"He's still not here."

I frown and sit up. I open my satchel, take out the ale flask and take a long swig. It was cool and clear when I started the race; by now it's a warm sludge. I bite a piece of bread. Audulf takes out a sausage from his bag, tears it in two and gives a half to me and Ursula.

"It's been too long," worries Gille. "What if something happened?"

We were supposed to spend the whole afternoon on the island; after the race, practice some wrestling and swim in the sea — clearer and wilder on Tanet's eastern shore than in the muddy channel between it and the mainland; but for this, I need all of my friends together, and so, with a heavy sigh, I stand up.

"Let's have a look," I say. "Maybe he's lost the oars. Again."

I first see Bana's boat, still there on the beach where we left it, and breathe out in relief — at least the boy didn't drown in the channel. Moments later, I see Bana himself; he's not alone.

There are six of them, standing on the foreshore, waiting; one of them holds Bana's arm in a tight grip. I can guess who they are before we get close enough to see their faces: sons of the Iute warriors. Fathers of two of them are members of the *Hiréd*, the king's household guard: the most elite fighters of the tribe. They have names, but I could never be bothered to remember them; they all have the same pudgy faces, turning deep pink in the sun; the same thatch of pale, almost translucent hair — they might as well all be siblings.

I raise the oars, slow down and nod at the others to catch up to me so we can prepare for the inevitable brawl.

"Will they really dare to fight you?" asks Ursula.

"I can't hide behind my father forever," I reply. "If it's a fair fight, there's no reason for me to avoid it."

"They'll crush us," says Gille. "Look at their arms. They're as big as my legs."

"They may have brawn, but they don't have our brains," I say. "Give me a minute to come up with a plan."

I'm boasting to raise their spirits, but for the moment, I don't have any idea how we can get out of this without a sound beating. Gille is right to fear the six boys. They're taller and stronger than any one of us, except Audulf, and have been spending all their free time in combat training, hoping one day to succeed their fathers. We brawled with some of them before, in smaller groups, but have never yet had to face all six at once.

Bana cries out, his arm twisted behind his back.

The Blood of the Iutes

"Hey, you mongrels!" yells one of the six, "if you don't hurry up, we'll just have to beat up your friend, instead!"

"What in *Hel* do you want from us?" I call back, though I can guess why they're here. I'm playing for time; I need a plan, and fast.

"You've desecrated the sacred place of our people," the pale-haired boy replies. "Disturbed the spirits of our fallen with your foolish playing."

"We haven't done any such thing," replies Gille. "We just rowed there and back."

"Hengist's grave is not some arena for you to race around! But of course, you wouldn't understand it — none of you is a real Iute!" He spits.

This is the main reason why the warriors' sons loathe the five of us; this is why they really came here today. At last, we've given them enough of an excuse; but they've been itching to make us suffer for months for the perceived crime of trying to live among the Iutes as if we belonged here.

Ursula, dark-haired and dark-eyed, is the worst offender; she isn't even a barbarian — she's a *wealh*, a Briton, a native of this land, daughter of Dorowern nobles, representing the Cants at *Rex* Aeric's court. Little Gille, his face as pale as his short, spiky hair, is a Frisian; his parents, a family of horse traders, settled near Dubris a few years ago, and now provide mounts for the king's guard. Audulf's father arrived on Tanet from Frankia to help in the war with the Britons. And Bana, squirming in the grasp of his tormentor, was born into a family of Saxon smiths in the Trinowaunt land to the north; they moved across the Tamesa to sell their metal ware to the Iute warriors.

Myself, I'm a half-breed. My mother was a Briton, a native of this land. I have her bright red hair and green eyes. People tell me I have my father's slightly bulbous nose, and the ruddy complexion of his kin; but it's not enough to make me pass for a Iute in the eyes of those whose parents came here on the sleek *ceols* from the Old Country.

This is a new world for most of the Iutes, this stew of tribes and races; they lived for too long in the crowded squalor of Tanet, and some of them had grown used to only ever seeing and talking to others like them. Back in the Old Country, before the wars and the great upheavals of peoples that forced them out, they would rarely see anyone other than their neighbours, or a passing Anglian or Saxon merchant. Even long after leaving Tanet and settling down on the mainland, their villages and farms were only peopled by the Iutes; the war with the Britons — a terrible, bloody conflict which pitted the Iutes and their Saxon and Frankish allies against the armies of the *wealh* — further cemented the bonds between the tribesmen and made them feel that they could only count on each other for support.

But that war ended years ago, and in the time of calm and relative wealth that followed, people from across the Narrow Sea began to see Britannia as a safe haven from the many conflicts that continued to shake the Continent. Much like the Iutes a generation earlier, others would now land on the friendly shores of the easternmost province of Cantiaca — or Cantia, for short, as the newcomers have begun to call it—

The Blood of the Iutes

seeking peace or fortune; and much like the arrival of Iutes, this new migration has spawned a new conflict with those already here, if only for a generation.

"If you want to one day be in the *Hiréd*, you should watch how you talk of my father," I say.

The Iute scoffs. "By the time we're in the *Hiréd*, your father will be long gone," he says ominously. "We'd rather serve under Haesta."

"Then maybe you should go join him now," I reply. "I'm sure there's space in his filthy mud huts!"

The boat grinds on the shoal; the tide is ebbing, and there's a good hundred feet of dark, wet, heavy sand and gravel between us and the enemy, enough to slow down any charge. A head-on attack is out of the question, and though the six Iutes are far from the smartest boys in Rutubi, I doubt I can goad them to run towards us.

"I could just whack them over the heads with the oar," offers Audulf. The Iutes are unarmed, as far as I can tell — and anyway, even they wouldn't dare attack me with blades — and an oar in Audulf's hands would be a deadly weapon.

I shake my head. "Not while they have Bana. They came here for a fist fight, and we have to honour that."

"Not much honour in fighting six against four," says Ursula.

"True," I admit. "It does seem like we have a bit of an unfair advantage," I add with a smile as we start wading through the surf. "Now, listen carefully…"

"Your father wants to see you," the guard at the gate says. She eyes my bruises but says nothing.

"Good. Where is he?" I ask. She points towards the *stofa*, the wooden bathing hut. Steam rises through its thatched roof.

"Again?" I roll my eyes. "How many times a month does this man need to wash?"

I cross the wide-open yard of Rutubi. It's a memory of a Roman fortress, still surrounded by an ancient, crumbling wall of striped stone. The Iutes live on a borrowed land, a land of the dead, and we are surrounded by the reminders of that fact everywhere we look: lines of raised dirt and patches of stone pavement mark the foundations of the barrack houses, officers' halls, warehouses, water cisterns. In view of the fortress walls stands the great stone circle of the amphitheatre, and between the two, more grassy mounds and outcrops of stone mark a garrison village that had once sprouted here. The only Roman building that still stands is the small chapel by the cemetery, rebuilt in Hengist's time as a symbol of peace between the pagan Iutes and the Christian *wealas*, to serve the natives who still tilled their old scraps of land scattered among the new Iutish farms.

The Blood of the Iutes

The Romans, too, built their stone dwellings on someone else's land — that of the native Britons, whom they subdued, conquered, ruled for centuries, and then abandoned when the Empire's fates turned. There are no more Romans in Rutubi. Iutish buildings now stand where once the Legions dwelled, made of wood, dirt and thatch set up atop cracked stone pavements — the mead hall, the guest house, the granary, the brewer's hut, the blacksmith's forge… In the middle of it all, a few of the *Hiréd* train spear-fighting under the watchful eye of their *Gesith*, war chief, Betula. I nod at her respectfully, and she nods back, brushing silver hair from her eyes with her one remaining hand; she lost her right arm fighting the Britons. Her daughter, Croha, a pretty twelve-year-old with golden mouse-tails, stands at her side; she's holding a long stick, and imitates the movements of the spearmen as best as she can.

The *stofa*, built at my father's command, stands in the corner where the Legion's bath house once stood, back when the Legions were still garrisoned within the walls of the fort, to guard Britannia's shores from raiders and pirates. But it's been almost fifty years since a Legionnaire was last seen anywhere near Rutubi, and longer still since the Legions resided here permanently, and their bath house was long ago dismantled for building stone to repair the palaces of the *wealh* nobles. Now, even these are falling apart…

I enter and wait for my eyes to adjust to the dim light of the oil lamp inside, diffused on the thick steam. This is nothing like the Roman baths of old: great buildings with heated floors and separate chambers for cold and hot water, the remains of which I'd seen in Londin — and that my father would still have used in his youth; like everything else around us, this one's just a memory, a dream, a twisted mockery of the past: a simple lead tub, dug into a hole in the ground, that a servant fills with water heated up in a big cauldron.

I find my father sitting on the rim of the tub, with his back to the entrance and his legs in the water, drying himself with a towel. In the light of the lamp, I can see all his old scars. The mess of badly healed skin along his right side and arm is where he stopped a great stag from trampling Wortigern, the *Dux* of the Britons, on a hunt in the West. The deep cut on his right shoulder is from a duel with Wortigern's son, Wortimer, at the Battle of Crei, where the Iute *fyrd* beat a Briton force sent from Londin. A spear wound in his left side — a duel with Brutus, Wortimer's commander, at the Battle of Eobbasfleot, where the combined armies of Iutes and Saxons defeated the alliance of Britons marching to destroy the barbarians at the end of the great war. There are other scars and bruises from minor skirmishes and fights that were not important enough to talk about or sing of in the songs of the *scops*. Each marks a different time in history when he fought for the future of the tribe. His tribe.

Few people see him like this, other than the bath servants. He took no wife after both women he loved died in short succession; I am his only remaining family. When he's not at home or in the bath, he wears a white woollen tunic, plaid breeches and a rich cape lined with bear fur: a gift from Frankia; a thick golden armband, carved with dragons and wolves, adorns his right arm, and a long *seax* sword hangs at his waist, to complete the look of a powerful barbarian warlord.

The Blood of the Iutes

This isn't how he looked the first time I saw him. I was twelve years old then, and terrified, and he was just another young warrior, one among a massive host of Iutes and Saxons gathered on the shores of the Narrow Sea not far from Rutubi's ancient walls. I watched him fight a Briton general on the beach, and win, but I didn't understand anything of what was happening.

Two years earlier, soldiers in odd uniforms and speaking in strange accents, invaded our village, slew the man I thought was my father, burned down our house, and took me away, far to the West. During those two years, I lived in a community of Christian hermits on some distant seashore, a place of faith and learning. The hermits taught me to speak the Imperial Latin and were just about to start preparing me for a baptism, when another man arrived to take me away yet again. This one was old and grey, but with a majestic demeanour and the taut muscles of an old soldier. He told me that his name was Wortigern and that he was going to take me back home.

But my home was gone, and I never returned to what was left of my village. For reasons I did not yet understand that young Iute warrior, whom I watched kill the Briton general on Rutubi beach, took me into his care, even though my mother, Eadgith, still lived. He took me to stay at the Londin Cathedral with Bishop Fastidius, while my mother, until now a village blacksmith, moved to a distant island of Wecta. There she ruled a colony of Iutes — and there she fell, fighting for her people.

Two years ago that Iute warrior — not so young anymore — brought me the grim news of her death. That same day he announced that *he* was my real father… and that the gathering of tribal elders, the *witan*, had just elected him as *Rex* Aeric, King of the Iutes.

He turns around.

"What happened to your face?" he asks.

"A mock fight, turned real," I reply with a shrug.

We talk in Latin, the High Imperial tongue, rather than Iutish; my father insists that we use it whenever we're alone, so that I sharpen my skills and that he — surrounded by barbarians — keeps alive the memory of a better time, a time when he lived among the *wealh* as one of their own.

"Did you win?"

"…no."

It started well enough, but it was always going to be a slim chance. I took to the fight as I would to a battle, using all the knowledge of strategy and tactics I gained from the books my father and uncle had me read. We rushed the leader of the six boys, all four of us, in a diamond formation — there weren't enough of us to form a wedge — Ursula and Gille at my sides, Audulf at the back; we kicked him down and sent Audulf through the gap before the others piled on us. Bana, encouraged by our help, wrestled with the boy fighting him, reducing the enemy's numbers to equal ours. I punched one of the Iutes squarely in the face, scraping my knuckles on his

The Blood of the Iutes

nose; Ursula bit and scratched at another ferociously, forcing him back, and Audulf grappled the third by the neck and brought him to the ground.

But none of that was enough. There were too many of them, and they were too strong. Gille was the first to lose his fight, thrown back into the surf and kicked in the stomach until he pled surrender. Bana soon followed, choked, his arm twisted almost to breaking. In the end, with Ursula pinned to the sand by the strongest of the Iute youths, only Audulf and I remained standing against a flurry of kicks and blows, until at last we, too, succumbed and fell; I curled up and covered my head with my hands until our tormentors at last grew bored; they trampled our satchels, broke the flasks and left, laughing and calling us cowards and weaklings.

I sniffle and wipe blood trickling from my nose. The bruises still sting.

"I'll have Betula punish whoever did this," my father says.

"Please, don't. It's fine. It was a fair fight."

"You're an *aetheling*. A king's son," he says. "You can't go around getting beaten up like this. What if next time you get really hurt?"

"I can't just sit at the court all day, afraid to come out."

"And I'm not asking you to — I'm just saying, you should be more careful."

"What did you want to see me about?"

"I was going to tell you not to go to Tanet anymore — but looks like I was too late."

"I'm afraid so."

"At least stay away from Hengist's grave. Things have been a bit… tense since he died."

"I've noticed."

"We may not have seen eye-to-eye, but he was a calming presence while he lived…" He looks up. "Is that why they attacked you? Because you went there?"

"They attacked me because I'm not one of them," I say ruefully. "Because I'm a half-breed. And so are my friends."

He scoffs. "They called me a half-Iute all my life," he says. "Or a half-Briton, depending who you ask. You just learn to endure it. You will rule them one day — then they won't dare call you anything other than their *Hlaford*."

I sit down next to him at the edge of the tub. "Why?"

"Why what?"

"Why should I rule them? They're right — I *am* a half-breed. I don't even look like any of them." I touch my flame-red hair.

He laughs. "We talked about this. You're my son. That's why."

The Blood of the Iutes

"I know that's good enough reason for you," I say. "But it won't be enough for the others. There are other Iutes — *proper* Iutes — who would make as good rulers as I would, if not better. What if someone challenges me when you're gone?"

"I'm not going anywhere yet."

"You can't promise that, Father. Every pirate raid, every border skirmish — every time you ride a horse or go hunting — you could suffer an accident and die. What then would become of me?"

He looks at my face. He takes me by the chin and studies my bruises and cuts carefully.

"You're shaken," he says. "Some of those blows could've really hurt you if they had fallen just a couple of inches away. Are you sure you don't want me to send Betula after whoever did this to you?"

I shake my head from his grasp. "That would only make them loathe me more," I reply. "I can't go through life protected by the *Hiréd*, no matter how loyal Betula is to my mother's memory. How did *you* make them respect you? You weren't anybody's son — you were a slave, a foundling. And you weren't even a strong warrior. You told me so yourself."

"No, I wasn't." He nods. "I got beaten all the time when I was your age. I lost more fights than I won — and I have scars to prove it." He chuckles. "Look, I don't know what you want me to tell you. You're still young. You'll have time."

"But I'm not *that* young! When you were my age, you were already a warrior, and a Councillor in Londin not much later — the hero of Saffron Valley… I know the saga — gods know your *scops* sing it often enough for me to have learned it by heart."

"It was a different time," he says. "A time of chaos, of war. It was easier to be a hero then — but also easier to die. We have peace now. There are other ways to prove oneself."

There is an odd, longing quality to his voice, and a glint in his eyes which I don't often see.

"You miss those days," I note.

"A part of me does," he admits, staring into the water, cool and dark by now. "It may be just because I was younger — and happier… Sometimes I think I had more freedom as a *wealh* slaveling than I do now, as a *Rex*. Besides," he adds with a wistful smile, "I lived in Londin, then. And we both know nothing can compete with *that* place."

"Then why did you abandon all this? Ambition?"

"Ambition?" He scoffs. "I never wanted any of this." He glances around. "Don't tell this to anyone but being a king of the Iutes is… *boring*, most of the time. And wearisome. No, it was never my choice. It was forced upon me — by Fate, by our enemies, by a sense of duty…" He blinks and looks back at me. "It is not a light burden, son."

I am, perhaps, the only person in the tribe who understands my father's complaints. For everyone else, being

The Blood of the Iutes

a *Rex* — or even a mere *Drihten*, warchief, as Hengist was before my father forced him out — would be the greatest, unattainable achievement of their life. But for him, who served at one point, if briefly, as the right hand of the *Dux* of Britannia, at the court in the great city of Londin, it must have felt like a demotion.

I don't ask him why, if being the king is so bad, he wants me to succeed him; we have, indeed, talked about this many times before. I understand his reasons, and I am resigned to my fate as much as he is to his, but it doesn't mean I have to like it.

"It would be lighter if I knew how to carry it," I say. "I have no authority, other than among my handful of friends. I have no knowledge of the world, other than what I've read in the books. I don't know how to lead men, how to make them respect me, how to make them fight *for* me, rather than *with* me. You say there are less opportunities now to be a hero — but that doesn't mean there aren't any! How long are you going to keep me sheltered here, like a hatchling in the nest?"

He runs his fingers along his chin, neck and the back of his head, ending with a scratch at the balding patch at the top.

"That was a fine speech, but your accent is slipping. Anyone in Londin would be able to tell you were a barbarian."

"Is that all you have to say?"

"Hand me the cloth, please," he asks.

He towels himself dry in silence. The light of the oil lamp has all but died out by the time he puts on the white tunic and the plaid breeches; still, he says nothing.

"Father —"

He stops. "You have a point," he says at last. "You're not a hatchling anymore — you're a fledgling, and you need to start spreading your wings. I will talk to Betula about what we can do with you."

"You make it sound like she's my mother."

"No, son." He smiles, pensively, as he tightens the sword belt. "Nobody could ever be like your mother."

I lie on the grass of the old Rutubi amphitheatre, reading a new book Ursula sneaked out from her mother's library at Dorowern: a description of a journey from Rome to Gaul, in verse couplets, by some Roman poet called Rutilius; I don't get to read many books now that I live with my father among the Iutes, rather than in Londin, with its great libraries; yet this one might be my favourite of all. Rutilius's description of travel along Italia's coast in the wake of a Gothic invasion forty years ago is supposed to invoke in his reader a sense of loss and destruction: forest encroaching on abandoned farms, rivers no longer bound by bridges, harbours silent and empty; but in me, it only stirs a longing to see more of the world outside the borders of my father's kingdom. All the names sound exotic: Arelate, Tolosa, Pisa, Triturrita… all the cities, even in their ruinous state, remind of the glories of Londin

The Blood of the Iutes

and the Briton towns I remember passing on the way back from my western captivity. The language of the book, a High Imperial Latin, is flowery and difficult, at times, to decipher, but it is so beautiful that I find myself reading the verses aloud, just to let the words, no doubt mangled in my mouth, caress my ears with their melodious sounds.

As always when I read about Rome's glories, I ponder the unfathomable choice the Britons made more than fifty years ago, when they decided to throw out the Roman magistrates and to rule the island by themselves. And they fared badly at it: civil wars, rebellions, breakdown of all trade and civility. In the end, they split into tiny, conflicted factions, first by provinces, then by the *pagi*, and up in the North, perhaps even into smaller shards, reverting to the ancient animosities between the tribes and clans older than Rome itself. In my brief captivity in the West, I saw how the part of Britannia that did not remove all its ties from the Empire prospered in peace and unity; but they, too, were cut off from the old network of trade and diplomatic routes that the island was once in the centre of. And by the time I found myself a war orphan in the old monastery on the windswept western cliff-side, there, too, the Empire became little more than a memory, the Briton officials and nobles merely playing at being Romans.

Somewhere out there, beyond the Narrow Sea, the Empire still exists, still survives; surely, it's still not too late for Britannia to one day return into its fold, like the Prodigal Son of the Christian Scriptures? I can't understand why the Britons are more interested in their petty island conflicts than taking part in the greater events unfolding on the Continent. My father doesn't want to talk about it; he may have once been one of them, but after all that the *wealas* did to him and the people he loved, he can no longer bring himself to care about their fate. The fate of the Iutes is now all that concerns him. And there isn't anyone else in Rutubi with whom I can discuss these matters, except maybe Ursula.

A jarring, thudding sound interrupts my meditation; a pony appears over the ridge of the amphitheatre's crumbling auditorium. One of the *Hiréd* warriors rides up and tells me to join him in the saddle. "You're wanted back at the fort," she says.

The rest of Betula's men are already at Rutubi, gathered in the centre of the courtyard before my father. He's wearing his full regalia — the silver circlet of the *Rex* and the boar-skin cloak of the *Drihten*.

"It looks like you may get your wish sooner than either you or I expected," he says, when I dismount. "I'm sending you with Betula to the South. Pack your bags; the ship departs in an hour."

"An hour? What's happening?"

"There's been a raid on the villages near Leman. A large one. If we hurry, we can still intercept them."

"A raid — Frankish pirates?"

"I hope so — I'd like to get my hands on them." His eyes flash with anger. "Gods know how many people we lost to those slavemongers."

The Blood of the Iutes

Other than the Picts and the Brigants coming in from the North of Britannia, the pirates from across the Narrow Sea have always been the main threat to Cantia's shores; the fort at Rutubi was raised to defend the harbours from them back when they hailed mostly from the lands of Saxons and Frisians. But the Saxons have now settled in Britannia peacefully, and Frisia's coast is being swallowed by swamp and flood, and so the pirates are now Franks — or at least, that's what they call themselves, since the crews are usually made up of whatever bunch of rustlers, bandits and adventurers they can gather on the shores of Gaul and beyond.

There isn't much left to plunder in Britannia other than men, so the pirates' main trade these days is slavery. It usually takes them only a couple of days to round up all the suitable serfs at their landing place; it's rare that we get a warning advanced enough to catch them in the act.

"I'll go get my friends," I say.

"There's no time — or space," my father says. "The *ceol* in the harbour can only take twenty riders." He notices my hesitation. "Unless… You've changed your mind?"

"No, Father. I'm going."

"Good. I'd go with you, but I need to prepare for the move to Robriwis." He clenches and unclenches his fists.

"Already?" "It's that time of the year. Go, son. Kill one of them for me. Nobody takes Iutes into slavery and gets away with it — not while I'm the king!"

James Calbraith

CHAPTER II
THE LAY OF HROTHWULF

"Are you sure this is the right place?" Betula asks the *ceol*'s captain.

"This is Bilsa's Stead," the man replies. "Just like you asked."

I step up to the ship's edge and look at the remains of a cluster of fishing huts, clumped together around a small, shallow inlet of the Narrow Sea. The sight of land should calm me down; we've been chasing a strong, northerly wind all day. The storm season may have just ended, but the gusts are still powerful enough to make one's stomach churn. The little ship heaved and leaped in the waves like a bucking pony. A journey that would take us two days on horseback, took us less than six hours along the coast — and I feel each of these six hours in my guts.

But the burnt-out shells of huts make me feel just as queasy as the rolling waves. I haven't seen a village destroyed like this since the Britons invaded my childhood home, and I realise my father has sheltered me from the harshness of the world for too long. Yes, there's been mostly peace in Cantia since the war with Wortimer ended; but the farms are still being raided, the ships are still lost at sea, and people are still being killed, especially in these frontier lands, between *Rex* Aeric's Iutes and *Rex* Aelle's Saxons, where neither warlords' power reaches quite far enough.

"What's wrong?" I ask the *Gesith*. I can sense the colour and warmth slowly returning to my face.

"There's no trace of any ship," she replies. "Not so much as a landing mark on the beach."

"Maybe we're too late? Maybe they've gone back to Frankia?"

She shakes her head. "We would've seen them pass us by. And look," she adds, pointing, "the huts near the shore are the least damaged. Whoever attacked this place, came from inland."

She turns to the captain. "Take us south. And hurry."

"South?" I ask, when the captain leaves to order his crew. "You don't think — Aelle?"

"I don't think anything. If they're pirates, they must have landed somewhere else. If not — we have a chance to catch them before this northern wind calms down for the night."

The single grey sail unfurls again and fills out on the breeze. The oarsmen start their rhythmic song and heave at the oars, launching the ship south-west, towards the darkening sky. The boards creak under the strain. The crew is as eager to find the raiders as the *Hiréd*. The *ceol*, named *The Swallow*, still smells of fresh wood and tar; she's one of a handful of new ships built at my father's order, to help deal with the pirate raids and assist the renewed trade with Gaul and Frankia, but, so far, with little success.

The Blood of the Iutes

The next few farmsteads we pass along the shore appear plundered and abandoned as well, though not burned — whoever raided them was not interested in mere wanton destruction. These are Briton farms as well as Iutish, as this far south along the coast the Iutes have only begun to settle; it makes no difference to us — according to treaties of alliance, King Aeric's warriors are tasked with defending the *wealas* and their own kindred alike, in exchange for the land.

We reach a broad river estuary, and the muddy shore begins to arc back towards the south-east. To the south, the land rises over the marsh into a low plateau of dunes and sharp rocks. The setting sun touches the dune-tops.

"That's Limenea," says the captain, nodding at the river. "If we go any further, we'll cross into Haesta's territory."

"We'll sail to New Port if we have to," says Betula. She looks towards the estuary. A couple of well-built timber huts stand on the northern shore, surrounded by crab apple trees in bloom; neither the huts, nor the orchard bear any sign of damage. "Who lives on this river?" she asks.

"Swineherds, mostly," the captain replies. "Good pasture land."

"Iutes or Britons?"

"Iutes," he says. "They came here even before the war. Survived by hiding in Andreda."

"How far to the nearest ford?"

"Five miles, maybe. I can land by those trees, if that's what you want." He glances up. "And I'll have to stay there for the night, it looks like."

"Do what you must," says Betula. "Just be quick about it. And keep an eye out for any passing ships. Those pirates might still be out there."

There is no village here — just a number of small farms, most consisting of single-room huts with enclosures for pigs and goats. Some are roundhouses in the old Briton style, but a majority are Iutish rectangles, sunken into the ground, with thick thatched roofs. They're simple but well kept.

We pass a swineherd, returning from a nearby hazelnut grove with his drove. He greets us, raising his stick in the air.

"*Hael*," replies Betula. "Where can we find your clan's elder?"

"Hrothwulf lives in the big house to the north, by the river bend," the swineherd says, pointing his stick. "With the stone chimney. Can't miss it."

"Why do you think we can find something out here?" I ask Betula, after we leave the swineherd and start climbing a low hill.

"If the raiders came from inland, as I suspect, they will have to cross this river on their return," she replies. "The captain mentioned that the locals hid in Andreda during the

The Blood of the Iutes

war. They might know a thing or two about what the bandits are up to around here."

"You don't think it's really Aelle — or Haesta?"

"If it's either, it's usually both," she replies. She stares at the dark line of Andreda forest. "Though I do hope it's just some bandits. We haven't had any trouble from the Saxons since last summer. This must be the place," she adds.

The stone chimney mentioned by the swineherd is all that remains of a Roman iron bloomery, raised on the river's edge. A large house of lime-washed walls with a carved gable stands around it, using stone from the furnace as foundation. A wooden watchtower atop a low mound next to it overlooks several farm buildings, a round-walled *stofa* and a large barn, all surrounded by an earthen wall.

"Someone's doing well for themselves," I note. It's rare to see such affluence in a Iutish village this far from Tanet.

"Someone knows to expect danger," says Betula. She seems more interested in the earthen wall and the watchtower than the rich house.

A single spearman guards the entrance through the earthen wall. He takes one look at our warband and runs off to summon his master. Moments later, the clan elder emerges from the big house, tying the rope in his breeches and wiping crumbs from his moustache.

"*Hael, Gesith!*" Hrothwulf calls. "And, if I'm not mistaken, young *aetheling?*"

Betula frowns. "You know us?"

"I saw you last year at Leman, at *Rex* Aeric's court. I invited him to move here," he says, spreading his arms. "He shouldn't have to live among those dirty *wealas*. Have you come to review the place? There's plenty of good, solid land to build a mead hall anywhere between the river and the forest."

"We still haven't finished the hall at Robriwis," I say. "Maybe later my father will consider your offer."

"Oh —" He stutters, perplexed. "But then — why did my king's son and his best warrior come all the way here, unannounced?"

"We're here to help you with the raiders," says Betula. "Or have you not noticed them passing through your land?"

He falls silent and wipes his hands on his tunic. He turns to the guard. "Go get Penga," he orders. "Wake him up if you have to."

"Come with me inside," he then tells us. "I'll get the mead. Your men can set up camp on the riverside — just look out for the fish traps."

"How did you find out about the raiders?" asks Hrothwulf as he pours us the mead. "I only got the bad news yesterday myself."

The Blood of the Iutes

"Horse courier from Leman," replies Betula. "One of *Rex* Aeric's new ideas. First time it worked."

It wasn't a new idea — indeed, it was a very *old* idea: a network of mounted couriers, passing messages between the forts of the Saxon Shore along the old Roman roads — but it was my father who decided to revive it, more than a generation since its demise, to connect his three courts at Leman, Rutubi and Robriwis.

"I didn't think it worth your trouble," says Hrothwulf. "We can take care of ourselves here. I was just about to gather the clan militia to hunt that band tomorrow."

"Then I was right," says Betula. "It wasn't pirates."

Hrothwulf laughs. "Pirates? By the gods, no. Pirates rarely sail past Leman, and if they do, they go straight for the Saxon lands. There's nothing here to take but our pigs."

"And men," I say. "Do you not fear the slavers?"

"The men know to flee into the woods at the first sign of danger. We survived Wortimer's war; we won't be threatened by some pirates — or forest bandits."

The door opens into the night. The guard lets in an old, grey-haired, bent man with dark eyes and nose like a hawk's beak.

"Penga," Hrothwulf introduces him. "He's lived here longer than anyone."

"You're a Briton," I notice.

"Am I?" the old man chuckles. "I've lived among you fair-hairs for so long, I almost forgot."

"Why did you drag this poor old man out of bed?" asks Betula.

"He saw what happened at Bilsa's Stead."

Betula turns to the old man with a raised eyebrow. "And you survived?"

"The slavers have no need for someone like me," the Briton replies. "And when you reach my age…"

Betula nods impatiently. "I know. You learn a few tricks. I've heard it before. What did you see?"

"They came from the West, *Hlaefdige*," Penga says. "Some on ponies, most on foot. The village folk resisted as well as they could, but the fight was short against well-armed warriors. The raiders killed all men, took women and children — and all the supplies they could carry. Food from the winter stores, firewood, tools…"

"Ponies? Not war horses?"

"There was only one man on a horse… Their chief. A dark-skinned, bald man clad in leathers and fur. Didn't seem to be from around here."

"Haesta's mercenaries." I spit out the despised name.

The Blood of the Iutes

There isn't a man alive that I hate more. Hengist's cousin, scion of one of the most noble of Iutish clans, Haesta always believed it was he who should have succeeded his uncle as ruler of the tribe, not my father. His failed revolt against Hengist was the spur that launched my father's bid for the kingship... More importantly to me, it led to my mother's death on the distant Isle of Wecta. My father fought him, and beat him and his army of mercenaries, marauders and outlaws three years ago, but he could never vanquish them for good. The warband settled on the border land between us and the Saxon kingdom, under protection of the Saxon *Rex*.

"Maybe," says Betula. "How many of them were there?"

"Twenty, maybe thirty? About twice the size of your camp outside," the old man replies.

"And the others were all fair-hairs?"

He nods.

"That doesn't mean anything," says Hrothwulf. "There are a lot of fair-hairs living in Haesta's settlement. He's been attracting Iutes who disagree with *Rex* Aeric, or those fleeing from his punishment — and Saxons seeking freedom from Aelle."

Betula turns sharply to the chieftain. "You seem to know a lot about them."

Hrothwulf shrugs. "They're our neighbours, for better or worse."

"If the raiders came from the West, they would have passed through your land."

"The river is easily crossed further upstream, deeper in the forest."

"But that would mean they went out of the way to avoid this ford. Don't tell me they were so frightened of your clan militia."

Hrothwulf smiles a dishonest smile. "You're assuming they came from Haesta's land. Maybe they came from the West. Or the Downs to the North."

"Somehow I doubt they did." Betula scratches the tip of her nose with her thumb. "Have you heard them say anything?" she asks the old man. "What did they need those supplies for? Where were they taking them? It's not easy to sell a Iutish slave in Britannia."

"They didn't seem to have a plan," Penga says. "They kept arguing about it. Some spoke of going to New Port; others said it's too far to march with the captives — said they should find some Franks to trade with. I don't know what they decided in the end."

"There you go," says Hrothwulf with a satisfied grin. "If they came from Haesta's land, why would they go to New Port?"

"I don't know." Betula leans over to me. "Something's not right about this."

The Blood of the Iutes

I nod but have nothing to reply. I feel like I'm disappointing her with my silence. She's used to my father's company on these campaigns; he would know what to say to either confirm or refute her suspicions — but I don't even know what those suspicions are. This is my first time marching into combat, and I have no idea what's expected of me, other than to carry a sword and, hopefully, help get rid of a few enemies. To me, the matter is clear: Haesta sent his men to harass the border villages, not counting on our fast response. If we hurry, we may have a chance to intercept them before they get rid of their captives, one way or another.

"May-may," I stutter. "Maybe we could send out some patrols across the river."

"In the middle of the night?" Betula chuckles.

"No — of course not. Never mind." I stare at my feet.

"No, wait, you're right," she says.

"I-I am?"

She looks out the door. "The moon is bright; the land is flat. We might surprise them. I'll go tell the men. Can the boy stay here tonight?" she asks Hrothwulf.

"Of course — I have a guest room in the back, safe and warm," the chieftain replies. "I'll give him my best covers. It's not often we get to host a king's son!"

I don't know if it's the bad mead, the unfamiliar surroundings, the excitement of the sudden journey, or everything combined; I can't sleep — I thrash and twitch in the bed, under the thick, embroidered blankets given to me by Hrothwulf's wife. I stare at the thick, thatched roof above me and I study the knots in the wood of the rafters.

I reach for the sheath of my *seax*, lying next to the bed, and feel the comforting, rough cool of leather binding on the hilt. If Betula's patrols find the raiding band, tomorrow I might face the enemy for the first time. I may have to kill my first man. I have trained for it, but am I ready?

My father slew his first enemy when he was sixteen, fighting in what the *scops* are now calling the Battle at Aelle's Ford — though it was only some forest bandits attacking a passing caravan. In the years that followed, he would go on to kill dozens more, in many battles and skirmishes; but, he once told me, he would remember that first woman forever: the way his knife entered her stomach, the way her neck spurted blood on his hands, until they were so slippery he could no longer hold the hilt…

What will my first kill be like? I hope it will be quick, so that I don't have to think about it too much. Maybe it won't happen tomorrow — not every warrior in a battle gets to slay an enemy, and I will be far from the front line. But eventually, it will come, and it will have to come soon — I can't possibly be a leader of a warrior tribe without ever ridding a man of his life.

A leader.

The Blood of the Iutes

Soon after my father first brought me to Cantia and explained who he was and what he wanted my destiny to be, I revolted. I hid in a fishing village, then tried to make my way back to Londin. Betula's warriors found me before I reached Robriwis — but they didn't take me back; they just asked that I allow King Aeric to meet me one more time.

It was there, in a tiny, dark, stuffy fisherman's hut that my father told me his vision of the future — not just of the Iutes, but all of Britannia, even the Empire itself — and my role in his plan.

"The world everyone knew for generations is falling apart," he told me. "It's not just Britannia that is splitting into small kingdoms. Gaul does, too, and so does, I hear, Iberia… Christian kingdoms, heathen kingdoms… It happened before, a long time ago, when Alexander's Empire fell. And it doesn't end here. The weak kingdoms will fall apart further — and the strong ones will gobble up the pieces between themselves. And what makes a kingdom strong?"

"A strong king?" I guessed.

"*Continuity*," he said. "Rome suffered through countless weak Imperators, yet it thrived for centuries because of the continuity of its laws and institutions, because transition of power remained uninterrupted, even between tyrants, even between fools. It survived Caligula, it survived Commodus, it survived even Elagabal." He knew I'd read enough ancient writers under Bishop Fastidius's tutelage to follow his lecture without much trouble. "The Empire floundered not when the Imperators were weak but when the institutions failed. A gap between dynasties meant chaos, civil war, fire at the borders, loss of provinces. This is what will happen to us if we don't establish continuity. The Britons, the Saxons, the Picts, the Franks — each will want a slice of the Iutish meat."

"Then all you need from me is to be a symbol for your grand idea. An accident of birth is to decide my destiny, not my talents, not my desires."

"You will always have a choice, my son. A choice I never had. My promise still stands — you're free to do with your life what you want. But —" He lay a hand on my shoulder and gave it a strong squeeze. " — I truly believe you *are* the best contender to be the next king. Otherwise, I would've just adopted someone more suitable." He chuckled. "Not because I'm your father but because Eadgith was your mother."

His words rang true, but I had no way of knowing if his prophecy was accurate. The Iutish kingdom had no borders, other than the ones we shared with the Briton province of Cantia, so there was no frontier for anyone to swallow. The various Briton tribes in Londin and beyond quarrelled and squabbled with each other, but then, there was no threat of open conflict — they were too weak after Wortimer's war, too afraid of the heathens on their doorstep to risk wasting their energies on fruitless conflicts. I had little idea about the situation in Gaul, and much less about Iberia, or lands further away.

But no peace lasts forever. The pirates, the sea raiders, Haesta's outlaws — there are enough of these attacks now to keep Betula's warriors and the clan militias busy throughout the year. I'm not sure what's causing this rise in hostilities; harvests have been good, trade is thriving, the serfs are fed

The Blood of the Iutes

and content... Is it simply an inevitable circle of time, passing from peace to war and back to peace again, or is there something more sinister going on? My father and his advisors would know more, but he's not sharing this knowledge with me and, until now, I haven't really been all that interested.

I must have dozed off as my mind wandered, for when I open my eyes again, there are pale white wisps coming through the thatched roof above my head. I hear crackling. I smell wet smoke. Groggily, I wonder what's going on. Is it a dream — or a bad memory? I remember a burning hut like this six years ago, when Wortimer's men attacked my home village. My mother was away, selling her tools at the Saffron Valley market. My mother's husband — the man I then believed to be my father — ran outside with a meat cleaver to face the invaders. He never returned. I waited — until it was too late. A falling roof beam barred my way out; I was trapped. The flames roared around me; the smoke filled my lungs. I crawled through the rubble like a lizard, in poisoned daze, as the house was falling apart around me. The smoke was black and thick but brightened within by the fire licking the walls and sparks bursting with each shattering beam.

When I at last found my way out, I saw my foster-father dead, pinned with a dart to the ground, the cleaver still in his hand. A hand in iron gauntlet grabbed me by the hair, picked me up and threw me onto a wagon. Most of the other children of the village, my playtime friends, were already there. Soon, the wagon would carry us away to the West, where each of us would be taken to a church or a hermitage, and I would never see my foster-father again. To this day, I don't know where — or if — his body is buried.

Again, I lose a few precious minutes to brief sleep, my mind not yet adjusted to the urgency of the situation. It is only when an arrow with a flaming rag tied to its shaft pierces the roof and hits the floor a foot from my head that I fully wake up, instantly sober and alert.

I hear shouts outside, but they come as if through fog. Cold sweat covers my hands and my brow. My vision narrows. My head spins, either from the smoke or from fear. I grab the sword and rush, naked, to the door. It's a solid barrier, made of thick oaken boards — and it's locked. I rattle at the handle. It won't budge. Behind me, the thatch begins to fall through in fiery clumps. The blankets catch fire. The holes in the roof act like chimneys. Smoke fills the room. I start coughing. In the darkness, I stumble, seeking the pitcher of water I prepared for morning ablutions. I pour it over myself and go back to the door. I start banging on the boards and call for help. My throat aches. My voice grows weaker, thinner, more desperate. It turns into a panicked wail — then a sob: "It's locked! Help me! Save me! I can't get out! Open up, somebody, *please…*"

Somebody rams into the door from outside. I fall back. They ram again. The door bursts open. I can't see who it is — and I don't care. I run outside, naked, coughing, weeping, screaming. I spot Hrothwulf and, not paying attention to why he's holding a large axe and why he's bleeding from his shoulder, grab him by the collar and shake him.

"Why did you lock me up!" I yell through tears. "Why did you lock me up?"

The Blood of the Iutes

Betula runs out of the burning house, pulls us apart and slaps me in the face.

"Stop your blabbering, Octa! It was latched from inside," she tells me. "*You* locked yourself up. Brave Hrothwulf almost died trying to get you out. Now get that sword and make yourself useful — we're under attack, if you still haven't noticed!"

It's a disaster.

Not for Betula's warriors who, after initial confusion, gather around the farmstead in a tight formation; I watch them spread into a crescent, then a wall — not of shields, for there's no need for such complex tactics when fighting a bunch of bandits — but of spears, swords and flesh. The attackers emerge from the darkness in waves of four, five, six; the assault doesn't seem coordinated in any way, there is no war chief shouting orders, no order to the chaos. It looks like the bandits put all their hopes in the element of surprise, and when that failed, they could think of no other way to defeat us — and now that they've committed to the attack, they can't figure out how to untangle themselves from it. As soon as she gets the situation under control, Betula sends out a few men along the riverside to strike at the bandits from the rear. Before long, they realise their way of escape is cut off; some make an attempt to fight their way out towards the woods. Others drop their weapons and surrender.

Not for Hrothwulf; the flames consume the roof over the guest room and part of the kitchen, but the rest of the big house, built on the solid brick foundation of the old smithy, can easily be repaired. Nobody on the farm suffers any serious injuries, apart from Hrothwulf's arm, shattered in rescuing me from the fire. His farm is safe, his clan victorious, his honour undiminished, though it's the *Hiréd* that did most of the fighting.

It's a disaster for *me*. As soon as my head clears enough for me to realise what's going on, I rush into the brawl with nothing but the sword in my hand. But my actions are too hasty; the smoke is still in my lungs and in my eyes. Dizzily, through tears, I stagger towards the nearest enemy. I slash at him with the sword but miss. He parries with his axe, easily throwing the weapon out of my weakened hand. I stumble back, trip and fall. He stands over me, raises the axe in both hands over his head. I cover myself and cry out in fear. The bandit cries, too — in pain. I look up: a small throwing axe juts out of his chest; blood spurts from the wound all over my naked body. I don't need to look to know who threw the axe — it's Betula's favourite weapon, and she can launch it as precisely as an archer launches an arrow, even if she can throw it only with her left hand.

The bandit makes two staggered steps back and disappears from my sight; a thud tells me he hits the ground, but I have no time to feel relieved when another warrior takes his place. This time, two of Betula's men appear above me; one fights back the enemy, the other drags me away. The sharp gravel digs furrows in my bare back. After a few paces of this, the warrior picks me up and carries me to the safety of the camp, and leaves me there, like a mewling child, before returning to the fray.

The Blood of the Iutes

Abandoned to my own devices, I putter around the camp as the fight rages on outside. I find some breeches to put on; my clothes perished in the flames. I wash myself from the soot and blood in the river. The cold water sobers me up and I face the enormity of my humiliation. So much for being a warrior; so much for being a leader of men. So much for ever becoming anything like my father. I was never going to be a hero of this expedition — not in the company of the tribe's finest warriors — but I certainly did not expect that everyone would witness me as a naked, weeping coward.

The sounds of combat are dying out, and soon the first injured return to the camp. Their wounds are light, and they are still exhilarated by the battle rush. They're laughing, boasting, telling each other how they slew one enemy or the other in a particularly gruesome way — but then they see me, by the campfire, and their voices turn to subdued whispers and grunts.

They will never say this to my face — they are my father's guard and know better than to insult his son openly — but I know, after tonight's performance, they will never respect me again.

I remain by the campfire until dawn, unmoving, silent, wallowing in my shame. The others all avoid talking to me, busy tending to their wounds, fixing their equipment, washing their clothes in the river; Betula asks only if I'm alright, and brings me a spare tunic and a woollen cloak — the morning turned cold, with the breeze blowing in from the sea and mist rising from the river. From the snippets of conversations around me, I gather the story of what happened at night.

The attack came as soon as the patrols departed to seek the enemy's camp. They crept up to the big house from the west, shot flaming arrows and threw flaming darts on the roof to sow chaos and confusion, while the main assault came from the north — but whoever planned it, failed to take into account the training and cold blood of Betula's warriors.

At daybreak, the patrols return. One of them had discovered remains of a camp some five miles north, and a track, splitting in two, one branch heading west, the other south, back to Hrothwulf's farm.

"You have a rat among your household," Betula tells Hrothwulf. "It takes a few hours to organise an attack like this. Somebody must have informed them as soon as we arrived."

"I figured as much, *Gesith*," the chieftain replies. "I have a few suspects. You can leave this in my hands, I'll deal with it swiftly."

"I intend to — we're not staying here long."

She orders the men to break up camp and prepare to ride out.

"It wasn't the entire band," she says to her officers. "There were no mounted warriors, only untrained footmen."

The Blood of the Iutes

They speak standing over my head, as if I am not here. I stare into the fire with my arms wrapped around my knees. My sword lies beside me, mocking me with its unblemished blade.

"They distracted us while the main host fled into the woods with the plunder and captives," says one of Betula's men. "They couldn't have gone far in the darkness."

"I fear it might be too late," says Betula. "If they are the forest bandits, they will know the secret paths. Get me a few of those prisoners," she commands. "Send the rest back to the ship. I need to find out who's leading this band, and why."

"I still think it's Haesta," I murmur quietly, when the others depart with orders.

"This was too sloppy for Haesta," she replies. She squats beside me and reaches out to warm her hand in the fire. "We must have taken out more than half of that band tonight, with barely any casualties. It may be that one of Haesta's men is in command here, but he himself is too clever to try something like that."

"You praise him? After everything he's done to us?"

"It's a grudging respect. Not even your father could have defeated him without Aelle's help. Above all, he's a survivor. He escaped Londin when Wortimer was purging the city from Iutes. He lived through the war, defending Tanet. I fought him and his men many times after Wecta; he escaped unscathed every time. This —" She nods towards the smouldering farm. " — is not the way he does things."

I fall silent. Even Betula has more respect for Haesta than I could ever count on. If my father died today, what would she do? She was my mother's friend, and I'm sure she would protect me from harm, but that doesn't mean she would necessarily support my right to the circlet. Would she join Haesta instead, or at least let him do as he pleased? I know she understands my father's ideas, and agrees with the need for continuity, for establishing the new, enduring laws and traditions — but the Kingdom of Iutes is no more than five years old; things can still change without too much harm. If it was Haesta who started the new dynasty instead of Aeric, would anyone care — or even notice? In the long run, it wouldn't matter. The sagas would need a quick rewrite, that's all. A hundred years from now, even if anyone remembered the brief rule of *Rex* Aeric, no one would ever mention his cowardly son — unless as a joke…

"Does Haesta have a son?" I ask.

"If he does, the child would be very young," she replies. "He didn't have one when he was exiled. Why do you ask?"

"I — nothing. Doesn't matter."

One of the officers returns. "The prisoners are ready, *Gesith*," he says, pointing to the big house. "So are the men. We can ride out as soon as you give the word."

"Good." Betula stands up. She wipes her hand from the dirt. "Have them eat something first — and eat well. It might be a long ride."

"What do we do with him?" He nods at me.

"What about him?"

He lowers his voice, but not enough for me not to hear him. "He's in no shape to ride. Or fight. And the men —"

"I understand." Betula touches my arm. "Octa, I'm sending the captives back to *The Swallow*, to your father — and I need a few men to guard them —"

I shrug my arm from her grasp. I stand up and stare, furiously, at Betula and the officer. "Don't treat me like a child. I know what you mean. I'll go. I'd only be in your way, anyway."

James Calbraith

CHAPTER III
THE LAY OF URSULA

Left side — top — right side — step back. Left side — top — right side — ow!

I drop the wooden sword and rub my bruised fingers. Audulf throws his weapon to the ground in anger.

"Focus, *aetheling*!" he shouts. He only uses my title when he's angry with me. "Today you fight worse than when I first started training you."

I walk away and sit on the bench under the wall. The stone curtain around Robriwis is in much better shape than at Rutubi; the fort overlooks the old bridge over Medu, the only paved highway linking Londin with Cantia and the harbours of the east coast, and as such was once one of the most important in Britannia. It was manned for a time, even after the Legions departed, by soldiers in Londin's employ, and was among the first strongholds given to the Iutes after they were allowed out of their refuge on Tanet. Excepting the brief interlude of Wortimer's war, the fortress at Robriwis has been in Iute possession for more than a decade now, and out of all Iute places in Cantia it is said to most resemble an Old Country fortified settlement.

The Iutes are a scattered people — settled among the fields abandoned by the Britons, on forest clearings and in drained marshes, not keeping to the network of metalled

Roman highways that the Briton settlements are strung along. A *Rex* who wants to reach all of his subjects needs to travel all around his domain and needs more than one court. My father, after some trials and errors, devised a system in which he, his *Hiréd*, his circle of advisors, and everyone else who sees it their business to always be close to the king, spend a third of the year in each of the three capitals of the Iutes — Rutubi in the East, Robriwis in the West, and a temporary one at an inn in Leman, until a more suitable place is selected for the southern, autumnal court. In Robriwis, we spend the finest part of the year — from *Thrimilce* to *Weod*, or from May to August by Roman reckoning, when the storms quieten and it's appropriate for the king and his warriors to stay as near to the busy harbours of the northern coast as possible. Usually, I look forward to our moving here, since it means the long, warm days of summer are near: the days of bathing in the Medu and hunting in the Andreda, long evenings of telling stories and singing songs. But this year, I find no joy in any of these pastimes.

"What's the point?" I say. "I'll never be the warrior that my father was. I'll never get to lead an army. Not when all my men know I'm a coward."

"We all know you're anything *but* a coward," says Bana. He breaks off his mock duel with Gille and sits down next to me. "It was just a stroke of misfortune. You could have died in that fire — it's a miracle you survived."

"I almost died because I didn't see that the door was latched from my side. Because the fire made me panic. Like a weakling that I am. Like a child."

The Blood of the Iutes

I glance towards the middle of the yard, where other young warriors are training today, while the *Hiréd* rests. Five of the boys who beat us up at Tanet are here — the sixth one remained with his family back at Rutubi; they see me looking at them and grin back mockingly. Our forces are equal now, and I should be thinking of ways to wreak our vengeance on them, but my spirit is crushed enough to not want to risk yet another humiliation, so I just look away.

"There will be other opportunities to show your bravery," says Bana.

"Not while we're stuck here in Robriwis. We're even further from the frontier or the pirates here than we were at Rutubi."

"You just need to ask your father to send you on another mission with the *Hiréd*."

"My father won't talk to me," I scoff. "He's too busy. Or so he claims. Everyone wants to speak to him about some urgent matter or other — they've been waiting eight months for the court to be back. You can imagine how many court disputes that left unsolved, how many trade deals and friendship treaties unsigned…"

"What about the feast tomorrow?" asks Gille. "Nobody should bother your father there — and he's bound to be in a good mood after a few barrels of mead…"

"I-I don't think I'll be going to the feast. I don't want to see Betula and those officers of hers again."

Yesterday, Betula and her men returned from the South. Tomorrow, at a feast thrown in their honour, they will present their findings — and their captives — before my father and his advisors.

They will also, no doubt, bring the story of my humiliation with them. I haven't told it to anyone yet except my friends, and that after much prodding when they saw me brooding after my all-too-soon return from the mission. The warriors who came with me on *The Swallow* were not interested in spreading rumours, but somehow, I sensed everyone in the fort already knew exactly what happened…

"You have to be there," says Audulf brusquely. He draws a real blade and swishes it through the air a couple of times. "You're the *aetheling*. If you don't go, then everyone *will* think you're a coward."

I leap up to him with fists clenched. He steps back, pointing the tip of his knife at my chest, and laughs. "Get your sword out, Octa!" he says. "Maybe a threat of real injury will help you focus better on the training."

"That's quite enough, you two." Gille steps between us. "I swear, as soon as Ursula's away, you both turn back into children."

"When *is* she coming back from Dorowern?" I ask, gritting my teeth. I push Audulf away, unclench my fist and sit back on the bench. I notice my right hand is trembling and hold it in place with the left hand.

The Blood of the Iutes

"She was supposed to be here today," says Gille. "I'm sure she's not going to miss the feast."

"She'd better be," I say. "I need to talk to someone grown up." I pick up the wooden sword and thrust it in my belt. "I'm done training," I say. I mean to say "for today", but I make it sound as if I'm done for good. "I'll read a book, instead. I still haven't finished Rutilius. Reading's the only thing I'm good for, anyway."

The mead hall in Robriwis, standing on the foundation of the *Praetor's* office, is the oldest of the three raised for my father's court, and the most lavishly decorated. It's the size of a clan barn, as long as a warship and as tall as a young pine tree, with walls of oaken beams and a shingle roof in the shape of an upturned boat, topped with horse heads carved in the wood of the gable rafters.

It was built large enough to accommodate the greatest feasts the Iutes can throw: to mark their holy days, like Eostre or Yule, to celebrate the start and end of harvest, or to mourn the death of a seasoned warrior. But today's feast is a minor one. The list of guests is limited to those already staying at the fortress; no clan elders arrive from distant corners of the province, no envoys from across the Narrow Sea, no delegates from the Briton towns. The long table, covered with deerskins, running in a horseshoe along the walls, is half-empty when we all sit down to the first meal: a stew of carrots, barley and hare meat, sweetened with spring honey.

Betula and two of her officers enter to loud cheer and cries of *was hael!* They take the seats of honour opposite my father and me. I can't look the officers in the eyes; I recognise one of them as the man who asked that I be sent away. Three more Iutes enter, dragging in bandit captives and throw them on the floor. The bandits prostrate themselves before the king.

The three Iutes are not of the *Hiréd* — I haven't seen them before in my life.

"Are these some of the would-be slaves you freed?" my father asks.

"Yes, *Rex*," Betula replies. "They wanted to come to show their gratitude to you."

"You're welcome," my father says with a smile. "But save your gratitude for *Gesith* Betula. I wasn't there."

"You are our *Rex*," says one of the Iutes. A confused, servile grimace appears on his face. "Your men do as you command."

My father leans towards me. "Three years ago, these people hadn't even heard the word *Rex*," he says, quietly, in Latin. He smiles again at the Iutes and invites them to sit at the far end of the table. "They're still not sure what it means. Am I just a *Drihten* by another name? Or am I more someone akin to gods? Do I speak for Wodan and Donar now, or do they speak through me?"

"And are you?" I ask. "Sure, I mean."

The Blood of the Iutes

He chuckles. "I don't think I'll ever be sure of that. No ancient writer wrote a guide for being a king." He tears off a chunk of bread and gestures at Betula to speak. "Tell us of your victory, *Gesith*."

Betula recounts first the part of the story I was witness to, from landing by the crab apple orchard to the night battle. She omits any mention of my shameful misadventure, but judging by a few snickers scattered around the table, the rumour has already reached Robriwis.

"We rode out in the morning, following the trail closely," she continues. "They moved through the woods, using the paths only bandits know — but as you can imagine, it's not easy to hide a train of captives and mules carrying plunder, even in Andreda."

The few warriors familiar with the forest nod appreciatively; my father among them.

"We tracked them for hours, until the sun started descending behind the pine tops," Betula continues. "They tried to slow us down — they'd leave prisoners behind them, beaten up and tied down, so that we would need to take care of them. They'd leave archers in the trees to snipe at us from above and force us into hiding. But still we went on, and at last, we caught up to them on a charcoal burner's glade, near the High Rocks."

"That's Aelle's land, isn't it?" my father interrupts her. "You crossed the border in pursuit?"

"We must have," Betula admits. "But there are no borders in the forest — and we did not care for it at the time."

"Understandably so." My father nods. "I'm sure Aelle will see it the same." I can hear in his voice that he's sure of no such thing. The king of the Saxons has for long been a thorn in our side, and though ostensibly a friend and an ally, he never wastes an opportunity to annoy my father with some ridiculous demand or perceived grievance.

Clearing her throat with mead, Betula proceeds to tell of the battle on the charcoal burner's glade. The *Hiréd* surrounded the bandits in a tight crescent and moved to attack; the fight turned into a series of individual duels, the finest of which Betula retells in more detail. The gathered warriors murmur, nod, grunt and cheer in appreciation, reacting to Betula's tale as if they were in a theatre. I'm only half-listening. I know the story of the battle will be told and retold many times over in coming months, maybe years, woven into sagas and poems by the king's *scops*; had I been there, my name would be in it — just like my father's name is mentioned in the retelling of every battle he took part in, no matter how insignificant his actions.

But I missed my chance. And I doubt I'll ever get another.

Maybe I *should* become a priest, like my uncle. Nobody accuses priests of cowardice when they don't want to fight. I am ready to be baptised — I can read and write in Latin like any Briton; I've read the Scriptures and the Church writings. It would ruin my father's plans, but I know he'd adjust them if he had no other choice. He'd name some other warrior or

The Blood of the Iutes

courtier as his successor; not Betula — she's a Christian, and she only fights for the Iutes out of loyalty to the tribe and my parents. She wouldn't be interested in ruling a heathen kingdom. But there are others, just as suitable, among the *Híréd* and among his advisors…

Betula's story nears the end. Alas, the chief of the warband, the bald, dark-skinned man riding a Gaulish war horse, and a few of his men on ponies, ran away, while the rest of his warriors held the rear; the forest paths were too narrow for Betula to break through without great losses, and so she decided to let them all go free, once she secured the main prize — the prisoners and the plunder from the villages.

"Running away from a battle — that does sound like Haesta's training, alright," my father remarks. "What did the captives tell you? I assume you interrogated them thoroughly."

Betula nods at a guard. He kicks one of the captured bandits, prodding him to speak.

"We are Haestingas, it's true —" the man says to a few murmurs. My father raises an eyebrow.

"*Haestingas?*" he asks. "You took a clan name after the traitor?"

"We are no mere handful of bandits," the man replies, and there's a shadow of wounded pride in his voice. "We're a clan now, just like any other. Three villages strong and growing stronger by the day."

My father frowns. He makes a gesture at one of his advisors — "we need to talk about this later" — and then nods at the prisoner to keep talking.

"Why is Haesta attacking our villages now? He knows I will be forced to crush him if he goes too far."

"*Hlaford* Haesta did not order this attack," the bandit replies. "It was our own idea. A foolish one."

"No need for you to defend him now. You're not going back to your '*Haestingas*' villages no matter what."

"It's true!" The bandit slams his chest with his fist. "*Hlaford* Haesta couldn't give us the order — he… he isn't even in Britannia anymore."

My father stands up from his seat. His frown deepens into a dark lattice of furrows. "Not in Britannia?"

"He's right, as far as we could confirm," Betula interjects. "Haesta took most of his mercenaries with him a while ago and left for the Continent again. These men have no chieftain. They are leaderless and restless. And there is something else, too."

"What is it?"

"The Iutes were not the only prisoners we freed in the battle," says Betula. "There were a few of Aelle's Saxons there, too."

"What did you do with them?"

The Blood of the Iutes

"We sent them back home."

My father sits back down and rests his cheek on his fist. "Curious," he says. He waves a hand. "Take them away," he says. "Give them some food. I'll interrogate them tomorrow myself."

The bandits are removed from the hall, and the servants bring in the main dish of the feast: a couple of fine-looking wild piglets, and a whole young lamb, tender and gleaming with spring fat. As we dig into the meat, an old man in the long, frayed robe of a *scop*, enters the hall and stands at the raised platform at the far end of the hall; he plucks at the strings of his lyre and proceeds to tune it, waiting for us to finish eating.

"A brand-new song, *Hlaford*," one of the courtiers remarks; fat drips from his chin. "Written especially for tonight's feast."

My father nods. "A new song? I'm intrigued."

The wandering glint of disinterest in his eyes tells me he's anything but. His thoughts are already elsewhere; no doubt wondering what to make of the *Haestingas* and their random attacks. At last, there's some new mystery that can sufficiently occupy his quick mind.

For now, however, he must return to the mundane reality of running a tribe. Between the lamb dish and the *scop*'s performance, there is time for petitioners to request a hearing with the king. There are only a few of them here tonight — this isn't a formal audience, of which there will be plenty throughout my father's stay in Robriwis — but the few that did come bring lavish gifts and equally lavish praise to heap upon the king; hoping, just like Gille predicted, that the delicious spring lamb washed with heady western mead will help keep my father in a considerate mood.

The scene reminds me of how the ancient writers described the courts of the Eastern tyrants, or Imperators of old; it's astonishing how quickly the Iutes — and the Britons, for I see a couple of Cants waiting in the line of supplicants — became used to the new situation, with my father replacing the *witan* as the sole representation, even an embodiment, of the tribe. The Cants are here hoping, no doubt, to gain some amicable trade deal or for him to judge favourably on a land dispute between them and their Iutish neighbours. The Britons have their own ruling Council in Dorowern, but when it comes to disagreements with the Iutes, they prefer dealing directly with my father, rather than appeal through the ineffective Councillors.

As I watch the petitioners present their cases, I'm struck by a sudden idea. I excuse myself from the table. My father barely acknowledges me leaving, with a slight nod, wearily listening to a Frankish merchant describing his demand for better prices on his fish. I leave the hall, borrow a hooded cloak from a guard outside, and return, standing at the back of the line.

When I at last approach my father, a hush falls on the hall. The herald does not announce me, not knowing who I am; I come alone, in a soldier's hooded cloak, without a chest of silver or a servant bringing gifts. My father leans forward, curiously, but when I throw back my hood, he scoffs and sits back.

"What jest is this, son?"

"It's no jest, Father. I have a petition of my own," I say to sniggers and chuckles around the table.

"And you couldn't have just told me when you were sitting beside me?"

"I didn't think you'd find the time to listen," I say. "You've had a busy day."

"I have a busy *life*, boy. Fine." He waves his hand. "I'll indulge this. What do you want?"

"I want to go back to Londin."

The murmurs and chuckles stop. I feel the eyes of everyone around me.

"Why?" the king asks.

"I will be of more use there. I tried being a warrior, and I failed. But I will make a good clerk, or-or a priest…"

"No, I mean — why would you humiliate me like this?" His eyes drill into my skull. "In front of everyone? At *my* feast, in *my* hall?" He rises from his seat. "I thought we had an understanding. Yes, you can do whatever you want, boy. How many times have I told you this? If that is what you truly wish for — we can discuss this. But in private. Now sit back down beside me. You're still an *aetheling* and you will behave like one until I tell you otherwise!"

I reel from the outburst. It's rare for me to see him this angry. The others stare at us in stunned silence. My father sits back down and runs his hand across his face in a weary gesture. He sighs.

"Sit down, son. Please." He points to my seat invitingly. "I've heard your request. I will address it tomorrow. Now, let us hear the *scop*'s song in peace."

"I'm not sure I'm in the mood —"

"Sit. Down. You've embarrassed me enough."

I make my way around the table — I need to walk back all the way, then up again, to reach my seat, past the guests, past Betula and her warriors. When I pass her, the *Gesith* grabs me by the sleeve.

"Octa," she whispers. "Whatever it is that's bothering you, let me sort this out with your father. Don't do anything you'd regret later."

"Thank you, Betula," I whisper back, laying my hand on her one shoulder. "But I can manage this on my own."

I sit down, take a deep breath and calm myself down. The *scop* stares at us nervously.

"I can… I can perform some other time…" he says. "The song might not be —"

The Blood of the Iutes

"Nonsense," my father scoffs. "You've worked hard on it, I'm sure. Let us hear it."

The *scop* gulps a mug of ale, wipes his moustache and, when the hall falls silent, begins his song with a brief invocation to the gathering, to King Aeric, and an appeal to Wodan to bless his efforts, before moving on to the story proper.

Then said Hengist, of boar-helm:

"Come out, Finn Folcwalding,

Come out, chief of the Frisians,

Honour thy fathers, hide not behind walls,

Take up thy war-board, and thy blade-lightning!"

There's no need for the *scop* to explain the situation he's describing. It is enough for him to mention the two names. The story is well known to all in the hall; he sings of the time *Drihten* Hengist spent in Frisia as a young mercenary, leading a warband of Iutes and Danes in service of a Danish chief. Through a series of unfortunate events, Hengist and the Danish chief turned against their host, the Frisian Finn, son of Folcwald. The saga is old — my father first heard it sung nearly twenty years ago, when he first came to Tanet, and it was already a famous story even then.

It appears the *scop* wishes to describe only the last part of the tale, in which the Danish chief is already dead, Hengist took over the command of the Danish and Iutish warband and, after slaying most of his warriors, besieged Finn in his own mead hall with the remnant of his retinue.

"It's an odd choice of subject for a song," I say quietly. "I was expecting him to describe one of the recent raids, not an old story everyone knows about."

"Maybe he thinks there are no new stories anymore," my father replies. "We won all the wars, vanquished all the enemies. All that's left are some forest bandits, some pirates… Nothing worth singing about."

In the *scop*'s tale, Finn Folcwalding has just refused to leave the mead hall for the third, and last time. This marks him as a coward who would rather sacrifice his men than fight an honourable duel. It leaves Hengist no choice but to destroy him and all the remaining Friesians.

The Danes string their bows of sturdy yews,

And the Iutes nock the pain-wasps.

They wrap them in wound-bindings

Soaked in pitch, dripping with tar;

The flame-serpents, the ruiners of houses,

The Blood of the Iutes

Fly through the air, the bearers of fire

    The *scop*'s voice shakes as he describes the burning roof of Finn's hall; I stir in my seat. I don't like where this is going. I don't remember the story of Finn's demise involving fire arrows or burning down the mead hall. I glance to my father and notice a slight frown; he, too, is unfamiliar with this part of the tale.

The door bursts open; the lord runs out:

Gold-breaker, treasure-giver,

With no gold to break, no treasure to give,

No tunic on him, no breeches, no belt,

No helm and no steel-shirt; naked as a babe.

    Sniggers and chuckles ring out around the table. I feel my cheeks and ears burning.

    "Stop him, father," I say.

    "Calm down, son. It's only a song."

Folcwalding charges with war-twig in hand,

But Hengist's men laugh; they surround him

And watch as he trips and falls in the mud,

Weeping and cursing; a child, not a warrior,

Not worthy of being a king, he wallows…

"Enough!" I cry. I stand up, throwing the stool down. I throw the mead mug to the ground and run out of the hall as it erupts in laughter.

I spot a light coming from the *stofa*. My father had one built here, too, bigger and more comfortable than the one at Rutubi, with a tub large enough for two or three people, for when he wanted to talk to his courtiers in private or impress his envoys in an imitation of old Roman style.

    In my anger, I pass the hut at first, but then I stop, intrigued. A bath suddenly sounds like a great idea. It would help me calm down and consider what to do next. I wonder who's using it at this time of the night — everyone should be at the feast. Whoever is in there right now, at least they're not laughing at the *scop*'s song and at my humiliation. Maybe it's one of my friends, Audulf or Gille — though I'd rather expect them to be at the sailors' tavern outside the fort, throwing a feast of their own with the local girls…

The Blood of the Iutes

"Ursula!" I exclaim upon entering the hut. "When did you get here?"

She splashes over the side of the tub. "Just now," she says. "A long journey from Dorowern."

"Why aren't you at the feast?" I ask, disrobing.

I feel no shame standing naked before her, and she feels no shame before me; our bodies have no secrets from one another, though it's been a few years since we lay together; it was the first time for me, just as I was beginning to find interest in such matters, but she lay with Audulf before me, and with Gille after. Neither of us could satisfy her. Just to make sure, she even tried one of Betula's shieldmaidens, before deciding it all wasn't for her, and it would be better if we all just stayed friends.

"I could ask you the same question," she says. "Shouldn't you be at your father's side?"

"Don't even remind me…"

I slide into the bath, close my eyes and let the water calm my nerves. I don't mind that it's no longer hot and oozing with the dirt of Ursula's journey.

I tell her of what happened at the feast.

"Oh, Lord's mercy!" She gives me a slippery embrace. "I'm so sorry."

I shrug, enjoying her wet warmth. "It doesn't matter. I told my father I don't want to do it anymore. I'm not going to be a king — I'm going back to Londin, to Bishop Fastidius."

She pulls away.

"But — that would mean you're no longer with us."

I chuckle. "Londin's not across the sea. I would still come visit. And you'll be welcome to see me in the capital."

She sulks and submerges up to her shoulders. "It won't be the same."

"I mean it. Nothing's going to change. I just won't be training to be a warrior anymore. No burden on my shoulders."

"But you'd make a good warrior. Out of the five of us, you're the second strongest after Audulf. And the cleverest by far. And you're giving up after one misfortune?"

"You don't understand. They wrote a *song* about me. They mocked me in front of the entire hall. Tomorrow, every man and woman in this fort will laugh when they see me. How can I ever be a king to these people?"

"They will all forget about this in a month. In two, you yourself will be laughing at the memory. You just need to go on more assignments, fight more battles. Let this be just one of many."

The Blood of the Iutes

"I don't think I can do it again. Not with Betula and her men. And I don't think they'd want me going with them."

"They will if your father commands them to."

"My father thinks I'm a joke, too. He did nothing to stop that *scop*, even though he knew very well what was happening." I pick up a soapy rag and start to wash my arms. "I don't want to talk about this anymore. Why don't you tell me why you were so late to the feast?"

"It's because of my mother," she says, rolling her eyes. She leaps out and sits on the edge, drying herself with a towel. "Some news came yesterday from across the sea, and the magistrates had to gather urgently to discuss it."

"News?" I sit up, intrigued. "What news?"

"I'm not sure." She shrugs. "There's something going on in Gaul…"

"There's always something going on in Gaul. My father says ever since the Goths sacked Rome, the Empire is like a wounded wild boar: it's dying but it doesn't know it yet… and Gaul is like its bleeding heart."

"This time it may be serious. Mother said she hasn't seen the magistrates this worried since the Huns."

"You don't think… the Huns are back?"

"No, I'm sure she would mention something if they were. It's probably the Franks, or the Goths… There are so many of those little kingdoms now, it's hard to keep track of them…"

"I wonder if Haesta leaving Britannia has anything to do with that." I turn serious. "This is exactly what my father's always saying. All those little kingdoms, clashing with each other, all those dynasties vying for power and recognition — and the Iutes among them…" I scratch my balls. "Maybe I *am* being too rash about this. If the Iutes have to start again a generation later than everyone else, we'll be swallowed whole. Aelle's got a son now — an heir. So does Ambrosius in the West, at last."

"He's waited a long time for this — how old is he now?"

"I don't know — fifty? And his son is ten, I think?"

"I'm surprised he could still get it up at that age."

We both laugh. I climb out and start putting on my clothes. "Thank you for this," I say. "I knew I should've talked to you. I feel better already."

"I know what will *really* cheer you up," she says. She slips a white linen tunic over her head and reaches for the woollen plaid breeches. Sometimes I wonder how she'd look in a dress; I don't think I've ever seen her wear anything other than a shieldmaiden's garb — or nothing at all. "A chase. It's been eight months since we raced across these moors."

"I don't know… I'm tired, after everything…"

The Blood of the Iutes

"Come on." She punches me lightly on the arm. "There are no sacred Iute graves anywhere around here," she adds with a grin. "And we'll get some mounts this time, so Gille's got a chance to win."

"Mounts, huh…" I scratch the side of my nose. "It *has* been a long time since we rode together."

"See? Leave it to me, I'll arrange everything. And no more talk of going back to Londin — at least not until the race. Promise?"

I smile. "It's good to have you back, Ursula."

James Calbraith

CHAPTER IV
THE LAY OF AEGIDIUS

I have never ridden a moor pony before. The beasts, bred from a herd discovered by my mother's people in the heathlands surrounding our colony at the River Meon in the West, are reserved for the *Hirēd* and the king's courier service. My father prefers his moor mare, called Frige, to any other mount at his disposal. Even as an *aetheling*, I could ride any other horse or pony — I once rode a Gaulish war horse around Leman, to see how it felt — but not this one.

I've heard legends of how easy they were in the saddle, how smooth their ride, and how resilient they were; sturdy, yet fast, these beasts are supposedly able to travel longer distances and on less feed even than the famous Gaulish war steeds. The tales have all come true. On the flat plain stretching between the tall shores of the Medu and the sand-spits and moors of the peninsula the locals call the Heel, it feels almost like I'm gliding in the air; the occasional bumping of the saddle wood on my rump the only reminder of the pony beneath me. Instead of an effort, this is more like a well-needed rest after the first stage of our chase — a foot race around the Robriwis wall and an arduous swim across the Medu. This isn't Cantia anymore — the land beyond the Medu belongs to the Briton nobles of Londin; but scarcely anyone lives in these soggy fields, except a few scattered farms we pass along the way, some of them Iutish, some of them Saxon, and a handful still toiled by descendants of the native Briton serfs.

I could almost doze off in the saddle if it wasn't for the sight of Gille's back, a hundred paces before me. Son of Frisian horse traders, Gille is a natural in the saddle and, just like Ursula predicted, quickly made up for the losses in the foot and swim races and shot ahead of the rest of us. With the boat race still before us, I don't worry about catching up to him — just keeping close enough to make up for the distance on the sea.

Ursula was right about one other thing. The chase *does* make me feel better. I feel like the innocent youth I was three years ago, when all five of us met at Rutubi for the first time. Shunned by the Iutes our age, we came up with the idea of the chase as training that we could do on our own, away from the court halls, away from the villages. I can't remember who was the first to propose it — either me or Audulf; but since then, we have tried to organise a chase at least once every time my father's court moves to a new place.

If I move to Londin, we'll never be able to do this again. My father reminded me of this when he intercepted me on my way to the stables.

"Off to the race?" he asked. I nodded silently.

"I'm envious of how close you are with your friends," he told me. "I could never hold on to mine."

"What about Betula?"

"She was always more your mother's friend than mine."

"If you treated your friends the way you treat your family, I'm not surprised."

He winced. "I'm sorry about the feast, son. But you shouldn't let it bother you so. It was a harmless jest."

"*Harmless?* You call all that sneering and jeering harmless?"

"You'll have to suffer far worse insults in your life. And take them with dignity. Treat this as a lesson in leadership — even a king must allow his subjects to laugh at him once in a while."

"You should have stopped them."

"The men were weary. They deserved entertainment. They would have been angered and insulted if I denied them this little diversion. I spoke to the *scop* — he will not sing that song again. As far as I'm concerned, the matter is closed."

"And what about *my* concerns?"

"What more would you have me do? You told me yourself you didn't want to hide behind my authority — I can't punish anyone for what happened. Trust me, if you forget about it, so will everyone else. They are warriors. They don't have time to dwell on such trivialities. Next time, you'll just have to…"

"And will there ever *be* a next time?"

He smiled. "I'm afraid there will be plenty of next times — if you decide to stay here, that is." He looked to the sky and sighed. "I need to gather the court." He nodded towards the stables. "Your friends are waiting. For now, don't worry about any of that. Enjoy yourself."

I didn't need his encouragement to enjoy myself on the chase. As soon as I mounted the moor pony, all my worries seemed to fade away. Nothing could mar my enjoyment of this day.

The waters here are more shallow than at the Tanet Channel — I could almost walk along the bottom — and calmer. It's only a mile to row, but it's a maze between the islands of rushes, sand-spits and reefs of smooth boulders. I can't see Audulf, but he can't be too far ahead. Ursula is right behind me, but I can't see her, either, hidden in the narrow bends.

In a few more thrusts of the oar, I reach a dune spur, prodding deep into the sea. I steer with one oar and, to save strength, let the current, stronger in this stretch of the sea, push me around the promontory. The strait soon widens; here, the canal between the tidal islets meets the mighty Tamesa estuary, a stretch of brackish water many miles wide, reaching out into the Narrow Sea.

When we don't race, this is a good place for watching ships plying the Narrow Sea as they sail to and from Londin's quays. Sleek *ceols* from the Saxon lands, broader, heavier vessels from Frankia, and once in a rare while, a long, bulky merchant galley from Gaul, whose owner, disbelieving the reports of his competitors, ventured on the long journey to Britannia in futile hope of finding some goods they could get a decent profit on back home.

But I have never seen a ship like this. A hundred feet long, at least, two rows of oars, two tall masts rising from the deck, with crimson sails hanging loose in the quiet air; some kind of siege machine on a raised deck on the bow, and a bronze spur, gleaming patina green in the sun, peeking from the waves aft of the hull. A row of red shields lines the side above the deck.

"Don't tell me you've… run out of strength… already!" Ursula shouts between breaths. She's just emerged from around the bend and, judging by how strained she sounds, she's too focused on rowing fast to look up; I know how she gets in these last few moments of the race. I look over my shoulder; just as I thought, she's even got her eyes closed. Her puffing cheeks are deep red. "I always tell you…," she rasps, "fortitude over speed…!"

"Be quiet," I say, "and look where you're going."

She opens her eyes and gasps. She lets go of the oars and lets the current drift her boat past me as she stares in awe at the ship. At that moment, a gust of easterly wind fills out the sails. An Imperial Eagle spreads its golden wings across the crimson cloth, as twenty-five pairs of oars strike the water.

"I need to tell my father about this," I say. "Go get Gille and Audulf. The race is over."

I enter the mead hall and the eyes of my father's advisors turn towards me. A few of them are members of the old gathering of the elders, the *witan*, those whom my father trusted enough to be here. Betula, just back from some patrol along the coast, sits on my father's left side. Ursula's mother, Adminia, a delegate from Dorowern, sits on his right, next to old, one-eyed Haegel, a man my father brought from his adventure on Wecta; he was the one who put the *Rex*'s circlet upon my father's brow. A few more men among them — the master of shipbuilders, the master of brewers and the old *scop*, whose task it is to memorise the proceedings in case something worth mention in a saga happens at the hall — complete the assembly, sitting at the far end of the horseshoe-shaped table.

It wasn't always like this. Until three years ago, before my father declared himself the *Rex*, the tribe was ruled by the *witan* of clan elders, who only elected a warchief, *Drihten*, to command the armies during wartime. But King Aeric disposed of all that, replacing the elders with his court, a small Council of Advisors he appointed himself. He patterned the gathering on the only court he knew, the Londin Council, in which he once served under *Dux* Wortigern. It wasn't a completely smooth transition; my father spent most of the first year of his reign quelling small rebellions against his rule, pacifying the villages led by the elders who opposed him, and fending off sea raiders trying to make use of the chaos; but for the most part, the Iutes shrugged the change off and got on with their lives. It did not matter much who ruled them, as long as they could dwell on their land in peace, tend to their farms without having to worry about pirates and bandits and, if needed, trade their produce in the *wealh* towns without disruption.

The Blood of the Iutes

"What is it, son?" my father asks. "I understand you have some urgent news."

The servants pour us all mead — except the king and Adminia, who drink imported red wine from glass goblets.

"I just saw a *liburna* out on the Tamesa," I say.

"A *liburna*?" one of the elders asks. "What's that?"

"A Roman warship."

"A warship? Are you sure?"

"Of course." Momentarily, I'm angry at him doubting me. It's not like any of these old men ever had a chance to see a real *liburna*. None of us have, not even my father, despite all his many experiences. There hasn't been a ship like this in Britannia's waters in a generation. "Just like in the old writings. A *ballista* on the bow, two masts, fifty oars…"

I describe the ship with as much detail as I can recall, to a few gasps of disbelief.

"There was only one of them?" asks Betula.

"As far as I could tell, yes."

"Could you tell if the ship was new?" my father asks.

"It… didn't look new," I reply. "Except for the sails and the siege machine on the bow, it looked like it has been through a lot."

"Apologies if I speak out of turn, *Rex*," another advisor interrupts gruffly. He's one of Hengist's old companions, retained at the Council as a sign of reconciliation with those who rebelled against him. One of the boys we fought at Tanet is his son. "But is this news really important enough to interrupt our gathering? Some *wealh* ship arriving at a *wealh* city? What does it concern any of *us*, Iutes?"

My father's lips narrow. He scowls at Hengist's man. There's no love lost between the two.

"I remember you were with us at Andreda beach, *Elder*," he says, coldly addressing the man by his old title. "When Aetius threatened us with an invasion. Even he would not send a war galley to these shores. This is an unprecedented event, and it affects everyone on this island, Briton, Saxon or Iute."

"What do you think it means?" asks Betula. "War? Should we mobilise the *fyrd*?"

"They wouldn't send just one ship to start a war," my father replies. "I'm guessing it's a diplomatic mission to the Londin Council. But why now, of all times? And what could they possibly hope to gain from it?" He rubs his forehead. "Do you know anything about this?" he asks Adminia.

"I haven't heard anything about any warship," the Briton replies. "But then, Londin doesn't inform us of their moves anymore. We are independent of the Council, so they feel they don't need to tell us anything."

"Any news from Gaul?"

The Blood of the Iutes

"There's always news from Gaul." Adminia shrugs. "I lost count of the usurpers and *magisters* that came and went over these past few years. But nothing that would explain…" She waves a hand towards the sea. "…this. I'm as surprised as you are. I thought the Legions were busy in Italia."

"That's not what I heard from your daughter," I say. "The magistrates at Dorowern are more anxious than they've been since Maurica."

"Is this true, Adminia?"

"Ursula needs to learn to hold her tongue," the Briton replies. "But yes," she admits reluctantly, "there have been some disturbing developments lately. There may even be a new civil war in Gaul. It's possible one of the sides is looking for allies even here, in Britannia…"

"If they sent a ship here, they must have sent one to Ambrosius, too," I say.

Father looks to me with gratitude. Adminia and I are the only people in his court aware of the politics outside Cantia's borders, though neither of us can match with his understanding. He spent most of his life in Londin, as a close advisor and sometime friend to the last great *Dux* of the Britons. Wortigern even offered to adopt him as his son and heir, before the war ruined any chances of a Iute, even one as thoroughly Romanised as my father, ever becoming the ruler of a *wealh* province.

"They don't need to send a *liburna* to Ambrosius," he replies. "They don't have to scare him or impress him into loyalty."

"So you think this is about loyalty? Are they trying to get Britannia back?"

The Iute elders observe our exchange with bored and confused looks. They are clearly out of their depths; their only experiences are in governing the tribal matters, judging conflicts between the villages, settling market disputes, or, when words fail, leading men into war against raiders and bandits. But a Roman warship on the Tamesa is beyond anything they have ever had to concern themselves with, and they are keen to turn the discussion to things they know, and care about.

"What about the raids on the northern coast?" says one of them. "We were just about to discuss this when the *aetheling* interrupted us. The pirates are becoming ever bolder. They say there was another bad harvest in the North. Is this not worth our attention more than some *wealh* boat?"

"You're no longer at a *witan*, Essa," my father replies. "I decide what's worth my attention. Besides, my *Hiréd* has already dealt with the raiders, has it not, *Gesith*?"

"We routed a band of Northerners near Duroleo today," Betula replies. "At least, I think they're Northerners. We captured a few but didn't have time to interrogate them properly. It's hard to understand their mumbling."

The Blood of the Iutes

The king nods. "I remember. Ask the *wealh* for help. They are more familiar with the speech of the Northerners." He looks to Adminia and waits for the Briton to offer her service, then turns back to the Iute elder. "As you can see, Essa, the raids are no cause for concern. This warship, however, very much is."

"Clearly, you've already decided on your course of action," says Hengist's companion. "I don't know what you expect *us* to do about it."

"I was hoping for some advice. But if you can't offer any…" He shrugs. "We should at least send a man to Londin, to hear what the Romans have to say to the Council. We need to be prepared for anything that may happen — we don't want to be surprised by another Wortimer."

"They would never agree to one of 'our kind' attending their Council," the elder scoffs. "Unless you're planning to go yourself."

"I can't leave my people. And my standing at the Council is not what it once used to be," my father replies.

"Then I will go," I say.

Their eyes turn to me again. "The disgraced child? To represent us at the Londin Council?" scoffs the elder. "He's barely weaned off his mother's teat. Do you want him to humiliate himself again?"

A few men laugh, but this time, my father's glare silences them. This matter is too serious to indulge their jeering.

"I'm eighteen, elder." I reply with a deathly stare. "And my mother is long dead. I speak the *wealh* language like a native, and I am friends with the Bishop. There isn't anyone else here who can speak to the Councillors as equal."

"Ignore him, son," my father says. "He's just trying to rile you. I think this is a great idea. You said you wanted to go back to Londin. This is your chance — not as an acolyte or student, but as the *Rex*'s envoy."

"Thank you, Father."

I try to sound casual, but I can barely contain my excitement. Back to Londin! The great city! No more cramped and dirty mud huts, no more being surrounded by the same Iute pale, fair-haired faces, no more stews and pea-flour bread. My father may be a king, but he's only a king of the Iutes; our life can't compare to that of even the poorest of Londin nobles, and I can't wait to live like one of them, even if for a couple of days.

"Prepare your pony, then. There's no time to lose. That ship will already have moored by now," my father says. "It's a fortunate thing we were all here today. If that *liburna* had come just a couple of weeks earlier, we'd still be in Rutubi!"

I enter the city through the Bridge Gate and halt. I breathe in the unmistakable smell of manure and overflowing gutters, cf brick dust from crumbling walls, of sweat coming off the horses and people, of strange food prepared in the inns lining Cardo Street that links the Bridge with the Forum. To anyone

The Blood of the Iutes

unused to it, the stench must be unbearable; to me, it means I'm finally back home.

Though I lived there only for three years, I think more of Londin as my true *home* than any other place in Britannia. Orpeddingatun, the village I grew up in with my mother and her husband, was destroyed by Wortimer's army, and though it's since been rebuilt and peopled by a handful of Iutes, Saxons and Britons, I have never felt the need to return there since everyone I knew is now gone. And with my father's court constantly on the move, there is no one place in Cantia that I can call "home" anymore.

The three years I spent within the mighty black-and-white-striped walls of Saint Paul's Cathedral, and in the walled complex of buildings around it, were the happiest days of my life. Under the tutelage of Bishop Fastidius, I learned to read and write Latin, history, geography and arithmetic — and was introduced to the tenets of the True Faith of Rome. But more importantly, for three years, I got to live in the greatest city in Britannia.

Everyone I talked to in Londin, then, felt it necessary to point out that the city was a mere shadow of its past glory even before Wortimer usurped the throne of the *Dux*. Ravaged by war, cut off from its trading partners on the Continent, abandoned by its rulers and elites, it was a hollow shell of a settlement. Wind blew dust and waste through the vast, empty avenues. The trade that went on in the markets had dwindled to a fraction of what my father's generation remembered. Whole tracts of tenements in the poorer districts, where my father, my mother and Betula once fought running battles with Wortimer's city guards, had been dismantled for building material for great palaces of Wortimer's loyalists, which, in turn, lay abandoned and unfinished.

    I did not care about any of that. Without knowing how it was in the past, I was free to enjoy what was left of the city. The uncounted layers of history, visible in the *insulae* of tenements, built-up, expanded, then shrunk, finally half-razed to make place for smaller huts. The inns, each filled with more people than lived in an entire Iutish village, serving food that tasted like nothing any Iutish kitchen ever cooked, from ingredients the names I could only guess at; broad highways still bustling with traffic on market days; the ruins of grand public buildings, looming like cliff sides above the narrow streets; nestled between them, smaller, single — and two-storey — stone houses, busy with the kind of life that goes on only in the big city, half-sordid, half-industrious: craftsmen, merchants, bakers, butchers, gamblers, whores, beggars — all mingled together, like ingredients in a stew; sprawling gardens surrounding the crumbling palaces, overgrown with weed and ivy, but still witnesses to the glory and riches of their owners.

    Most importantly, instead of being surrounded merely by Iutes and an occasional passing Briton merchant, in Londin I once lived among a multitude of peoples and races, all looking different, all speaking in different accents and, sometimes, even different tongues, if I happened to stumble upon the crew of a Gaulish, Frankish or Iberian ship on shore leave. I've been missing all of this ever since my father came and took me with him into the country of muddy villages and farmsteads, green fields and wooded hills — and I know he misses it, too.

The Blood of the Iutes

A hurrying merchant brushes grumpily past my pony's flank. "Get a move on, country boy!" he grunts. "This is Cardo Street, not a bridle path in the Downs!"

I smile. Everything is just as I remembered.

The Bishop is surprised to see me at the doorstep of his Cathedral. The people of Londin have themselves only just awoken to the presence of the great *liburna* in their harbour, a ship so great it took the space of three merchant galleys at the pier. Few had the time to process what its arrival might mean for the city, and for the island as a whole.

"Have the Iute priests learned how to see the future now?" he laughs.

"I saw it sail past Robriwis," I say. "My father sent me here to investigate."

"Then you've arrived just in time," he says. "The Council is just about to gather to meet with the Roman delegate. I assume you'll want to join us."

"Then it is true? The ship has come from Rome?"

"South Gaul, I would guess, judging by the markings on the sails," he replies. "But I'm sure we'll find out soon enough." He puts a hand on my shoulder and looks me in the eyes. "You've grown, boy. You're as tall as me. How's Ash?"

I could never quite grasp the relationship between my father and the Bishop. His Grace was the only person I knew who still called my father "Ash" — his old slave name, one he used before he joined the Iutes as the war chief of Hengist's household guard. The two of them grew up together in the same *villa* where my mother worked as a bladesmith's apprentice; when I first saw both of them together, they acted like estranged brothers. Something happened between them that made them grow apart, though they were still on friendly enough terms to meet once in a while, whenever time allowed. Once Ash now Aeric became the king of the Iutes, however, it was no longer seemly for a Bishop to associate himself with a leader of a pagan tribe, and I don't think they have so much as spoken since.

"Hasn't changed much," I reply. "No, I lie. He's grown more… *barbaric*. He's wearing furs now, and thick cloaks, and gaudy ornaments of gold. He's grown a beard and wears his hair long. I don't think you'd recognise him now. Even his speech has grown rustic."

The Bishop chuckles. "Duties of a king. He always had a hard time being accepted by the other Iutes. They saw him as a *wealh*, a Briton, rather than one of their own. So now he needs to be more Iutish than any of his subjects. Is it working?"

"He's quelled all the rebellions, so I guess it is." I shrug.

"*All* the rebellions? Even that cousin of Hengist's… what was his…?"

"Haesta settled on Aelle's land, on the border by the sea."

The Blood of the Iutes

"A screen between the Iutes and the Saxons." The Bishop nods. "Smart move. Don't worry. Remember your Greeks: 'the gods' millstones grind late, but they grind fine'. Haesta will get what's his due yet."

"Shouldn't you be telling me to forgive him?" I say.

He smiles a sad smile. "You are not one of my flock, young Octa," he says. "And thanks to your father, you never will be."

The tall, dark-haired man in a white linen tunic and crimson cape trimmed with golden thread, whom I presume to be the Roman messenger, looks around in confusion.

"Why is the Council of Britons meeting in… what is this, a chapel?" he asks. He speaks in as pure an Imperial Latin as I've ever heard. None of the Londin Councillors sounds as clear and noble as he does. I imagine this is what the words of Rutilius and other Roman writers I've been devouring should really sound like when spoken.

We are crammed inside Saint Peter's, a small church hall adjacent to the Forum. It was once one of the chambers of Londin's *basilica*, the greatest such edifice north of the Alps, as the city folk were always keen to point out, though I doubt any of them have ever been able to confirm that claim in person. Now, the rest of the *basilica* stands in majestic ruin, as does any other public building in the city that wasn't converted into a church.

"The *Praetorium* was destroyed in a fire a few years ago," explains Bishop Fastidius; he omits to mention that the fire was started by my father and his Iute warriors as one of the final acts of the Great War. "We haven't fully rebuilt it yet."

"You mean you haven't rebuilt it at all." The messenger shakes his head. "I know how it is. There are still swathes of Gaul we haven't recovered since the Huns. Never mind. As long as there are enough of you here to hear what I have to say and decide upon it, it doesn't matter *where* we are."

Fastidius's gaze sweeps around the gathered Councillors. Our eyes meet and he acknowledges me with a slight nod. Without his vouching, I would never be allowed inside Saint Peter's, even if I am a son of the Iute king — or maybe *because* I am one. A few of the Councillors might remember me as the Bishop's young ward, but I was just one of many students at the Cathedral and didn't have much chance to make friends among the nobles. A few more would know my father from his Londin days, but that's not something any of them would want to admit to.

"We're all here," says the Bishop. "Say what you've been sent to say."

The messenger unpins his cloak and throws it over the chair, then stands up onto the rostrum which, for the duration of the Council's meetings, replaces the chapel's altar.

"My name is Aegidius Syagrius," he starts. "I am *legatus vicarius* of Gallia Lugdunensis Prima and Secunda. I was sent here on behalf of Imperator Maiorianus."

The Blood of the Iutes

"Maiorianus?" asks one of the Councillors. I know this Councillor as Riotham; he's a Westerner — a representative of *Dux* Ambrosius on the Council, and one of the most learned and powerful members of the gathering. If the quarrelling factions ever allowed election of another *Dux* in the East, he would be the most likely candidate. "What happened to Valentinianus?"

I'm surprised any of the Councillors are able to follow the messenger's introduction. From what my father told me, Londin nobles paid little interest to what happened beyond the borders of their domain. Clearly, things have changed somewhat since his days at the court.

Aegidius shakes his head. "*Valentinianus?*" he asks incredulously. "Are you so unaware of what goes on beyond your borders? Next thing you'll tell me you haven't heard of Gaiseric the Vandal sacking Rome."

The news strikes like lightning. Agitated murmurs rise into a rumble, like a southern wind turning into a storm. A sack of Rome — *again?* I remember my history readings. Forty years ago, the news of an army of Goths sacking the Eternal City triggered the vote that pushed Britannia out of the Empire. Rome was rebuilt after that, and since then great men like Aetius helped to restore some of its power and glory, until the Legions once again marched across Gaul and, at one point, threatened even to take back Britannia — but the Empire never returned to its former greatness.

And now, if the messenger is to be believed, it has happened again — twice in one generation. By someone nobody has even heard about — this "Gaiseric the Vandal"?

My father always expected the unstoppable horde of horse archers, the Huns, to be the ones who would bring down Rome one day. Judging from the agitated, confused whispers, few, if any, of the courtiers have ever heard of these "Vandals". How many more barbarian armies are hiding in the immeasurable forests and steppes of the East?

The Bishop calls for calm. He doesn't seem as surprised as everyone else. He is the only one who, through his contacts in the Church, would be closely familiar with the events in Rome.

"Bishop!" calls Riotham. "You are aware of this?"

"I did receive the terrible news a while ago, yes," says Fastidius. "But it didn't seem something that would be of relevance to the Council…"

"And you were right to think so, your Grace," says Aegidius. "The city soon recovered, and the Vandals were eventually defeated. My lord Maiorianus beat them back and liberated all of Italia… But it wasn't the Vandals who wreaked the most destruction throughout the Empire, and it's not against them that the Imperator is now gathering forces."

"Who is it, then?" asks Riotham. "The Huns?"

"The Huns?" Aegidius guffaws, genuinely surprised with our ignorance. "No, we dealt with them a long time ago… It is the Goths at Tolosa and their allies, followers of the usurper, Avitus, in Gaul, who are Rome's enemies. And it is against them that we are looking for your assistance."

The Blood of the Iutes

There are blank stares throughout the gathering. This is too much information even for the learned Councillors — but they understand the last sentence all too well.

"Assistance?" one of them asks. "Rome… asks for our help?"

"Yes. Your position is uniquely suitable for what we require."

"We have no soldiers to spare," says the Bishop. "You took the last of them forty years ago, if you remember? We have barely enough warriors to defend our own land from barbarians."

"You should've gone to my master, *Dux* Ambrosius," says Riotham. "He will gladly share a few *centuriae* with you — if you can provide the transports."

"We have been in contact with your *Dux*, Councillor — as, I note, has the Usurper," says Aegidius, his voice lowered at the last part of the sentence. "And we are aware of the Council's precarious situation. We've all heard of the terrible losses you suffered from the heathen hordes a few years ago, and how much land you've lost to them." His eyes fall on me, the only fair-hair in the room, and he stares at me far longer than at anyone else. Has anyone told him who I am, or did he single me out just because I don't look and dress like a Briton?

"We are merely looking for a harbour to refit and resupply our ships for the war in Gaul," he adds, after a pause.

"And Britannia is the ideal place for it. One of the old *Classis Britannica* harbours on the southern coast would suffice."

"This is how it always starts," a Councillor harrumphs. "First a naval harbour, then a fort to defend it, then a road to supply it and, before we know it, the Legions are marching up and down the province again."

"We don't do that anymore," says Aegidius. "We are prepared to officially recognise this Council as rulers of a Free Britannia in exchange for your help. And we would, of course, pay for the use of the harbour."

He raises his hand. Two slaves enter the chapel with a great iron-bound chest. They open it up and spill the contents on the floor: it's full of gold and silver coins, jewels and trinkets. The heap raised before the Council is a fortune, even compared to the riches of the city's wealthiest nobles.

"You cannot buy our freedom with such trinkets," somebody scoffs.

"Rome has no right to decide who rules Britannia," intervenes another. I'm guessing he's been sent here to represent one of the *Comites*, rulers of Briton tribes surrounding Londin. "The coast belongs to the Cants and the Regins. This Council has no authority beyond the city's walls."

"With our help, it might have it again," says Aegidius slyly.

The Blood of the Iutes

"*Divide et Impera!*" one of the men shouts. "This is Rome's motto! You'd have us fight each other again and then come to pick up the ashes!"

"Please, my noble lords," Aegidius raises his hands, "I understand your fears. But perhaps, you are misjudging how far Rome's arms can reach. Winning back Gaul — or what's left of it — is a difficult enough task. It seems to me that you need some time to decide the answer. I'm willing to wait until Easter. If any of you sirs would have any questions, I'll be staying on my ship."

He steps off the rostrum and in confident strides walks past the Councillors, past the heap of gold, and past the Bishop, towards the exit door.

Bishop Fastidius leans down to me and whispers in a conspiratorial tone. "Well, we know how *this* will end, don't we?"

"I'm sorry, I don't follow…"

I feel an oncoming headache and dizziness. It would've been difficult for me to follow Aegidius's High Imperial tones even without the torrent of new names and events he introduced. I'm trying to remember as much as possible for my report before the king's court, but I feel the details are already fleeing. What was the name of the new Imperator? Maior…inus?

The Bishop raises an eyebrow. "Oh, right. I'm sorry. For a moment there, I thought I was talking to your father." He sucks air through his teeth. "It's times like these that I wish we could use his mind on this Council…" He waits until Aegidius leaves the chapel before continuing. "I doubt this is the only chest of treasure he brought with him to Londin. The likes of Riotham or Celanius might scoff at the gold, but not everyone here is as rich as they are."

"Bribes?" I guess.

"You catch on quickly." He smiles. "I think you'd better go back to your king and tell him what happened here. If Rome wants a port on the southern coast, the Iutes might end up involved in this whether they like it or not…"

CHAPTER V
THE LAY OF INGOMER

It's an odd feeling, standing on the deck of a ship as large as Aegidius's *liburna*. Though my mind tells me I'm on water, my senses tell me otherwise. The ship doesn't roll on the ripples of the tide, like a Iutish *ceol*; if I focus on my feet, I can sense a gentle wobble, but otherwise, it's indiscernible from walking on dry land.

Aegidius's cabin is furnished like the finest room in a Londin inn, and the large oaken table at which we meet is stacked with soft bread, several kinds of cheese and meat, some strange sauces in little bowls, small plates of preserved fruit, and pitchers of fine wine.

"I know you," the legate says. "I saw you at the chapel. Odd fair-haired boy. What were you doing there? Aren't you too young to be a Councillor?"

"I'm too Iutish to be one," I reply.

"*Iutish*," he repeats, and bites on a piece of cheese in thought. "One of the heathen tribes on this island, isn't it?"

"Not just any heathen tribe," I say. "We hold most of the southern coast, in Cantia… Cantiaca."

My stomach rumbles. He nods at me to sit down and gestures around the table invitingly. I take a piece of chicken

— a delicacy which I've only ever tried in Londin. I missed its sweet taste.

"What do you mean, *hold*?" asks Aegidius.

I feel cold. The chicken sticks in my throat. I asked Bishop Fastidius to help me prepare for this conversation; I wanted to impress my father with something more than just a dry report from the Council's meeting with the Roman messenger. From his tales, I know it's the sort of thing he would've been doing all the time back in his Londin days. If I can't make him proud of my prowess as a warrior, maybe this, at least, would make him appreciate me more? But now, I'm not certain I can handle the situation, even with the Bishop's training.

I finally swallow the chicken.

"Whoever it was said the Council has no power outside Londin's Wall, was right," I say. "The *pagus* of Cantiaca is independent of the Council — but the Iutes are independent of the Cants. We have our own land, ruled by our own king, and we man the forts of the Saxon Shore. Dubris, Leman, Rutubi… We control access to the old naval harbours, such as there are."

"And you are telling me this… why?"

"It just so happens that the king of the Iutes — is my father."

"I see." He smiles knowingly. He pours me some of the wine. "I wonder… It's possible you just saved me a lot of gold — and Lord knows Rome could find a better use for it than bribing some backwater magistrates."

I gulp the wine and let the alcohol rush through my veins to gain the courage for the next question. Still, it comes out with a stutter.

"Wha-what makes you think dealing with us will be any cheaper?"

He gives me a sour wince. "Leave these things to the adults, boy. I can tell you've been prepared for this by someone else. You're out of your depth! Why don't you tell me instead where can I find this… *king* of the Iutes?"

"Robri —" I blurt out. "I mean… I need to know more before I tell you."

He waves his hands. "Keep your secrets. It can't be that hard to find out. But you've impressed me, and I'll indulge your youthful curiosity. What do you want to know?"

"What is *really* going on in Gaul? Why is an Imperator preparing a fleet to attack it? Are there no harbours in Gaul?"

He laughs. "I could explain, but if those educated fools at the Council couldn't keep up, I doubt you'd understand."

"Try me."

He sighs. "Very well." He stands up and walks up to a map of the Empire, rendered in gold and jewels on the wall of his cabin. "This is Gaul." He points.

"I know *that*," I scoff.

"The Goths, much like your Iutes, I'm guessing, have settled in this corner, around Tolosa and Burdigala, first as allies of the Empire, now rivals," he says. "The Burgundians, another troublesome tribe of fair-hairs, are here, West of the Alps."

"That leaves only a narrow corridor to link Italia to Gaul," I notice.

"You're quick! Yes, others have noticed that, too… Including the previous Imperator, Avitus. When he was deposed, he fled to Gaul — and to cut off the route of his escape, he granted that narrow corridor, called Lugdunum, to the Goths and the Burgundians."

"Then it's a civil war," I say. "A clash between the Imperators. I've read about these things."

Another of my father's predictions coming true — the bleeding beast of Rome is eating itself, while Gaul, the jewel in the Empire's diadem, ruptures into ever tinier splinters.

"Avitus is gone," Aegidius continues. The way he says it, I can't tell if the Imperator died of natural causes or was dispatched on the new Imperator's orders. "Maiorianus's rule in Rome is unopposed. We just need to pick up the pieces after Avitus's unfortunate rule. Beat back the Goths, pacify the Burgundians… and take Gaul back from Agrippinus, his *magister militum*. You're still keeping up?"

The Blood of the Iutes

"I... I think so," I say. I pick up one of the strange, dried fruits: a small, brown disc. It's the sweetest thing I've ever tasted. For a moment, I can't speak as saliva fills out my mouth.

"Of course, there is something else I haven't told the Councillors. I saw the way they reacted to any mention of armies and fighting..." He comes up behind me and lays his hands on my shoulders.

"What is it?"

"A good navy harbour is a useful thing to have," he says, "but what we really need are warriors. Fine barbarian warriors like yourself." He gives my arm muscles a squeeze.

"Even heathens?"

"God guides the arrow's shot even from heathen bows. Rome knows full well how useful your kind can be in battle — and how to reward such service."

"I will... relate all this to my father."

"You do that, boy." He pats me on the shoulder. "I've got the feeling we'll be seeing each other soon."

"Why would you do something like this?" my father fumes. "Why would you invite a Roman official *here*?"

I don't understand his anger. I was sure I did everything right. The Bishop even praised me as I departed Londin. "You have your father's mind," he said. "I always knew that. I just pray you haven't inherited his… other traits."

"I have enough trouble without your interference," Father continues. "I don't need to get entangled in Roman politics."

"Trouble?"

He waves his hand. "Nothing you need to concern yourself with. I just received an envoy from Aelle. He's playing his war of words again. It's all just a game for him."

The erstwhile alliance between Aelle's Saxons and the Iutes turned into a hostile truce after the Saxon ruler gave assistance to Haesta's rebellion; but the two have been waging a silent war of words and influence ever since, competing ceaselessly over who is the superior leader of the heathens in Britannia.

"The border raids," I guess.

"He claims *I* sent the men who attacked the Saxon farms, not Haesta. And spreads rumours that I'm selling my own people to the slavers, to fund my lavish feasts. If I don't deal with it soon enough, he'll set the frontier burning all over again."

"This is why we need this alliance, Father!" I say. "You should've seen the amount of gold in that chest. We could hire an army of mercenaries to deal with Haesta once and for

The Blood of the Iutes

all. And the prestige — dealing with the Imperator himself over the heads of the Britons... This would surely silence Aelle for good!"

"You're young, Octa," the king replies. "It took me years to grasp the complexities of Roman politics, and I was *in* the Council, at the right hand of the *Dux*."

"Aegidius didn't seem to think I was too young to talk to."

"He was just playing with you. Filling your head with words and ideas. And you were so quick to believe him." He shakes his head. "I can't have the Iutes get involved in a clash between Imperators, son. We would be crushed like grain between millstones."

"Imperator Avitus is dead. This is just..."

"Avitus, Honorius, Valentinian... Yes, Fastid keeps me well abreast of the goings on in Rome. There have been at least three Imperators in the past three years. At least! These men come and go, but we must live with the consequences of our choices." He catches himself. "Don't tell anyone about this, boy. As far as everyone knows, Bishop Fastidius and I don't speak to each other."

"Of course, Father. But I still don't understand what the harm is in making a deal with Rome. We give them a harbour; they give us some gold. And if we don't offer them that harbour, Aelle might. New Port is better suited for the purpose anyway."

He grimaces. I can see mentioning his rival riles him, but not enough to make him agree with me.

"We don't even have a harbour to offer. Dubris and Leman belong to the Cants."

"Aegidius doesn't know that. And I'm sure you could use your influence on the Dorowern Council…"

"Staying so long with Fastidius poisoned your mind," he says. "You've grown too fond of Rome — or rather, what Rome imagines herself to be. You've become susceptible to her lies."

"Why are you so bitter, Father? You were a Roman yourself, once. You've lived in a *villa*, among old books, among the remains of civilisation. You told me once how sad you were to see the old glory perish in war and flames. And now this very civilisation is pleading to be saved, and you would do nothing?"

"Do you not remember what the men who called themselves 'Romans' did to your home village? To your family? To my… to Rhedwyn? Yes, I saw the glimpse of the old glory when I was your age… But I have also seen what it's become in my lifetime. There is nothing left worth saving."

"Maybe not here, in Britannia, but in Gaul there must still be…"

The Blood of the Iutes

"Enough," he says. "I don't want to hear about this anymore. If you want to make yourself useful, go help Betula with those pirates she captured."

"What's wrong with them?"

"Turns out, they're not Northerners. It looks like they came from the Continent, maybe from the flooded islands north of Frankia. And they came here for the slaves captured by Haesta's raiders. A proper little business enterprise." He rubs his tired eyes. "I thought Meroweg was supposed to take care of those bastards…"

"You know who *could* help us with the pirates… A Roman fleet."

"Gods, give me strength." He raises his hands and eyes to the hall's ceiling. "If you don't —"

There is commotion outside; animals braying and people shouting in wonder rather than fear. Father walks to the door. He stands in the frame and looks outside in silence. My father's house in Robriwis overlooks the harbour on the Medu River and a stretch of the shore reaching all the way to the Tamesa's estuary.

"When did you say this Aegidius was going to come here?" my father asks.

"I'm not sure… He said *soon*. Why?"

"Because there's a damn *liburna* standing at anchor on my doorstep."

James Calbraith

"Why are we doing this, again?" asks Ursula.

We're crouching in the shadow of the wall of the Robriwis fortress, where it crumbles down to meet the river. In the distance, the *liburna*'s position is marked by two lanterns, one aft and one on the bow. The fishing boats are strung out on the beach among the drying nets. One of them should be enough to transport all five of us to the Roman ship, if we're not caught — and there's nobody around to catch us. With the warship at anchor so near, a pirate raid is out of the question, so there's no need for shore patrols, and all the fortress guards are busy tonight, protecting the mead hall where Aegidius is presenting his plea before my father's court.

I was there in the beginning. To my father's increasing annoyance, Aegidius spoke more about the need for warriors than of the naval harbour. I thought I'd try to break my father's resistance again. Surely, I repeated my earlier appeal, if Rome needed our help, and was willing to reward us for it generously, we should give her what she asked for, for civilisation's sake? But that only made him grow more furious.

"Reward? Let Aegidius tell you how Rome rewarded her allies after Maurica. If they hadn't betrayed the Goths and the Burgundians, they wouldn't need our help against them now."

With a soured face, Aegidius tried to explain that whatever happened at Maurica, where an alliance of Rome and barbarian tribes defeated the Hun army — neither of them got into the details of what they were talking about, and everyone except the two of them looked as puzzled as I was — had nothing to do with the new Imperator and his government, but my father would hear nothing of it.

"I admit, I was willing to hear you out regarding the harbour," he told the Roman envoy. "It was a harmless enough request. But you had to get greedy. You had the audacity to come here asking for *men*. You'd think taking all the Legions would have been enough, but no — Rome is an insatiable maw which digests uncounted peoples and then spits them out. It serves her right if she chokes once in a while."

To that, Aegidius could only apologise, bent in half in a deep bow, and withdraw his request for troops. Placated somewhat, my father agreed to resume discussing the needs of the Roman navy, but anyone who knew him could see he wasn't going to agree to anything. I wondered, was he in fact secretly enjoying talking to Aegidius? The Roman spoke in an old-fashioned, literate manner that only I and Adminia understood fully. They exchanged quotes from the Ancients and from the Scripture, as equals in learning, and from time to time, when Aegidius found an accurate response to the king's ancient quotation, I could see a rare glint of excitement in my father's eyes. Still, he remained stubbornly opposed to changing his mind, and I soon grew bored of their increasingly incomprehensible conversation.

That is when I decided to find my four friends and invite them to my little adventure.

"How often do you get to see a Roman warship up close?" I say. "This is the first one in these waters in forty years."

"What do we do once we get there?" asks Audulf.

"Just look about. Check out that siege weapon on the bow… It would be great if I could show you Aegidius's cabin. It's like nothing you've ever seen."

"Aren't there guards? Won't we get caught?" asks Bana.

I shrug. "So what? I'm the king's son. I'll just tell them my father sent me."

"Then why can't we just go there by day?"

"It's more fun this way."

We rush to the boat and push it into the sea, careful not to make too big a splash. It's a moonless, clouded night, and except for the lanterns on the *liburna*, the only other lights are coming from within the fortress and the hall. Audulf and I, the best rowers in the group, take to the oars, while the others make themselves as invisible in the shadows as they can. It doesn't take us long to reach the warship. I slow us down, so that our boat meets the ship's side with only the gentlest of bumps. I grab a thick rope running the length of the ship between the first and the second row of oars and hold onto it until we're certain that no guard heard our arrival.

There are enough holding points on the ship's side — ropes, protruding boards, a decorative eye carved in oak —

The Blood of the Iutes

for us to climb to the deck with little trouble. The stern of the ship is raised and fortified with a wooden rampart; this is where the passenger cabins are. The rampart is empty and quiet today since all the Roman officials are at the mead hall meeting.

I spot a watchman, in sky-blue uniform, no more than twenty feet away. I gesture at the others to duck in the shadow of the rampart. I count only four guards on the main deck. The ship doesn't appear fully manned; some of the crew must have remained in Londin for the duration of this brief journey. The sails are furled and lashed to the masts, which means the ship is moving only by the power of the oars, so there's no need for as many mariners on board as during a true ocean crossing.

"There must be fifty men sleeping underneath our feet," I whisper to the others.

"Slaves?" asks Gille.

"I don't think so," I reply. "Free men are more reliable."

We wait for the watchman to move to the other side of the ship and tiptoe along the line of red-painted shields towards the stern. I expect the *ballista* to be closely guarded, since it's the most valuable thing on the ship outside Aegidius's cabin — but there's only one soldier there, leaning on a spear and staring at the sea, with his back to us. A lantern of polished horn hangs off the end of his spear.

The weapon is almost as big as the ones standing on Londin's Wall. At its feet lies a stack of bolts, each as thick as my arm, a heap of stone rounds, and a large black cauldron, tightly closed, which I'm guessing contains pitch for lighting the missiles on fire. The power contained within the *ballista*'s sinews is terrifying. One shot from it could tear right through a *ceol* or blow my father's mead hall into pieces. What need would an Empire wielding such power have for a handful of barbarian warriors?

I want to sneak closer to examine the weapon's mechanism. Ursula tugs on my sleeve. "Careful," she hisses a whisper. I tear my arm out of her grip, and stumble; I trip over a rope and tumble into the pile of bolts.

"Hey!" the guard turns. "Who goes there?"

He raises the lantern. In the shadows, he can't quite tell who we are. "Pirates!" he shouts and raises the alarm.

"We're not pirates," I tell him in Imperial Tongue. I come out into the light, hands outstretched. "I'm the king's —"

The guard lets out a panicked grunt. He grabs the spear with both hands, whirls it and strikes me on the head with its iron-tipped butt.

A splash of cold, stinking water brings me back. I squint while my eyes adjust to the surroundings; it's already day, judging by the light coming in from the hatch above my head. I look around — I'm the last of our group to wake. We're in the ship's hold, thrown among crates and *amphorae*, with our hands tied behind our backs. The soldier who poured the

The Blood of the Iutes

water on me now stands by the hatch ladder, helping a man in rich clothes descend from the deck above.

Aegidius stares at us for a second, before issuing a curt order: "By Lord's wounds, man, release them!" The soldier's *pugio* cuts through the binds. I rub my wrist and notice something odd about our surroundings. The ship is rolling from side to side, much more noticeably than when it was at anchor.

"We're at sea!" I say.

"Yes, my apologies," replies Aegidius. "I'm afraid the negotiations with your father took longer than I planned and I had to leave in a hurry in the morning. The captain only remembered to tell me about you when we were already well on our way…"

"You've abducted the king's son!" exclaims Audulf. He jumps up with fists clenched. The soldier reaches for the sword. "Do you want a war with the Iutes?"

"Calm down, boy," says Aegidius. "We're only going to Londin. I'm sure you'll be able to find your way home from there. I'll leave you a few coins for the journey back."

"No," I say. It is a sudden thought, but it's clear like a crystal goblet. Seeing the *liburna* up close made me realise something that until now was only a faint, lingering thought: I was just as bored with life in Cantia as my father before me. Maybe, if I had lived all my life in my parents' village, I'd be satisfied with following the king's court around the villages. But I have tasted a life in Londin, and I yearn for more. I could never afford to live in the capital on my own, and I know there is no other place like it in Britannia. But there is a whole other world outside, a world which my father never got to see, other than a few official visits to Frankia and Armorica. A world I've only read about until now; a world of war and chaos, of entire tribes and nations marching against each other, of godlike Imperators vying in titanic struggles, sending armies of thousands to perish in the flames of countless battles. A world where a simple barbarian soldier could become a king-maker, where a youth like me could prove his worth in a myriad different ways, if only he put his mind and muscle to it. And while it is my father's duty to stay with the Iutes in Cantia — I am free to do what I want, and go wherever I wish.

"I'm sorry?"

"Take me with you," I say firmly. "Take me to Gaul."

Aegidius laughs nervously. "I admire your enthusiasm, but I fear your Frankish companion is right — that *would* jeopardise everything I've agreed to with your father."

"You convinced him?" I ask, astonished.

"A mere preliminary agreement, but it sounds promising. I was as surprised as you are. I think he waited until everyone else got bored or fell asleep… In the end, when there were just the two of us awake at the table, he changed his entire demeanour. I got the feeling he *does* want to help the Empire, even if he doesn't yet know it himself… Of course, you'll find out all the details as soon as you return —"

The Blood of the Iutes

"I'm not going back," I say. "And the king can't do anything about it. A long time ago, we made a deal. He would never order me to do or not to do anything against my will. My fate is mine alone to decide. He already agreed I could go live in Londin — he won't care that I have changed the destination. Trust me, he won't even notice I'm gone."

Aegidius scratches his head. "I was hoping to bring back a troop of seasoned warriors," he says, "swordsmen and shieldsmen for which the barbarians of these islands are so renowned. Not one brash youngling with a knife in his boot."

"My mother made this knife," I tell him. "And I can handle myself with a sword and shield just fine, if your men have any to spare. Why not think of me as my father's envoy? Maybe I could persuade him to send you more help if I saw with my own eyes what's happening in Gaul."

"You make a convincing point — and one I see no reason to argue with. There's plenty of space on the ship, though I'd expect you to do your share of deck duties." He points to the others. "But what of them?" he asks. "Shall I at least send your companions back?"

"I don't expect any of you to follow me," I say, turning back to my friends. "I already got you into more trouble than I expected. We were only supposed to see the ship, and now…"

"How often do you get to see *Gaul*?" Ursula mocks me with a chuckle. "Sailing across the Narrow Sea sounds like a much better adventure than anything you've ever come up with until now. And I'm sure my mother will send a ship for me when I decide I've had enough."

"I will go wherever Octa goes," says Audulf, standing beside me. "If you're certain that this is what you want."

Ursula joins him at my other side, as does, reluctantly, Gille.

I look to Bana. The Saxon boy retreats into the shadow.

"Come on, Bana," says Ursula. "We're not going to leave you here."

"No, wait," I say, stopping her. "Don't force him."

"My parents…" Bana stutters, "…they need me in the workshop…"

"I understand," I tell him. "It's fine, Bana. I'd hate to push you into doing something you don't want to do. Besides, I need someone to take a message to my father…"

Aegidius tells us that the harbour town at which we stop for the first night of our journey is called Epatiac. It was once one of the home ports of the Gaulish navy; like Dubris on the other side of the Narrow Sea, it's now just a small market town with a few piers large enough to accommodate the *liburna* and a handful of merchant ships. But unlike at Dubris, and almost any other small town in Britannia, its stone buildings still stand tall, the grid of its streets is still perfectly readable, and there's a crowd of traders and buyers at the market. A flame tower in the harbour belches a thick column of smoke to guide even more ships to the waterfront.

I already feel I've made a good decision.

"Can we really stay here?" I ask Aegidius. "I thought Gaul was occupied by your enemies."

"This is a frontier backwater. Frankia's border is less than a day's march away. Agrippinus's hand doesn't reach this far. By the time he learns of our visit, we'll be safe in Iberia."

"Then why not use this place for your navy's needs? It looks like it's in much better shape than any port in Britannia."

"We can sneak past with one warship. An entire fleet is a different matter. Besides, we need to secure the surrounding land for supplies, a pool of skilled, friendly men to replenish the lost sailors…"

"Then the Councillors were right. You *would* like a colony."

He winces. "It's a little bit more complicated than that. Anyway, I've got things to do here, people to meet — why don't you and your friends go to the market?" he says, keen to change the subject. "There are things even here that you can't buy anywhere on your far-flung island."

"I don't have any money. This is all I've got on me," I say, pointing to the clothes in which I was captured.

He reaches into the chest in the corner of the cabin and pulls out a small cloth sack. He throws it at me. It jingles heavily.

"I was going to try to bribe your father with this, if I deemed him susceptible to that sort of thing," he says. "But he was too honourable. I might as well give it to you."

I untie the purse and look inside. There are a few silver coins among the bronze, and a single gold one.

"It's good you didn't try," I say. I feel my cheeks grow red. I feel insulted on behalf of my father. "He'd have thrown it back in your face. He carries more gold on his person than there is in this sack."

"I may have misjudged both of you," he replies, chuckling. "You must forgive me, young Octa. We don't get much news from your island. According to the scribes and chroniclers, Britannia outside Londin is all but lost to a barbaric darkness."

"Maybe in Aelle's land, or in the North," I reply with a wry smile and, making sure my Latin accent doesn't slip, I add, proudly: "We Iutes are a civilised people."

At first, I notice nothing unusual about the market at Epatiac, other than how busy it is. The first few stalls sell the kinds of goods one would normally find at a market in Dorowern: farm produce, pots, bread. There's a slightly greater variety of food, and the pots are of a better quality, as far as I can tell, but this is to be expected in a busy harbour town. The first novelty I spot is a wine seller, pouring his product from a great amphora straight into the flasks of his customers. In Britannia, wine only appeared on the tables of the nobles; the poor drink ale and milk, and the warriors have their mead. Here, it seems, it's a drink enjoyed by rich and poor alike.

But as we enter deeper, I notice that not only do the goods on sale change, so does the entire market. The merchants wear finer clothes, the stalls are more richly furnished and further apart, and each is guarded by a warrior or two. The stands form a grid of broad avenues, all meeting at a raised platform at the centre.

Every stall sells some kind of weapon or armour. Axes, spearheads, swords in all sorts of styles and shapes. There are Frankish flying axes, Frisian spears, *angon* javelins, twice-curved bows of the horse archers; there are *seaxes* and *spathas*, and a variety of other blades I'm not familiar with. There's one stand that sells only metal bosses for shields, and another with arrowheads and lead slingshot missiles.

The merchants don't hawk their wares to the passers-by like us; instead, they speak only with other merchants, shadowy dealers with bulging purses and muscular bodyguards. Once in a while, a buyer exchanges his purse for a stack of weapons that are then loaded onto a foot cart and taken speedily out of the market.

"What's going on here, Octa?" asks Ursula, staring at the spectacle with wide eyes. "Who are all these people?"

"I'm not sure," I reply. I can't tell any pattern to the purchases. The men who buy the weapons look like Franks, Saxons, Gauls, Britons, Iberians; there's even a thin-eyed, fat-cheeked Easterner, browsing through the bowyer's stand with interest. They all speak the same Vulgar variety of Latin, mixed in with their own tongues and accents. Most of the equipment on sale is used; a lot of it is quite old. The swords are notched and pocked with rust. The spear blades have been torn from their shafts with little regard to how they'd been fitted. The helmets are dented; the mail coats are in tatters. But none of this seems to deter the buyers.

"These must be weapons from Maurica and other great battlefields," I say at last. The greatest battle in living memory took place only seven years ago. If the numbers I've heard rumoured were right, there would have been tens of thousands of weapons lost on that field; enough to sustain a market like this, and many others scattered throughout Gaul, for years. And there has been more fighting since then, wars I'd only hear in gossip about: Franks against Alemanns, Goths against Suebians, Saxons against Burgundians, Roman Legions against all of them… Men were numerous and easy to replace. Weapons were valuable. The buyers in this market would be the representatives of the very tribes and armies who fought in those battles, aiming to reclaim some of the lost property, scavenged from the dead by slavers and corpse thieves.

One of the merchants, passing us by, stops and looks greedily at the sword at my side. It's a Legionnaire's *spatha*, given to me by Aegidius for protection. This weapon, at least, is brand new.

The Blood of the Iutes

"How much would you like for that *sweard*, boy?" the man asks.

"It's not for sale."

"I'd trade you for four of my own," he probes further. "One for each of your…" He looks at my friends, uncertain whether to call them my guards or my slaves. "…companions."

"That's very generous of you, but I'm not interested."

"Wait, you're from that ship that moored today, aren't you? Tell the captain I will buy every weapon he can spare. The River Franks will pay in gold! Just tell him to ask for Probus!"

"Octa, look!" Ursula points to the podium in the centre of the market, while I'm trying to tear my sleeve out of Probus's grasp.

A column of fair-haired slaves, chained to one another, is pushed onto the podium by a burly guard. The slave trader waits for the small crowd at the foot of the podium to calm down, before announcing his new wares.

"What we have here," he says, "are fifteen fine men and women, fresh from the island of Britannia." He touches the muscles of the slave in front. "Sailors. Warriors. Child minders. Supple girls for your pleasure. And this one's a good cook!" he says, pointing to an elderly woman at the back.

"These must be the Iutes captured by Haesta's men!" I say. "The ones they sold to the Frankish pirates."

"We have to save them!" says Ursula. "I know that girl on the right; she's from Robriwis!"

"And that old woman is from a village near Leman," adds Gille. "He's right; she *is* a good cook."

There are far more onlookers than interested buyers in the crowd. I push through to the front. "How much for the lot of them?" I shout.

The slave trader laughs. "They don't come as a set, boy. Did everyone in your *villa* just run away and you're looking to replace all your servants?"

"How much?" I repeat.

"Five solids, if you must know. Five solids, everyone!" he addresses the crowd. "That's a discount if you buy them all together — if you can afford it!"

I peruse my purse. There isn't even one whole solid in it. Aegidius really didn't appreciate my father's worth…

"I'll take them all," a gruff voice calls. I search for the buyer in the crowd. He's wearing a cloak of black fur over a narrow tunic of fine, bright green cloth. A diadem of silver wire adorns his long fair hair.

The Blood of the Iutes

"My lord Ingomer," the slave trader bows with an uneasy smile. "What need does your king have for a Briton cook? Or a cloth weaver?"

"You're not getting out of it so easily, Hypatius," says the man in the fur cloak. "I know you'll get more if you sell these slaves individually, but you said five solids for all, and that's what I'm paying."

The slave trader gives me a vicious stare, then goes back to arguing with the man in the fur cloak; but "lord Ingomer" is a shrewd merchant, and he ends up negotiating himself an even greater discount.

"I will prepare them for you for tomorrow, my lord," the slave trader ends with a miserable look on his face. "And you, boy," he turns to me, "I better not see you on this market ever again!"

"Five solids is a decent price for fifteen Iutish slaves," says Aegidius, nodding, when I tell him what happened at the market. "Especially if some of them are strong young men — or fine-looking girls…"

"That's not the issue here," I interrupt him.

He sighs. "Son, I'm not going to buy out your kindred for you. I know what you're going to say —" He raises his hand. "It would be a favour to your father. It would help to get him on our side… But that's not how things work in Gaul. That man bought the slaves in a fair transaction, and it's not my, or anyone else's, problem what he's going to do with them."

"Then just lend me the money. My father will give it all back to you, with interest."

He lays a hand on my shoulder. "I'm sorry to be the one to tell you this, but… If your father cared so much about his people being sold to slavery, he would send his own merchants to Epatiac. I'm sure he knows what's going on here. It's only a day's sail away from Britannia, after all."

I want to protest, but I realise he's right. Maybe back in the day, when pirates and raiders ruled the Narrow Sea, and the Iutes struggled for survival on Tanet, such a thing was unthinkable; but it's been relatively easy to reach Gaul for a few years now, and my father is not a poor man. He told me often of the pot of gold coins buried on the grounds of the *villa* where he grew up. Why hasn't he been buying back his own people from the pirates?

"See, even your father understands the economy of the Empire. And really, a slave's life is not as bad as you think, especially if he's sold to a good Christian home. Now, if it's one of the barbarian lords that took them…"

"His name was Ingomer."

"Ingomer of Tornac?"

"Maybe. Big man, black fur coat, silver diadem…"

The Blood of the Iutes

"Ah, that's different." Aegidius taps a finger on his lips. "You don't want to involve yourself with him. And *I* definitely wouldn't want to get on his wrong side. You'd best forget about those Iutes, Octa. Anyway, we're leaving tomorrow for Iberia. You'd do well to get used to seeing your people on the slave markets. There'll be plenty more of them in the South."

I return to Ursula and the others, waiting for me at the pier. "We're on our own," I tell them.

"What do we do?" asks Gille. "We can't just leave these poor people there."

"We can't buy them, and we can't *steal* them. The town is crawling with guards," says Audulf. "Not to mention the bodyguards of that fur-cloaked merchant."

"Maybe not while they're in town…" I rub my chin. "But I may have a plan. We just need to find out where he's taking those slaves…"

"What are you thinking? We can't fight through an armed guard," says Ursula. "We're just four younglings — and we don't even have weapons, other than your *spatha*."

"This, we can remedy right away," I say. "Let's go back to the market and find that Probus."

James Calbraith

CHAPTER VI
THE LAY OF HILDRIK

"I can't believe we're doing this," says Ursula excitedly. "A week ago, I was helping my father finish his accounting in Dorowern. Now I'm a forest bandit!"

"You realise we can *die* here, right?" asks Gille.

"Try not to," I answer with a grin. I hush them and we sneak through the scrub. I, too, can't quite believe I managed to convince them — and myself — to this mad plan. We've been following Ingomer's caravan for half a day along a Roman highway out of Epatiac. They are now decamping for the night in the grounds of an old, ruined, halfway *mansio*. A part of me is strangely content to see the ruin. Not everything in Gaul is in better shape than Britannia.

The slaves are ordered to shuffle to the road side and sit there under protection of two armed guards. I notice they're being treated with surprising leniency. Three more men guard the two tents set up within the *mansio*'s walls for the merchant and his servants.

"There doesn't seem to be that many guards for a caravan that size," notices Audulf.

"The roads here must be safer than in Britannia," I say. "No bandits around here."

"Except us," grins Ursula.

"There's still five warriors to deal with," says Gille. "And the only combat experience we've got is beating up some Iute boys in training."

"We can do it. We are Iutes."

"No, we're not," says Audulf.

"We are my father's subjects. That's what makes us Iutes," I say. "Not blood. And that's why we are freeing these slaves. Because they're our tribesmen."

I explain my plan to them in detail. Audulf is to stay in reserve, to draw the attention of Ingomer's guards, while the rest of us will rush to free the slaves. "I don't plan that we will fight all five of them," I say. "I just want to get the Iutes and us out of here as quickly as possible."

Unlike my friends, I feel oddly optimistic. We may have no experience, but we're well trained and have surprise on our side. The Iutes were captured only a few days ago, and apart from the slaver's whip marks and being tired from the day's march, they seem to be in good condition. Some of them look like they might even help us in the fight. If we can all get into the dense forest on the other side of the road, there's a good chance we'll lose any pursuit.

I draw the sword. It's one of the beaten-up, rusted blades from the market. Probus made good on his promise, and even threw in knives for the other three, to match the one my mother made me.

The Blood of the Iutes

"I've never killed a man before," says Ursula, growing suddenly sombre.

"None of us have," I remind her. Her remark makes me pause. Why am I doing this? She is right — I am not a Iute. My mother was a Briton bladesmith. My father may have been born in a Iutish village, but he was raised as an heir to a Roman *villa*.

Ever since I saw that *liburna*, I've been acting like a shield-biter on henbane. I'm not surprised the others have followed me on this adventure — their lives were tedious enough back in Cantia; son of a fort guard, son of a horse trainer, daughter of a minor nobleman from a backwater town… But I'm the *aetheling*, the heir of a king. I should not be playing forest bandits on a country road, somewhere in northern Gaul.

"Octa?" whispers Audulf. "Are we doing this or not?"

"Let's go."

I launch into a charge. Ursula and Gille follow after me. I cross the stone road before the surprised two guards manage to react. One of them, too slow to strike, raises his spear to a parry. I grab my sword in both hands and slash through the shaft with full force.

The blade snaps in two.

"There haven't been bandits on this road since Aetius," says Ingomer. "Who are you, younglings, and what are you doing here? Did Hypatius send you to pester me?"

I make a feeble attempt to wrestle out of the guard's hands, but it only results in him tightening his grip. I say nothing. I haven't said anything since telling my friends to stand down and keep silent, as soon as it was clear we were not going to defeat Ingomer's bodyguards. I managed to cut one of them with the shard of my broken sword, and Audulf gave the other a bruise on the head, but with our weapons broken, we were soon overpowered.

Ingomer picks up the blade from the ground and studies it intently. "Curious," he says. "You're rich enough to buy swords from Probus, but not smart enough to know when he's cheated you." He then looks at the rest of us. "What even *are* you all? You're a Briton girl, aren't you? What are you doing with these two?"

I lick blood from my lower lip. The guard searches my clothes and finds the purse from Aegidius. He throws it to the merchant.

"Wait, I remember you now," says Ingomer, after browsing through the contents of the purse. "You're the boy who asked about the price of the slaves. What is your interest in them?"

"He's —" Ursula starts, but I grimace at her to stop.

The Blood of the Iutes

"I don't have time for this," says Ingomer and turns to his guards. "Kill everyone except the girl. She'll fetch a good price in Tornac."

The guard draws a long knife.

"Stop!" I blurt. "I am Octa, son of Aeric, king of the Iutes."

The merchant laughs. "The son of a king! Ha! I haven't heard that one before. And what is a king's son doing in a forest in Gaul?"

That's a great question…

"I'm saving my people from slavery."

Ingomer laughs again, then his eye falls on the chained slaves. He orders the guard to bring me before them. "If you're their *aetheling*, shouldn't they recognise you?"

"Most of them are serfs," I say. "I doubt they've ever seen me."

"Then it looks like I have only your word."

"I don't know if the boy is who he says he is," says an old woman, sitting at the far end of the group. "But I know the girl. She's Ursula, Adminia's daughter. Her mother owns a wharf in Leman where our ship sometimes moors."

"And that's Gille, Brinno's boy," says another slave. "The best pony tamers between Rutubi and Dubris."

I notice one of the girls sitting at the back — the one Ursula said was from Robriwis — is staring at me curiously, in silence.

"What are the chances of them recognising you?" asks Ingomer dubiously.

"We are a small tribe," I reply. "My companions and I travel with my father's court."

"Hmm." He throws the broken blade to the ground. "Fine. I'll take you with the others to Tornac. If you really are King Aeric's son, somebody there will recognise you."

"What? No!" I protest and struggle again. "We need to get back to the harbour. Our ship is leaving in the morning!"

"And you thought you'd just steal my slaves and take them back to your ship before then?" The merchant laughs again. He puts a hand on my shoulder, in what I take for a fatherly manner — then pushes me down to the ground. "Sit down, '*aetheling*'. You're leaving in the morning, alright — with me, to Tornac."

Here is another thing I've never seen in Britannia: a Roman town that has outgrown its walls. Where Briton towns shrank over generations so much that many of them needed to build second, smaller walls to better contain the receding grid of streets, Tornac spilled out of what was once essentially just a Legionnaire fort guarding a river passage, into a sea of wooden houses and mud huts, sprawling across the bridge to the other side.

Is this what a capital of a barbarian king looks like? Is this what Rutubi or Robriwis will eventually turn into? I have already seen the beginnings of this transformation in these towns, with Aeric's mead halls raised on the grounds of the old fortresses, surrounded by huts of the court followers. But Tornac is different. It is not just a Frankish town — Gauls live here, too, maybe even in greater number than the Franks. It is as if my father built his court in the middle of Dorowern. And the seat of the king is not a mere mead hall. It is a *palace*.

I don't know much about the Franks of this region, other than they have had their *Rex* for a whole generation longer than the Iutes, and Tornac is the chief seat of their court. Some decades ago, the Franks crossed the Rhenum in force, like so many other barbarian tribes, and were "allowed" to settle in the northern marches of Gaul — a tacit acknowledgement of the fact that Rome was too weak to unseat them from the land they occupied, even after Aetius defeated their warbands in a series of battles further to the South. With only the Narrow Sea separating them from Cantia, the Franks have been a traditional ally in our struggles with the *wealas* — as long as it suited their interests.

The fort's walls are far from crumbling; the Franks — the work is recent — filled out the gaps with rubble from the dismantled barracks. Beyond the twin-towered gatehouse spreads a compound of long, low timber buildings, culminating in a grand hall, at least twice as large as the hall in Robriwis, with a roof of slate tiles, its gables and edges decorated in patterns of gold and silver foil.

For five days, my friends and I march tied to the Iute slaves. I wonder how we are going to get ourselves out of our predicament, but I don't worry too much — I am certain once we got to Meroweg's court, my identity will be confirmed by one of the envoys who visited my father over the years. I've grown to know a few of the Iutes as we march down an old Roman road, passing settlements scattered along it between Gaul and Frankia — Seawine, a sailor, who once fought at Crei; Ulfa, the old cook; they are a curious, varied group, thrown together by Fate and the slavers: some, like Ulfa or Odilia, the girl from Robriwis, were captured on a ship heading for Leman, others were taken by the "Haestingas" from our villages on the south coast.

Many of the hamlets we pass have been recently ruined, houses burned, farms plundered and abandoned. I guess these are the remains of the war with the Huns. The frontier land itself was devastated far more thoroughly than anything I remember from Britannia, even at the height of Wortimer's rage. On the worst stretch, on the border between Gaul and Frankia, for one full day we don't see a single farm or a village that wasn't touched by the destruction. But whereas in Britannia the morbid scars of past wars and rebellions remain visible forever among the empty fields, crumbling into dust without anyone taking the slightest interest in ever rebuilding them, here in Gaul, life was slowly returning to the ruins. Scaffolding rose to support the collapsing walls, thatch and animal hides were thrown over the leaking roofs, fields turned green with fresh oat and barley.

As we enter the fortress, Ingomer nods at the guards. They set us all up against the wall.

The Blood of the Iutes

"What are you doing?" I protest.

The guard approaches me, presses my head to the wall and manipulates my wrists. The chains fall. One by one, all of us are released from the shackles. I turn around, rubbing my chafed wrists.

"You're all free," says Ingomer. He throws a jangling purse to the slaves. "Find yourself somewhere to stay the night. My men will pick you up on the morrow. Except you, Octa, son of Aeric. You come with me."

I look to my friends. "Find an inn close to the gates. Stay together."

I follow the merchant down an alleyway, between two timber walls. The guards stand at attention as we pass them.

"What was all that about?" I ask. "What's going on here?"

"Haven't you figured it out yet, *aetheling*?"

We reach the great hall in the centre. The guards bow before Ingomer and open the gate wide.

"Has the king returned yet?" Ingomer asks. Their Frankish speech is similar enough to Iutish for me to understand most of the words, even if I haven't heard it often enough in my father's court, spoken by merchants, envoys, mercenaries — and Audulf's family.

"Not yet," the guard replies. "But *he* has," he adds with a meaningful nod. "That's his horse over there."

I follow the guard's nod to see a tall, haughty, white Thuringian steed tied down before the stables, next to an equally haughty white mare.

"The Gods have blessed us today," says Ingomer. "He's been gone for eight years, and he's back on the exact same day I arrive with the prince of the Iutes!"

There's more gold leaf and silver plate inside the hall, in the carved, insect-like patterns on the pillars and supporting beams and decorating the plates and goblets on the long table. Shields of fallen warriors hang under the eaves, and below them, ancient tapestries line the walls. The tapestries must have been taken from some nearby *villa*, since I doubt a Frankish warlord would order cloth showing scenes from Roman farm life, as do a couple of beat-up plaster statues of Mars and Mercury which the Franks must enjoy, as they resemble their gods, Donar and Tiw.

A seat at the far end of the hall, made from a Roman magisterial chair with intricately carved oaken supports, sits empty.

"So you do believe me now?" I ask Ingomer, as we stand in the vestibule, waiting for our mysterious host.

He nods. "I sent a rider yesterday to ask around. It wasn't difficult to find someone who's been to Cantia recently. It's fortunate that you're so easy to recognise. You should make a sacrifice to whoever of your ancestors gave you this fiery head of hair."

The Blood of the Iutes

"It was my mother," I say quietly. "But then, what about the slaves?"

"Meroweg and the king of Iutes are allies," he replies. "We help your father free them and return back to Cantia. He provides the gold; we provide the dealers."

Have I misjudged my father this badly? Aegidius was wrong — King Aeric *does* care for his subjects. How much gold from the pot in Ariminum has he spent on this enterprise?

"And the chains...?"

"I have a reputation to maintain." He smiles. "If the slavemongers of Epatiac found out what I was doing with their merchandise, they'd never sell me anyone again."

The door on the other side of the hall flies open. A young man enters, with a broad nose, sharp eyes, shoulder-length flaxen hair and a black cape embroidered with the same strange insect-shaped pattern as is carved onto the beams and pillars, thrown over what looks like a Roman officer's clothes. The hilt of his sword is gilded and studded with garnets; the pommel moulded in the shape of two dragon heads. He strides purposefully across the aisle and approaches Ingomer. They pat each other on the arms.

"Uncle," the young man says. "It's been too long."

"You must tell me all about Thuringia, Hildrik," says Ingomer. "I see you got yourself a new horse. *And* a new sword."

"These are not the only gifts I brought," Hildrik says with a mischievous smile. "And who is this?" he asks, turning to me.

"I am Octa, *aetheling* of the Iutes," I say, before Ingomer can speak.

"Then Aeric responded to my father's request!" Hildrik exclaims. "How many warriors have you brought? Is Haesta with you?"

"*Haesta?*" I frown. "Why would that traitor…?"

Ingomer laughs and squeezes my shoulder. "Why don't we all sit down and discuss this with some wine? Your father is coming soon, I hear?"

"His cup-bearer and *maior* are already here, preparing for the court's arrival."

"Excellent. That means the *good* wine is already here, too. I'm sick of that swill they drink at Epatiac."

I've never met a man with more fascinating past than Hildrik, son of Meroweg. Even my father's life seems grey and uneventful compared to what this young warrior, not much older than myself, managed to achieve in the eight years that he was away from his father's domain. Hearing his tale, I'm beginning to understand what drove *me* to flee from Britannia. I feel a growing affinity to the man sitting on the opposite side of the table. He and I both belong to a new generation, a generation born of great movements of people. For centuries, our ancestors lived in the broad pastures and dark forests of their homelands, hemmed in by the Empire's walls, never needing or willing to move further than was needed for the fallow fields to turn fertile again, or the burnt forests to regrow — until the winds of Fate, and the unstoppable steppe warriors coming from the East, forced them out. My father's people sailed to Britannia across the dark and stormy whale-road, searching for a new land to settle. Hildrik's tribe crossed the great Rhenum River and entered Roman land in pursuit of the same. And now, both he and I are driven by the same desire in our blood: to see more of the world, to experience what none of our ancestors could.

The only difference being, Hildrik set out on his adventure years before me, and not of his own accord.

When he was my age, he tells me, he went with his father to fight the Huns at Maurica. On the edges of the main battle, the Salians — the tribe of Franks settled at Tornac — fought a civil war of their own, between Meroweg, allied with Aetius, and his elder brother Adalbert, who sided with Attila. Meroweg won the conflict — but at a cost. For the price of peace, and unity of the tribe, he had to send his firstborn son to the East, to live among one of the tribes forming Attila's Empire: the Thuringians.

"For two years, when Attila was away fighting in Italia, the tribes remained peaceful, and I was busy taming wild horses and fighting the occasional Saxon raiders," Hildrik says. "But then, Attila died, and the tribes united against the Huns under the king of the Gepids. A great battle was met at

Nedao, in the fields of Pannonia. I was on its left flank, leading a small group of Frankish riders."

He pauses for the slave — a beautiful girl, with bright blue eyes and long, braided hair the colour of dried straw — to pour him more wine and put some carved meat on his silver plate, then continues to describe the battle in detail, using goblets and bits of bread as markers.

"We heard of this battle," says Ingomer. "I did wonder if you were there."

"We haven't," I say. I feel left out. Most of what Hildrik talks about goes over my head, except the story of the Battle of Maurica. "We barely get any news from the Continent, beyond what goes on in Frankia."

"And we only know of what happens in Britannia when your father sends us one of his envoys," says Ingomer. "They may call it the Narrow Sea, but it's wide enough for all tales to perish in its waters." He turns back to Hildrik. "With the Huns defeated, you were free to return," he asks. "Why didn't you?"

"There was a war to win," replies Hildrik. "The Huns left an empire to be divided. It was every tribe for itself. The Thuringians gave me a unit of cavalry to scour the Goth lands, all the way to Rome's border. I won great spoils. This sword —" He taps the scabbard at his side. " — was taken from a Goth warlord. For all I know that war is still going on."

"Then why have you returned *now*?" asks Ingomer, and I sense suspicion in his question. "What's changed?"

The Blood of the Iutes

The hall gates burst open. There is a strong resemblance between Hildrik and the man who storms in, except the new visitor is older, stockier and wearing a golden circlet, studded with jewels, upon his head. Ingomer stands up in a bow.

"Father!" Hildrik stands up, too, and extends his arms in greeting. His father slaps him on the face.

"*You!* You dare come back here! After what you've done to poor Bisin!"

I don't know what's going on, but I know I'm standing before Meroweg, King of the Franks, so I bow the deepest of the three of us, trying to introduce myself; they all ignore me.

"Father, you don't understand," pleads Hildrik. "If you only saw her…"

"*Her?*" Ingomer raises an eyebrow.

"You dishonoured your host. You dishonoured your clan, and you dishonoured *me*. I should banish you again."

"Brother, brother." Ingomer wraps his arm around the king's shoulder. "Control your wrath. You should celebrate your son's return, not scold him. And celebrate the arrival of our ally, *aetheling* Octa of Iutes."

"You, boy?" Meroweg recoils as if seeing me for the first time. "Aeric sent his son to us? This is more than I ever asked for. Is the Hammer of Saxons with you?"

"The Hammer of Saxons?"

"Haesta, boy. Haesta and his mercenaries. Where are they?"

Why is everyone asking me about Haesta?

There's enough space at Meroweg's great table for all of us: my three friends, whom I introduced as my followers, some of the freed Iutes, whose presence at the feast I requested as a personal favour, and scores of King Meroweg's courtiers, advisors and family. Meroweg's son sits at his right hand, his wife, Clodeswinthe, at his left. I sit next to them, opposite the king's brother.

The story I tell of my arrival in Gaul, and an attempt to free Ingomer's slaves, amuses the gathered but disappoints the king. As it turns out, he asked my father to send another band of warriors to assist in keeping his borders safe, the way Haesta's mercenaries did some years ago.

"I was hoping Haesta himself would return," he tells me. "He helped us greatly with the border raiders last time."

"My lord, Haesta…" I pause to scratch my nose, "rebelled against my father one time too many. He is now with Aelle and his Saxons."

"The Hammer of Saxons allied with them?" He frowns. "This is troubling news. But I'm sure you and your men will be a worthy replacement."

The Blood of the Iutes

"I'm not here in place of Haesta. This is a misunderstanding. After his feast, I'm taking my companions back to Gaul, as we originally planned."

Meroweg winces. "*Gaul*... Rome... Nothing good ever comes of us allying with them, boy."

"It might be different this time."

He scoffs bitterly. "The hopefulness of youth. You remind me of Hildrik when he was your age." He looks at his son. "It was he who convinced me to join Aetius instead of aligning with my brother. And look where it got us."

"To a hall dripping with gold and silver, Father," says Hildrik. "Bisins's halls are like pigsties compared to yours."

"Do not let your mouth taint this man's name after what you've done to him."

"What *have* you done to this Bisin?" I ask Hildrik.

The young man looks questioningly to his parents. Queen Clodeswinthe puts her hand on her husband's hand and whispers something in his ear. The Meroweg sighs. "Fine." He waves at the guard at the door. "Let her in."

I hear her approach first, before I see her; I hear her in a wave of agitated murmurs rolling up the long table, of whispers of awe and bawdy shouts of approval, which turn into silence as she passes. She is a moving statue of sharp, aquiline features and impeccable proportions; she has a tall, striking brow, pushed far back, bound by long black hair flowing down to her waist; her dark eyes pierce anyone who meets her gaze.

It's impossible to tell her age. She might be not much older than me, or she might be ageless, like an ancient goddess. She approaches the king's seat and takes a deep bow. Every man behind her takes a deep breath of amazement.

"My *herrs* and noble guests," says Hildrik as he stands up and accepts the woman's hand. "I present to you *Frua* Basina of Thuringia. My betrothed."

The gathered wait in silence. Everyone stares at Meroweg.

The king rubs the top of his nose. "You took the wife of the man I was hoping to make my ally. Now I will have to go against the Alemanns alone."

"He was old enough to be her father!" exclaims Hildrik.

"This is no reason to disrespect him so!"

"My king," Basina speaks in a soft, husky voice, leaning sensuously on Meroweg's table. "Your son didn't take me. No man ever did. I went with him freely."

She turns around to address the rest of the gathering. "My husband lost the war against the Gepids. He is a doddering old fool, and I had no more need of him. I sought the hand of the mightiest man in the land," she proclaims and holds Hildrik's hand high. "And I found him in King Meroweg's son."

The Blood of the Iutes

She leans to kiss him, and twenty men imagine themselves being kissed by her at the same time, and sigh.

The feast in the hall ends by midnight — but that doesn't mean the feasting itself is over. The gates of the fortress are flung open, and the king invites the townsfolk, Franks and Gauls alike, to join the reluctant celebration of his son's return by the bonfires and meat-roasting pits scattered throughout the fort's grounds. My friends and I find a small pig spit, turned by a golden-haired slave boy — he might well be a brother to the girl who served at Meroweg's table — to sit around and dip our bread in the fat dripping into the flame below.

"How are we going back to Gaul?" asks Gille.

"I will ask the king tomorrow. I'm sure there are merchants sailing from some harbour in his domain."

"Do we have to go back?" asks Audulf. "The king said something about needing warriors. And I think I found some family here."

"I promised Aegidius," I say. "And the whole reason we came here was to convince my father to help the Empire, not assist the king of Franks in some border skirmish."

I notice the servants around the spit are suddenly bent in bows. I turn around to see Hildrik and his betrothed approach us.

"Is there a place for two?" Hildrik asks. I move away from Ursula. Basina sits beside me. Our knees touch, briefly. My breath shortens.

"I hear you, too, are the son of a king," she says. I can almost feel her breath on my cheek.

"King of the Iutes," I say. I thrust forward my chest. "The mightiest tribe in all of Britannia."

"Then it looks like my father chose his allies well," says Hildrik.

"Your father is not the only one who chose us as allies," I say.

"Ah, yes. I've heard." He nods. "The invasion of Gaul."

"I'm surprised the Romans didn't ask you to help them," I say. "Your kingdom is in the perfect strategic position for a pincer manoeuvre."

"A student of war, I see," Hildrik says with a smile. "They have. My father refused."

"Refused? Why?"

"Because of Maurica, no doubt," says Basina. "The tale of Rome's betrayal reached even us in Thuringia."

"Not just that," says Hildrik. "My father spent his childhood among the *walhas*. He was a hostage in Arelate. He admires them. He knows this is how Rome works, and he never expected them to behave otherwise. Divide and conquer. Lie and cheat. They have been too weak to win through sheer force of arms for generations." He shakes his head. "If it was up to him, I believe he *would* send an army to help Maiorianus."

"Up to him?" I ask. "Isn't a king free to do as he pleases?"

Basina scoffs at my ignorance. I feel my cheeks burn red and bury my face in my knees.

"A king has a duty before the gods and the people," she says. "I don't know how they do things in Britannia, but here if a king doesn't lead his armies to glory, he loses the respect of his subjects. This is why I had to leave my husband."

"Glory, spoils, land to settle," muses Hildrik. "There is nothing to gain from helping the *walhas* win this war. Not with this Imperator."

"What's so different about this one?"

"His predecessors gave away Rome's land to whoever asked. Goths, Longbeards, Franks… This is how we got this town in the first place. Maiorianus comes to take it all back, and he's not going to share any of it with us. His envoys told us as much. This is why he can't find any allies in these lands; this is why he had to send his *legatus* all the way to Britannia. Indeed, I would be surprised if my father wasn't planning to march *against* him, if an opportunity appears. We haven't had time to discuss the war plans yet."

I stare into the fire. It explodes in little bursts every time a drop of pig fat falls into it. I turn to Hildrik again.

"Thank you. I think I understand now."

"Understand what?"

I straighten my back. "I lied. We weren't sent to Gaul by my father. King Aeric was also raised among the *walhas* — or *wealas*, as we call them. He also admired them, once… But then the Britons attacked us and nearly destroyed us. Now he just mistrusts them. Or so I thought. But now, I wonder if this was the only reason why he didn't want to send his warriors here."

This catches Basina's attention. "Your father fought against Rome? Were you in this war?"

"I was only a child," I reply, and the interest in her eyes fades. "But I've heard plenty of stories," I add hastily. "My father led the allied army of all fair-hairs against the Britons. I could tell you all about…"

"Then you're here against your king's will?" asks Hildrik. There's a brusque roughness to his question which takes me aback.

"We stowed away on the Roman legate's warship," I reply. "I was hoping I could convince my father to help the Imperator this way."

"Maybe you could convince *my* father, while you're at it," he says with a wry smile. "Gods know I've tried enough."

The Blood of the Iutes

He stands up and wipes his hands on the cloak. "I need to talk to my uncle. Are you coming with me, Basina?"

"I'll join you later," she replies. "I want to hear Octa's tales of the war."

A moment later, Audulf also stands up. "I think I'll go look for my relatives. I'm sure I've seen some over by the stables. Gille, Ursula?"

"I'll stay," says Ursula with a mischievous grin. "I also want to hear Octa's *tales of war*."

"So, your fathers fought on different sides in this war?" asks Basina, once I finish retelling the Battle of Eobbasfleot.

"My parents are magistrates, not soldiers," replies Ursula. "My father didn't take part in the fighting. Neither did my mother. But they were enemies."

The spit servant offers us slices of freshly roasted meat. Ursula bites into hers with vigour.

"And now you are…" Basina looks from me to Ursula. "…lovers?"

"Lovers?" Ursula chuckles. "No — just friends."

"Do you have a lover back in Britannia?" Basina asks me.

I spit a piece of gristle and lick fat from my fingers. "Why have you come with Hildrik?" I reply with a question.

"You heard me. My husband dishonoured himself with a failed campaign. I no longer wished to be with him."

"I know, but… Why Hildrik? Why not any other victorious commander? Why not whoever it was that defeated your husband's armies?"

She smiles. "Back home, I saw the tribes fighting each other for scraps of Attila's legacy. But whatever treasures the Huns had, came from Rome's chests. Trinkets, thrown at us by the envoys. The true power and glory is here, within the Empire's borders. This is what the Huns came for, and countless others before them."

"And now you. Do you think that Hildrik's Franks will be the ones to grant you the power you seek?"

She shrugs. "If not, I will seek further. At least here, I am closer to the source of the power than I ever was in Thuringia."

"Then you don't love him?" asks Ursula.

Basina laughs "*Love?* I *love* gold. I love conquest. I love hearing the skulls of enemies crushed under victorious boots. And I will *love* the man who brings me the most of it."

Ursula tears off a strip of meat with her teeth. "So… Even our Octa here might have a chance, if he proves himself a capable leader?" she asks with a chuckle.

The Blood of the Iutes

Basina puts her hand on my shoulder and runs her finger under my ear. I shiver in bliss.

"He's young. Who knows what the future may bring him?" She stands up. "I must find my betrothed. I hope we can talk again."

I give Ursula a furious stare. She shrugs it off.

"What a woman, huh?" she says after Basina leaves. "Almost makes *me* want to become a king, just to have a chance with her."

"What was all that about?" I ask.

"Come now, Octa. I was only helping. I saw the way you looked at her."

"Every man with healthy eyes looks at her the same way. But she is the betrothed of our host. I'm not going to bring him dishonour."

"*She* didn't seem to mind," says Ursula, scratching her nose.

"We need to leave this place," I say, "before we get ourselves in trouble."

PART 2: FRANKIA

CHAPTER VII
THE LAY OF ODO

I hear familiar accents as we cross the town's gates. I see familiar-looking faces. It's almost as if we are back in Britannia.

We are back on the coast — a day's march further north than Epatiac, in the small harbour town of Bononia; or rather, what's left of it. The town itself, protected by two remaining walls of a Roman fort, rises on high land above a broad river estuary. Looking down, I see remains of houses, fortifications, temples and *basilicas*, and, further downstream, stone wharves and port warehouses. An entire sunken city spreads below us, several times greater than current Bononia, swallowed by the ravenous Narrow Sea. One of the few structures still standing is a mighty lighthouse, maybe even greater than the one at Dubris on the other side of the sea, overlooking the ghost of the harbour from the top of a nearby cliff. The maze of ruins makes it impossible for any ship larger than a *ceol* to penetrate further upstream, to where the moorings now are, and so, what looks to once have been a mighty harbour, capable of supporting an entire war fleet, has been reduced to a small Saxon port.

It is the Saxon and Iute voices I hear everywhere on the town's narrow streets and market place. This is a Saxon town now, but unlike any in Britannia — the Gauls had abandoned it as soon as the port ceased to function, and the Saxons simply moved into their place, to live among the *wealh* ghosts. It is a clear day, and I think I can see Cantia's shores on the

The Blood of the Iutes

distant horizon, though it might be just the trick of the sun and clouds. It would be easy to change my mind now, to reconsider my mistake, hire a ship from the harbour below and go back home. Forget the brief escapade ever happened. Forget Basina's dark eyes, gleaming like garnets in the hilt of Hildrik's sword…

I look to my companions. They seem content. They are well rested, fed on roast pig and ale. We haven't yet suffered any great hardships on our adventure, other than being led in chains through northern Gaul for a few days; but that now seems a harmless setback, which served only to whet everyone's appetite for more exploits. They expect me to take them further on, to southern Gaul, as promised; what I haven't told them yet is that I have no idea how to get there — wherever "there" is. And even if we do reach some southern port, how would I find Legate Aegidius and the Imperator's army again?

One thing's certain — we are not going to get anywhere near southern Gaul from Bononia. The small ships that land here ply only the Narrow Sea. And it is not why we are here. I agreed to come to this town as a favour to King Meroweg. I'm here as his representative, to send off the freed Iutes back home, and to welcome a ship arriving from Britannia. A ship sent by *Rex* Aeric.

"That looks like one of the royal *ceols*," remarks Gille, pointing to a small vessel being drawn out on the beach.

"Too small," I say, remembering the size of *The Swallow*. "But it's one of ours."

"How many warriors can fit on something like that?" he asks Audulf as we descend the cliff path. "Twenty?"

"I doubt my father is sending warriors," I say. "He promised 'assistance'. Knowing him, it's just some supplies and iron for weapons."

There's a man on the beach, waiting for the ship to reveal its load. Tall, with long black hair with specks of grey in it, bound by a diadem of gold and silver, wearing a purple-trimmed cloak marked with an emblem of the Imperial Eagle.

"I thought we were the ones supposed to meet the ship," I wonder out loud. "What's a Roman official doing here?"

"I'm no Roman," the man replies. "I'm a Gaul, and I'm a friend of *Rex* Aeric. Who are you, and what are you doing here?"

"If you are *Rex* Aeric's friend, you should recognise his son," says Audulf.

The stranger stares at me with a puzzled frown. "Little Octa?"

"Clearly, not so little anymore," I say, annoyed. "And who might you be, to be so familiar with me? I don't remember ever meeting a Gaul like you."

"No, I don't suppose you'd remember. We haven't seen each other in… what was it, six years? So, you finally came to see the famous Gaulish horses!"

"You're Odo!" I recall at last. "The cavalry *Decurion*!"

"The very same." He bows and, in response, so do my friends, though they appear confused. "Now that we remember who we are, how about answering the second question?"

"We come on behalf of King Meroweg," I reply. "What about you?"

"I own this wharf," he says, nodding towards the *ceol*. "And everything on it."

The crew lowers a gangway from the deck, and a Iute sailor emerges, leading a pony in full tack. Another pony follows, then another, until a whole score of them stands in a row on the foreshore.

I can tell at one glance: these aren't just any ponies; these are the moor ponies. The finest treasure the Iutes possess, worth more than their weight in gold. I recognise my father's wisdom; anyone could provide Meroweg with men or swords. Only the Iutes could offer him these mounts.

"It feels like a waste to have these ponies ridden by the Franks," I tell Odo.

He nods. "I know what you mean. The Franks have their own mounts that they know and love. They will not appreciate these little beasts."

One more gift emerges from the ship's hold: a large, iron-bound chest. Odo orders it opened. I peer inside and see twenty fine *seaxes*, twenty lance-heads, and a stack of helmets and mail shirts. I pick up one of the *seaxes* and swish it around. It's a long blade, of the kind my mother used to make, good for fighting on foot as well as from horseback.

"It's enough to equip a full wing of cavalry," says Odo. "All you need now is men."

"And an officer to lead them," I say, giving him a pressing look.

"Don't look at me," he protests. "I fought my last battle at Eobbasfleot."

I turn my gaze towards the freed Iutes, waiting to board the *ceol* before it sails back to Britannia. Though there are some civilians among them, at least half of them are mariners, and a Iute mariner is as good a warrior as any. In this remote part of the world, with no king or *Gesith* to command them, I, the *aetheling*, am the only one whose orders they should heed. All of it is almost too much of a coincidence — if I was as superstitious as an average Iute, I'd almost think it's the gods telling me what to do next…

"I know that stare," says Ursula. "You're thinking of doing something mad again."

"I'm just wondering… Wouldn't it make more sense if, instead of just four unarmed younglings, what we offered to the Imperator was a battle-hardened cavalry squadron?"

"Your father sent these for the king of Franks, not for the Imperator."

"And I will bring them to the king of Franks — with a band of warriors to carry them. This is my best chance to prove myself, to erase the shame of that dark night. None of these Iutes will have heard about my embarrassment. They only know me as their *aetheling* — and will follow me like they'd follow my father."

She shrugs. "Listen, we already told you we will go with you wherever you take us. Neither I nor Gille have any reason to return to Britannia in a hurry — and Audulf seems glad to be here, in his home land. The only person you need to justify your decision before is yourself. If this is what helps you pretend there's another reason why you want to go back to Tornac…"

"I have no idea what you mean."

At Odo's signal, we charge onwards. There's no formation, no wedge or line, just four riders on four ponies crossing the swampy meadow in a haphazard manner, raising fountains of mud. We reach the line of hay bales, each stacked to the size of a warrior, and strike.

Only I and Audulf reach the hay with our swords. I slice through the top of the bale and let the pony's momentum push it forward, before turning back for another strike. Gille tramples the hay under the hooves of his pony. Ursula misses by a few inches, then stops and whacks repeatedly at the bale until there's nothing left of it. Audulf does the same.

"Break!" shouts Odo. "Turn for another charge!"

Ursula and Gille heed the order, but Audulf struggles to make his pony move. I ride up to him and pull on the reins. At last, his pony rears and canters back, with Audulf holding barely on its back. Fortunately, the ponies seem to have received some cavalry training back in Britannia; they certainly know what they're supposed to be doing better than we do. Eventually, we manage to execute the second attack, this time more or less in single line, before returning to the grassy knoll where Odo stands.

He rubs his eyes with a sigh. The other group of four riders, selected from among the freed Iutes, ride out to the field, as servants set up the hay bales again.

"Gille — good control, but your enemy will not be a bale of hay, but a man with a spear. Ponies don't have the chest of a war horse. If you charge like this, your mount will get skewered on the blade," Odo says. "Audulf and Ursula — your main weapon as a rider is speed and manoeuvrability. If you stop to fight, or to finish someone off, you're dead. Always be on the move. Always turn."

We nod eagerly, but I can see Odo's exasperation with our lack of talent eating him inside. We may all be decent riders when it comes to simple travel, but we were never trained to fight on horseback; even the *Hiréd* prefer to dismount for fighting — one of the reasons why my father had such a hard time dealing with Haesta's mounted mercenaries.

"I should show you how to use the light lance," he says, "but it would take weeks to learn how to use it properly. If you must, just use it as a javelin, or a club. Better yet, don't use it at all. You'll only hurt yourselves. Well done, Seawine!" he shouts as one of the riders executes a perfect charge-and-turn.

He's one of the few Iutes who have some skill in riding. The other one is Odilia, the shy girl who stared at me so keenly on that first day, after our failed rescue attempt. She hails from a small farm on the outskirts of Robriwis that we'd pass in our races; she'd watch us play while she toiled at her family's fields.

"I wondered what you were all doing," she told me. "I didn't know you were the king's son, but I knew you had to be a noble to have so much free time to play. I wished I could play with you."

"And now, here you are," I said, smiling. "A Iute warrior in *aetheling*'s service."

I watch her make the same mistake as Gille — charging straight at the hay doll, instead of to its side, for a sword strike — but she's keen to try again, and so are the others, though they fare much worse.

I did not order them to follow me, even though I had the power, if I wanted to — I asked them to join me as volunteers, though I could not tell them what missions I would take them on, or what spoils we could count on winning.

"I was thinking of turning to mercenary work anyway," Seawine replied to my request, while the others nodded in agreement. He had a natural authority about him, which made him overnight a leader of the freed captives. "Those pirates took our livelihoods, and with the situation in Britannia as it is, there's little chance for a brave, honest man to win himself some gold." He shook the newly gifted *seax* in his hand to confirm the gravity of his decision.

I was hoping for a handful — I got them all, even the old woman from Leman; I had to send her and a few others, too old or too frail to be of any use, back to Cantia, but enough of them remained for the "cavalry wing" of my imagination to come true. A dozen freed slaves, the four of us — that left us with four ponies in reserve and to carry supplies, a proportion Odo said was proper for a well-equipped squadron.

"I can't teach you anything more here," he says, observing the riders. "You can't build a cavalry unit overnight. You'll just need to train with these few manoeuvres every day, until you've perfected them, and hope for the best."

"Are you sure you can't come with us?" I ask.

"I'm done with war," he says. "Hopefully, where you're going, what I taught you should be enough. Most tribes here are like the ones in Britannia — they don't fight well on horseback. Just pray that you don't stumble on any horse archers. There are still some left in Gaul, roaming the countryside like hawks."

"We will try to stay out of their way," I say and smile. "Right, you lot," I say to the others, "back on those ponies, and let's try again. The day is still young."

The Blood of the Iutes

"I will let your father know what I saw here," Odo says as I turn away. "I'm sure he will be proud."

The forest reminds me of Andreda.

The great Roman highway, paved with crushed limestone, gleaming white, skirts its northern edge; to our left spread the fields, pastures and farms, scattered among the moors and hills, smouldering slag heaps and smoking chimneys of the smelters. To our right rises a dense barrier of ancient, gnarled oaks, sprawling hornbeams, and slender, silver beeches. Though the spring sun is high up, it doesn't penetrate beyond the first few lines of trees and scrub. Anything could be hiding in that darkness; and though our guides assure us there are no bandits in these woods, at least not in large enough numbers to threaten us, I find it hard to stay calm. There's no way a forest like this isn't teeming with outlaws, runaway slaves — and worse.

I would be even more concerned if it was just the handful of us, riding down this exposed stretch of highway. We are a vanguard of a greater force, a troop of infantry led by Hildrik. Our mission is the same as Haesta's and his mercenary band a few years ago: to patrol the frontier along the Rhenum River and intercept any Saxon or Aleman incursions; they continue to harass the villagers in that region. It's not a particularly exciting or glorious expedition, but neither I nor Hildrik expect our small army to stay long on the Rhenum border. King Meroweg has greater plans for this summer's campaign season, and the skirmishes with Saxons should only serve as combat exercise for Hildrik's troops, and as a way for my cavalry wing to gain experience and unity. As Odo said, we should have little to fear from the Saxons.

"They arrive in small packs, on foot," Hildrik explained, when I asked him what sort of enemy we can expect. "They are the easiest prey when they've already done some pillaging. Then they're weary and laden with plunder. But of course, it's best if we intercept them before they cause too much harm."

The spirits of my men are high. The Iutes sing a marching song; I'm familiar with the melody, but neither I, nor any of my friends know the words. Still, I remain tense. Another dark wall of forest approaches from the north. Soon, the Roman road will descend into a ravine, carved through the trees like a river gorge cuts through rock. I can only hope that Hildrik is right, and that there are no bandits waiting for us in what would be a perfect ambush site.

I look back. A hundred paces behind us is the front of the Frankish column: ten men, marching in a neat line spread across the width of the road. Hildrik's force is no mere barbarian warband but a *centuria*, organised in the manner of a Legion, divided into squads of ten, each commanded by its own officer and carrying its own tents and supplies on the backs of mules. It's clear Hildrik, and at least some of his officers, have been studying the Roman art of war — maybe even been on its receiving end themselves?

Hildrik rides at the head of the column on his white Thuringian steed; next to him, on the white mare, is his betrothed. Like Hildrik, she's wearing a long mail shirt and a silver helmet topped with a figurine of a bull; she's got a lance slung across her back, and a Hunnish bow, double-curved, of glued wood and horn, resting in a leather arrow bag at her saddle.

The night before our departure, Basina visited me in my room in Tornac's guesthouse. She came alone, wearing a hooded cloak, sneaking in like a night thief. Her presence made me uneasy. Why would she keep the visit a secret from Hildrik and the king? I was a guest at Meroweg's court. She was his son's betrothed. She could request that I see her whenever, and wherever, she pleased.

"I'm impressed," she said. She sat down on my bed, only a couple of feet away from me. In the damp cold of the night, the thin cloth of her tunic left little to the imagination. "You came here in shackles, unarmed, with just your three companions. Now you're in command of a cavalry unit, marching alongside my Hildrik to battle."

"I am a king's son, after all," I replied, mustering a proud smile.

"But why have you returned from Bononia?" she asked. "I thought you wanted to go back to Gaul."

"I'm going to, eventually," I replied. "I thought I would try to gain some experience in combat before throwing myself into the Empire's war."

She nodded. "Sounds reasonable."

"I will be back soon," I blurted, a bit too hastily. She laughed.

"Oh, but I'm coming with you!" she said.

"You are?"

"Of course. A Thuringian woman always accompanies her man to the battle."

"That means…" It took me a second. "…you were there when your husband was defeated."

"Yes. I witnessed his disgrace," she replied. "I saw his armies wither before the enemy. I was forced to flee the field of the battle with his entire household." She laid a hand on my shoulder. "I don't think I would survive such a humiliation again."

I swallowed. "I'm sure Hildrik will prove himself more than a capable leader in battle."

"But what if he doesn't…?" With this, and a touch of fingers like a butterfly landing on my face, she left me to my uneasy dreams.

I look over my shoulder again. For a moment, our eyes meet; from the distance I can't tell the expression on Basina's face. I still don't know what she was trying to tell me. Did she want me to protect Hildrik, to make sure he would never lose a battle on this campaign? Or did she mean that if her betrothed fails to meet her expectations, I was the next in line in her quest for power?

She raises her hand, clad in kidskin glove, and gives me a slow wave. I feel my cheeks glow red and turn away. I hear

Ursula giggle. I tut at the pony and ride to the front of the formation.

The dark walls of the Charcoal Forest hem us in on both sides. A lone kite shrills in the sky.

We spot the column of thick, black smoke a mile off, rising high over the treetops. I order the men to ride onwards to investigate. Soon, we leave Hildrik's force far behind.

"What if it's a trap?" asks Ursula.

"Who here would set up a trap for an entire army?" I laugh nervously. "I'm sure it's nothing more than a charcoal burner's hut on fire…"

The forest parts onto a broad clearing on either side of the Roman road. A large village sprawls onto the road itself, leaving only a narrow, paved passage between the houses, leading to what looks like a small marketplace or village square. The houses vary in shape and size; the largest one is a long, timber hall, built along the axis of the highway. The others are similar to the Iute and Saxon huts in Britannia, of daub and wattle, with thick thatched roofs, or smaller dug-in huts used for storage. Charcoal pits and several iron smelting furnaces line the edges of the forest.

The timber hall, and several storage huts beside it, are in flames. I feel a surge of panic; I close my eyes and force my breath to calm down. It's alright. I'm on the outside. These flames can't hurt me.

I focus on the bodies on the road to keep my mind from the fire. I count eight dead, hacked with axes. A few more are scattered among the huts. I tell Audulf and Ursula to dismount and order the others to stay vigilant while we search for clues.

"There's a lot of footprints disappearing into the forest," says Ursula. "Everywhere."

"That would be the villagers fleeing," I guess. "The bandits wouldn't be interested in them once they got what they came for."

I nod towards the smouldering grain store, raised on stone piles over the damp ground, its door stuck open, a trail of barley and oats strewn around the foundations. Of the pile of iron ingots by the foundries, only a few remain, forgotten by the plunderers.

Whoever attacked the village, made no effort to hide their route. None of us is a tracker, but it doesn't take a tracker to follow the trail of dragged dirt, spilled grain, muddy footprints, all leading east, up the Roman road.

"It can't be a large band," I say, looking at the prints. "Twenty men, maybe."

I order Odilia to ride back to Hildrik with news of what we found here, then tell the rest to mount up and make ready — for battle.

"Shouldn't we wait for the others?" asks Gille.

The Blood of the Iutes

"We don't need them. It's just some bandits, heaving with plunder." I'm surprised by my own confidence. Moments ago, I feared meeting an enemy. Now, I'm looking forward to it. "We'll wipe them out. For *Rex* Aeric!"

I raise a fist and the Iutes join me in a war cry.

Half an hour after we set out from the burnt-out village, Odilia, sent out to check the road ahead, returns in a hurry.

"I saw them a mile away," she says, "beyond the great bend. You were right, *Hlaford*. There can't be more than twenty of them, and they march slowly."

"Did they see you?"

Odilia scratches her head. "They… may have."

"No matter. They can't set up a defence line in the middle of a paved road."

I ride out in front of the group and set the pace. A trot first, then, as we near the bend, a quicker step. My breath hardens. I focus all my thoughts on the task before us, in an effort to stem the doubt creeping in.

I am about to lead fifteen men and women into battle. I, whose only combat experience is getting myself almost killed by some random bandit. What makes me more suitable to command the Iutes than anyone else in the squadron? Seawine radiates more authority than I ever did; Audulf is a better fighter, Gille a better rider, and Ursula shows more calm and common sense. Is an accident of birth really all it takes to be a leader?

As we emerge from beyond the bend, I see the bandits lined across the breadth of the highway. I frown, seeing some of them have shields and spears, and form into a primitive shield wall. These are no normal forest bandits; they should have dispersed into the forest, seeing the approaching cavalry, not prepare for a fight. But it's too late to turn back now. An accident of birth or not, the Iutes entrusted me with their command, and I can't disappoint them now. I spur my pony into a gallop and raise the sword high. I glance over my shoulder. Ursula, Audulf, Gille and Seawine form arms of a wedge behind me. The rest of the Iutes ride behind in a loose crowd, not even attempting to shape a formation. Some draw swords, others, too certain of their skill, reach for the lances. I'm reminded of Odo's words — a lance is the weapon of a trained rider. I can only hope we'll manage to vanquish the enemy before any of my men hurt themselves…

"Remember your training!" I shout at them. "Charge and turn. Don't stay in place. And avoid those spears!"

The Iutes respond with another war cry. I look to Ursula. Gone is her usual levity. Deadly serious, she nods, and tightens the chin-strap of her helmet. Audulf draws a lance; I shake my head, but he just grins.

"Spread out," I tell my friends. "Attack the flanks."

At a hundred paces from the line of shields, I launch into a full gallop. I focus on the tips of two spears in the middle of the enemy line. I guide my mount at the shield raised between them and brace myself. The pony's chest strikes the shield; I hold on to the reins as the force of the impact propels me forward. I would be in trouble if my enemies were trained warriors; but the man I charge into drops the shield and covers his head with his hands. I strike down. My sword cuts through his arms and splits his skull. I have no time to ponder the man's death — my first kill. I push forward to attack the warrior in the second line. He swirls an axe. I parry the blow and tug on the reins. The pony rears and, as it drops back on all fours, I bring down my sword. The blade crashes through the shaft of the enemy's axe, his fingers, and ends in the collarbone. The man falls down with a howl.

To my sides, Ursula and Audulf break even further through the enemy line; Audulf holds a broken shaft of the lance and uses it as a club. Ursula stabs and whacks at the shields of the men around her as her pony pushes forward. Seawine, having ridden around the enemy's flank down the roadside, turns around and charges at the bandits' rear.

Furthest to my left, Gille is struggling, entangled between the spears and axes of the enemy, unable to reach anyone with his blade. I kick away a man trying to strike at me with a long knife, then ride around to help Gille out. I sheathe the sword and draw a lance. I throw it at the chest of the man charging at Gille from the flank. The bandit throws his arms apart and falls backwards, breaking the shields behind him. Just at that moment, the rest of my squadron smashes into the enemy. Eleven war ponies, crushing the men under their hooves at full speed, destroy what little unity there was left of the enemy line. The bandits abandon any pretence of standing their ground. Dropping their shields and weapons, they scatter in all directions. Most run in panic down the Roman road. These ones are easily dispatched by Audulf, Ursula and Seawine, catching up to them and slashing across their backs. Others try to flee into the woods, where they think horses can't follow. But we are not riding horses — we ride moor ponies, used to finding their way through thick undergrowth. Within minutes, all but a few of the bandits lie slain by our swords and lances. What few have managed to disappear among the oaks and beeches can't be worth a pursuit.

I return to the road. Hildrik's host emerges from beyond the bend. They're running towards us, but they're too late to share in our glory. I look around. All of my men are alive, and only two are lightly wounded. We destroyed a band of some twenty warriors. I killed three of them myself — a feat worthy of song. I raise a triumphal yell, echoed by my men.

I dismount to examine the fallen. I pick through the shattered shields, trampled spears and the long, single-bladed knives. I study the patterns embroidered into their capes and images painted on the shields, and my concern deepens.

"What are you looking for?" asks Ursula.

"Something doesn't add up," I say. "I don't know what kinds of bandits they have in Gaul — but these are no ordinary forest roughs. Look at these patterns and designs."

"Saxon, aren't they?" notes Audulf. "We knew we'd meet them sooner or later."

"Not just any Saxons," I reply. "These are Aelle's men. Some of them, at least."

"Aelle? Are you sure?" Ursula's mouth twists in doubt. "What would they be doing here?"

"I'm *not* sure — and I don't know. But if I'm right, then this mission just turned into something other than a mere border patrol…"

"The Saxons have never ventured this deep before," says Hildrik with a concerned frown. "The River Franks would have stopped them long before the Charcoal Forest. I don't like this."

According to our guides, we are only a few miles from the forest's end. I still observe the trees with unease, though I doubt the Saxons would send two raiding parties into the forest. I won't breathe with relief until I see open plain again.

We dug no graves for the slain warriors. We had no time, and they did not deserve a warrior's funeral, having fared so poorly in battle. We piled them all on the side of the road and left them for the wolves and the crows. I then dispatched one of my riders back to the burnt-out settlement, to tell the returning villagers of our victory and assure them it's safe for them to return to what's left of their homes and pick up the spoils we won back from the Saxons.

"The River Franks?" I ask.

"That's what we call the clans who live along the Rhenum," he says. "They have their own chieftains, and are not subject to my father's rule, but they remain our friends. We should soon meet them."

I meet Basina's gaze. She nods with a smile. I straighten my back and puff up my chest. All my doubt is gone. I washed off my shame in Saxon blood. I am a proud commander of a victorious cavalry squadron. I can't believe our first triumph was this easy. I'm aware that these were just some foragers, split off from the main host to gather supplies; but there were warriors among them, better trained and more experienced than any of us. I pat my pony's neck. What a difference having a war mount makes!

I glance back and notice Gille's pony slow down. The Frisian boy lowers his head in a sulk. I ride up to his side.

"What's wrong?"

He raises his right hand, trembling, still red with Saxon blood.

"I've never killed a man before," he says.

The triumphant song in my heart turns into a mournful dirge. The battle rush recedes. I realise my own hands are trembling, too. I also just killed my first man. Several men. It all happened so fast, I didn't even have time to think about it.

"All those Saxons we slew would have been somebody's fathers, sons or brothers," says Gille. "There was a woman there who was my mother's age. I let her run away."

"Those villagers they killed, they also had families," I remind him. "And they didn't even get a chance to defend themselves."

I look at Gille again. The boy is still shaken, and I wonder if what happened today is at all what he expected when he joined me on this adventure. We were supposed to see the great cities of Gaul, not fight Saxons in the dark forests of Frankia.

"We all trained ourselves to be warriors," I say. "This is what warriors do. It's not all just one, long, exciting adventure filled with glory and treasure."

"It is in the *scops* songs."

"Life is not a *scop*'s song, my father always says. There will be more blood in our path — and more death. Somebody must always pay for the warrior's glory. Perhaps it's better we learn this truth while we're still young."

"Perhaps," Gille says. "I just hope it's not we who will one day pay for the glory of someone else. I'm not ready. There isn't anyone who'd mourn me, other than my parents and you three — and no one I could mourn when they die…"

I nod in agreement. We were fortunate today. We may not be so fortunate next time. I know many Iutes would make a show of mourning my passing if I was slain by some Saxon's spear — but who among them would do that to ingratiate themselves before my father, and who would be truly sincere in their regrets? I can think of a few who would be *relieved* by my death — maybe even rejoice in it.

One unhappy thought breeds another. The doubt creeps back in. We *were* fortunate that our first enemy proved so weak. I gambled the lives of my men on that, and this time, I was successful — but if the shield wall held just for a moment longer, if there were just a few more trained warriors in the line, how many of us would have perished, and how much worse the mood in the squadron now would be? Perhaps even some of the Iutes would decide they did not, after all, want to follow my lead on this adventure — and I wouldn't blame them…

I need to be more careful. Who knows how long this mission is going to be, how many more battles we'll have to fight? Next time, we might not be so blessed.

The Blood of the Iutes

CHAPTER VIII
THE LAY OF WELDELF

We soon learn what the passing of a war really means to a countryside. We catch the first glimpse of the destruction at Mosa, a river almost as broad and deep as the Tamesa in Londin. The Romans built a bridge here, a long time ago, and it still stands, with only a few holes and gaps — not as grand as the one in Londin, but still an impressive piece of engineering. Many of the Iutes in our band have clearly not seen anything as magnificent before, judging by their gasps of awe and disbelief.

The bridge was once a blessing for Traiect, the small town which grew around it, and the Legions' fort guarding the vital passage. But, when the enemy came marching down the Roman road, it turned into a curse. The low walls and round towers of the small outpost on the far side of the river stood little chance of stopping the invading army. The enemy poured across the bridge and sacked the fort, the town, and the *villas* around it.

This is the first of the ravaged towns we pass on our way, though it was the last on the path of destruction. West of Mosa, the rampaging hordes made their way quickly down the Roman road, avoiding fortified towns as if they were in a hurry to be somewhere. But the countryside between Mosa and Rhenum is a burnt-out shell of its old self. This must have been once a land rich beyond measure, dense with settlements and all sorts of industry. It would have made

Cantia look like a barbaric wilderness. There is barely anything left of it now. We pass miles after miles of sacked towns, ruined *villas*, fallow fields, farmsteads of which only stone chimneys remain. People still live here, eking out a sorry existence among the fields and pastures, but unlike further south, they make no effort to rebuild the ruined dwellings. Vine grows over the charred stone; young trees sprout where wheat once grew.

We reach the edge of one such collapsing town by the end of the first day of marching after crossing the Mosa. The wall that surrounds it is breached and torn down in several places; through the gaps I see the ruin of a large bath house, and a wall of what would have been a *basilica*, looming over the small mud huts raised by the town's returning citizens within the perished *insulae*. I would like to explore more, but Hildrik tells me we are to camp outside the walls in a settlement the River Franks built along the northern edge of the Roman road. There's more activity here than in the town itself. Iron foundries and smithies bellow smoke and flame high into the evening sky. We've passed several such iron-making villages before, all busy smelting what must be enormous amounts of weapon metal.

"*Walhas* live in towns," he explains. "Franks live in the villages. Such is the custom here."

"At least as long as the *walhas* keep a garrison in Coln," says the chieftain of the village, coming out of his long house to greet us. "Gods willing, and with *Drohten* Hildebert's help, this won't last long!"

"I was there when the Huns came," Weldelf begins his tale. The burly Frank, his curly black hair bound with a silver band, is not just a village chief, as it turns out, but a chieftain of the local clan, and a relative of Hildebert, a *Drohten* of the entire River Frank tribe. The timber-framed, shingle-roofed long house built for him in the centre of the village is a smaller, simpler imitation of a mead hall, without any decoration inside, and only furs and animal skins spread on the floor around the hearth in place of table and chairs.

"It was just a large foraging band, really," Weldelf continues. "Attila's main host moved south, towards Mettis. He sent a smaller force to the north, as a diversion and to gather supplies for the main battle with Rome. We had been fighting Aetius for several years before, and were too exhausted to stop them, so we hid in the woods and the marshes. The *walhas* had nowhere to hide."

"They fought well when the Huns besieged their walled towns," says another Frank, with a face marked by a deep diagonal scar. "Like badgers in a sett. And like badgers, they died in their hundreds when the Huns breached the walls."

Other Franks hum in morose agreement.

"My brother was in that Hunnish band," says Basina, unexpectedly. Everyone stares at her in surprise, and I'm reminded of the fact that her people were allied with the Huns, before Attila's death and the demise of his empire. "He died at Coln."

"*Ja.*" Weldelf nods. "Coln held. Many Huns fell at her walls."

The Blood of the Iutes

"Where is this Coln?" I ask.

"On the Rhenum," says Hildrik. "The greatest city the *walhas* ever built in this land. An impregnable fortress."

"As long as there were warriors enough to man the walls of Coln, the city could withstand any enemy," says Weldelf. "Legend has it that our ancestors once besieged it for a full year, and only got inside when a traitor opened the gates."

"There's a city in Britannia by that name," notes Ursula.

"There are many cities by that, or a similar name all over the Empire," says Hildrik. "They were all called *Colonia*-something-or-other in Imperial Latin. But," he turns back to Weldelf, "if Coln is as impregnable as you say, why is your *Drohten* planning to wage war against it?"

Weldelf grins. "I know you and my Salian brothers well," he says, "but I never met this one or his... *Iutes*, you said?" He nods at me. "Your allies will need to earn our trust before we begin to share our war plans with you."

"There may be a chance of that soon," says Hildrik. "What do you know of the Saxon band, that..."

"I've heard enough men talking of war tonight," Weldelf interrupts him. "I want to hear women singing. I want see girls dancing." He claps his hands, and a group of young, fair-haired women stands in the middle of the hall. One of them, clad in a white flowing dress embroidered with red flowers, starts playing a lute and singing a cheerful tune in some language I don't recognise, while the other two dance around her.

I look to Hildrik and notice him scowl in impatience. All through the night, Weldelf had been dodging the subject of the Saxon incursion, and now, it seems, he's evaded the conversation for good, at least until morning.

During a pause between the young woman's songs, Hildrik stands up, bids everyone good night and leaves the hall. A moment later, Basina stands up also — but instead of leaving, she sits down on the deer hide beside me.

A monotonous, rhythmic, humming sound, like a deep, crackling breath, echoes in from the outside, underneath the young woman's eerie song: the noise of the village's iron foundries, working ceaselessly through the night. From a further distance comes a metallic ringing of a blacksmith's hammer. Many of our ponies need looking after, their shoes and hooves damaged from all the charges and tight turns on the hard stones of the Roman road. It calms me down to know someone is taking care of them.

"I saw your reaction when I mentioned my brother," says Basina. "Why were you so surprised?"

"I keep forgetting your people were allied with the Huns," I reply. I spit the name of the tribe with such disgust that it takes her aback.

"It was either that or be conquered," she says with a shrug. "Enslaved. Like her people."

She nods to the dancing girls. The young woman's song turns mournful. She sings in broken Frankish now, of the warriors slain by the Hunnic army.

"I understand. It's just that to the Iutes…" I turn my eyes away from Basina's face. "…the Huns were just a myth, demons from a distant legend. I never thought I'd talk to someone who actually lived among them."

"I didn't know the Huns ever got that far north," says Basina.

"They didn't have to," I say. "They were a great stone thrown into the pond of peoples, the ripple of which threw us out of our homeland and washed onto Britannia's shores."

"It was the same with the Frisians," says Gille quietly. "I remember my grandfather's stories. The floods were bad enough… The sea swallowed the beaches and the fishing villages, flooded the fields, soaked the pastures, drowned the livestock. My grandparents had to move ever deeper inland, ever closer to the Saxon and Frankish lands… But then they stumbled on the Saxons and the Franks moving the other way. Nobody knew why. We were too weak to fight. Our only choices were to flee south or be enslaved."

"The Thuringians had to fight the Saxons because the Goths and the Longbeards were encroaching on our land from the south," says Basina. She opens her eyes wide. "And the Goths were on the march because the Huns were forcing *them* out!"

"We knew nothing of those movements up north," I say. I recall the few times my father and Hengist would reminisce of the life in the Old Country, before the whale-road and the songs of the *scops* telling of those ancient days. "The first thing my father remembers from his childhood were strange riders attacking his clan's lands. Now I wonder if they were Thuringians, or maybe Alans — but back then, all we knew was that they were fleeing from some unstoppable force. And so we, too, had to flee — to Britannia."

"What was life like under Attila?" asks Ursula.

"I never thought of it as living *under* him," says Basina, after pausing for thought. "The Huns were just always there, living among us, with Gepids, Rugians, Longbeards, Goths and so many others. I liked all the attention I was getting from them as a child. I got this from a Hunnic chieftain on my tenth birthday." She reaches into her tunic and takes out a pendant in the shape of an eagle, made of gold and encrusted with garnets. "Sometimes I miss those days," she says. "Before all the tribes started warring among each other."

"Sounds like the old days of Rome," I muse. "I wonder if we'll ever see a world like that again."

"There will be other men like Attila," says Basina. "I'm certain of it." She puts the pendant back between her breasts, and briefly, I wish *I* was that pendant. "This is an age of great upheaval — and great upheaval breeds great warlords."

"You hope Hildrik will be one of them?" asks Ursula.

"I hope my husband will be one of them," Basina replies with a playful grin. "*Whoever* they may be."

We march out the next day — not quite at dawn, as the feasting had gone long into the night. I pack some of the food left over from the feast into my saddlebags: freshly baked bread, matured cheese and pork sausages should make a nice change from the usual travelling fare for a couple of days.

I find Hildrik already out on the road. He's wearing a wry scowl on his face; his left eyelid is twitching, a result, I'm guessing, of a pounding headache we all suffer after drinking too much of the River Franks' heady ale.

"Where are we heading?" I ask.

"South," he says.

"You managed to get something out of Weldelf, then?"

"Something's not right about him and that Saxon band," he says. "But I spoke to other men in the village, and I went to town in the morning." He nods towards the crumbled walls. "Another of those foraging packs passed through here the day before us. If we hurry, we might catch them before they join the main host. And this time, we should keep some alive."

Hildrik splits a small group of fast walkers from his *centuria*; men who can keep up with a trotting pony. We're launching into a pursuit, and this time, Hildrik is not going to let me and my riders have all the glory.

Another, smaller Roman road crosses the town from north to south. Following it, we enter deeper into what was once the centre of the province of Germania Secunda and is now the land of the River Franks. The traces of the destruction left in the wake of the Hunnic horde are not as severe here — the foraging army kept mostly to the east-west road, leaving these southern villages aside.

There's still more industrial activity here. In every cluster of farmsteads, there's either a smelting furnace, a charcoal pit or a blacksmith's forge working all through the day. The entire land is making ready for war. With each village we pass, the scowl on Hildrik's face grows deeper.

"Why do you think Weldelf didn't want to tell us about the Saxons?" I ask. My voice is hoarse and breaking. After an hour of hurried trotting, even on a moor pony, my bottom is aching, and my breath is short.

"I hope it's because he's too busy preparing for the war with the *walhas*," Hildrik replies with an equally weary voice. "And not because he's allied with them."

"The news of the war surprised you."

"I would have thought *Drohten* Hildebert would consult such action with my father," says Hildrik. "Antagonising the Romans when there's an Imperial army marching for

The Blood of the Iutes

Gaul..." He shakes his head. "It's just stupid. If Rome lashes out, they will not care if they're fighting us or them. They'll just want Franks to suffer — and we're closer."

"You think Rome still has enough power to make us suffer?" Basina asks, overhearing our exchange. She surveys the ravaged fields around us with a doubtful eyebrow, and I remember all the ruined towns we passed on our long journey from Tornac, and earlier, as we marched with Ingomer from the coast.

I know nothing of what the rest of Gaul looks like. Perhaps in the South, where the Huns never reached, it is still as prosperous and populous as it always has been, and it might still be worth fighting for. But I can't imagine any Legionnaires willing to travel all the way up here, to wage war over some barbarian villages and crumbling towns. I imagine the same thought must have occurred to this Hildebert; surely, he must have thought the time was ripe to conquer the last vestige of the *walhas*' presence in his land.

"Even a lame wolf can bite," Hildrik replies, then snarls out a litany of swearwords. "And Rome is the greatest wolf there ever was."

"You admire them," I say. "I noticed you made up your army in the Roman manner — and you seem to speak some Latin?"

"And a bit of Greek," he replies with a satisfied smile. "So does she," he adds nodding at Basina. "We had tutors from both Imperial courts in Thuringia."

"Have you seen much of the Empire itself?"

"Only once," he says. "When I accompanied the Gepid king for annual tribute. We crossed into Pannonia and entered the great city of Sirmium. I have never seen anything like it before or since — even Coln doesn't compare. I thought *that* was Rome, at first."

"You paid tribute to the Empire?"

"The Empire paid tribute to *us*." He chuckles. "Or rather, not so much a tribute as a salary — the Gepids kept other tribes away from Rome's borders, and Rome didn't need to waste its own men on holding the Pannonian frontier." He clenches his fist. "If only I could convince my father to join forces with Rome, instead of that fool Hildebert! We could be like the Goths and the Gepids, sharing in Rome's riches and power, instead of fighting for scraps in these mist-shrouded marshes!"

"I know exactly how you feel," I agree, glad to find a common subject with the Frank. "Fathers can be so stubborn! If only…"

Hildrik raises his hand. I follow his gaze down the Roman road. Before us, a mile or so ahead, rises another walled town, somewhat larger than the last two we passed. Once again, I feel like a serf from some barbarian backwater; how many towns have the Romans built in this land? And if this is a remote northern frontier of the Empire, what must the rich South look like?

The Blood of the Iutes

Several columns of black smoke rise above the town — and, mysteriously, right in the centre, one thick, expansive column of white steam, dissipating into a mist over the fields.

The gates are broken open, but the damage is not recent. It seems more like the wood of the door has rotten through so much the hinges no longer could hold it in. We enter the town with caution. There is little damage within the walls, and what there is, like at the gate, appears to come from neglect rather than intent. The town resembles more the places I know from Britannia, with its stone tenements abandoned, the street grid obscured, the crumbled foundations built up with wooden houses and mud huts.

The locals pay little attention to us at first. They're busy running around with wooden buckets of water, extinguishing the fires scattered throughout the town. The water flows out of a large, shallow pool, lined with marble, dug in the middle of the central crossroad. I have never seen anything like it. The water is the colour of pure azure, smells of sulphur, and produces bellows of white steam, as if heated from below, but I can see no furnace or hypocaust pipes.

What I do see, instead, as we march further into the town, are not one but four great bath house complexes, one in each corner, each as large as any in Londin. It is from inside these bath houses, and from several more shallow pools I now spot at other crossroads, that the odd cloud of white steam rises above the city. There are other large public buildings attached to the bath houses — temples, hostelries, taverns, a *Praetorium*; all far too grand for a town this size, and all abandoned a long time ago, judging by the remains of pagan statues and frescoes still adorning the porches and the walls. Between them rise ruins of grand porticoes, atriums and gardens, now filled with waste or built up with huts. There isn't a church anywhere in sight.

"What is this place?" I ask Hildrik. He shakes his head.

"I don't know." He grabs a passing townswoman. She looks up, startled, as if she's just noticed us.

"You!" he asks in rough Latin. "What do you call this town?"

"*Ake*," the woman replies, "Waters."

"Why is the water steaming?" I ask.

She shrugs. "Who knows? It comes like this from the ground. Maybe it flows through the flames of Hell. Now let me go, I have a fire to take care of."

"Wait — the fires — was it the Saxons?"

"It wasn't the damn Huns!" she replies with a sarcastic scoff. "Why would they bother burning down these ruins? I don't know. Lord knows they took everything they wanted anyway."

"Nobody tried to stop them?" I ask. "Have you no town watch?"

She laughs bitterly. "The *vigiles* were the first to hide! Now, will you let me go?"

"We should help them," I tell Hildrik.

"We have Saxons to catch," he says. "They can't be far."

"If the fire spreads from that bath house's roof, it will engulf the entire town."

In my mind, I see the flames consuming a village. I hear the screams of people being burned alive. My hands tremble, and I start into a cold sweat. Hildrik must see it too, in my eyes, for he ceases his protesting and orders his Franks to form a bucket chain from the nearest steaming pond to the blazing bath house. I tell my friends to join them, then rush into a nearby house and grab a tin tub from the hearth. I cast it to the first man in line.

"No!" shouts the townswoman. "Not the tin!"

It's too late — the Frank fills the tub, then drops it with a howl of pain, spilling the scalding water over himself and the nearest comrade. The townswoman runs over to them.

"Take off your clothes! Quickly!"

The two Franks look to me in pain and confusion.

"Do what she says," I order. "The rest of you, grab these," I throw them two wooden buckets I found around the house. "Is there any *cold* water in this town?" I ask the woman. She takes me to an ornamental wellhead, carved in marble in shapes of naked goddesses. I struggle with the chain, until somebody grabs it from me and draws the bronze bucket, full of, mercifully, ice-cold water. It's Basina; her face is tense, her lips tight, her eyes dark and focused. She runs back to the two Franks, shirtless now, writhing in agony in the dirt, and pours water over them. They scream again, even louder than before, but before long, they calm down. The skin on their chests and backs is bright red, covered in blisters and lesions.

Hildrik grabs me by the tunic. "Now look what you've done! Your mercy just cost me two of my best men!"

Basina reaches out and pulls him from me. "He did the right thing," she says. "We'll gain more from it than your two men are worth, you'll see. Now get in that line yourself and start passing those buckets!"

The Saxons do not care for stealth. They set up in a rambling, lazy camp on both sides of the road, blazing with a dozen campfires, with only the slightest guard, more to ward off thieves and wild beasts than any attacking army. The mood in the camp is merry and reckless. Among the plunder taken from Ake were *amphorae* of old, heady Gaulish wine, reduced almost to jelly, leftover from the town's glory days. Judging by the loud singing and bawdy laughter coming from the tents, there's very little left of it now.

"Just as I thought," says Hildrik. "They're not afraid of pursuit."

The Blood of the Iutes

"What does it mean?" I ask.

"It means the River Franks are giving them a free pass," says Basina. "As long as they only plunder the *walh* towns."

We found the Saxons a few hours past the town of the steaming waters, on the narrow, unpaved road leading back to the limestone highway. The land around us is a landscape I'm unfamiliar with from Britannia, but one that forms swathes of northern Gaul: a perfectly flat plain, a sea of grass and clumps of low trees, with little place to hide — another reason why the Saxons don't appear worried of ambush. The three of us had to crawl through tall grass from a hazel thicket where we left the rest of our troops.

"Has this happened before?" I ask.

"Not that I know," replies Hildrik. "But then, I haven't been in this land in years. I only know as much as my father told me."

"When my husband let the Rugians pass through his territory without harm, it was because they were marching against one of his own enemies," says Basina. "The same thing must be happening here."

We study the camp in silence, to learn the patterns of the guards and the setup of defences. The Saxons threw a barrier of logs and brambles across the Roman road, which means they aren't completely oblivious to the possibility of an attack, but they can't be expecting anything more than a band of Gauls seeking revenge for the destruction of their towns.

"At least we know Weldelf didn't warn them of our coming," says Hildrik. "Or they wouldn't be so careless."

"Have you noticed," I ask, "for a raiding party, they haven't actually been doing a lot of *raiding*? They seem a very disciplined band. Other than the wine, they only took the necessities — food, fodder, metal for weapons. Where are the women? Where's the gold?"

"Maybe they're in a hurry," suggests Basina.

"Or maybe they're under strict orders, and expect to obtain the real treasure elsewhere," I say. "Where does that road lead to? Back to Coln?"

"To a crossroad at Tolbiac," replies Hildrik. "You can go anywhere from there — east to Coln, back across the Rhenum to the north, or south, deeper into Gaul."

"Perhaps the Saxons are marching on Gaul, then," I say.

"They would need a massive army to try something like that," says Hildrik. "We would know about it."

"Not if they had allies in the South…"

"This is idle talk," says Hildrik. "The sooner we attack, the sooner we can capture ourselves some tongue and find out everything we need."

The Blood of the Iutes

We crawl back to the hazel thicket. Our entire host is gathered here — and more; Hildrik's numbers have increased by a dozen men: the *vigiles*, watchmen from Ake, who joined us in gratitude for saving their town — in hopes of wreaking some revenge on the Saxon raiders. Nobody expects them to fare well in the coming battle, not least the *vigiles* themselves — they are more used to chasing thieves and dragging drunkards out of the gutters than fighting a trained warband. But if they're keen enough not to flee at the first sight of blood, they might at least prove a useful distraction from the main attack.

The townsfolk wanted to throw us a feast after the flames died down, but there was no time, no matter how much I may have wanted to bathe in the steaming waters — the first proper bath I'd partake of since leaving Britannia; so to find out more about the strange town and its mysterious springs, I had to talk to their leader, *Praefect* Paulus, as we marched in pursuit of the Saxons. He told me that the Roman nobles believed the sulphur-smelling waters were good for their health, and back in the days of his ancestors, the rich and powerful would come to bathe in the great bath houses from all corners of the Empire.

"Actually, the only other place like this I've ever heard about was in Britannia," he said. "Ake Sulis, I think; you may have heard about it?"

I had to admit that, to my shame, I had no idea of a town of this name anywhere on the island.

"The nobles would build palaces and *villas* all over the town," he continued to reminisce, "dripping with gold and marble; gardens with exotic birds and individual pools filled with the steaming water, so that they could bathe whenever they pleased. Legionnaires would come here on leave, to rest and heal after battles. The taverns were full of song and beautiful women."

"Do you remember any of it yourself?"

"No." He shook his head sadly. "All of it was gone long before even my father was born. The *villas* dismantled, the treasure sold for food in times of famine and plague. The last tavern shut down after the Franks crossed the Rhenum. Sometimes we would get visitors from Coln or Trever, but they just stayed as guests in the houses of the townspeople."

"And yet you still had enough valuables stored in the town for the Saxons to consider you worth plundering."

"They probably took the last of it. I'm not sure if the town will survive much longer. People are moving away: to the South, or to the countryside." He smiled ruefully. "This might well be the last ever fight of the Ake town watch."

"Better make it count, then."

Paulus and I watch, or rather, listen, to Hildrik's column as it moves out, slowly and carefully, of the hazel thicket. Hildrik did not want the Ake *vigiles* joining him; he doesn't trust them or their training enough, so it was decided they would march with my vanguard. I turn to my riders and order all Iutes to leave their ponies tied to the trees.

"We strike just before dawn," I say. "None of you has trained to even ride in the dark, much less to fight, and the ponies are not used to being ridden in the darkness."

They murmur in agreement. I can't see their faces clearly in the gloom — we dare not light torches for fear of being spotted by a Saxon patrol — but I can hear in their voices that the confidence they gained after the previous battle is all but gone. It doesn't take much combat experience to know that attacking a large, armed war camp, in the middle of the night, is a completely different kind of battle to charging a pack of foragers by day.

"We are not alone," I tell them. "The Franks will do most of the fighting tonight. We're only expected to assist them and pick out the survivors. Just stay close to me and keep a tight formation. We'll get through this together. Donar leads us."

"Donar leads us," the Iutes repeat in a loud, subdued whisper. It would be better if this was a heartfelt war cry, but it must wait until we're in range of a charge.

By the time we reach the position in which Hildrik's men are lying in wait, the eastern sky is already beginning to grow grey. A mist rises from the ground, thickening fast in the still air. Only a few campfires are still burning, and most Saxons are drunkenly asleep in their tents or on the grass under the stars. But there are more guards around the camp; the chief of the warband must have grown wary of spending a night in hostile territory. A hesitation rises in my mind. What if it's a trap — what if the River Franks *did* warn the Saxons of our pursuit? What if the warriors are not sleeping in their tents, but waiting with spears drawn?

But excitement soon replaces doubt. The Franks are moving to attack. I haven't seen them fight a battle before; indeed, this will be the first pitched battle I will have seen since witnessing Wortimer's war as a child, and the first one I will be taking an active part in. This is my Saffron Valley — at long last, and this time, I'm ready.

Hildrik may have spent the last couple of years in command of Thuringian troops, but he is just as skilled leading his kin. In the gloomy, hazy darkness, it's impossible to see the Franks clearly as they sneak through the tall grass. Hildrik's men carry axes and long knives, having left the spears, useless in close combat, back in the thicket. They spread out in a broad crescent around the camp, invisible to the guards; if I didn't know they were there, I don't think I would be able to spot them myself. I wonder how they're managing to stay in formation in the darkness — my Iutes and I have to walk in single file, each warrior holding on to the arm of the man before him, like blind leading the blind. I'm in front of the column — Ursula's hand rests on my shoulder. Once in a while, she gives me an encouraging squeeze. We move in a broad arc around the camp, until we reach the road on the other side.

Just then, I hear the echo of a distant war cry. Hildrik has launched his assault. The time for secrecy is over. I command my men to spread out across the road and move in the direction of the camp, but not to charge; not yet.

The Blood of the Iutes

"Look out for any Saxons running your way," I tell them. "Our main task is to pick off the survivors."

As the Iutes and the *vigiles* move forward, I gather my friends around me. "We need a few of them alive," I say. "I have to know why there are Aelle's men among them. Audulf, you're the strongest of us all. Try to find me someone who will talk."

"I'll do my best," says Audulf. I pat him one last time on the shoulder; he draws his sword and disappears into the dark fog.

She runs out of the shadows straight at me, half-naked, wild-eyed, with her hair loose, holding a short *seax* in a bloodied hand. She spots me and slashes at me without stopping. I take the *seax* on the shield — I picked it up from one of her dead kinsmen back in Charcoal Forest — dodge aside and cut her across the back. She cries out, runs a few steps more, then stumbles and falls. She jerks twice, before turning still forever.

I take a deep breath and hold my right wrist with my left hand to stop it from trembling. This is the third Saxon I have slain today. The second one took me longer to kill, an exchange of several blows, before I got in with a fortunate thrust to his arm. So far, I haven't yet stumbled upon any hardened resistance. It's clear that my doubts were misplaced. The attack appears to be progressing with little trouble. I can hear the cries of pain and death, the gurgles of agony, the clash of weapons coming from the direction of the Saxon camp, but I can't see any of the fighting clearly, now that the campfires and braziers have been trampled down by the fighting warriors.

I see the backs of three men before me, and I drop to the ground. They're moving slowly backwards, their gaze focused on the direction of the camp and to their flanks; one is holding a spear, the other two have axes. The left arm of one of the axemen hangs loose; they're all splattered with blood and, judging by the red on the blades of their weapons, some of it, at least, must be the blood of the Franks.

When they get within ten feet from me, I leap up. I strike at the nearer of the axemen. I stab him through the kidney and pull away as he flies his axe before my face. I immediately regret having launched the attack. Though I managed to quickly dispatch one of the three, the other two now focus all of their attention on me. The spearman charges at me with great skill, and I can only dodge and block the blade as I back away before his onslaught. His thrusts get around my shield and under my parries; one well-aimed strike reaches my outer thigh. I don't know how deep the wound is, but it hurts more than any injury I've ever suffered. I hiss and stumble away. In the corner of my eye, I spot the second Saxon approaching on my flank, with the axe held in both hands, raised to strike.

Paulus appears behind the axeman, and jumps on him, pulling him to the ground. This distracts the spearman enough for me to shorten the distance in one leap and plunge my *spatha* in his stomach. The Saxon gurgles blood and slides off my blade. I turn around. The *praefect* wrestles with his enemy in the mud. I run back to them and grab the Saxon off

Paulus. I whack him across the head with the pommel of my sword. The Saxon sways, concussed, and collapses.

I help Paulus off the ground. "You saved me," I say. "Thank you."

"I guess we're even now," he replies.

I kneel down by the fallen Saxon. His cloak and brooch are of the Briton style; I've seen men in Dorowern wear similar garments. It's of course possible he obtained his clothes from a trader or in a raid on the Cantish coast, but I decide to take my chances.

"He's coming back," I say. "Give me the other one's belt."

I tie the Saxon's hands with his own belt, and his legs with the belt of his fallen comrade. "Can you keep watch over him?" I ask Paulus.

"It's what I do for a living," he replies with a grin.

I look to the south. The morning mist is clearing, and the dawning sun shines a dim, grey light on the grassy plain. Smoke rises over the Saxon camp in thin, black wisps. The Saxons still fight for their lives in pockets around the trampled tents, but most survivors have now decided to flee. Now that the cover of darkness and fog is gone, they are easy pickings for my Iutes, hunting the enemy in groups of three and four. I notice the Iutes, where possible, just beat the Saxons down into submission; they have no hatred for the men they fight, and no desire to kill. The Saxons are beginning to notice that, too, and as they flee from the Franks, they surrender to my men for protection.

One of those Saxons runs towards me, with no weapon drawn, his hands spread wide apart. I make ready to accept his surrender, when I hear the whistle of an arrow and a thud of missile hitting flesh. The Saxon falls dead just a few paces from my feet.

I search for the archer: it's Basina, standing on the edge of the Saxon camp. She draws the bow again and scans the field for a new target. She shoots, and another fleeing Saxon hits the ground.

I run to her, waving my hands and shouting for her to stop. Before I reach her, she downs yet another fleeing Saxon. She sports a broad, satisfied grin on her face, which turns to surprise when she sees me.

"They're surrendering," I tell her.

"We don't need slaves," she replies. "And we can't let any of them warn the others."

She raises the bow to her eye again. I push it away.

"We've killed enough. Save your arrows."

"What are you, a *Christian*?" She scoffs. "And here I thought you were strong."

I tell her something Bishop Fastidius taught me: "Only the strong can show mercy."

She stares at me with a puzzled expression. Behind her, Hildrik's blade pierces the last of the Saxon defenders — a giant of a man, wrapped in a cloak of bear fur, with a bear's head for a helmet. He's already bleeding from many wounds; shafts of several arrows stick from his body. The Frankish prince watches him fall, slowly, to the ground, then approaches us, wiping blood from the sword and sweat from his brow.

"It's over," he says. "That was the last one."

Basina scowls and lowers the bow. "A few got away."

"It's fine," says Hildrik. "We won't be able to keep what happened here a secret for long, anyway."

"If you say so," says Basina. Just then, she spots a movement in the grass: the wounded Saxon, trying to crawl away from us. Before either of us can stop her, she draws the bow and shoots him in the back.

"He was suffering," she says, and looks me straight in the eyes. "It was *mercy*."

CHAPTER IX
THE LAY OF PINNOSA

By midday, we are joined by a group of Ake townsfolk, arriving to pick up their fallen and to help us bury ours.

Praefect Paulus got his revenge on the Saxons, but at a heavy price. The enemy warriors, even in panic, even in flight, proved too fierce an enemy for the inexperienced *vigiles*. Half of Paulus's men lie dead on the battlefield; of the rest, many bear crippling wounds, rendering them unable to ever return to their duties. The town watch of Ake is no more.

"Was it worth it?" I ask Paulus as he begins to dig a grave for his men.

"Of course," he replies. "The town is dying. *Gaul* is dying. One day, some other barbarian warband will come and raze Ake to the ground, with us in it. At least this way, we got our chance to die in a fair fight."

"You weren't always a watchman," I note.

"I was a centurion once," he says. There is darkness in his voice, of a man who saw everything he once held dear destroyed. "At Mogontiac. A long time ago."

The soil is wet and loose, and digging the graves is short work. Before long, a pit is dug large enough to fit all the fallen Saxons; we drop them in, stripped of weapons and jewels, and cover with a thin layer of dirt — all of them except four, whom Hildrik deems worthy of a separate burial, with their weapons beside them.

These four were the last to succumb to the Frankish assault. They all wore the thick coats of bear fur over fine mail shirts, and carried long, good quality *seaxes*, unlike the rest of the Saxons in the band, who wielded only spears, axes and clubs.

"They fought like wild beasts," says Hildrik. "Even with their limbs cut off, they still stood their ground. It cost me six men to finally bring them down. I've never seen anything like it."

Like wild beasts...?

I limp back to the camp — the spear wound in my thigh, though cleaned and wrapped to the best of Hildrik's shieldmaidens' abilities, erupts with pain at every step — and search through the belongings of the four Saxons. I find a suspicious-looking water skin. I take a sniff.

Henbane.

The secret brew, the dangerous brew that gives Iute warriors their nigh inhuman powers of resisting wounds and battle madness. We learned how to use it from our northern neighbours in the Old Country — the Danes and the Geats. Once, it was commonly used by the Iute *Hiréd* warriors, whenever there was a need to make a breakthrough in the enemy lines, or stand ground against overwhelming odds —

but my father decreed that not only the recipe, but the very existence of the brew be kept a secret, to be made and used only as the last-ditch surprise, just as it had been at Eobbasfleot.

This isn't a discovery I want to share with the Franks. I bring the finding to my friends, instead.

"I thought the Saxons didn't know how to brew henbane," says Ursula.

"They don't," I say. "Someone must have revealed the secret. They only had enough for four men, this time — but it was just a foraging pack. If they're able to brew more, this campaign suddenly turned a lot more dangerous."

"You should let your father know about this," says Gille.

"I will — as soon as we find out more about it." I throw a bloodied bearskin cloak to the ground. "The men who drank the henbane wore this," I say. "Better stay clear of them if we ever meet them again."

I turn to Audulf. "Have you managed to learn anything?" I ask.

More than a dozen Saxons survived the battle with enough clarity of mind to be worth interrogating. Of these, I picked two whom I believed to have come from Britannia and, while Hildrik's men tortured the others to discover the whereabouts of the main Saxon warband, I ordered Audulf to find out what they were really doing here.

"I have. But you won't like it."

He leads me back to the captives. One of them is lying on the ground, unconscious, his face a bloody mess; I glance to Audulf's fists — his knuckles are covered with blood and torn skin. The other one, the Saxon I captured with *Praefect* Paulus's help, is sitting up, tied to a hazel tree, staring defiantly at us over a broken nose.

"You were right," says Audulf. "They are from Britannia. This one says he's from Anderitum."

"Does your *Drihten* know you two are here?" I ask him.

He spits a tooth out. "*Drihten* Aelle sent us here. What's it to you, Iute? We're both a long way from home."

"The Franks are our friends and allies," I say.

"We weren't sent here to fight the Franks. It was *you* who attacked us."

I pause. The captive is right; the River Franks had no quarrel with the Saxons, and they didn't ask for our help. Hildrik marched out against them to assist the River Franks against the raiders. But once we discovered *Drohten* Hildebert's indifference to the Saxon expedition, what reason was there for us to continue the pursuit, other than a chance for glory and plunder? Who was more at fault for this conflict — the Saxon warband, crossing the River Franks' territory by mutual agreement, or the Salians, chasing after the warband without the slightest threat or provocation?

Somewhere deeper in the hazel thicket, I can hear the screams of the other Saxons, tortured by Hildrik's men. No doubt, after this ordeal, Hildrik will know where the Saxon band was going, and why. I don't see the point in asking my captive the same questions, so I focus on what's more important to me and the Iutes.

"How many of you are there?"

The Saxon shrugs. "Why should I tell you anything? You'll kill me anyway."

"I'll let you go free if you swear an *ath* to return home."

He looks up. "I'd be dead before I got to the coast. This isn't a safe land for a lonely, unarmed man."

"At least you'd have a chance."

He mulls my proposition over for a while.

"One full *ceol*," he says at last. His tone's changed. I sense he's telling the truth. There would be some thirty to fifty men on a *ceol*. "One of our large ones." Fifty, then. "Most of them are with the main host."

"Who gave you the henbane?" I ask.

"I don't know anything about the henbane," he replies with a shrug.

"The bear-shirts."

"Whatever the bear-shirts took, they already had it when we arrived."

"Was there anyone else in the warband who may have given it to them? Some Danes or Geat mercenaries?"

"There was a unit of cavalry with the main host," he says. "The horses were Thuringian, but the riders were Franks, Friesians — and Iutes."

"*Iutes?*" I give him a sharp look. "Are you sure?"

"As sure as I am that you're one."

I know of only one Iute who leads a band of mercenary riders, is friends with the king of the Saxons — and was reported to have left Britannia recently.

Haesta.

The revelation intrigues me but doesn't surprise. I can't help but notice the irony; Meroweg asked my father to send Haesta to his aid against the Saxons just as the rebellious cousin was sailing to *join* the very same Saxons he fought before. I couldn't blame Haesta for changing alliances. He's a mercenary. Hemmed in between the Iutes and the Saxons, settled on an inhospitable, marshy land on the south-east coast of Cantia, the Haestingas needed to find a new source of income.

But betraying the secret of the henbane was a different matter. It endangered the entire tribe. If more of Aelle's warriors learned how to use it, like those bear-shirts in the camp, the fragile balance of peace between the two kingdoms would be shattered.

"Escort him back to the road," I tell Audulf. "And then give him his knife back."

"What about him?" the Saxon captive asks, nodding at his unconscious comrade.

"Is he your friend?"

"A brother in arms. We fought at Eobbasfleot together."

"You were at Eobbasfleot?"

He nods. "I killed two *wealas* there. One of them with my bare hands," he boasts, raising bloodied fists high. "And I would have killed more of them here in Gaul if you hadn't stopped us."

"Fine, take him with you," I say, "if you think you can carry him all the way back to Britannia."

"I will not let him rot in an unnamed grave in Frankia."

I watch Audulf lead the two Saxons away, and then go off to find *Praetor* Fulco. He's making ready to depart back to his home town, with the bodies of the slain watchmen laid out on biers.

"Can I ask you one last favour, *Praetor*?"

"Anything you ask."

"I need you to send a message to my father in Britannia."

"I can certainly try, but I'm not sure how easy it will be to reach him…"

"It shouldn't be that difficult. Just address it to Aeric — King of the Iutes."

Shortly after nightfall, just as I start preparing for sleep, Ursula enters my tent, holding something small in a clenched fist.

"I found something that you might find interesting," she says.

"What is it?"

"Give me your hand."

I reach out. She puts a small metal object in my outstretched palm: a golden eagle, studded with garnets.

"It's Basina's pendant! Where did you find it?"

"In her hand," says Ursula. "She gave it to me. But if anyone asks, I found it in the grass on the knoll to the north of the camp."

"I… I don't understand."

"She's still there, searching for it, if you want to give it back to her."

"What does it mean?"

"If I had to guess, I'd say it means Hildrik has grown impatient with her night visits to your chamber," she says with a grin. "Don't act so surprised. Did you really think no one would notice?"

The tips of my ears burn. "Does it mean I… shouldn't go to that knoll?"

"No, you fool. She's waiting for you. Just do it discreetly. This gives you an excuse if anyone's asking," she says, pointing to the pendant. "Hildrik is not stupid. He knows there's nothing going on between you two, it's just Basina teasing him, and teasing you — but his honour is at stake, so all of you need to keep up the pretence. Otherwise, he'd be forced to kill you."

I lick my lips and swallow. "*Kill me…*"

"They're all warriors here, Octa. Killing is how they deal with most problems."

"How do you know so much about this?"

"Audulf explained to me a little how things work in this country… The rest I've learned from Basina herself. Now go, before she grows bored with waiting. The night is cold."

I pass the guard with a nod, and enter the dark, empty, featureless field outside. To the north, a thin line of pale orange dots is spread along the dark horizon: the lights of the city of Coln. We have camped half a day's march from its walls, on the edge of another old stone road, linking Coln with Trever and southern Gaul. To the east, I can hear the lapping of the mighty Rhenum against its muddy shores. I didn't have much time to admire the famous river before the quickly coming dusk forced us to make camp, but I can already tell that what I managed to glimpse in that brief moment will stay with me forever.

Tamesa is an imposing, broad current that turns into an inlet of the open sea not long after passing Londin's walls, but it's a sea of mud, silt and sewage, an aqueduct of waste and sludge, sometimes resembling nothing more than a trench filled with manure. It is impressive, but it is not *beautiful*. Rhenum is a wild, gleaming marvel. It spills broad and lazy across the meadows, clear and calm, like an old man who has lived a full life and now spends his twilight years just watching the clouds roll by. A dark, dense forest grows on its distant right shore, a ribbon of shadow, reflected in the pure waters, highlighting the river's elegant beauty like a line of antimony powder on the eyebrows of a woman of the night.

Somewhere along that shore, between us and Coln, is the camp of the Saxon warband.

After finding all there is to find out from his Saxon captives, Hildrik stood before a difficult choice. The Saxon host we pursued was far stronger than we had expected. It wasn't even the main Saxon army — that one, a couple thousand men strong, we are told, is marching along the right bank of the Rhenum, to cross at some point further south. There is nothing we can do about an army that large, except maybe warn the Roman garrisons along its path. But even the one here is powerful enough to give Hildrik pause: two hundred footmen, reinforced by Haesta's cavalry wing, and at least a dozen of those bear-shirts, drunk on henbane. They have engineers among them, veterans of Attila's army, ready to build siege engines if the situation requires. Meanwhile, our Frankish band now number less than a hundred men, and it is clear we can't count on *Drohten* Hildebert and his River Franks joining us against the Saxons.

But it isn't just the fear of failure that impacts Hildrik's decision. We know now where the warband is heading — more or less, the men we captured were not high ranking enough to know the exact route of the expedition, only its target — and we know they are no longer a direct threat to Meroweg's kingdom. Is there still any point in pursuing them, in risking the lives of our men?

"My father would have us return," said Hildrik. "He doesn't care what happens to the *walhas*."

"And you do?"

The Saxon army is waiting on the outskirts of Coln for the return of the foraging packs, like the one we just destroyed, but soon they will move on to their final target. It isn't Coln — that one they were leaving to Hildebert's Franks — but an even greater and richer city in the south, the capital of all Gaul, the seat of the *praefect* and a residence of Imperators when they visited Gaul: Trever. In the chaos brought on by the feuding Imperators, with hostile Roman

The Blood of the Iutes

armies roaming the province, the city must have been left poorly defended, or at least the Saxons believe it to be.

"Rome makes better neighbours, whatever my father might think," Hildrik replied. "Once they sign a treaty, they keep to it. The Saxons are unpredictable and can only be beaten into submission. They're already settled to our West, along the coast, and to our East, across the Rhenum. If they gain a foothold on our southern border, if they ally with the Alemanns and Burgundians, we'll be surrounded on all sides."

"Wouldn't your father prefer a weakened Rome?"

"He may well do — but you already know I don't agree with him about everything."

Hildrik may be growing suspicious about my relationship with his betrothed, but he has also grown to realise we share a common affection for Rome, and a wish for the Empire to survive strong and healthy through the many crises it has faced. Like me, he believes the heathens need Rome as an ally and a friend to profit from, not merely as an enemy to be feared.

"Some say this Maiorianus is like the new Aetius," he said, when I asked him if he truly believed Rome could yet recover its lost might. "My father saw him fight many years ago, when Aetius's Legions stopped *Drohten* Clodio's advance into Gaul. If he can't do it, no one can."

"What if he's also as shrewd as Aetius? What if he'll have you fight his battles for no reward?"

"Peace and stability on our borders is reward enough. If Rome could stop Alemanns and Saxons from crossing the river, the Franks would flourish where we are."

"What about conquest? What about glory? What about plunder?"

He smiled. "All in due course. Haven't you seen how ravaged Gaul was after the Huns? What's left may be good for the Saxons, but it will take years for it to be rebuilt into something worth conquering."

I could never tell if he was jesting when he was saying these things.

"How long are you going to stand there? I'm getting cold."

Basina's voice brings me back to the present. I can't see her in the dark, so following her voice, I limp up to the birch tree on top of the grassy knoll. She's sitting under the tree with her arms around her knees; unusually for her, she's wearing a long robe of thick wool, and a woollen cloak, as if she was a shepherdess.

"Why did you want to see me?" I ask. "I thought you were angry with me."

"Of course I was angry."

"Then, I don't understand…"

She laughs. "Ursula told me you had little experience with women, but I didn't think you were *this* naïve."

"Ursula —" I remember. "I think I found something of yours."

She reaches out. I put the pendant on her palm, and before I can take it away, she covers my hand with her other hand and holds. Her fingers are soft and warm.

"Sit down," she commands, and I obey. She moves closer, until our bodies touch through thick cloth.

"I was impressed," she says. "No man ever stood up to me like that, except Hildrik."

"I only did what I thought was right."

"And you did the same in Ake, convincing Hildrik to save these poor people from fire."

I remain silent.

"*Are* you a Christian?" she asks. "It's the sort of thing I've heard Christians preach about."

"Would you respect me less if I were?"

"I respect a man of conviction."

"I'm not a Christian," I tell her. "But I spent a long time among them in Britannia. I was tutored by the Bishop of Londin."

"A *Bishop*, no less!" She chuckles. "We always believed Christians were weaklings — not worth a place at Tengri's table — until Aetius and the Goths defeated the Huns at Maurica."

"Tengri?"

"It's what the Huns call the one you'd call Wuotan."

"Wodan, in Iutish," I correct her. "It's strange to think that these… beasts worshipped the same gods as us."

She laughs. "They were just men. Except Attila — he… he was more like a god. As if Tengri himself came down to Earth. But he died just like any other man, and after his death, there were no more gods in the East."

"Were there Christians in Thuringia?"

"A few," she says. "Even among the Huns. But most went south with the Goths. The Goths are strange ones. They're Christian, but they are fierce warriors. Just like the Romans. How does it work with all that talk of mercy and forgiveness?"

"I told you. Mercy is a virtue of the strong. The weak must destroy their enemies. The strong can afford to let them live."

"Hmm."

She falls silent, and we listen to the distant lapping of the Rhenum, and the northern wind picking up on the empty plain.

"Kiss me," she says suddenly.

"What?"

"Kiss me."

"But you're Hildrik's woman!"

"I don't see him here. Don't you want to kiss me?"

"I... I dream of nothing else."

She turns towards me and closes her eyes. I lower my head and our lips touch. She opens her mouth and pulls me in; her tongue twirls and dances inside me. The thick wool of her sleeves tickles the back of my neck. I lose myself in her embrace; I don't know how much time passes before she releases me, gasping for breath.

"Why?" I manage to utter.

"I told you. I was impressed. Consider how you can impress me further next time," she says.

She stands up and walks away, leaving me breathless in the darkness.

The letters above the gate state proudly: "C.C.A.A." I do not know what that inscription resolves to, except that the first word must be "Colonia"; the Franks mangled the word into the simple "Coln" — but I imagine like most Roman cities it once had a more majestic, convoluted name, invoking some Imperator or a victorious general in whose name it was founded.

The countryside around the city still bears the familiar scars of the many wars and barbarian invasions that rolled through the land — burned farms and ruined *villas* reaching almost up to Coln's tall walls. But nearer the city, the suburbs are in surprisingly good shape. The stone houses lining the highway still stand, with roofs freshly mended and walls recently white-washed. Wheat shoots green in the fields. Orchards are bursting with leaf and budding fruit. Even a few of the marble-lined pagan memorials on the main cemetery still remain, gleaming white in the sun, though most are crooked or overturned in the mud.

The guards at the gate study us suspiciously, but they wave us through without questioning. Clearly they don't feel two youths on ponies are any threat to the city, whose mighty walls are manned by a garrison strong enough to make even the Saxon warband keep their distance.

I only have Ursula with me on this journey — figuring a Latin-speaking, Christian Briton could convince the Gauls where an uncouth son of a barbarian king failed. Only my friends know of my mission; as far as anyone else knows, Ursula and I are out patrolling the riverside, spying on the Saxons. In reality, we have ridden as far away from the Saxon camp as we could, trampling the wheat fields and the pastures still tended by the few Gaul serfs who remain in the land trod on by so many heathen hordes in living memory.

All night, after seeing Basina, in between dreaming of her tongue in my mouth and her hands on my body, I was racking my brain about what more I could do to "impress" her again. Having seen him fight — and win — against the bear-shirts, it was obvious I could never compete with Hildrik in battle prowess, neither could I prove a better war chief with my handful of Iutes against his trained *centuria*. As the moon crept slowly up the eastern sky, it dawned on me. I remembered how my father came to be respected as a leader, how he would sort out all the difficulties that came to him in his life. Not through beating his opposition in combat — like me, he was never a great warrior, though he could always hold himself in a fight — but by thinking about the best solutions and, most of the time, simply *talking* to people; forming alliances, or provoking enemies against each other... He was a better diplomat than he was a general, and he was a better general than he was ever a fighter. It was time for me to find out if I had inherited any of his talents...

Coln is a much smaller city than Londin, but it's more densely built. Having trundled for days through Gaul's empty rural landscape, I immediately feel at home in its packed streets. There are none of the empty, barren spaces that plague so much of Londin's western and northern reaches, and although parts of the city bear some of the same wounds of barbarian raids as the countryside, the ancient fabric of Coln remains intact: the grid of the streets is untouched, the *insulae* of the city folk have not been turned into palaces and gardens for the nobles.

There are obviously fewer people living now in the city than it was originally built for; many of the flats in the stone tenements are boarded up, especially the more expensive ones downstairs; the wide avenues carry a fraction of the traffic they were designed to accommodate; the guest houses are empty, and the door to the bath house is barred with a chain, its vaulted roof rotten through and fallen in. Even the large church by the Forum has seen better days. But the city still lives: a lonely island of civilisation in the sea of poverty and barbarity.

Cardo Street takes us to the Forum, still surrounded by several levels of galleries and a semi-circular portico, though there's only a handful of stalls nestled between the columns. As I observe the market-goers for a while, I note that, shrunken and impoverished though it may be, the city's population is as diverse as it must have been in its glory days. I have never seen as many face types, skin hues, eye shapes and hair styles and colours, not even in Londin. There's a man with black curly hair, full lips and skin the colour of a chestnut, studying intently a knife blade. Here's a woman, dark-eyed and deeply tanned, with nose straight like a mason's square and dark hair tied with a ribbon in a bun a foot high, smelling a bottle of some balm or ointment. Behind her, a silver-bearded spice merchant adjusts a piece of red cloth wrapped around his head. Syrians, Iberians, Greeks, Gauls, Germans… This was once a town of the Legions, a frontier fortress guarding the gates of the Empire, and the descendants of the Legionnaires from all corners of Rome had settled here over the centuries, long after the Legions themselves marched off to fight Rome's distant wars, long after the exotic trade routes dried up.

The Blood of the Iutes

Ursula watches all this with her mouth agape; she hasn't been to Londin as often as I have, and a lot of this is new to her. But she is the first to remember why we came here. She tugs at my sleeve and points down the main avenue to the east, to an arcade façade of a grand building — the largest we've yet seen in Coln, taking up an entire *insula* by itself — looming over the riverside.

"This looks like the *Praetorium*," she says.

"Then that is where we must go."

It is a testament to Coln's reduced strength that one man holds all the temporal, spiritual and military power in his hands. Pinnosa, a grey-haired, balding Gaul, with a jagged scar across his face and cauliflower ears, is the city's Bishop, *Comes* and *Praetor*, all at once, dividing his time between the church, the palace and the garrison quarters.

Even combining so many duties, Pinnosa is not a busy man. We find him returning from an inspection of the city walls. There is no queue of supplicants awaiting his audience, except two merchants arguing about some deal gone foul. Pinnosa gives them a tired look, then notices us and a faint smile lingers on his lips. He nods at the guard to let us enter first.

I have never seen Londin's *Praetorium* in its full glory. The building was razed by my father during the war with Wortimer, and all that was left in my time were burnt-out, blackened ruins. In line with the rest of the city, most of

Coln's palace still remains, including its great octagonal audience hall in the centre, though its walls are cracked and charred with the memory of some recent fire, and the Council table is a mere plank of fresh pine wood supported by piles of terracotta tiles.

"You're not from around here, are you?" Pinnosa asks.

"I am Octa, son of Aeric, *Rex* of the Iutes. This is Ursula of Dorowern," I introduce us.

"Iutes? Dorowern?" He scratches his head. "I'm not sure…"

"We're from Britannia," says Ursula.

"Britannia! We haven't had anyone visit from there in… I can't remember how long. What is a pair of Briton youths doing here, of all places? And why would you want to see me? Do you want some food?" He waves at a slave. "I was just about to have my dinner."

"Thank you," I say. "We *have* been travelling long…"

"Of course. Wine! Meat! Bread!"

As the meal is prepared before us, I tell Pinnosa briefly of our arrival in Gaul, and of our joining Hildrik's force in pursuit of the Saxon warband. I don't dwell on details — the moment he finds out we came as part of the Frankish horde, he loses interest in my tale.

The Blood of the Iutes

"I know all about Hildrik's army," he says, waving a quail bone in the air. "And about the Saxons he pursues."

"Then you also know that the Saxon band is greater than any before, and includes mercenaries from Britannia?"

"I did not know that last part," he replies, "but I don't see how that changes anything. Is that why you're here? To settle some old score with your enemies from home?"

"We're here to ask you to help us fight the Saxons. I understand you still have a powerful garrison here — between them and Hildrik's host, we would make short work of the Saxon band."

"We could," Pinnosa nods. "And if the Saxons were a threat to my city, I might consider your proposition... But they passed the walls of Coln without stopping. Why should I waste my troops on them?"

"Are you not worried what they might do to the rest of Gaul?" asks Ursula. "To Trever, and other cities?"

"Trever is a greater, stronger city than Coln," says Pinnosa. "If it can't hold against the Saxons, what chance would we have?"

He wipes his hands in cloth, stands up and walks to a window. He invites us to join him. The audience hall is on the second floor of the octagonal tower rising in the centre of the *Praetorium*, with a commanding view over the surrounding area. In one window, we see the Rhenum, flowing proud and calm along the building's arched foundations; a few flat-bottomed merchant barges stand in the harbour. In the window opposite, the rest of the city, the walls, and the fields and pastures beyond.

"If you travelled here from Tornac, you must have seen Hildebert's forces, preparing for war," he says.

"We did," I admit. "The weapon smithies are belching smoke all over the country. Warriors gather in the villages. Fodder is taken from the fields."

"They are poised to strike the city at any moment," says Pinnosa. "The Franks have sacked this city before, more than once. My father came here from the East to help it recover after the last time — he rebuilt the Basilica of the Martyrs, and a few other public buildings." He points to the great edifice looming over the centre of the city. "Every time, we came back; every time, Rome pushed the barbarians away. But now, Rome is far away. The *magister militum* of Gaul is busy fighting the new Imperator; there are no Legions stationed along the Rhenum — I'm not even sure if there are any troops left in Trever. Nobody's coming to our help. If we lose, I fear it may be the end of the city."

"The *praefect* of Ake said the same thing," says Ursula.

"You've been to Ake? How did you like the baths?"

"We had no time to take the waters," I answer grimly. "We were too busy fighting the Saxons. Defending the towns and villages of Germania from their roving bands. Something your soldiers should have been doing instead of us."

The Blood of the Iutes

Pinnosa scratches his chin and looks longingly to the walls.

"There was a time when two thousand soldiers manned these ramparts," he says. "If you had come to me then, I would've sent a *centuria* or two to deal with your Saxons without hesitation. But now, I barely have two hundred men to face the Franks. I have none to spare."

"What happened to all those soldiers?" asks Ursula. "Did the Huns kill them all?"

"There are more dangers to a soldier than the Huns in these parts, dear," Pinnosa replies. "Franks, Saxons, disease, desertion… The last one's the worst. A mercenary life pays more than the meagre salary I can offer them. They have enough conscience to not fight their own comrades-in-arms, at least, but that is a small blessing."

"Then our trip was a waste of time," I say. "I wish I had known sooner how dire your situation was."

I return to the table, pick up a piece of bread and chew it slowly in silence.

"Does Hildrik know you're here, boy?" asks Pinnosa.

"He does not," I reply.

"I don't suppose he would have appreciated you coming to beg the *walhas* for help."

"Do you know him?"

"I met his father." He points towards the western gatehouse, looming over the wall. "He was there, with a small band of Salians, helping us to fight back a Hun raiding party. We were still allies back then, before Aetius called him off to Maurica — to use him and betray him."

"And you still could be," I say. "Hildrik is not as bitter with Rome as his father is. He wants you to be his friend, not an enemy."

Pinnosa smiles sadly. "Maybe in another time… If we all survive these next few months, everything is possible. For now, though, each of us must look to their own."

He reaches for a pitcher and pours wine into our goblets. It is warm, smooth and sweet like mead.

"Enjoy it while you can, young Iute," says Pinnosa. "This might be the last of Mosella's white this world will ever see, if those Saxons have their way."

The Blood of the Iutes

CHAPTER X
THE LAY OF ASHER

In grim moods, we ride the streets of Coln back to the southern gate. I initially planned to stay in one of Coln's taverns for the night — it would have been the first real bed I slept in since leaving Meroweg's capital — but now, I no longer wish to spend any more time in the city than necessary. Looking at it with a disillusioned eye, I can see now it's in much worse shape than I first noticed. The red render has fallen off almost every wall. There is no roof that is not patched with straw or board. Only the main streets are paved — the back alleys are just gravel on dirt and feeble grass on mud. Away from these broad, paved avenues, I spot some plots of empty land, left after razed houses and never built up again, turned into vegetable patches or pigsties.

We pass by some large public building of sandstone and red tile; this one, at least, is still well kept — I can't tell if it's an old temple or some kind of *curia*. Its door flies open. A boy runs out, fair-haired, wild-eyed and clad in furs, clutching an oblong bundle in his arms. He's chased by an old man, with a long, curly beard, dressed in white woollen cloak rimmed with black and a small, pointed hat, which falls off his head as he runs.

"Thief!" cries the old man. There is desperation in his voice, more than greed. Whatever the boy is holding is more precious to the old man than any treasure. "Stop him!"

The Blood of the Iutes

I have no side in this quarrel but, seeing how nobody is rushing to help the old man, I spur my pony and charge after the boy. I reach him in a few short leaps. I grab his fur coat; the boy slips on the cobbles, drops the bundle, and stumbles to the ground. My hand entangled in his coat, the falling boy drags me down with him. I cry out in pain as I hit the stones with my wounded thigh. The boy extricates himself from his coat and scrambles up, but as he launches into a run, he bumps into Ursula's pony and falls again.

The old man rushes up to us and picks up the bundle with great care, mumbling words in a language I don't understand. He then looks to Ursula, who's holding the boy in a tight grip.

"Let him go," he says. "He is just a hungry child. Lord forgives him."

I nod at Ursula. She puts a few coppers into the boy's hand and pushes him away. The old man turns to me and notices my pain.

"Your leg!"

I look down. The fall opened the spear wound. A dark wet patch grows on my breeches. I feel faint and stumble.

"Come with me, quickly," he says. "I will take care of that for you. It's the least I can do."

I bite hard on the piece of wood in my mouth as the old man pierces the skin on my thigh with a needle.

"You should've had this wound mended when it was fresh," he says. "It will take much longer to heal now."

I take the wood out to speak. "There are no… *arse!* …surgeons in a Frankish warband. I hoped poultices and… *ah, fuck…* wrappings would have been enough."

"They may have been, if you had rested for a week."

"How do you know so much about mending wounds?" asks Ursula.

"I was a surgeon's apprentice in the Thirtieth Legion," the old man replies. "When such a thing still existed."

"You were with the Legions?" she asks excitedly. "What battles did you fight?"

"Battles…?" The old man bites through the thread and spits out the end. "I saw the Goths cross the river, fifty years ago, sweeping all men before them like wheat under a sickle. Cities ravaged from here to the ocean. Entire cohorts vanquished overnight. The Thirtieth Legion, gone. This made me lose all interest in fighting. I turned to the Lord, instead."

"You're a priest?" I ask. I look around. The building doesn't look like a church, though now that I can study it with more attention, there is a sense of holiness about it.

The Blood of the Iutes

In the centre of the room stands a small alcove with a pedestal. The ceiling and the floor are covered in mosaic, showing scenes from some familiar-looking story, but inscribed with black writing I have never seen before. All the walls are lined with bookshelves, filled with bound tomes and scroll cases. At the far end of the room stands a decorated cupboard, bound in gold and silver.

"I am, but not the kind you'd be thinking of. I am Rav Asher," the old man introduces himself. "And this is the city's library — and a temple of my people."

"You're a pagan, then?" asks Ursula.

The old man's beard shakes in laughter. "No, my child. My faith is older than any pagan god — or a Christian one, for that matter. To me, you are all heathens," he adds with a mischievous smile.

"A *Iudaeus*," I say. I recognise now the images on the mosaics — they show stories from the Scriptures. There's Abraham and Isaac, Moses and the Red Sea, Garden of Eden. But no Christ, no Mary, no Apostles anywhere to be seen. "I've never met one of you before."

"There aren't that many of us this far north," Rav Asher says with a nod. "Where did you come from?"

"Britannia."

"Britannia! I have a cousin who's a gold merchant in Londin," he says. "But I doubt you'd know him."

[246]

He finishes wrapping my thigh with cloths. "That's all done. Give it a few days, and the stitching should hold even in battle."

"I may not have a few days," I reply. "I expect to ride to war any day now."

"Then at least have a night's rest. Do you have a room in the city?"

"We do not."

"Then you must stay with us! Esther!" he shouts, before I can protest. "We have guests tonight. Prepare the first-floor bedroom!"

"What was it that the boy was trying to steal?" asks Ursula. She glances around the room. "One of the books?"

She picks one of the tomes at random; opens it, blushes, shuts it, then peeks into it carefully again, before putting it back on the shelf. Her fingers linger on the spine as she's remembering where she put it.

"Not just any book." The old man walks up to the cupboard. He whispers a brief prayer before opening its doors. He takes the oblong bundle out and unwraps it gingerly. Inside is a cylinder of silver, studded with jewels.

"The boy wanted it for the silver and the gems," says Rav Asher. "But the real treasure is inside. The word of God."

"The Scripture."

"A part of it, for you Christians. All of it, for us." He puts the cylinder back and closes the cupboard shut.

"I'm not a Christian," I say.

"You talk like one," the old man says, surprised. "And you act like one. I saw you throw coins to the boy."

"I lived among them long enough."

"Did they teach you to read as well as speak like a civilised man?"

"And write."

He smiles broadly. "Then I think you might enjoy spending the night in this house." He points to the walls. "There is no greater library than this one anywhere north of the Alps. All the knowledge the Lord saw fit to bestow to men is within these walls."

"Thank you," I say. "But I don't think I will have the time to enjoy them as well as I should."

"I know, I know — you're in a hurry to die in some battle, like all young men. Still, have a look through my tomes after the *cena*. So few people do these days."

"No book can help me find a way to defeat the Saxons," I say. "Even my father, with all his strategies and learning, could not prepare for what's coming. There are simply too few of us to stand against them."

Rav Asher runs his fingers through his long beard. "Is that why you came to Coln? To seek help?"

I tell him the same story I told *Comes* Pinnosa. He nods, sagely, as I describe Pinnosa's answer to my pleas.

"Pinnosa is a wise man, and a good commander," he says, at the end. "But he doesn't have my people's *hope*."

"Hope?" asks Ursula.

The Rav's wife, Esther, enters the room with plates of flat bread and pickled fish. She smiles, hearing us talk. "There is always hope," she says. "The Lord is our shepherd. He will provide."

"Wisdom of a woman," the Rav says and embraces his wife's waist with a smile.

"In the next life, maybe," I say. "But how can you hold on to hope in this world?" I nod outside. "The Saxons are marching on Trever. The River Franks are gathering to conquer Coln. Romans fight each other. Everyone thinks the Empire is dying, and sooner or later, it will fall forever."

He points to the cupboard. "That scroll represents millennia of unwavering hope, against odds more dire than either you or I can imagine. Before Rome rose, there was Israel. After Rome falls, there will be Israel… One way or another."

The Blood of the Iutes

"I do not know the stories of your people," I say. "So they cannot give me consolation."

"And yet you fight," says Esther with a gentle smile. I have no answer to that.

"You are not, yourself, of Rome?" asks Rav Asher. "And Britannia is far away from the wars on the Rhenum. What do you care if there is hope for us or not?"

I look to the book-filled shelves. "My father told me how he and his people had to burn books and scrolls like these in Londin, to survive a harsh winter, in the middle of a war. How they hacked ancient statues to pieces, to sell them for food. How they wrapped themselves in cloaks of purple silk, and then tore them into wrappings for wounds."

Rav Asher and his wife nod sadly. "Such things happened here, as well, when the city was besieged."

"He said this was the second, most tragic thing he's ever witnessed — after the death of my mother. He told me — 'Men can always breed more men. It takes no skill, no training. But civilisation, once lost, takes generations to rebuild'."

"Your father is wise," says Esther, "but he is mistaken to think a man can stop the passage of time, if it is ordained by the Lord."

"'Alas, Postumus, the years fleet quickly by'," Rav Asher recites some old poem. "'Not even prayer can stay their passage.' Even the heathens knew this truth."

"I do not hope to hold back Rome's fall forever," I say. "But I would like my children to see what I have seen. What my father saw before me. I would like my son to still have books to read when he's my age."

"There will always be books," says Asher, again smiling at the gilded cupboard. "Of that, I can assure you."

"Where in *Hel* have you been?" Audulf punches me in the shoulder. "We thought you were dead!"

"We had to hide all night in a ruined farm," I say. "We weren't the only ones who sent patrols along the river."

"Get your shield and lance," says Audulf. "We march out."

"What's the hurry?"

"The last of the Saxon foraging parties returned today," says Gille. He's strapping the sword belt to his waist and slings a Saxon shield over his back. "Hildrik reckons they will break camp in the morning."

"Gather the riders," I order. "Wait for my word."

I search out Hildrik, already on horseback and in full armour. Basina is beside him, as always. Her gaze, when she sees me, is indecipherable. The Franks gather around them in force, grim faced and silent. The mood in the camp is dark and heavy. They expect no triumph.

"The Saxon camp is fortified with wood and ditch," I say to Hildrik. I did not waste my entire journey — I did ride close enough to the Saxons on my way back to gain at least some intelligence. "What is your plan to capture it?"

"There isn't one," replies Hildrik. "They did not come here to stay behind a palisade forever. There's only one road leading to Trever. We will meet them there."

"A pitched battle?" I may have no experience of command, but even I see the folly of his plan. "In an open field, with nothing to guard our flanks, against an enemy with horses?"

"We, too, have riders."

"They are sailors and peasants on moor ponies. They have never fought against real cavalry."

He glares at me. "Do you have a better idea?"

"We could pull back. Let the *walhas* deal with the Saxons first. They will not capture Trever overnight. Gather a greater army, and then come back."

"Run away, you mean," says Basina.

"There's no dishonour in retreat against such odds," I reply. "The situation's changed. We were supposed to pursue a raiding warband, not a conquering army."

"I don't know how you do things in Britannia, but the Franks do not retreat from the Saxons," says Hildrik.

I glance to Basina. Her stare is defiant. Is Hildrik doing this because he wants to impress her? Or does he really believe a warrior's honour obliges him to lead us into this forlorn battle?

"Why are we doing this, really?" I ask.

He bites on his lower lip and stares at the low-hanging clouds coming fast from the East, laden with rain. "If we go back to Tornac now, my father may not let us march out again any time soon," he says at last. "And Hildebert may not look fondly at an army of Salians at his back when he's busy besieging Coln. This could be our only chance to slow these Saxons down. Our only chance to do anything."

I nod and make my way back to my men.

"When I asked you to follow me out of Meroweg's capital," I tell them, "we were hunting a band of Saxon raiders out on plunder. Today, Hildrik is asking us to fight a pitched battle against a seasoned army, maybe twice as large as ours. Therefore, I feel I must ask you again if you are still willing to follow my lead."

The faces of the Iutes grow pale at the news. They knew the Saxons we faced were a stronger force than we first expected, but I doubt they were aware just *how* strong. Our two easy victories gave them a sense of invincibility. Now, I was telling them we were likely to suffer defeat, if not death.

"Do you think Hildrik can win this battle?" asks Seawine.

"I don't know," I answer. "He's earned a name as a capable commander in Thuringia, but I have only seen him fight once, just as you have."

"Would *you* win it?"

"I don't think I would," I reply. "But I'm just a youth with little experience in war."

"What else can we do?" asks a burly Iute, called Oxa. "We're in the middle of hostile land, weeks away from home, and the only road back is through Tornac. If we defy their call to arms, won't the Franks hunt us, like they did the Saxons?"

"There are other roads back to the coast than through Tornac. If we go south, it will take longer, but we'd cross through Gaul rather than Frankia."

"I don't like the sound of that." Oxa shakes his head. "I think I'd rather face the Saxons with the Franks at our side, than the *wealas* without them."

"We came here to fight," says Audulf, shaking his sword. "A warrior knows death awaits him, always."

The others join him in a war cry.

"I say we take the chance," says another rider, a girl called Haeth. "And if it looks like the Franks are losing, we can always run away," she adds, patting the neck of her pony.

The other Iutes murmur in agreement.

I shake my head. "It's harder to flee from a losing battle than you may think," I say. "But if this is what you all want, I will lead you once again, to the best of my abilities."

"Then what are we waiting for?" says Audulf. "Let's go kick some Saxon rears!"

We march all night down the Trever Road, in the pouring rain, seeking a suitable place to make battle, until Hildrik at last decides on a location. About halfway between Coln and the crossroad of Tolbiac, we find a low, wooded hill rising to the north of the road. To the south, a large, abandoned farm, surrounded by a solid drystone wall. The rain has turned the fields around the farm into a mire, which we hope will at least slow down Haesta's horses. It is not a mountain pass or a ford, but it's as good a choke-point as can be found in this flat, featureless country.

Late in the morning, Odilia returns from patrol with news of the Saxon horde approaching. Hildrik's line unravels slowly across the Roman highway: fifty men in a double *fulcum* formation, with the second line ready to press their shields against the backs of the first. The rest of the Frankish force remains in reserve, tasked with defending our southern flank and rear in case the Saxons overrun the farm.

Only two corner walls remain of the farmhouse, with the ruins of a stove built into one side. I see myself making a final stand between these two walls, once everything fails, spears piercing me from both sides. I shake my head to get rid of the grim image. Instead, I try to imagine the fight itself. This is not going to be a battle of manoeuvres. Neither Saxons nor Franks are used to such refined tactics. The two forces will clash on the road, and push against each other with shields and spears until either of the lines breaks — or until Haesta's horsemen fight their way through our flanks, to rip at the rear of Hildrik's spearmen. I remember my father telling me how just three of Haesta's riders almost destroyed a Saxon shield wall twenty-men strong. It is the task of my pony riders to see that it does not happen again.

It is unlikely that we will succeed.

"Have you planned our escape yet?" asks Ursula with a wry smile.

"We could reach Tolbiac's gates in an hour, if we ride fast," I say. "I wonder if they'd let us in or watch us get slaughtered."

"Do you really think Haesta would slay his fellow Iutes?"

"I doubt he'd even know who we were. To him, we're just some fair-hairs on ponies. Mercenaries, like himself."

"You could surrender to him. He'd spare your life for ransom, I'm sure."

"Or send my head to my father." I scowl. "Don't tempt me. If we die, we die together."

"But you're more important than any of us. You're an *aetheling*, the only heir to your father's title. We're just some commoners. You shouldn't even be here."

"My father became the *Rex* by accident of Fate, not by blood right. I am no more a noble than any of you." I draw my sword and test the sharpness of the blade on my finger. "How can I prove that I deserve to inherit my father's circlet if I run away from danger?"

"You don't need to prove anything to anyone." She puts on a helmet and fastens the strap under her chin. She lays her hand on my shoulder. "But I'm glad you decided to stay and fight with us. God willing, we shall prevail."

"Oh, right, I almost forgot," I laugh. "We're not just two bands of heathens, fighting it out for Wodan's pleasure. With you, we have the God of Rome on our side!"

First, two lonely riders appear on the horizon. They spot our shield wall and ride closer to investigate; too close. Basina's bow twangs, and one of the riders falls off his horse. The other turns around in place and gallops away, before Basina can draw her bow again.

Before long, the entire Saxon host marches up towards our line. The short train of ox-driven wagons and porters sets up at the back, waiting for the warriors to clear the way. The front of the army spreads out across the road, at a distance of a hundred paces — twice as long as ours, and three men deep — and stops. Haesta's cavalry pulls up the southern flank, opposite the farm. A handful of archers and javelin-throwers moves in front but, seeing the shields of the Franks perfectly raised to counter their missiles, they pull back. A single rider splits from the line and stops at the midpoint between the two armies, waiting. I notice Hildrik putting on his bull's helmet and mounting up to meet the enemy envoy, and I ride out to join the two of them at the meeting point. The Saxon gives me a wary stare.

"*Hael dir*," he greets us. He's surprisingly young, roughly Hildrik's age, with dark eyes, short dark hair under a plain helmet, a pointy chin and a thin moustache. Up close, he doesn't look much like a Saxon. "I am Odowakr of Skiria, son of Edeko," he introduces himself, speaking with a hard accent I don't recognise. "Why do you stand in our way, Frank? I have no quarrel with you."

"*Hael*, Odowakr," Hildrik replies. "I am Hildrik of Tornac, son of Meroweg. You have no right to be here. This isn't Saxon land."

Odowakr looks around. "Neither is it Meroweg's," he replies. "Have the *walhas* hired you as their guard dog, Hildrik of Tornac?"

Hildrik's face twitches at the insult.

"I don't need the *walhas* to tell me a Saxon army on our southern border is a threat," he says. "Go back where you came from, or raid somewhere else. You will not take Trever while I'm alive."

"Why not join me, son of Meroweg?" Odowakr waves an inviting hand. "I remember your name from Nedao — you led your cavalry with great skill and courage."

"You were at Nedao?" Hildrik raises an eyebrow. "You must have fought on the Hun side."

"The Hun side, the Gepid side — it doesn't matter anymore. It's our turn for glory now. Come with me, son of Meroweg — together, we could take all Gaul, and share the spoils as equals."

"Is this what you promised Hildebert for letting you through his lands?"

"Hildebert was just happy not to have to waste his men on fighting me, and for me to draw the *walhas*' attention away while he takes Coln," replies Odowakr. "He's a more honourable man than you give him credit."

"You speak like a *Drihten*," I say, "but we know this is only a raiding party — the main force is still across the Rhenum. Who's the real commander?"

He turns to me with curiosity. "And who might you be?"

"I'm…" I hesitate. If he doesn't know who I am, neither would Haesta, and it might be best not to let them know there's a potential hostage among the Frankish host. "…Beormund of Cantiaca."

"Another visitor from Britannia?" He smooths his moustache. "You know much, but you don't know all. I *am* the commander of this expedition. The army on the other side of the Rhenum is marching on *my* orders. And it's not just Saxons that are in it. We are Alemanns, Rugians, Longbeards, Werns… Salians could come with us, too."

The Blood of the Iutes

"I do not share my glory with others," replies Hildrik. "Franks don't need alliances. We will take what we please, as we please — and make sure nobody else reaches out for our plunder."

"Oh, is that what it is?" Odowakr smiles. "You want Gaul all to yourself? I'm afraid I can't let you have it." He looks at the line of shields, then at the open field to the south of the farm. "You know, I could just have my men march around your little blockade."

"You could try."

Odowakr grimaces impatiently. He smacks his lips. "Fine. Make sure you keep that helmet on. I want to send your head to your father when this is all over."

He turns the horse and trots slowly back to his men. Hildrik and I do the same.

"Either he's very arrogant, or he knows his worth," Hildrik tells me. I nod. "Either way, this one won't be easy. Have you seen that cavalry?"

"Yes."

"Great horses," says Hildrik. "Thuringian mares among them. I wish I could have taken more with me when I... went home." He pats his own mount on the neck.

"There were fewer of them than I feared." I counted only twelve horses. More must have accompanied Odowakr's greater host. One of the men may have been Haesta, but I have only ever heard about him in tale, so I could not recognise him from other helmeted riders.

"Will you cope?"

"Donar will decide."

"Indeed."

We reach our lines. Hildrik leaps off the horse and looks over his shoulder. The Saxon wall is already on the move.

The earth shudders as the two lines of shields clash. The two hosts are well matched. The Saxons are more numerous, but they are a mass of different warriors from different clans, mismatched in training and equipment, whereas the Franks are some of Meroweg's finest, trained both in Roman and barbarian manner, almost as fine as the king's household guard itself. Odowakr's line is loose, disordered; Hildrik's men stand in a Legion's *fulcum*, a solid wall of mail and sword. They don't budge an inch under the Saxon onslaught; indeed, it seems that as long as the attack comes only from the front, the Franks might withstand it all day. From the second line, Hildrik's men reach out with spears and long-shafted axes between the shields of the first line; once in a while, one of them reaches a target and a Saxon disappears from sight, trampled under the feet of his brethren.

The Franks may be standing their ground valiantly, but soon enough the sheer numbers of the enemy are beginning to make a difference. The extended flank of the Saxon line reaches the farm's unguarded drystone wall. The warriors clamber over the stones, pushing against Hildrik's reserves. Just as the first Saxons leap into the enclosure, I see Haesta's cavalry ride across the rain-sodden meadow to our south, the hooves of their mounts raising great clumps of fresh mud.

I tell my Iutes to prepare. We are hidden among the trees of the wooded hill. I'm certain Odowakr knows we're here — his spies would've told him of a detachment of pony riders among the Frankish host — but I hope the cover will give us at least some element of surprise amidst the chaos of the battle.

The Haestingas, formed into an arrowhead, draw a wide arc around the farm, and reach the paved road on the other side of Hildrik's line. The Frankish reserves line up to brace for the charge, but they are wavering. They are not as good warriors as the ones in the shield wall: the line is not straight; the shields are held all at different levels, in trembling hands. They pull back too far, leaving themselves exposed, and with too little space between their backs and the backs of the front line. But it's not all bad. By pulling so far back, they leave my riders space for an attack on the flank of Haesta's charge.

The cavalry wedge shatters deep into the Frank line. The rider in front — he must be Haesta — reaches almost to Hildrik's rear, before having to turn back in fear of being cut off from the rest of his men. The horsemen whip the Franks with their *spathas*; blood spurts from the heads of the fallen. Haesta waves a sword over his head — a signal for the others to retreat for another charge. That is also a signal for us.

"Iutes, with me!" I cry. "May Donar lead us to victory — or death! For Aeric!"

As they raise a cheer, I turn to Ursula. "And may your Roman God preserve us."

Though surprise is on our side, as soon as we clash into Haesta's flank, it becomes apparent how hopelessly outmatched the Iutes are compared to the mercenaries. One of my men falls in an instant, without even touching the enemy, pierced with two lances. Another manages to exchange a few blows with his foe, before having his chest sliced right across by a cavalry sword. If it were just us fighting Haesta's men, we would have been annihilated in a few quick moments. But we're not alone; our attack allows the Frankish spearmen to catch breath and regroup around the slowed-down riders. The momentum of their charge extinguished, the mercenaries find themselves suddenly surrounded by spears and shields. Still, it is not enough to stop them from delivering a fatal blow after a fatal blow. A third Iute falls off his pony, but this time, he drags one of the Haestingas with him. Another mercenary's stomach is gutted by a Frankish spear. Axes clash against *spathas*, lances batter against the shields; blood and guts mix with rain and turn the road into the floor of a butcher's shop.

Haesta looks around and spots me behind him. For a moment, his eyes gleam in a flash of shocked recognition, which quickly twists into a puzzled grimace. With my red hair hidden under the helmet, I must resemble my father in his youth more than I realised. A stream of Frankish shieldsmen

The Blood of the Iutes

flows between us, separating me from Haesta, and threatening to cut him off from the rest of the Saxon horde. He lets out an angry roar. He spurs his horse, and leaps over the heads of the Franks. The others follow after him, either fighting their way out, or forcing their horses to high, dangerous jumps, to avoid the spears and axes. One of the mares slips while landing on the pave stones, slick with blood, and breaks her leg. Her rider is clubbed to death before he can even draw breath. Haesta leaves three of his men dead on the road, but the rest of his band manages to break away. I take quick stock of my Iutes — three of my twelve are fallen, too. I look to my friends. Ursula and Audulf halt on the side of the road, bloodied, waiting for my orders. I search for Gille in the chaos. I cannot find him, or his pony.

A new war cry erupts to our south, from the direction of the farm. My heart sinks as I spot four black shapes: the bear-shirts, tearing through the Frankish reserves, as if they were, themselves, bears. The rest of the Saxon line follows after them, and shortly, the enemy overruns the entire farm. I look to Hildrik. The right flank of his *fulcum* is now laid completely bare.

"On me!" I cry with my sword raised high. The surviving Iutes gather around me. I glance to Haesta's riders; they're galloping towards us again, but I have no time to pay them attention this time. The bear-shirts are a more immediate threat.

I leap over the drystone wall into the farm enclosure; it's tight quarters here, and I can sense the pony under me is nervous to be surrounded by walls, other ponies, and a crowd of warriors. I press on, slashing and hacking, until I reach the nearest of the bear-shirts. He turns to me with a roar; I see the madness of henbane in his bloodshot eyes. He holds an axe in each hand. A knife is stuck in his side up to the hilt, but he pays no attention to this wound, or any of the others visible all over his body.

I tug the reins and the pony rears; for a moment, it stands so tall, I fear we will fall backwards. But then it drops back on its forelegs, and I let the momentum add to my falling sword. The bear-shirt raises both axes, crossed, to block the blow. My blade slices through the crossed shafts but doesn't strike the Saxon's chest with enough force to dig in deep. Still, the power of the blow is enough to send him to the ground. My pony stumbles, trying to avoid trampling the man under its legs, just as it was trained. I pull back, not wanting to damage its hooves.

All around me, the Iute riders and the Franks are desperately pushing back against the Saxon assault, but all we can do is slow it down; behind us, Haesta strikes again. We are pushed from three sides now, with nowhere to go but into the forest. Now would be the time to flee, if I wanted to save myself. I spot Ursula and Audulf to my left in the midst of a brawl. I notice the crowd of Saxons splits around them, leaving a passage I could take if I wanted to run away.

I look back to Hildrik's wall and find Basina; she's still on her horse, squashed from two sides by retreating Franks, launching arrow after arrow, until the quiver at her saddle is empty. She holsters the bow and draws a long, curved sword. She glances towards me. Our eyes meet. There's a stark warning in her bloodshot gaze.

The Blood of the Iutes

If you flee, I will never again think of you as a man.

I look over my shoulder once more. While I vacillated, the gap through which I could have ridden to my salvation closed down. I can now only fight. Or die.

My sword arm grows weary, the hilt slippery with blood. I see another of the bear-shirts disappear in the brawl, having taken too many spear thrusts and axe blows, but the other two are still standing strong, ploughing their way through Hildrik's flank. The Haestingas split away for another charge, with nobody able to stop them this time. Odowakr and his guard have already broken through Hildrik's last line of defence and are now crowding through the gap between us and the Franks, pushing Hildrik's warriors into the forest.

When I hear the thundering of hooves, and spot another wedge of riders, cloaked in crimson, coming from the direction of Coln, past Odowakr's wagons and porters, I lose all hope; with another detachment of cavalry, coming to their help, the Saxon victory is certain. I parry a spear blade, and block a mace with my shield, but I have no more strength to strike. I can almost see Wodan's flying riders coming down from the sky to pick me and the others up to his Mead Hall…

The crimson-cloaked riders lower their lances and smash into the rear of Odowakr's shield wall with the strength of a charging wild boar.

There are only ten riders in this new, mysterious detachment, and by themselves, they would still be too few to turn the tide of the battle. But they are not alone. Running close after them is a troop of what looks like fifty men, all in red cloaks, silver helmets and gleaming mail. They, too, form a broad wedge and burst deeper into the hole punched in the Saxon line by the cavalry. The battle turns in a blink of an eye. It takes Odowakr no more than a breath to realise he's lost the fight. I see him now, in the middle of the brawl, hewing a passage through the Frankish horde with his bloodied *seax*, until he breaks through to the other side. He's a shrewd commander, not willing to let his men die in vain. He raises a horn to his lips and blows a retreat. One by one, the Saxons break away from the fighting, heading towards their chieftain, or if that's impossible, turn tail and run across the field. Only the two bear-shirts remain, too deep into the henbane trance to know when to stop fighting.

The withdrawal is stunningly quick and, for the most part, an orderly one. Odowakr cuts his losses, abandons the wagon train, and directs his fleeing troops westwards, towards Tolbiac — and Gaul; still, it seems, not changing his plans of invasion, no matter how diminished his force now may be. Hildrik's Franks, relieved to have survived what moments ago seemed like a slaughter, drop their shields and heavy weapons, then fall to their knees or lie down on the stone road, with no strength left to pursue. Our saviours also appear exhausted. I see now that the men in the crimson cloaks are breathless, red-faced, as if they'd been running all day. The riders gather in the muddy field south of the farm and dismount, their horses foaming at the mouths and flanks. I call on my men, and when enough of them find their way to me, I command them to ride with me in pursuit of the Saxons.

"The... horsemen..." pants Seawine, pointing with his sword towards Haesta. The mercenaries form a tight screen between us and the fleeing Saxons. Ours are the only two groups left on the battlefield who are still ready and willing to fight. Haesta raises his helmet and lifts his sword high in a clear challenge.

"Don't do it, Octa," says Ursula.

"I know," I say. "I'm not a fool. I stand no chance in a duel against him."

I bite my lip. Looking at my men, then back at Haesta's, I see no way for us to pursue the Saxons without incurring heavy losses, even if we did somehow manage to break through the mercenaries. Suddenly, I feel tired again. The rush that came from having my life saved by the sudden arrival of the red-cloaked warriors, recedes. I can't even find enough strength to sheathe my sword — I let it fall to the ground. Haesta, seeing this, scoffs, puts the helmet back on and turns around.

"There will be another time," says Ursula, laying a hand on my shoulder.

"We live. That's all that matters," I reply.

"Not all live," says Audulf grimly. I follow his gaze and spot Gille's pony, walking away from the battlefield in a bloody daze, riderless.

"Poor boy," says Seawine, finally catching his breath. "He was a good rider, but not a strong enough fighter."

"And yet, he goes to drink with the greatest warriors of our tribe," I say. I'm too weary to feel the full shock of the loss yet, but I feel I must say something powerful for the men around me not to lose hope. "There will be a great feast at Wodan's Mead Hall tonight. For him, and for everyone we lost today."

The Blood of the Iutes

CHAPTER XI
THE LAY OF PAULUS

"**O**cta! Young Octa!" I hear a cry of joy. "Thank the Lord, you're alive!"

I turn to see one of the red-clad riders dismounting. He throws off his helmet, wipes his *spatha* from blood and strides up to me in confident, military steps.

"*Comes* Pinnosa!" I bow, hiding my surprise. Ursula bows beside me; the others, perplexed, glance from me to the rider and back. "I… don't understand… I thought you said —"

He smiles. "Let's just say, after you left, I had an inspiring conversation with my… librarian," he says.

"*Librarian*?" I ask, confused. "You mean — Rav Asher?"

Before he can answer, I spot Hildrik and Basina ride up to us.

"Who are you, lord?" Hildrik asks in his rough Latin. "To whom do we owe our deliverance?"

"Hildrik —" I say, "this is *Hlaford* Pinnosa. *Comes* and Bishop of Coln."

The Blood of the Iutes

Hildrik straightens in the saddle and looks to the red-clad men. "Then these men must be…"

"Coln garrison — those that could get here on time. More are coming."

"How — why?"

Pinnosa pats me on the back. "You owe it to young Octa," he says. I catch Basina's raised eyebrow and a smile. She seems suitably *impressed*, but as puzzled with what's going on as Hildrik.

I smile back impatiently. I want to look for Gille among the wounded, hoping he's out there somewhere, gasping for breath, bleeding, rather than dead in the field. I want to see the three fallen Iutes; perhaps they, too, can be saved.

The *Comes* takes a look around. "You have lost many men, chieftain," he says, as if reading my mind, "but some may still live, if you hurry. We can use the Saxon wagons to transport them to Tolbiac."

I look to Odowakr's supply train. The porters fled into the woods, leaving their sacks and crates behind. Some wagons lie overturned on the roadside, the load spilled, others got dragged by panicked oxen into the field, but a few still stand on the road, abandoned by their drivers in the retreat.

"They won't let a Frankish army into Tolbiac," Hildrik says grimly.

"They will if *I* tell them to," replies Pinnosa. "Gather your dead and your wounded, chieftain, and I will do the same, and then we must march onwards."

Hildrik hesitates. He looks westwards. "My men are weary. We need to rest."

"So do we. But Tolbiac is a small town. If Odowakr decides to take it, even with his depleted force, it shan't take him long, and we'll be trapped here. One more push, and we can rest — in beds. I'll introduce you to Tolbiac's best taverns."

"What about Coln?" I ask. "Shouldn't you be going back to defend it from Hildebert?"

He shakes his head with a sad smile. "Coln is coming with us."

He points to the east; in the shimmery haze of the evening, I see what first appears like a dark line of an approaching army. As my eyes adjust to the distance, I recognise it as a packed mass of marching men, horses and wagons, a few hundred at least, moving slowly, but surely towards us.

"This can't be the whole city," I say.

"No, it's not. But it's a start. Though it may also be the end, if we let those Saxons take Tolbiac."

I turn to my Iutes. "Get back on those ponies, warriors," I tell them. They raise a groan. "I know you're weary. But so are the Saxons, and they've just lost one battle. Wodan willing, all we have to do is show them we're serious to send them flying again."

How long can a single day last?

I'm certain I was never as tired as today in all my life. Indeed, I'm surprised I can still find strength to stand. A long march in the rain, followed by a long, bloody battle in the mud. Then, another, shorter march and another skirmish with the rear guard of Odowakr's surviving army; mercifully short, this time, since as soon as the Saxons realised we were serious in our pursuit, they abandoned their half-hearted attempt at capturing Tolbiac and fled again, leaving only a few harassing stragglers to make sure we wouldn't go after them.

There is no threat of that. We are so exhausted at the end of it all, that when the town, on Pinnosa's command, opens its gates to us, many of the Frankish warriors have only enough energy to reach the nearest open space — which happens to be the town's small market square — and lie asleep wherever they can, in the dirt among the stalls. Those of us with more strength left, help unload the wagons filled with dead and wounded and lay them out in the courtyard of the town's only church, helped in the gruesome task by the first of the arriving refugees from Coln.

It is there that I finally find Gille. He's still alive — barely. I doubt he's going to make it till morning. It's difficult to tell at first what his injuries are, until I find a blood-soaked wrapping on his inner thigh — a neat, well-aimed spear stab. Just one wound, not much bigger than any of the ones I suffered in the battle but placed so unfortunately that the boy would have bled out in seconds had some kind soul not taken care of him in the midst of battle, giving him at least this one day more of life. How many men did he fell before dying? I can't find his sword, but the legs of his breeches are splattered with the blood of the enemies he'd have hacked at from pony-back.

I, too, I notice, am covered in a layer of blood and dust as thick as the cloth of my tunic. I need a wash — and a bath. I can't process what happened while I'm in this state. As soon as we entered the town, my attention was drawn to one particular building, standing between the church and the market hall, with its unmistakable three vaulted roofs. It appeared to be in surprisingly good condition.

"Are these baths working?" I ask a church acolyte, skulking past in a drab robe.

"Yes, but they are only for the Church's use…"

I stop listening after he says *yes*. I grab an axe and stride up to the bath house's door. There is no guard here, but the door is locked. I hack through the lock — nobody around is foolish enough to try stopping an angry barbarian warrior from getting what he wants — and push the door open. I take a deep breath: the smell of mould, rancid olive oil and sweat tells me the bath has recently been in use. But the damp air inside is cold.

"You there!" I call out at who I at first take to be another acolyte. "Get me someone who can heat this thing up!"

The man looks up, startled, but also curious, not least at my speaking to him in Latin. "I can warm up a tub for you in the sacristy, warrior."

"You have a working bath house, and you want me to wash in a tub?" I snap. I grab him by the robe and notice embroidered vestments underneath. I realise this must be the priest of the church and let him go.

He staggers away. "Of course, lord," he says with a frightened bow. "I'll get the servants on it right away."

I feel sick at myself for threatening a man of the cloth over nothing; but the desire to wash off the grime of the battle is stronger than shame. "Make it quick!" I call after him. "I need to be clean for the feast."

The bath house is not heated by a wood-burning furnace, but by an offshoot of the same hot spring that powers the palaces of Ake. The acolytes only needed to roll away the boulder blocking the spring's outlet for the steaming stream to come gushing through the lead pipes into the hypocaust.

By the time the underfloor current heats up the water in the bath, there's already a small crowd of us waiting in the towel room. *Comes* Pinnosa, having found out about my discovery, brought with him one of his most senior officers, and old Rav Asher. I called for Audulf — and Ursula. Her presence makes the men of Coln uneasy.

"Is the girl bathing with us?" asks the officer.

"It's fine," says Audulf. "Ursula bathes with us all the time. She's used to this."

"But *I'm* not used to it," says Rav Asher. "What would my wife say if she saw me bathe with a young girl?"

"You could invite your wife," says Ursula. "There's enough space."

"Lord forbid!" Rev Asher raises eyes to the sky. "No man has seen Esther's bare skin in thirty years!"

"We owe today's victory to young Octa," says Pinnosa with a soft smile. "If he says we must bathe with his friends, it is what we shall do. Consider this a test of your character. A temptation we must suffer through."

"*Suffer?*" Ursula whispers and rolls her eyes. "I don't think I've ever made anyone *suffer* with my body before."

"Well, if the Bishop of Coln gives us dispensation, who are we to protest?" says the fourth man sitting on Pinnosa's side. He's not from Coln, though he came with the refugees — he's Paulus, the *praefect* of Ake. His arrival was a delightful surprise, and one that I have not yet had a chance to decipher.

The acolyte enters and announces that the water in the *caldarium* is ready. The men of Coln enter first, so that they don't have to look at Ursula as she disrobes and joins us. I have grown so used to seeing her naked that I rarely think of her as an object of lust anymore; it is only when I see how Pinnosa and his guests struggle to avert their eyes from her body, clad only in steam and olive oil, that I remember she is a woman. Her cheeks turn red as she senses all the men's gaze upon her, and she quickly submerges herself into the plunging pool to her neck.

Rav Asher clears his throat, and we all turn towards him in an instant, relieved at him drawing our attention away.

"The *Comes* mentioned you two met the night after I left," I say.

"Yes, indeed," the Rav says, stroking his beard. "We had an interesting conversation on the virtue of *hope*."

"I wasn't convinced by the Rav's philosophy at first," says Pinnosa with a wry smile. "As a Bishop, I believe in hope eternal, in God's gifts awaiting us — in the afterlife. But as a *Comes*, I view the world around us through a dark lens, much as yourself, I understand. The old world *is* dying. Maybe it is already dead, we just haven't noticed it. We made too many mistakes. We let our allies turn to enemies, and we let our enemies exploit our weaknesses. I did not think there was anything for us to do other than delay our demise for as long as possible."

"What changed your mind?" asks Ursula.

"I did," says *Praetor* Paulus. He scrubs his arms with the scraper. Of Pinnosa's men, he's the least perturbed by

Ursula's presence — I imagine the open steaming pools of Ake do not provide much in the way of privacy. "I brought news of what you and the Franks did in Ake."

"We didn't do anything remarkable," I protest. "We just helped you with the fire."

"It is more than any River Frank ever did," says Pinnosa's officer. "At best, they would have left Ake alone. At worst, they would have plundered what was left to plunder."

"Hildrik is not like that," says Audulf.

"Perhaps he isn't," says Pinnosa. "But it wasn't Hildrik who came to ask my help with the Saxon warband."

He picks up Paulus's scraper and applies it, with the oil, to his thighs. Dried blood and dead skin mixed with dirt sticks to the blade. I study his ablutions with interest — not even my fathered bothered to observe the Roman rites of bathing, preferring the Briton soap and rag. For a moment, I feel transported into the world of the Ancient writings, as if Caesar himself were to enter the bath at any moment.

Pinnosa must also feel like he's in another time and another place; without thought, he puts the scraper away for an attendant slave to clean and replace with a fresh one — but there are no attendants here, so the scraper falls to the wet stones with a soft clang.

"This place," he says, gazing around the *caldarium*'s walls, painted with ancient, faded murals, dancing in the faint light of the oil lamp, "it is much like yourself, young Octa. A curious remnant of Rome in the heart of a heathen land. I've never seen Franks and Saxons show any interest in our baths, or our libraries."

"My father was raised as a son to a Briton magistrate," I say and then remember another fact of my upbringing that is bound to make an impression. "My foster-uncle, who was my tutor in all Roman matters, is the Bishop of Londin."

Pinnosa guffaws. "Now I understand how it is that you could speak to me with such audacity! But it only confirms what I have already come to believe, after talking to Rav Asher and *Praefect* Fulco. The old world may be dying, but there is a new one being born. A world of men like your father and yourself. Men, Lord willing, like Hildrik."

"What does this have to do with the crowd of refugees outside?" I ask.

"Coln, the city, is just so many walls. Bricks. Stone. Tiles. Plaster. All of it can one day be rebuilt, like the *basilica* my father raised from the rubble. What cannot be rebuilt is here," he points to his head, "and here," he lays a hand on his heart. "I could send all my men to death defending these stones. It would be a glorious battle, but a short one. And then, the barbarians would prevail anyway, and raze the city to the ground. Melt the statues, burn the books, rip the marble, just as they have in so many other cities in Gaul, so many times. Just as they did to Rome herself, three years ago."

"Or we could try to save as much as possible, and find a new home in the South," says the officer. "Nearer to the centre of the Empire. Shorten our supply lines, compress our borders. Try to survive for a generation more."

"Only a generation?" I ask.

"Even I don't hope for more," says Rav Asher with a bitter laugh. "But a generation might be enough — to teach eager younglings like yourself what we know. To ensure that at least a memory of Rome remains."

"Your library," I guess.

He points to the outside. "All that was worth taking is on my wagon. The Franks are free to do what they want with the complete works of Statius." He laughs, but his literary joke is as lost on me as it is on everyone else.

"Not everyone agreed with you," I say. "Or there would be thousands more waiting to enter Tolbiac."

"It's not easy to evacuate an entire city overnight," says Pinnosa. "More will come over the next few days. Some are going by water, by way of Confluens. The others — most — will try their fortune with the Franks. To many of them, little will change with the new masters. You've seen how Gauls live in Tornac, under Meroweg. The plebs are no better or worse under the Frankish kings than under a Roman *Comes*."

"We left a *centuria* of soldiers to man the gates and keep order," his officer adds. "We're not going to let the Franks just march into the city without a fight."

"And where do you want to take all these people?" asks Ursula. "To Trever?"

"It depends very much on what your commander decides," Pinnosa says and wipes a thick trickle of sweat from his brow. He takes a deep breath. "I've had quite enough of the heat. What say you all we move to the cold room?"

"I would stay a while longer," I say. "My bruises need all the healing they can get."

"Of course." Pinnosa nods. "You've been fighting all day — we only joined you at the very end."

The men stand up, leaving me, Ursula and Audulf alone. The girl finally emerges from the water and sits up on the edge of the bath with a sigh.

"I like him better now," says Ursula. "Though he can still make milk sour with his voice."

"He's lived through a lot," I say. "I'm surprised he's managed to find so much energy at his age. When we first saw him, he was ready to die and take his city with him. Our visit must have shaken him out of some stupor."

"What do you think he meant, 'it depends on what Hildrik decides'?" asks Audulf.

"I'm sure we will find out tonight at the feast," I say. "I wonder if Gille —"

I pause. The room darkens. Gille was placed among the worst injured in the corner of a makeshift hospital of the church yard. The acolytes tending to the wounded made it clear that their skill was no longer enough to heal those that lay there — only God's miracle could save them.

"We must have hope," says Ursula.

"There's that word again, *hope*," I say. "I'm not sure there's enough of it for everyone. Hand me that scraper," I ask Audulf. "I think I'll skip the cold pool today."

It is a sombre feast; not one of those vulgar occasions we heathens are so fond of, with barrels of mead pouring all night, and youths humping each other in the shadows while *scops* sing songs of valour. We are not in a mead hall, but in the debating chamber of Tolbiac's *curia*, under a leaking roof, surrounded by stone walls of peeling plaster. Instead of a hundred celebrating warriors, only about twenty of us fit at the long table of venerable oak wood, dusted from mould and cobwebs for our arrival. Of my men, I brought only Ursula and Seawine; the rest of the table is divided between Hildrik's and Pinnosa's officers, with one lonely seat at the end for the representative of our hosts, a slightly miserable-looking chief magistrate of Tolbiac. The feast may be thrown at Pinnosa's orders, but it's the town that's paying for it; it's better than having the town plundered by rampaging Saxons, or razed by angry Franks, but it's still a substantial expense for a town this size, in the middle of a country ravaged so often by passing barbarian hordes.

The Blood of the Iutes

There is just enough ale and mead to keep everyone's spirits up, and a few flasks of wine to share among the officers. We should be celebrating a victory, but everyone is too weary and worried about their wounded comrades, out in the church yard, many of whom will not live to see the dawn.

"As the King of Epirus once said, 'another such victory and I'll be coming home alone'," quipped Pinnosa as we passed the makeshift hospital.

He is now explaining to Hildrik the presence of the Coln garrison on the battlefield, pointing to me and Ursula once in a while. Basina glances to me, smiling, whenever he does so. At the end of Pinnosa's speech, Hildrik asks him the same question I posed at the bath house: what now for the Coln refugees?

"What now for Hildrik's warband?" the *Comes* replies with a question.

"Nothing," Hildrik replies. "We will go back to Tornac. I don't have enough men to pursue Odowakr as it is, and there's a thousand-strong army waiting for him across the Rhenum. I will consult with my father and, if he so decides, gather a greater force to fight the Saxons."

Pinnosa scratches his cheek. "By the time you're back, Trever might be in Saxon hands."

"I cannot fight all your wars for you, Roman," says Hildrik. He picks up a strip of salted pork from the plate.

"And I would not ask you to. Not out of charity, at least."

Hildrik chews the meat slowly. "You would hire us as mercenaries?"

"I will need warriors to guard my people on the way to Trever. What's left of my own garrison is scarcely enough to fight through Odowakr's forces. A *centuria* of Meroweg's best would do just fine."

"You brought gold all the way from Coln?" asks Basina. "A risky move."

"I have brought a few chests with me, yes," says Pinnosa. "But it is not gold that I would like to buy your services with."

"Silver is good, too," says Hildrik.

"Not silver, either, though I have enough to cover your needs along the way. No, I was thinking of paying you in a different currency, one that none of our enemies could possibly outbid."

"What is it?" I ask, sensing an answer.

"Rome's friendship," replies Rav Asher, leaning over towards us so that the tip of his beard lands in the soup he's eating instead of the pig. "Rome's knowledge."

"Your books," I say.

"What would I do with books?" scoffs Hildrik. He grabs a carving knife. "I need iron for swords, and hands for holding them."

The Blood of the Iutes

"I know what *I* would do with Rav Asher's books," I say quietly.

All heads turn to me. I take a sip of the wine before formulating a response.

"My father once had a dream," I say. "He wanted to create a kingdom of the *walhas* and barbarians, united, combining the talents and skills of Rome and the strength and virility of the Iutes. Of course, that was before he grew disillusioned with Rome, like Meroweg."

"What happened?" asks Pinnosa.

"The Britons waged a war on us. Unprovoked. They destroyed farms, villages, killed innocents by the hundreds, or took as slaves. My home village was burnt to the ground. My mother lived only because she wasn't there at the time. I myself was abducted and put into a monastery, far from home and anything I knew."

The faces of the Romans turn grey as I describe what I saw as a child — of men, in uniforms imitating those of Roman soldiers, slaughtering innocent village folk, the flames, consuming the house around me; Hildrik grows grim, and nods, silently.

"This is not the story we were told," says Rav Asher, stroking his beard distractedly. "I got a copy of the latest Massalia Chronicle for my library. It tells of the barbarian levies rebelling and attacking the *Dux* in Londin, and the Britons forced to defend themselves from their onslaught."

"Wortimer would send his own messengers to Gaul, to ensure his version of events was what got into the chronicles," I say. "And worked with Germanus to spread the news from church to church."

Hildrik laughs. "If this is the quality of the *knowledge* you want to share with us, you can keep it," he says. "My father sent warriors to help the Iutes fight against the *walhas*."

"And we will be forever grateful for it," I say, with a nod.

"It affected him also," says Hildrik. "He, too, once hoped for a union with the *walhas*. When we crossed the Rhenum, we were just one of the barbarian hordes, raiding and plundering, much like the Saxons still do. But when Aetius beat us, instead of throwing us back across the river, he offered us land around Tornac for settlement… We thought this was the beginning of a great alliance. Maurica proved he was just using us for spear fodder."

"We have been paying for Aetius's betrayal of our allies at Maurica dearly," says Pinnosa. "The Goths and Burgundians have never forgiven us for it, either."

"What happened at Maurica?" Ursula asks me quietly.

"Aetius took all the plunder the Huns left on the battlefield," I tell her. "Leaving none as reward for his barbarian allies."

"He argued that Rome needed the gold more," says Pinnosa. "And he may have been right, at the time. But it was an ungodly thing to do."

The Blood of the Iutes

"It was enough to make my father forever suspicious of Rome's intentions," says Hildrik, "but Wortimer's war in Britannia was the final blow to his hopes."

I'm surprised — he never told me about this; I never even realised how much he was aware of the events in Britannia. Even in his exile in Thuringia he must have been kept abreast of his father's undertakings, and judging by what Rav Asher said, he had better access to this information than any of the Romans.

"It wasn't Rome," says Pinnosa. "That is what happens when Rome is *gone*. When the peace and order that Rome brings are destroyed."

"I wish I could believe it," says Hildrik.

"Then come with us to Trever," says Pinnosa. "And I give you my personal word that you will be sufficiently rewarded. Perhaps this could be a start of Rome regaining your trust."

"I need more than promises," replies Hildrik, and I notice Pinnosa's eyes glint. Hildrik talking about rewards means that now at least he's considering his proposal. "I got no plunder off of the Saxons, other than some supplies." He scratches his nose. The wagons we took were filled with odd load: thick ropes, long wooden beams, barrels of grease, blacksmithing tools, iron clamps and hinges. The iron could perhaps be forged into weapons, but the rest was useless to a warband. "If I leave now, I return with nothing, but at least I bring most of the men alive back to my father. If I go with you, I may lose even that."

"What if you left your gold and silver here in Tolbiac, for safekeeping?" I propose. "If neither of you returns for it, have it sent to Tornac in Hildrik's name, as spoils of the campaign — and *wergild* for the lost warriors."

Rav Asher and Pinnosa look to each other, then glance at the Tolbiac magistrate, staring glumly into his mug of ale. Pinnosa smiles. "I don't hate this. It's better than having to carry all that treasure to Trever through battle. How does it sound to you, chieftain?"

"Like Aetius's promises." Hildrik scowls. "I don't trust these magistrates to do what you ask. And what if Tolbiac falls to the Saxons, too? Or the River Franks? What of your gold then?"

"Bury it all in a secret place, and it will be safe," I say. "The *walhas* in Britannia did that all the time when war came near their homes."

"I need silver for the armbands to reward my warriors," says Hildrik, his resistance faltering. "And gold for the diadems. Otherwise, I may not be able to convince my men to continue this campaign. We are already far outside our borders, and Trever is further than we ever planned to go."

"I'm sure we can arrange something that will suit all of us," says Pinnosa. "Even if I have to reach into my personal accounts…"

As Hildrik and the Romans continue to haggle over the price with which to hire the Franks as mercenaries, I sense a hand on my thigh. I look down, startled, then up, to see

The Blood of the Iutes

Basina's eyes glinting with mischief. I freeze as her hand moves up my breeches, and to my quickly bulging crotch. I glance to my left. Ursula has also noticed what's going on, and she's struggling to stifle laughter. She moves closer, to cover me from the eyes of others sitting at the table, even as Basina's hand reaches inside. My heart quickens.

Ursula leans to talk to Basina over me. "You must try the baths here," she says. "Maybe tomorrow they can heat them up for us again."

"I never understood your *walhas* obsession with baths," Basina replies. "A river or a pond is good enough to get clean after the battle."

"Trust me, nothing beats a good hot soak," says Ursula. "You're never as refreshed and invigorated as after a session in a *caldarium*."

They continue this hollow conversation for a time; all the while, Basina strokes me under the breeches. I'm covered with sweat, and I can feel my face grow red; I pray that neither Hildrik, nor anyone else, spots my predicament, but the Franks and the Romans are too busy arguing. I can no longer pay attention to what they're saying, only that for some reason, they are unable to reach a compromise that moments ago seemed so close.

"You are just as deceitful as all Romans," cries Hildrik. "Like Aetius, you would have us die for you, but you're not willing to part with any of your precious gold!"

"Your price is unreasonably steep," replies Rav Asher. "It is one thing to ask for payment for services rendered, but to bleed us dry in exchange for protection — why, that's tantamount to extortion!"

"The gold on the wagons you mention is not mine — it belongs to citizens of Coln," adds Pinnosa. "I will gladly give you my share, and so will Rav Asher, I'm sure, but if you want more, you'll have to take it from us by force."

Their quarrel grows hotter just as Basina's fingers go faster, until at last, Hildrik slams his goblet on the table — and I explode into his betrothed's hand.

"Come, my beloved," Hildrik says. "Their wine is as sour as their tongues, and their meat is as rotten as their hearts. Maybe tomorrow these *walhas* will come to their senses."

He stands up and bids Basina do the same. She leans over and kisses Ursula and me on the cheek for good night — and wipes her hand in my tunic.

"We bury our fallen in the morning," she says. "I will meet you at the church yard."

"Of course," says Ursula. "Rest well."

"Rest… rest well, both of you," I stutter, catching my breath.

The Blood of the Iutes

Honour. What a strange idea it is. An idea that makes people fight, and die, and yet provides no tangible benefit to anyone.

People fight for plunder; they fight for mercenary pay; they fight to defend their homes and families; they fight because their chieftain wants to conquer a swathe of land. All this, I get. But this… this *honour* thing? This, I could never understand.

My father always hated it. "It's a useful tool for a leader," he'd say. "It makes men die for you without you having to pay them or promise them favours. But once the leader himself starts to be guided by honour, or glory, or some other futile endeavour like it, his people are as good as lost."

It was honour that made the Franks stand against the Saxons, despite the overwhelming odds. It was honour that killed the many warriors we are putting into the damp ground on this dreary, drizzly, grey morning. Poor Gille is among them, one of the two warriors I lost in this battle, the other the young shieldmaiden, Haeth; both died before dawn, just like the acolytes expected. No god saw it fit to save them. Gille will never put a fresh saddle on another untamed moor pony. He will never entertain us with one of his odd Frisian jokes. Few of the wounded survived the night; those who did, including two of my Iutes, are bound to make a recovery quick enough to return to our ranks soon. The others are all waiting on the biers; the acolytes and the surviving Franks work hard on digging the many graves needed to accommodate the fallen. The town does not have a separate cemetery for the heathens; at Pinnosa's insistence, they're all buried in the empty corner of the church's hallowed ground.

There will be twenty fresh graves today in this corner: all victims of Hildrik's pride and honour. And now, because it is never rational, the same honour is forcing Hildrik to refuse Pinnosa's offer of continuing the fight against the Saxons, a fight so many of his men already gave their lives for.

I know this isn't about the gold — at least, not *just* about the gold; Meroweg's Franks are a proud, wealthy people. They don't need trinkets from Coln's refugees. When we departed Tornac, to pursue what we then thought was just a raiding Saxon warband, there wasn't even any talk of spoils. If we caught the Saxons at the end of their raid, we would take what they plundered back to the villages they took it from. If, as we hoped, we intercepted them before they did too much damage, there wouldn't even be anything to take. It is, then, nothing but Hildrik's stubbornness and pride that made him leave last night's feast in such anger. Pinnosa's offer, as far as I can make it out, is more than fair; moreover, I'm almost certain Hildrik *does* still want to pursue Odowakr; to avenge his fallen, to prevent the enemy from capturing Trever. All the same, he can't be seen as weak by his men, accepting what may be mere scraps from the *walhas* table.

I need him to go after the Saxons, too. I haven't come all this way just to lose a friend. I want a part in Pinnosa's deal. Hildrik can keep all the gold; I have glimpsed a little of Rav Asher's library and know it's worth more than any treasure. The books and Rome's friendship are what I'm after, but I'm not going to get any of it if we now decide to return to Tornac.

"My father would know what to do," I whisper to myself, wiping the drizzle from my brow.

"About what?" asks Ursula. She's the only person standing close enough to hear me through the rain.

"Hildrik and his cursed *pride*." I explain the dilemma to her in a few words. "This is exactly the sort of problem my father used to deal with at the Londin Council. Even when he was my age, he somehow convinced Hengist to accept the settlement deal offered by the magistrates, even though it was far more insulting than the one Pinnosa is offering Hildrik."

"Can't you do the same?"

I shake my head. "I don't have his skill with words. He was raised in a Councillor's household. He could read the Ancients at half my age."

"I think it's about time you got out of your father's shadow." She glances across the field of graves, where Basina stands solemn, watching the ritual Hildrik conducts over the dead; we have no priest or rune-maker, so Hildrik must perform their duties. The rite is simple and not very different from the ones performed by the Saxons and Iutes. For every dead, Hildrik throws a sprig of oak, and a splash of bull's blood, now blended with rain, from a small clay basin.

"Maybe your new… *friend* could help with your problem," she says, nodding at Basina. "She certainly seemed keen on helping you yesterday."

My cheeks burn, but I admit there's merit in Ursula's advice. There's more than one way to play on Hildrik's pride. As another body is brought up, I walk slowly over to him and his betrothed.

"How soon are you going back to Tornac?" I ask.

"Now is not the time to discuss this," Hildrik replies, then adds: "In two days, if the wounded can walk by then."

"We will miss your company."

He looks at me sharply. "What do you mean?"

I feign surprise. "We are coming with the Coln refugees, as guard."

"Alone?"

"My friends and I came to Gaul to help Rome," I say. "It's too early for us to go back home while there's still a war on."

"You took Pinnosa's gold?"

"I did not," I say. "I do not need his gold. There is glory and plunder enough to be found at Trever."

"There is *death* to be found at Trever," he says. He glances at Basina. She smiles faintly. He must hate me now. He knows he's right; going with Pinnosa is a great risk, hardly worth any reward. And he must suspect I'm bluffing — I would never dare to follow the Romans on my own with the handful of Iutes that I have left. We would barely make a dent in Odowakr's forces.

But admitting all of this would make me look like a coward. And while I might not care about that, pointing this out to me is what makes *him* look like a coward, in his men's and Basina's eyes.

He scowls.

"Do what you want with your men," he says. "I can't stop you."

"Maybe I should go with Octa," says Basina.

"You are *my* betrothed," Hildrik seethes.

"But not your slave," replies Basina. "I always wanted to see Trever. And so did you, from what I remember. They say it's almost as great a city as Sirmium. We talked of it even in Thuringia."

"And we will see it. As soon as I get enough men from my father."

"We will be waiting for you," I say. "But try not to take too long, or there may not be much left to see."

As I walk away, I hear Hildrik roar and smash the bowl of bull's blood against the church's wall.

CHAPTER XII
THE LAY OF ODILIA

Odilia returns from her dawn patrol in a hurry.

"Found them," she says, catching her breath.

She is soaked through; the dew rises in steam from her clothes and skin.

Odilia has not proven herself a skilled warrior in the battles so far, but she's a keen tracker, and discovered a surprising natural talent for horse riding, so I have often been sending her out as vanguard as we march south towards Trever. We've been marching for six days now, straight down the great Roman highway, at a moderate pace, careful not to catch up to Odowakr too quickly in fear of ambush. If he's been sending any rear guards of his own, and he's bound to have, he must know we are following him. It's impossible to hide the mass of Frankish warriors, Roman soldiers and Iute riders from spies: nearly two hundred men under the joint leadership of Hildrik and Pinnosa.

Hildrik is still furious with me for forcing him to join our expedition to Trever, even though we both know it was what he truly wanted all along. The broad bands of freshly melted Roman gold on his arm and the arms of his officers did little to allay his anger at my trickery. We have barely spoken a word since Tolbiac, other than to grudgingly coordinate our war plans. All through the march, he's been keeping Basina away from me, and from anyone else, under guard, though I'm certain no guards would hold her for long if she didn't wish to play along with the pretence of Hildrik having power over her. It is a dangerous game; she knows she's the main reason why Hildrik eventually agreed to march south, rather than return north. His honour and pride must be satisfied by her subservience, otherwise he might as well pack up and go back home. He may be the son of a *Rex*, and a war chief of many victories, but he will not command the respect of his warriors for long if they start to suspect he can't control his betrothed's virtue.

Pinnosa stays largely silent, too, but for a different reason. Three days after we set out from the crossroad town, a bloodied messenger reached us from Coln. The city had fallen to the River Franks after a battle that lasted one day and one night. Pinnosa's calculations proved right — Hildebert's warriors, elated with easy victory, spared the lives and freedoms of most of the city's inhabitants, except a handful who insisted on fighting to the last, barricaded inside his father's *basilica*. But the once proud and mighty Roman city was no more. Not even Rav Asher had enough hope left to think Rome could ever capture Coln again. And with Coln gone, it was only a matter of time before smaller towns like Ake and Tolbiac succumbed to the River Franks; the entire lowland province would become Hildebert's domain.

It was an inevitable consequence of Pinnosa's decisions, and he was well aware of what would happen when he made them — but that knowledge did nothing to alleviate his melancholy mood, which soon spread over his entire army. That mood did not improve when we entered a dark, wooded highland area, that the local guides called Arduenna. The

Roman highway now weaved up and down — though always due south, like an arrow shot — between fertile valleys, dotted with rich farms, windswept hilltops marked with watchtowers and small forts, and slopes covered with black forest of tall pines and gnarled oaks. The weather turned melancholy, too — what started as a grey drizzle at Tolbiac turned into a procession of violent showers and gale-torn mists, unseasonably cold and windy for this time of year; we marched even slower now, not wanting to leave the miserable crowd of refugees following us from Coln too far behind.

This is a land that's seen its share of barbarian raids over the centuries. The road from Coln is a natural corridor for any conquering horde, and the locals have learned to live with the invasions as if they were natural catastrophes. This time is no different. Each small hilltop fortress we pass is filled with people and their livestock, gathered from nearby farms and villages, huddling together in the walls of the ruined barracks, waiting for the Saxon warband to march past until it's safe enough to leave. The forts this far north are only manned by skeleton garrisons, enough to slow Odowakr's progress down, but not stop him. He doesn't pay attention to their walls. With his wagon train gone, he can afford to simply march around the forts, plunder the surrounding farms for food and fodder, and move on.

We don't have such freedom. In every fort, we stop for the night, waiting for the refugees to catch up. In every fort, our news brings sorrow, but no surprise. It seems the people of Arduenna have long expected Coln to fall to the River Franks. If anything, they are surprised Pinnosa managed to save so much from the fallen city, and with so few losses. In every fort, a handful of the refugees decides to stay behind, too exhausted to march any further. Pinnosa, still a superior officer to the local commanders, orders each garrison to split into two unequal parts. One, smaller part of each, he sends back north, to the border fortress of Icorig, guarding the entrance to Arduenna, in case Hildebert's warriors decide to try their fortune fighting their way deeper into Gaul. The remainder is ordered to join our army in its march to Trever.

"There's no point leaving good troops in these hilltop forts," he explains. "Icorig should hold any incursion for a while, but if Trever falls, none of it will matter. We need to get as many men to the city as possible."

By the time I send out Odilia on her mission, our army has grown by another hundred or so fresh soldiers. There are now more Romans in our midst than Franks, and Hildrik's unease only grows. We're a small barbarian band, deep in the Roman territory — if they turn against us, what chance do we have to fight our way back home? And if we reach Trever, will there be enough glory and plunder to share if the Franks are only an auxiliary force to the main Roman host?

The news Odilia brings is not related to Odowakr. We don't need any more patrols to track his movements. We know he's ahead of us — coming up to the outskirts of Trever now, less than a day away, having slowed down to avoid the last fort along the way. Odilia's mission took her across the Mosella River, to the other side of the Roman city, to find out the position of the greater Saxon army coming from across the Rhenum.

"They blocked approaches to all three gates," Odilia explains, drawing a crude map in the mud. "The main camp is on the northern road, two smaller detachments to the south and east. There is still one road left open, south across the river. I saw some *wealas* fleeing in that direction."

"They would have come through Mogontiac," says Paulus, who joined us on the side of the road, together with Basina and Pinnosa. As Pinnosa's army grew, so did the need for new officers to command the recruits, and so Paulus was promoted to his former position of a centurion. "The same way Attila's Huns did. There will be many in that horde who came with him the last time."

"I remember when Mogontiac was an impassable fortress," muses Pinnosa. "Guarding the Rhenum crossing since Drusus vanquished the barbarians in the days of Augustus."

"The Huns left it a smouldering ruin," says Paulus; I can see in his eyes he witnessed the destruction himself. "And we could never afford to rebuild it again. It is now merely a watchtower, maintained to warn Trever of approaching barbarian warbands."

"They can't have been here long," adds Odilia. "The south camp was still being set up when I saw it."

"Is the siege tight in the north and east?" asks Basina.

"It is porous as a sieve," says Odilia with a grin. "There is little to stop the men and the beasts from simply crossing the fields around the city and reaching the gates this way. There is a gap more than an arrow shot wide between the walls and the Saxon camps. I saw some barges sail up the river from the North, undisturbed."

"They still fear the might of Augusta Treverorum," says Pinnosa. A faint, triumphant smile appears on his lips, the first in days. "The barges must be from Coln. They made it all the way here, after all." His fist clenches in anticipation of battle.

"The army must be waiting for Odowakr to join them before they begin the siege in earnest," I guess. "Is there no chance of reinforcements from the South?"

"If there were any, they'd already be here," says Pinnosa. "There is a strong garrison in Mettis, but they would not risk sallying forth to meet a barbarian army in the field. We are the only help the city may count on."

"Before we take on Odowakr's entire army, we need to figure out how to get *them* into the city safely," says Paulus, nodding in the direction of the crowd of refugees, huddling in makeshift shelters and on the wagons along the road.

"We'll figure it out presently," replies Pinnosa. "It looks like we have a little more time to come up with the plan than I feared. As things stand, the city will hold for weeks. You have my gratitude, girl," he says to Odilia. "Yours is the first good news I've had in weeks."

"She's not a *girl*," I say, and wrap my arm around Odilia's shoulders in a proud embrace. "She's a Iute shieldmaiden!"

Trever spreads below my feet as if it was a mosaic floor, a perfect map of the city and its surroundings, each red shingle roof a separate tile, set out on a vast grid of streets, punctuated with several enormous compounds of imposing public buildings — a *basilica*, a *Praetor's* palace, an ancient temple turned into a church between them, a complex of bath houses in the distance.

I can see all this from the top of a tall, steep cliff that forms Mosella's left bank. It stretches all along the great bend in the river's course, in which the city itself is nestled, and guards Trever's approaches from the West like a solid wall of blood-red rock; the gentler slopes are covered in a patchwork of the same dense, dark wood as the rest of Arduenna, and oddly regular rectangles of empty land, especially on the south-facing stretch. I remember Pinnosa mentioning Mosella's wine, and I recognise these patches as remnants of vineyards, overgrown now with vine and brush.

Everything I see from the clifftop confirms Odilia's reports. The barbarian army set up several camps around the city, the two largest ones to its north and south, on the grounds of old cemeteries, cutting across the main highway from Mogontiac to Mettis. A smaller one guards the eastern road, disappearing into the hills, the slopes of which are covered with more vineyards.

On my side of the river, past a heavily fortified bridge, the road hugs the shore for the most part, but a spur winds up the slope to my north: the road to Coln. It is down this spur that Odowakr will come down upon the city. I can't yet see his band, but I know they're there, hidden in a bend in the road, waiting for something, I don't know what, before showing themselves to the city's defenders.

But there is something else Odilia wouldn't have been able to see from the ground. Trever's mighty wall encompasses more than just the densely built-up streets in the centre — it stretches from the remains of an amphitheatre and what I'm guessing might be a chariot-racing stadium — though it's the first time I've seen such an edifice — in the east, to the swampy banks and wharves of Mosella in the west; most of the land enclosed within consists of fields, pastures, farms and orchards, enough to keep Trever sustained almost indefinitely. Now I understand why the Saxons are not particularly worried about keeping their ring around the city shut tight. No siege can break Trever's spirit — the enemy will have to eventually break through the walls.

Nevertheless, some of the city folk don't seem to put much hope in the walls' ability to hold the barbarians at bay for long. A thin stream of refugees flows down the last stretch of road still free of the Saxons: the southern branch of the highway along the riverside. As Pinnosa explained, though it leads to the city of Remi, it's an arduous journey, even longer than the one we just made from Coln. It's not surprising, therefore, that only a small number of Trever's inhabitants have as yet decided to embark upon it.

"Something's happening over there," says Odilia, pointing south of the bridge. I too, now, spot a commotion on the road. A large carriage, with golden trimmings glistening in the sun, surrounded by what looks like an armed retinue, is trying to make its way *towards* the city, through the crowd of refugees packed on the narrow approach to the bridge.

Odilia, Ursula and I climb down for a closer look. The moor ponies take to the wooded slope like mountain goats. For a time, we lose sight of the city and the road below, hidden by the trees and the undulations of the earth. By the time we emerge onto another clearing, the commotion has grown to a panic. I now see it is not the carriage that is causing it; it only added to the original chaos, caused by the flow of refugees being reversed back into the city. I look to the south, to see in the distance a large troop of warriors, marching fast towards the bridge.

"Saxons," says Odilia.

"They must have crossed Mosella further upstream," I say. "They're shutting down the last way out of the city."

"This has to be what Odowakr's been waiting for," says Ursula. "We need to let Hildrik know."

"You ride back, tell him what you saw here. Be quick."

"What about you?"

"We still have an hour or so before we have to march out. I want to check something first."

Ursula turns and begins a climb back. Odilia stays to keep me company. We dismount and come closer still to the edge of the slope, to take one last look at the city below. The walls may appear mighty from a distance, but Trever, too, fell to Attila's Huns. I want to see what the passing of the barbarian horde did to its defences. I spot great gaps in the wall, filled with rubble and dirt. The round towers are crumbling, roofless, their windows gaping, charred. Even the bridge itself is in disrepair, the wooden deck raised on a lattice of wooden trusses over the black stone piers is full of holes, and one entire section of its span, nearest the city walls, is hanging in the air, supported only by thick ropes attached to timber poles and to the wall of the gatehouse on the city-side shore.

A small detachment of riders in crimson cloaks sallies forth from that gatehouse, rides past the disordered crowd and sets up a thin screen at the rear of the fleeing city folk.

"This won't hold them long," Odilia whispers.

I chuckle. "Are you a strategist now, too?"

Her cheeks turn beetroot red. "Apologies, *aetheling*," she mumbles.

"Don't apologise when you're right," I say. "Look, they've stopped."

The approaching Saxon band pauses but does not retreat. The barbarians clearly aren't keen on fighting their way through a Roman cavalry, no matter how few of them there may be — but they also have their orders, which must be to link up with Odowakr's forces further up the road. This gives some respite to the refugees, and soon a semblance of order is restored to the fleeing crowd.

"I never asked," I say, as the situation on the road below calms down, "what was a peasant girl from Robriwis doing on a *ceol* heading for Leman?"

"It was your fault, *aetheling*," she replies.

"*My* fault? How?"

She looks away and stares at the road below. "You and your friends. I watched you so many times over the years as you raced past my farm every summer. I kept wondering about the different life you all led. I didn't know why I had to toil in the fields, while you had time to ride around on ponies; I didn't even know why you were only there in the summer, and disappeared after harvest…"

"My father moves between courts," I reply. "In autumn, we all go to Leman."

"I managed to find out that much," she says. "And I figured that the different life you all had was somehow connected to that place. *Leman*," she repeats the word with an almost pious awe, and then laughs. "I thought it had to be some great palace at the end of the world, where all the nobles lived. I learned there were a few ships going there from Robriwis, and I stowed away on one of them, not really knowing what I'd do once I got there."

"And now you're here. A warrior, hundreds of miles from home, further away than any Iute has ever been."

"I'm no warrior. Not yet. I've heard songs about warriors. My father told me of how they are welcomed into Wodan's Mead Hall by the silver-haired *waelcyrs* when they die…"

"Was your father a warrior before he turned a farmer, then?"

"He fought at Crei," she says. "And... died fighting Wortimer, early in the war. My mother's new husband is just a farmer. I wish I was more like my father. I wish the *waelcyrs* would come for me when I die."

"You're doing fine, Odilia." I lay my hand on her shoulder. "Your parents would be proud. Both of them."

"My mother must be worried sick," she says. "I never told her where I was going..." She notices my hand and stirs. "My *Hlaford*..." Her cheeks turn red again.

I move the hand away, but she reaches out and holds it.

"Sometimes..." she whispers, licking her lower lip, "I would hide in the bushes by the shallow pond on the bend of Medu, and watch you from there."

"Shallow pond..." I try to recall. "We would bathe there after the race."

"And more."

Now I remember — it was on the bank of the shallow pond that I first lay with Ursula.

Odilia's boldness excites me. She no longer turns her gaze away; instead, she stares at me in a clear challenge. She is a plain-looking girl, with chains of freckles around a slightly squashed nose and large, watery-grey eyes, but there's a fire in her which shines through those eyes that reminds me of the fire in my own soul. I lean down to kiss her. She responds in kind, but then pulls back, and for a moment I fear I misjudged her intentions — but she only moves away to remove her tunic and lie down on the dewy moss, offering her small, pert breasts to me. A ruby crescent of arousal blooms around her neck, and another, smaller one, on her face, along the line of freckles.

Hastily, knowing how little time we have left, I accept her offering, just as the Saxons and the Romans crash into each other on the road below.

In any other land, it would've been impossible to hide a hundred-strong warband from the enemy's sight for long, especially one that already is aware of our presence and expects an ambush. But the Arduenna wood is so dark and dense, the hill slopes so riddled with folds and nooks, that at times, we can barely see each other among the tall scrub.

Sneaking through the forest is our only hope of surprise. Odowakr knows how close we have been following him, and he knows he's in the perfect place for a trap, where the Roman road narrows into a gorge before descending into the steep river valley. But we have no choice. Our plan is not to destroy his forces, for this we are too few, even with the reinforcements gathered in the forts along the way — but to distract them long enough for the rest of Pinnosa's scheme to succeed.

This is no place for mounted combat, at least not at first, so we leave our ponies on top of the gorge before climbing halfway down the slope. We reach our positions just in time. Odowakr's vanguard appears from around the bend, watchful, *seaxes* in hand. On one side, our side, the road is bound by a tall face of the red, crumbling rock that is so ubiquitous here; on the other, the slope descends into a steep ravine.

The outcrop of red rock we huddle behind is not just a random boulder. We chose this place carefully. There is a good path down to the Roman road here, easy to climb down and back up, if needed. More importantly, the winds, the rains and the tree roots have weathered the red boulder down into a cracked, crumbled mess with several large crevices at its base. Audulf and Seawine drag a trunk of a young pine tree and shove it into one of those holes, then wait for my command.

The Saxon vanguard moves past the narrowest point. They stop at the last twist, from which they have a clear view of the entire river valley. Their leader raises a horn to his mouth and blows a signal: the road is clear. Soon, the rest of Odowakr's host marches forth in a well-organised column, with Haesta's riders in front and a troop of heavy spearmen guarding the rear. I see no bear-shirts among the warriors — they must only wear these outfits when they're certain of battle, and ready to drink the henbane.

I raise my left hand. Audulf and Seawine lean on the pine trunk. I draw the *spatha* from its sheath by an inch. I close my eyes for a moment and calm my breath. When I open them again, the main body of Odowakr's army is right beneath us. I wave a signal. Audulf and Seawine heave with all their might. The trunk bends and creaks, and I fear it will snap, when at last, the wall of red rock leans forward and, with an almighty rumble and roar, snaps, crumbles and rolls down onto the road and the Saxon troops below.

I raise the sword over my head and lead my men charging down the path. All over the slope, Hildrik's warriors pour out of their hiding places. They smash into the rear and centre of the Saxon horde with such force that I almost believe we will prevail against it right there and then, and the whole precise plan, devised by Pinnosa and Hildrik, will prove unnecessary. But Odowakr even in this chaos remains resolute. He rallies his men into as good a ring of defence as is possible on the narrow pass; the Saxons draw their shields and form a tight wall around their chieftain, though with nothing but a sheer drop behind their back, they have little space for manoeuvres.

Haesta and his mercenaries trot in place at first, hesitant, uncertain where to attack. Odowakr is too busy saving himself to give him orders, and with the rubble strewn across the road, there is no clear route for a cavalry attack. But all doubt vanishes from his face when he sees me and the Iutes rushing down the slope. He lowers his helmet's visor and spurs his horse towards us. Only now does Odowakr shout an order to Haesta, but it's too late; the horsemen splitting away from the main host are a signal — not for the Saxons, but for the Franks, to also pull away from the shield wall in a feigned panic.

We're almost too slow to retreat before Haesta's chargers. Unlike Hildrik's Franks, we don't need to feign fear. The earth trembles under the hooves of the Thuringian beasts, and the cliff-side crumbles under us from the tremors. At last, we reach the safety of the wooded slope. Haesta doesn't stop. He guides the horse up the path after us. His men hesitate at first, before doing the same. It's not easy to scramble back up the narrow path — but it's still harder to do it on horseback. The hooves of Haesta's mount slip on the mud and rock.

The Blood of the Iutes

Now I have to urge my Iutes not to flee so quickly; otherwise Haesta's rage will subside too fast, and he will return to the road sooner than planned.

As I climb, through the trees to my right I glimpse the rest of the battlefield. The Frankish retreat breaks the line of the shield wall. The Saxons pursue, triumphant, heedless of Odowakr's hoarse warnings. Before long, only his household warriors remain with him, accompanied by the rear guard of heavy spears, who until now have taken no part in the battle, still wary of the Roman forces hiding somewhere further up the road. The Franks and the Saxons disappear into the woods. The crashing of arms and the cries of the fallen tell me the clash in the forest is bloody and deadly; even drawn into our trap, the Saxons are putting up a fierce fight. This is not a battle the Franks can win through sheer strength of arms.

I glance back, and my heart comes up to my throat. Somehow, Haesta has managed to force his horse to climb straight up the narrow mountain path, as if it was one of our ponies. He is now just a few steps behind me, the tip of his lance now-gleaming, now-darkening in between the rays peering through the leaves, only a thrust away. I slip on the wet stone and slide towards him, grasping at lichen and grass to scramble back up.

"*Aetheling!*"

I hear the cry and the tumult of hooves on stone before me. I look up, rolling away at the last moment. Odilia charges madly from above; she wields no weapon, just holds tightly to the reins of her pony as it rams into the flank of Haesta's horse. The two beasts tumble down, throwing off both riders into the bushes. I hear the nauseating loud crack of a spine; I can't tell whether it's one of the mounts or the riders. Haesta's horse rolls further down, blocking the way up for his companions.

I descend carefully to find Odilia. Her leg is crushed under the body of her pony. She's unconscious but still breathing. While I struggle to free her leg, Haesta scrambles up; so does his horse, with a pained snort. With rage in his face, Haesta draws his sword and starts climbing towards me again, when a desperate sound of war horns tears the air. We both look through the trees towards the battle below; I know what's going to happen now, if everything has gone according to the plan. Haesta, on the other hand, is up for a nasty surprise...

A dense, crimson wedge of Pinnosa's cavalry storms into Odowakr's rear guard. It is a suicide push, the last ever charge of Coln's *equites*, straight onto the enemy's outstretched spears. The shafts shatter on the horses, the horses tumble over the spearmen, the riders fall on the cobbles. The agonising whinnying of the fallen beasts reaches even my ears, up on a distant slope. I turn my eyes away from the bloody spectacle.

Haesta points his sword at me. Only Odilia's pony separates me from his blade. I draw the *spatha*, ignoring the stinging in my hand, torn on the rough stones. The anxious horn sounds again. It's Odowakr, calling back his men from the pursuit in the forest.

"We'll finish this later — *aetheling*," Haesta snarls.

He turns back, limping slightly — I remember now how my father crushed his right leg at Wecta, many years ago — and leaps back on his horse. The mercenaries ride down to face what's left of Pinnosa's cavalry after it punched through the Saxon spearmen.

I turn my attention back to Odilia. The other Iutes have by now returned, bringing the ponies back from the old oak glade.

"Help me!" I cry.

Audulf rushes to push the dead pony from the girl's leg. The pain wakes her up. She gasps and grabs my hand. A trickle of blood pours from her mouth.

"My *Hlaford*…"

"Hush, Odilia."

"I will dine… with Wodan…?" she whispers.

"Of course, Odilia," I reply. "Can't you see the *waelcyr*?"

"I do… my *Hlaford*… I see them… Flying on white horses…!"

She winces and her body goes limp in my hands.

"I'll carry her," Ursula offers. She picks up the girl carefully and puts her on her own pony. She hands me my mount's reins. "Lead us to glory, *aetheling*. For Odilia's sake."

James Calbraith

One final piece joins the deadly game. The last, and the largest, army enters the battle, if only briefly, and in a great hurry: the Coln refugees.

Flanked by Pinnosa's Legionnaires, crowding around the wagons and horses, nearly two thousand men and women, tired and hungry, rush down the winding road, squeezing past the narrow corridor cut through Odowakr's forces by the *equites*' last charge. With most of the Saxons still busy hunting Hildrik's Franks deep in the forest, the only warriors able to stop the thundering multitude are the Haestingas; but they took too long chasing after us and return to the road too late to make a difference. The roaring torrent of men sweeps past them and threatens to engulf them. Haesta's men can only retreat into the shadow of the cliff face and wait as the human river rushes past them. Across the road, Odowakr's guard tightens the ring around their chieftain; they appear stunned by the sheer audacity of our undertaking.

It sounded like the plan of a madman the first time Pinnosa presented it to us, after we gathered to hear the reports from all the returning patrols. But at length, we were forced to agree there was no other way; our priority was for the refugees to reach the safety of Trever's walls before the city shut its gates for good and hunkered down for the long siege. There was no alternative — all the roads south led through Trever, and the refugees were already too exhausted by the long march from Coln to try to wander across the hills and forests to reach any other safe haven — the next nearest city, Mettis, was yet another week's march away.

The Blood of the Iutes

The only way to get to Trever was to somehow break through the Saxon warband, on the last, narrow stretch of the old highway.

"Should we not try to negotiate the passage with Odowakr?" I asked. "He doesn't seem like the sort who would bring harm to unarmed civilians."

"Hostages," Pinnosa replied. "We can't risk him getting his hands on the noblemen of Coln. Many of us have friends and family in Trever. Lord knows what having us captured and threatened would do to the city's morale."

"It would be better for them to die as warriors, than to let themselves be paraded like cattle before the walls of Trever," Hildrik said grimly.

"A pagan sentiment, but in this case, I can't help but agree," said Pinnosa.

Many Romans perish before they get to the other side of this gauntlet, though not, as Hildrik would have preferred, as warriors. Dozens of bodies lie strewn all over the road; most trampled underneath the feet of their comrades or the hooves of the oxen and horses in the panicked tumult, others slain by a stray Saxon spear or sword. One overturned wagon tumbles into the ravine, pulling the dray horses with it. Another cracks an axle and flips over, crushing all within. But despite these tragedies, the losses seem lighter than we feared, and soon all that stands between Pinnosa's men and the safety of Trever's walls is just another mile of a winding, empty Roman highway.

Finally, the Saxons return; fewer in number and bloodied, but no less eager for it. Furious at having been tricked into a fruitless pursuit, they emerge onto the road just in time to see the rear of the refugee column soon disappear beyond the bend. The civilians present an easier target than Hildrik's warriors, and an opportunity for revenge and plunder. Even Odowakr realises he can no longer hold his men back. He shouts an order, and his entire horde launches, belatedly, into a chase.

Above, the forest rustles with movement. It's the Franks, racing after the refugees and the Saxons, desperate to also make it to the city in time. The slope coming down to the river is too steep for ponies; it's unsafe even for the warriors running on foot, and I imagine not all of them will make it to the shore in one piece.

Only Haesta and his mercenaries remain where they are. I order the Iutes to halt on the edge of the forest. The Haestingas form a line, separating us from the rest of the pursuit.

"What's he waiting for?" asks Audulf.

"He doesn't care about the *wealas*," I say. "It's us he wants."

"Then let's give them what they want," says Ursula, drawing a lance. There's a strange look in her eyes, one that I've never noticed before: one of bloody resolve. Witnessing Odilia's death transformed her in an instant. No — it wasn't just that. I look around my men; how had I not seen it earlier? The battle at Tolbiac changed them from Iute sailors and farmers into true warriors. Before Tolbiac, they may have been ready to fight — now, they are ready to die.

"We only want to get to the other side," I remind them. "Don't get tied down in a needless brawl. There's safety at the end of that road. Warm food. Warm bed."

Ursula stares down the lance shaft with a steely gaze. It's a look of someone who no longer cares for such trivialities as warm food and bed. She wants to kill someone, and she's just chosen her target. I follow her gaze — she's looking straight at Haesta. I put a hand on her shoulder.

"He's not worth it," I tell her, and nod at the dead girl on the pony's back behind her. "Odilia needs a proper burial."

"She'll get one," Ursula replies. "I'll make certain of it."

We form a narrow wedge — the rock rubble and the flotsam left after the refugees only allow five horses abreast — and launch into a trot. Haesta grins in a mocking smile. His men holster their lances and draw small, round bucklers and swords instead. I can tell they're not taking us seriously; head-on, in the open field, my small band of farmers-turned-warriors stands little chance against a trained squadron of war-horse-mounted cavalry. My only hope is for most of us to press on through and do enough damage for Haesta to break off his pursuit. As I spur to charge, a thought flashes in my mind: if Haesta wants only me, maybe I can occupy his attention long enough for the others to reach safety — even if it means my own death…

Two white shapes blur past me with a thundering noise. Two riders on Thuringian war horses, one to each side of me, storm towards Haesta's men, out of nowhere... Hildrik raises his sword high and strikes at the nearest of the mercenaries. The blade slices through the shield as if it was made of cheese and shatters the enemy's arm. Basina shoots, point-blank, at another of the Haestingas, and then whirls the bow and whacks him in the face. Within seconds, Hildrik and Basina carve a two-man gap in Haesta's line. I swerve into that gap.

"Single file!" I shout to my men. "Quickly!"

I glance behind. Seawine and Audulf ride close behind me and are the first to clear the gap. Two more Iutes follow, but then the gap closes, just before Ursula; Odilia's body is weighing her down, and she's too slow to make it.

I turn around. I yell at Audulf and the others to keep going, but they ignore me and ride with me back into the mercenary line. I shout a challenge to Haesta. Some of his men turn their attention to me. The line breaks, now facing the ponies from two sides. An arrow whistles past my ear and hits one of Haesta's men on the shoulder — Basina and Hildrik, too, are turning back again.

I charge at Haesta. Our swords clash; he strikes with such force it almost throws the weapon from my hand. With a great cry of rage, Ursula throws her lance at his side. He swerves to avoid it. The horse rears under him and whinnies in annoyance. Ursula uses the opportunity to sneak past the horse's hooves to the other side.

The Blood of the Iutes

"Get her out of here!" I cry, and this time, the men heed my order. Those who broke through surround Ursula's pony with theirs, and gallop away in this tight formation. Five more Iutes remain on the other side. But now Hildrik and Basina join us. On the narrow road, the Haestingas can't make use of his numbers, and for a moment, our strengths are equal. I strike at him again, and again we exchange blows to no effect, but as we do so, two more Iutes ride through the gaps. Hildrik grabs his enemy's lance. The mercenary lets go of the weapon and pulls away, leaving enough of a gap for another of my men to pass.

Haesta's sword finds an opening through my blocks and cuts me across the shoulder. One of the remaining Iutes — Oxa, I remember his name, a keen tavern brawler in life before Gaul — leaps on Haesta's horse and grapples him to the ground. In the chaos, the last two Iutes sneak past. I lean to help Oxa up, but I'm too late — Haesta draws a knife and stabs him in the stomach.

Basina tugs me on the shoulder. "Come now! Or it'll all be for naught!"

Two mercenaries close in on me from both sides, lances lowered to strike. I sheathe the sword, turn around and start off towards the city. With each beat of the pony's hooves, the wound on my shoulder spurts blood and pain.

It's not over yet.

A long, tightly packed column of men, wagons, oxen and horses, crowds the Trever Bridge from the western gatehouse to the eastern wall, stretching the crossing's capacity to the limit. At the western end of the bridge, on our side of the river, a small troop of soldiers in crimson cloaks — I can't tell whether they're Pinnosa's surviving *equites*, or a sallying squadron of Trever's own garrison — holds its own against a great horde of Saxons, pushing at them from the south. Their struggle is valiant, but desperate. As we race down the Coln highway, Odowakr's warband, some half a mile ahead of us, reaches the bridge from the north, squeezing the Roman soldiers in a pincer — and cutting off our retreat.

Just then, with a shrieking war cry, Hildrik's Frankish warriors finally descend from the wooded hills, and join the battle from the west. A chaotic brawl erupts, in which the Saxons, the Franks and the Romans fight each other over access to the bridge gate.

"The Romans don't know we're here to help them!" I shout to Hildrik. "Pull your men back!"

"The *walhas* will be slaughtered! And what about your own men?"

He points to the end of the bridge, just beyond the gate. My heart rises, then sinks, at the sight. Somehow, a small handful of my Iutes have made it past the Saxons, past the Romans — and past the gate. I spot Ursula among them. But the remainder is trapped in the same muddled fight on the shore as everyone else, struggling to push through.

The Blood of the Iutes

As the last of Coln's refugees reach the safety of the eastern gate, trumpets sound a desperate alarm from the wall towers. At this signal, the Roman soldiers begin to make a disorderly retreat. Some of the Saxons and Franks mix with them in the confusion, but nobody seems to be paying attention to them. As soon as the last of the Romans clears the western gate, the great door begins to shut — but it's too late. The Saxons pour onto the bridge, overrun the defenders and climb up the towers, to take control of the gatehouse.

The trumpets sound again — a different signal this time; the Roman soldiers halt at the edge of the last span of the bridge and turn back again. There's a change in the way they stand against the Saxon horde; they appear slumped, dejected, as if accepting some inevitable disaster — but determined not to let the enemy move even a step closer to the city.

I spot a troop of guards run out of the gatehouse, armed with axes. They do not rush to aid their comrades — I can't tell what they're doing at first, but then I spot it: they hack through the thick ropes tied to the bridge's weakened wooden span. As the ropes snap one by one, slowly, almost imperceptibly, the entire span begins to heave and buckle — with the remaining refugees, the Roman soldiers and the Saxons attacking them still on top of it.

"It will never hold. Now you *have to* pull them back," I tell Hildrik. "Get them away from that bridge."

He notices it too, now, and blows retreat on his horn. The Franks begin to draw away from the Saxon rear and fight their way towards us; I call on my Iutes — what's left of them — to do the same. Odowakr and his men pay no attention to us — their only concern now is to break through the Roman line. If they can reach the eastern gate, they will end the siege before it even begins. In the rush of the battle, they fail to notice the creaking of the ropes and of the wood underneath their feet.

With a great heave and a crackle, the weak wooden supports bend, then yield to the weight of the fighting crowd and snap. The entire span folds in on itself and crumbles into the river with a deafening splash, taking both the Saxons and the brave Roman defenders with it into the rolling depths of Mosella underneath, leaving only the ends of the ropes dangling in the spray.

For a few brief moments, everything is silent, as both the city folk and the barbarian horde are too stunned to react to what just happened. As the dust and mist settles down, I hear Odowakr's voice, calling for his surviving warriors to rally around him at the bridge's western, remaining, end.

"We should leave," I say to Hildrik, "before the Saxons notice we're the only ones left to fight."

He nods. "We will hide in the woods," he says, "until I figure out what to do next. With me, men!" he cries and blows a rallying call on the horn. "Gather your strength one last time — pull back, back into those cursed dark hills!"

The Blood of the Iutes

PART 3: TREVER

CHAPTER XIII
THE LAY OF WIRTUS

I hold my breath as the bee lands on my hand. I watch it turn in place, stroll across my knuckles, ponder its predicament for a bit, then fly away to join its sisters on a nearby briar bush.

An overturned, cracked beehive is still home to the swarm, though judging by its state no beekeeper has taken care of it in months, or of any of the several other beehives scattered around the cherry orchard. The trees are heaving with rose-blushed fruit, too small and sour for men to eat yet, but good enough for the great flock of starlings, whose incessant noise conceals our approach. The farm, its white-washed buildings gleaming through the trees, is not in ruin, merely abandoned by the owners when news of the coming barbarian army first reached Trever.

Though the cherries themselves are yet unripe, there's a chance the farm's storehouse might still contain some of last year's preserved fruit, or better yet — wine. The buildings appear untouched by Odowakr's foragers. It's a small miracle that we found this place, far off from any road, up on a south-facing hilltop. Whoever built this farm here preferred solitude.

There are only eight of my Iutes left now. Every night, I remember the names of the fallen, and light a scrap of tallow candle in their memory. Gille and Haeth, slain at Tolbiac. Oxa, the wrestler. Odilia, the eager young tracker, whose death shook me the most, and whom I mourned the deepest. But those unfortunate deaths happened early on in our adventure. The rest of us grew both in experience and a number of scars over time. We are all battle-hardened now, grim and resolute to see this war to its end, whatever it may be. We've built a small shrine in their memory — a simple circle of river-smoothed boulders on a glade overlooked by three mast-like beeches, which my Iutes renamed Wodan, Donar and Frige. And though I do not share the faith of my companions, raising the memorial helped us all to ease the pain of loss and focus our efforts on the task at hand.

Four dead and three missing — Ursula and Audulf managed to reach Trever before the disaster at the bridge, and I hope another of my riders, Nodhbert, is with them. I have not heard from any of them since; I can only hope the people of Trever took good care of them. Ursula, at least, with her good Latin and her Christian upbringing, should have little trouble finding herself something to do in the besieged city. Pinnosa would vouch for her and Audulf — but I have no way of knowing if the *Dux* survived the battle at the bridge. In the chaos of the fighting, unable to tell them apart from the crimson-clad soldiers of Trever, I lost sight of the *Comes* and his men.

I miss my friends. I am now all alone: the only one left out of the four who set sail on Aegidius's *liburna*. The city gates are closed shut now, not letting anyone in or out, even if I did manage to get past Odowakr's blockade — and across the river, now that the bridge is gone. The morning after the battle on the bridge, the siege started in earnest, with every road and path within the blockade's perimeter, no matter how small, patrolled by Saxon guards.

I gave myself a couple of weeks to make the final decision. If nothing changes, I will take the surviving Iutes and we'll try to make our way back to Britannia — even if it means abandoning Ursula and Audulf. Nine pony riders can't possibly do any meaningful damage to Odowakr's forces. Staying here will be a waste of effort and, ultimately, lives.

Even for the journey back, we need supplies, and so for the past few days, I've been sending the Iutes out on careful hunting and foraging missions all over the cliffs overlooking Mosella's steep valley. The cherry farm might provide us with plenty of sustenance.

There's just one problem — we're not the first ones here.

"Are you sure they're not Saxons?" I ask Seawine, who led the patrol that discovered the orchard.

"The Saxons wouldn't skulk around like that," he replies. "I could barely see them; they pop in and out of the huts like rabbits out of hutches."

"How many have you seen?"

"Two or three. Can't be sure. They all wear the same drab cloaks."

I draw the sword but tell the others to keep theirs sheathed. I order the men to spread out around the orchard's border and start moving towards the centre.

"We want them alive," I whisper. "They might be from Trever."

The Blood of the Iutes

We reach the farmhouse without seeing anyone. The single window is boarded shut, and the door is closed. I gesture at my warriors to surround the house from all sides, then approach the door.

"You're surrounded," I say in Saxon, then repeat the same in the Vulgar tongue. "Come out unarmed!"

A response is a Latin slur I'm not familiar with, which tells me, at least, that Seawine was right — these are not Saxon deserters or lost Franks. I sheathe the sword and hold up just the shield instead. I kick the door in. A short, heavy iron dart, fletched with goose feathers, flies out and bounces off the shield feebly: I've never seen this kind of weapon before, but I recognise it from descriptions as a *plumbata*, the lead-loaded missile of the Roman Legions; I barge inside, followed by Seawine and a couple of Iutes. We overpower the three men inside with little effort. They're too weak to resist us — one is injured, the other two appear just famished. The red spots on their fingers and faces, which I take for blood at first, tell me there's little chance of us finding any of the farm's stores intact.

Their cloaks are not drab — just turned inside out. Underneath the brown leather lining, I spot bright crimson. I look closer and recognise one of the men.

"You're from Coln," I say. "Pinnosa's soldiers."

"What's it to you?" the man replies. He stirs in Seawine's grasp. I nod for the Iute to release him.

"We are Iutes," I reply, pointing to my warriors. "We fought together at Tolbiac."

He looks me over, then the rest of the Iutes, with a glimmer of recognition, but remains untrusting. "I thought the Franks had all left," he says.

The messenger from Meroweg's court arrived two days after the battle at the bridge. By some accident of fortune, we managed to intercept him, bumbling along the Coln road on a tired horse, before he was discovered by Odowakr's patrols. The moment he told us what he'd been sent with, we regretted our fortune. The news was unwelcome, but not surprising — Hildrik had been expecting a message like that ever since we departed from Coln.

"Meroweg demands our immediate return," he announced. "He orders it as a father and as a king."

"Did he explain why?" I asked.

"I can guess why," he replied, downcast. "His rival, Hildebert, now controls Coln and the entire province between Rhenum and Charcoal Forest. Meanwhile, we're still crammed on the scrap of land given us by the Romans — while his son is off on some fruitless adventure in Gaul. He must be planning some new conquest."

"Why not just say so in the message?"

"He doesn't trust me enough — I could always say I didn't receive the messenger or find some other reason not to heed him. He will want to tell me his plans in person."

"Will you go?"

He shrugged. "There is nothing that would hold me here anymore. I have fulfilled my promise to Pinnosa and made sure his people reached Trever safely. And I got nothing for it in return."

"What about the siege?"

"I don't see what we could do about it. There're too few of us left. Besides, I wouldn't be surprised if my father told me to ally myself with Odowakr and move against the *walhas*, to divide this province between us once Trever falls."

"And would you do it?"

"I would advise him against it. But there's only so far that I can go in my defiance. I've already stained his honour and reputation once. He wouldn't forgive me the second time."

"Then the next time we see each other, we might be on opposite sides," I said.

This surprised him. "You're not planning to stay *here*? With your handful of men? What could you possibly achieve by that?"

"I don't know." It was my turn to shrug. "But my friends are in that city, and I still want to help the Romans prevail over Odowakr. I'm not leaving until I can figure out how."

"Then you're a greater fool than I thought." He shook his head. "I hope I will see you again, Iute — and that we *won't* have to fight each other."

He left us no men; but he did leave us some weapons and armour to replace those damaged in battle, and a little food, and Basina left me her Hunnish bow — something to remember her by, she said. I had no skill with the weapon, but I promised I would train with it as often as I could.

"Keep it well," she said. "There's no bow like it this side of Rhenum. I'll be back for it."

Hildrik was watching us as we bid farewell, so she just touched my forehead with her lips and turned away, leaving me alone with my beating heart.

"When you grow bored of watching the *walhas* get slaughtered, you and your men are always welcome back at Tornac," said Hildrik as he departed. "If there are any of you left."

Now, I tell the Roman soldier, "*They* have, but we stayed to hunt us some Saxons. You're welcome to join our hunt. Are there any more of you out there?"

He shrugs. "There should be. Plenty of us got scattered when the bridge fell. Do you have anything to eat?" he asks eagerly.

"Not much, but we will share," I say. "If you help us find the others."

The Blood of the Iutes

The woodsman's axe is a fearsome weapon. If it cut through a man with the same strength as it now carves through the trunk of a mighty beech, it would hew a limb clean off. With each blow of the great blade, another inch of wood flies from inside the felling notch. Judging by the depth of the notch, the axeman had been working on it for several hours before our arrival — and is almost done with one side of the tree. A charcoal line marks another notch, still to be made on the opposite side.

Hidden in thick bramble at the edge of the glade, I watch the woodsman's axe reach almost, but not quite, to the centre of the trunk, leaving a narrow wedge in the middle. He stands with his back to the tree and measures the depth with his own backside, then, satisfied, wipes the sweat from his brow and hands the axe to another man who immediately starts work on the other side, while the first one starts carving a wedge from a long piece of leftover wood. The notch here is lower and shallower, and the new woodsman is well rested, so the work goes quicker, but it will still take him more than an hour to carve out the hole marked by the lines of charcoal, so I leave my hiding place for now and go back to my warriors.

Apart from the Iute riders, I now have under my command ten of Pinnosa's men. It was only confusion and weariness, at first, that made them obey my orders. I am younger than most of them, a heathen with no experience of leading the troops beyond the few weeks in Gaul; it would have made more sense if one of them had taken control of *me* and my warriors. But, finding themselves far from home and without their captains, facing an army of barbarians, and with no good idea of what they should do next, somehow they accepted my leadership without so much as a grumble — for which I am grateful. They grasped immediately the kind of war I wanted to wage on Odowakr, faster even than my own men. No wonder — it was the Romans who invented it, after all, or at least, it was their ancient general Fabius Cunctator who was the first to use it against Hannibal; that chapter of Livy's history was always one of my favourites, more than the great battles.

We would strike at night, or at dawn, in quick, harassing assaults. We were necessarily limited in our operations by the vicinity of the woods, but there was plenty to do for us here: disrupting a foraging party; intercepting a messenger with orders; overwhelming a patrol on the forest road; feigning an attack at a fortified camp, to keep the warriors awake. Once in a while, if we were fortunate, we'd even manage to burn down a supply store or two, but soon Odowakr noticed our attacks and doubled the guards around his granaries. This, too, was a success in a way — more warriors delegated to guard the supplies meant less of them on the battlefield.

It took time and effort, and great knowledge of the woods — fortunately for us, one of Pinnosa's *equites* grew up in one of the wine-making *villas* around Trever and was familiar enough with the land to be at least a rough guide — but at length, I felt our force, as tiny as it is, was beginning to make a difference. The Saxons started to be wary of the forest and would only venture into it in large groups. The men we caught confessed that they thought us to be a vanguard of some greater army, coming to relieve the city. Fear and anxiety crept into their minds.

The Blood of the Iutes

It was high time for our efforts to bring fruit. At the beginning of the siege, Odowakr's warriors could do little to bother the city. The walls that bound it, despite the damage wrought by the Huns, were impenetrable to the barbarian horde. Daily assaults at the vulnerable points ended in failure and retreat. Running skirmishes with a sallying force, riding into the fields to gather some fodder or disrupt a half-hearted sapping effort, brought neither glory nor plunder. Sometimes, an attack from the river, archers and javelin-throwers approaching on hide-bound boats, would test the defences further, to no avail. If this was all that Odowakr could muster to threaten the city, he may as well have packed up and gone home. A siege like this — considering how well prepared and stocked Trever was to withstand it, even with the refugees from Coln to take care of — could last until winter, and no army away from home could have remained in the field for that long.

But Odowakr hadn't come all this way just to curse, helplessly, at Trever's walls. By the third week of the siege, one of the patrols I sent out daily to harass Odowakr's foragers brought news of the Saxons clearing out a great swathe of meadow at the western end of the fallen bridge, and building what looked like a settlement at first, but turned out to be a cluster of smithies and iron forges. Some time after, we started noticing small groups of Odowakr's men disappearing deep into the forest and returning after several hours with great trunks of oak and pine. Of course — I remembered then what the Saxon captives reported after we destroyed the foraging band at Ake; it seemed so long ago now... They told us Odowakr was bringing with him engineers, hired from what was left of Attila's army after

Maurica, men responsible for the speed with which the Huns razed city after city as they ravaged Gaul.

Siege engines.

Our stand at Tolbiac proved more important to Trever's fate than anyone realised. More than just the slight loss of men would indicate, the battle was nothing short of a disaster for Odowakr, who was forced to leave his wagons back at the muddy battlefield. I knew now what all the strange equipment carried on them was for — machine parts, ready to be assembled into engines, needing only the strong wood for the frames, of which there was plenty around Trever. It was the loss of the wagons that caused the many weeks of delay, during which Odowakr's blacksmiths, rope-wrights and carpenters were forced to toil all over again to recreate the missing parts from whatever scraps they could scavenge around the city.

But that work was slowly coming to an end, and now the engineers could at last focus their efforts on what they had been planning to do from the beginning upon arriving at the city's gates: gathering timber for the final phase of the construction of the machines.

I know next to nothing about these engines, other than reading some mentions in the Ancients. There was never any need for them in Britannia. Not even any of Pinnosa's veterans had ever seen one — the Hun warband which passed Coln did not bother building any machines along their march, content with plundering smaller, easier to overrun towns like Tolbiac or Ake. But we all know that we can't let Odowakr build even one. A single breach in Trever's walls would be enough for the Saxon horde to pour through and end the siege in a single bloody strike.

I find my warriors where I left them, in an abandoned settlement of wood cutters and charcoal burners, on top of a bald hill. We have been moving from one farm like this to another, from hamlet to empty hamlet, avoiding Odowakr's patrols, in search of food and shelter. Most of the villagers in the vicinity of Trever either managed to flee to the city before the gates were shut, or hid themselves even deeper into the hills, leaving all their belongings behind. All the woodsmen in Arduenna have been recruited to assist Odowakr's engineers as they venture deep into the dark forests, seeking the best, tallest, oldest trees for the construction of his infernal machines. I make sure that for every pot of grain or sackful of turnips we take, we leave a handful of bronze coins, in case the owners choose to return one day; there is nothing else that we can spend the money on in our exile, and we happen to have plenty of it, ever since we discovered the remains of the upturned wagon in the ravine it fell into during the flight of the Coln refugees; it was filled with silver and gold, no doubt belonging to the unfortunate family we found in the wreck. We buried most of it with them and took only as much as each of us could carry without hindering our movements in battle.

We've been staying in this particular settlement for two nights now, knowing that the woodsmen would be employed nearby. The handful of hacked bronze still lies on the bedding in the corner of the main hut, in exchange for two smoked haunches of deer we consumed for supper last night.

"They will be ready with the tree before the sun is high," I tell the men. "Looks like they'll be taking it down past the three beeches. An auspicious sign — Wodan, Donar and Frige will be with us."

"What's the guard like?" asks Wirtus. He's the man I first spoke to at the cherry farm — the most senior of the Roman soldiers, chosen by the others as their officer and representative while they remain under my command. As a Christian, he doesn't care much for pagan auguries, putting his hopes in preparation and strategy instead.

"Heavy," I reply. "A troop of Alemannic axemen — and at least three of Haesta's riders."

Wirtus and the others wince. The Alemanns came with the great warband from the East; since then, they traversed Mosella on their hide-bound boats to protect Odowakr's camp and the meadow upon which the siege engines are being built; lately, we've been seeing more of them. We haven't had a chance to fight them yet — but they look dangerous in their thick leather tunics studded with metal plates, helmets painted black, and great, two-handed axes on their backs. Even if we manage to ambush them in the dense forest, they're bound to put up a fierce fight — and we can hardly afford to lose any more men as it is.

"If only Hildrik had left us a few of his warriors before he left," says Seawine, and we all murmur in annoyed agreement.

With the wedges inserted deep into the spine of the trunk, the two woodsmen cry a warning and pull on the ends of a rope tied around the top of the tree. Like the piers of the Trever Bridge, the giant oak first leans, then snaps, and finally flies down, slowly, majestically, before shattering the ground with its tremendous fall.

All the labourers gather around the fallen trunk and make short work of lopping enough branches to make easy the work of dragging the tree down the slope to the broad path below, leading to the Coln road. Past the heath-spattered glade marked with the three beeches, where we raised our memorial to the fallen, the path runs along one of the many folds that divide this stretch of the Arduenna slopes. Most of my men are waiting there, in ambush, praying to their gods and the brave spirits of our dead for help in the coming battle. As the woodsmen begin to heave the tree behind them, grunting with effort, I send a messenger, letting the warriors know they need to prepare themselves.

Once the entire procession — the Alemannic axemen in front, the three Haestingas at the back, a couple of engineers and a dozen woodsmen hauling the great oak between them — moves out of sight, Seawine, Wirtus and I ride out onto the path. A narrow forest road is no place for a cavalry battle, but I hope we can distract Haesta's men long enough for the rest of the ambush to succeed. It's not going to be an easy task, and not just because the axemen are a fearsome enemy to face. I aim to bring as little harm to the woodsmen as possible, knowing they were recruited into this work by the enemy against their will, though I'm not yet sure how we can possibly achieve this in such close combat…

The party slows down as they approach the narrowing in the path, but we don't. We ride out into full view of the three horsemen. It takes them a while to notice us, so concerned they are with an ambush coming from the sides; even when they do, they're yet uncertain of what to make of three pony riders, one of them in the crimson cloak of a Roman officer, following them at a distance. I draw Basina's bow. My pony snorts and shakes its head, sensing the unease with which I sit in the saddle while trying to aim the arrow. I shoot — the missile flies over the heads of the three riders and disappears into the trees above. It's enough to get their attention. Two of the riders charge towards us, lances drawn. The third one shouts at the axemen in front to make ready for battle.

He's too late. The Iutes and the Romans leap out of their hideouts under the scrub. The Romans rush at the axemen, while the Iutes head for the tree itself. While the axemen push back against their attackers, the Iutes chase away the panicked woodsmen, grab the ropes and haul the trunk off the path. The tree rolls off down the steep slope, bouncing on the roots and shrubs along the way, until it hits the bottom of the ravine; it would take a whole army of woodsmen to bring it back up.

The two riders halt, uncertain which way they should turn. There's no overall commander on this expedition — the engineers have been directing the wood-cutting, and the Alemannic guards have their chieftain, but there's nobody to coordinate the defence effort. I shoot another arrow — at this distance it's hard to miss, but I still only manage to hit one of them on the shoulder. He cries out, more in anger than in pain, breaks the arrow off, and charges at us again. His companion rides after him.

The Blood of the Iutes

As Seawine and Wirtus face the two mercenaries, I notice that a few of the woodsmen pick up their axes and join the Romans in their fight against the Alemanns. Others run off into the woods. The Iutes are now fighting the engineers, who are proving to be skilled in more than just building machines of war. I'm surprised at how long they're managing to defend themselves, before I remember they would have taken part in Attila's entire war trail — and they wouldn't have survived this long without gaining some experience in combat.

I join the mounted battle from the side; once again, Haesta's riders can't make good use of their horsemanship on the narrow path. Under the low tree canopy, our short ponies have advantage over the tall Thuringian war horses. The riders' movements are hindered as they struggle to keep their lances from getting entangled in the branches above. I duck under the lance blade and pierce the side of the man I shot earlier. Seawine takes a sword blow on the shield, while Wirtus cuts from the back. The two mercenaries fall almost as one.

The third rider glances back and, noticing what happened, blows retreat on his horn. The only men who can still heed his call are the Alemanns and one of the engineers — the other one finally succumbs to the Iute swords. The rider picks up the surviving engineer and charges through the Iute line, past the Romans, the woodsmen, and the Alemanns, and doesn't stop until he disappears into the wood. Now, I also call a retreat; there's no point losing any more men fighting the sturdy axemen. The Alemanns wait a moment yet, to make sure we're not just regrouping for a renewed assault, and when they see us depart for good, they pick up their dead companions, turn around and march off in an orderly column, humming a mournful dirge.

A short time later, when all is quiet, I send men to get all the other fallen back for the burial — our own and the enemy's. Though I insisted on being careful, three of Pinnosa's soldiers gave their lives in the fight. I don't know how many Alemanns they took with them, but it doesn't matter; we got what we came for, and more — I didn't count on us ridding Odowakr of one of his precious machine makers. Nor did I expect any of the woodsmen to join our ranks. They're no replacement for the Romans — but their great axes might prove useful yet.

We throw the bodies of the enemy dead onto a pile under the three beeches. I notice an unusual bulge under the cloak of the dead engineer. I stoop down to investigate. The engineer is an odd-looking man, an Easterner, short and squat, with swarthy skin, small eyes and an unnaturally long forehead, not unlike Basina's. His cloak is trimmed with fur, and hidden underneath it is a leather bag, full of papers and parchments, scribbled all over with schematics and geometric formulas.

"The design of the siege machines," says Wirtus, looking over my shoulder. "The commander of Trever would give much to get his hands on those."

I rub my chin; I have grown an inch-long beard in the wilderness, and it's beginning to itch. "Then we must make sure he gets it, somehow." I look to the woodsmen who joined us. "Is there any way to get across Mosella, other than the bridge?"

The woodsmen look to each other. "You could try Iranc, ten miles upstream," says one of them. "There was a bridge there once, now just a ruin, but the current is slow there — I could swim across it when I was younger."

"It's too risky right now," Seawine opposes. "We finally showed ourselves to them. They know that we're here, and that there's more of us than just a handful of lost Iutes. That rider could've recognised you and warned Haesta that you're still here."

"I'm aware." I nod. "And before those machines are built, these plans may be of little use to anyone. But let's keep this option in mind, just in case. For now, let us bury the dead and find another place to stay the night."

"My farm is just an hour away," says the same woodsman who told us about Iranc, pointing vaguely to the north. "You're welcome to stay there, though all that's left is four walls and a roof — they took everything else…"

"It's more than enough," I say with a smile. "What is your name, woodsman?"

"They call me Kila."

"You have my thanks, Kila."

Wirtus shakes me by my injured shoulder — the pain wakes me. One of the Roman soldiers patched up the wound inflicted by Haesta as best as he could, but without Rav

Asher's skill, it's taking long to heal. I hope it will only leave a nasty scar; there is no pus or ooze, always a good sign.

I rub my eyes. It's the middle of the night. Wirtus leans over me, holding a small oil lamp, barely illuminating his face.

"What is it?"

"The woodsmen are gone."

I get up instantly and hit my head on the low ceiling beam. The huts of the woodsmen are tiny, forcing everyone to stoop down to move around. This is the second of their hamlets that we've been staying at, a bit further north than Kila's own farm. I moved here with a few of my men last night, to use as a base from which I could investigate the crossing he mentioned. He was right — the river, joined by another stream coming from the hills, spills slow and wide here, over a broad meadow, between two marshy islets, some three hundred feet apart. As I watched from my hiding place, I saw some of Odowakr's men traversing the river from the eastern shore, and I could ascertain the strength of the current. A man on a pony should not have much trouble crossing here, I decided. All I needed now was a calm, moonlit night, with no Saxons around to spot me.

"What do you mean, gone?" I ask, my mind still in a haze.

"I went out for a piss and noticed one of them sneaking away into the forest. I checked the other huts — they've all run away. Something's going on."

"Get the others. Meet me outside."

The Blood of the Iutes

I strap the sword belt on, put on the helmet and the mail vest — a parting gift from Hildrik. I grab Basina's bow and arrow bag and rush out. The others run out of their huts as confused as I am. I order them to untie the ponies and prepare for battle. I only took the Roman soldiers with me, a handful of them, leaving the Iutes with Seawine in the South, in case we stumbled into trouble with the Saxons.

And it looks like we just did.

All around the hamlet — five small, thatched huts and a goat pen, surrounded by a tall fence that guards it from wild animals — torches flicker up in the darkness. I count at least twenty of them approaching slowly up the hill. The ponies neigh nervously.

"They'll try to smoke us out," I say. "We have to break out to the west where the wood is deepest."

"No," says Wirtus. He hands me the leather bag with the siege plans. "You must get across the Mosella, while they're distracted. There won't be another chance."

"What about yourself?"

"We'll keep them occupied," he says, nodding towards the torches. They're within javelin throw now.

"I'll be back soon," I say hopefully. "Wait for me at the cherry tree farm where we found you and your men."

He nods and salutes me with his fist to his chest. I mount up, then draw the bow and aim in the direction of the nearest light. Wirtus draws the sword.

"We strike west," he tells his men. "While Octa rides east. *Roma Invicta!*"

I let the arrow fly. To my surprise, it hits the target. The warrior cries in the darkness and drops the torch to the ground. In response, the others start to charge. I shoot one more time, but this time, I hit nothing. Some of the torches fly through the air, landing on the ground and on the roofs of the huts around us.

Wirtus leads his men towards the western side of the village. They raise wild war cries, to make the Saxons aware of the direction of their attack. I retreat into the shadow of the nearest hut. The straw on its roof catches fire, but it does not yet blaze bright enough to reveal my position. For a brief moment, as I lose sight of the Romans, I'm alone in the silent darkness, with the flames crackling just a few feet away, and the old terror creeps back… Then the first of the Saxons run into the light, in pursuit of Wirtus's men. The sounds of battle erupt at the far end of the hamlet. I count — four, five, six warriors pass me by, not noticing me in the shadow. The seventh spots me and raises a shield and axe to face me. I ride out and strike at him before he can call the others for help. He takes my sword on the shield and staggers away. I leap out into the path. There are still more men here — how many warriors did Odowakr send to get us? I swerve between them, not slowing down, parrying the axe blows to my left and right. A spear blade hits my side but slides off the mail. I whisper a thanks to Hildrik for his gift. Eventually, I charge out of the encirclement into the open glade. I glance back — I hear the cries of the fighting men, and I recognise Wirtus's voice calling increasingly desperate orders to his men; his cry is cut short mid-word.

I turn back and ride down the hill. In the darkness, I need to move slowly and carefully — but so do my pursuers. I see three dots of torches behind me. The pony under me snorts, nervously, as it keeps tripping over the roots. The tree branches tear at my face. I close my eyes; sight is useless now, so I just let the pony guide me down. I hear one of the Saxons fall and curse.

At last, I sense a breeze on my face. I open my eyes again. I'm out on the swampy flood plain, a few hundred feet from the river. I spur the pony; its hooves splatter in the mud. I can now leave any pursuit far behind me. The torches follow me for a while yet, then give up, just as I splash into the freezing cold river. I gasp and cling to the pony's mane as I float from the saddle.

The current is strong; stronger than I expected. But it's the cold that gets me first. The water surrounds me. My teeth chatter. The skin on my fingers shrivels. My hands are cramped shut on the reins. I reach the first island and halt for rest. I take a deep breath before I take the plunge again. The current drags me away from where I think the second island should be; I feel an onset of panic. I can't see the other side, or anything, except the dark water around me. My limbs go numb. I can't feel my face. I hold on to consciousness with great effort, barely warding off sleep. My pony snorts, desperate to get out of the water. I pray that it holds on — racing in the Medu may have turned me into a decent swimmer, but in this cold, in heavy armour, I'm sure I will sink to the bottom like a stone as soon as I let go of its reins.

Suddenly, the pony stops. We're still in the middle of the river, but no longer in the water — the pony is standing on something, just inches above the surface: the half-sunken supports of the old Roman bridge. Built of wood, rather than stone like the great bridge at Trever, it must have collapsed a long time ago in some flood. But the supports are still here: a thick wooden board parallel to the current, linking the remains of two surviving piers.

We can't stay long here; I can sense the rotten wood giving way under our combined weight, but it's enough for the pony and me to rest briefly before taking another plunge. I think I see some lights in the distance, but my eyes are swollen with cold and tears, and I can barely see anything at all. Either way, there's only one direction left for me to go. The western bank is too far away to return, and my pursuers might still be there, patrolling the shore. I tug at the reins; the pony snorts and splashes back into the water, with me in tow.

It doesn't take long before it starts climbing out again: along the shallowing river bed at first, then up the steep bank, between two rows of rotting piers. We're out at last — the pony stops and shakes the water off. I slide from the saddle and into the mud. For a while, I can't move, catching my breath, the mail shirt heavy on my chest. I throw off the helmet and wait for a semblance of warmth to return to my body.

The Blood of the Iutes

Slowly, I rise back to my knees. The light of torches blinds me. I look up and see half a dozen spear blades aimed at my neck.

"I got you now, *aetheling*."

CHAPTER XIV
THE LAY OF ARBOGAST

Haesta draws the bow, aims carefully and shoots. The arrow flies an inch above my head and digs deep into the trunk of the ash tree to which I'm tied.

He studies the bow and nods, impressed. "This is a good weapon. Almost as good as Aelle's stick thrower," he says, referring to the strange device my father told me about so many times: a black repeating *ballista* wielded in battle by the Saxon *Rex*. "We don't have anything like it back home."

"No, we don't," I agree. "And I'd rather you took good care of it. It was a gift."

"A gift from that Hunnic wench?" He laughs and throws the bow into the grass. I wince, but notice he was careful not to damage it.

"So, you've been keeping friends with Aelle?" I ask.

"Aelle doesn't know how to keep friends," he replies with a scowl. "Or allies."

"He kept you close enough to send you here. Or did Odowakr ask for you personally?"

The Blood of the Iutes

"Nobody *sent* me," he snarls. "I was in New Port when the messengers arrived. I talked to them before they got to Aelle."

"Messengers — plural?"

"One from Odowakr, the other from Meroweg, both looking for mercenaries for this warring season. I'm glad I chose to go with the first one, otherwise I'd never have found *you*."

I'm surprised he's speaking with such honesty. I was expecting a brutal interrogation, but though I got the *brutal* part right — my nose and ears still hurt from the gratuitous punches he and his men threw at me as they carried me from the riverside to their camp — he doesn't seem interested in anything I'd have to say; instead, it's he who's been speaking all morning, as if for the first time in a long while he had somebody to talk to about his woes.

I sneeze. I'm still in my cold, wet clothes, shivering; I sense a fever coming. I sit too far from the campfire for it to warm me.

"What were you doing in New Port? Isn't your land near Leman?"

His face turns sour. "My *land* is a patch of sand and marsh. Nothing grows there but oats and glasswort. I have to go to New Port every year after the harvest, begging the merchants for help, and then look for work as a mercenary. I'm in debt up to my ears." He speaks with such sorrow that I almost feel sorry for him and his men, until I remember what he did to my people — to my mother. "But not anymore," he adds. "Not now that I have *you*. Now I can go back home, and I don't have to fight for Odowakr's silver anymore."

"What do you need me for? I'm as poor as you are. Even if you get my father to pay the ransom, that's not going to last you for long."

"I won't need your father's gold when I get you back to Cantiaca. I will demand that he gives me the throne in exchange for your life."

The audacity of his demand is so absurd, it makes me laugh out loud.

"I think you put too much faith in my father's fondness for me," I say.

He comes over. His limp is even more pronounced than when I saw him last time. I flinch, expecting another blow, but he crouches, clumsily, beside me.

"And I think you don't appreciate his love enough," he says. "I don't know Aeric all that well, but the only time I've ever seen him truly angry was the first time I tried to abduct you."

"The first time?" I frown.

"He never told you?" It's his time to laugh now, with bitterness. He sits down, cross-legged, picks up an arrow from Basina's arrow bag and uses it to pick at his dirty fingernails.

"It was a few months after he brought you back from Londin," he says. "He took you to New Port, to show you off before Aelle."

"I remember." I nod. "Nothing out of the ordinary happened, other than Aelle being silently furious at my father's circlet. The *witan* had just refused naming him *Rex* again."

"It was the last time they dared defy him," Haesta remembers. "When you were coming back, you camped in a village at the Downs, on the edge of Andreda — close to my land. Too close. I took it as an open challenge and struck at the camp at night."

"I don't recall anything of the sort."

"Somehow, you must've slept through it all." He shrugs. "We *were* trying to be stealthy… Until I got too close to the hut where they kept you. Aeric came down upon us like a wounded boar." His eyes glint. "I thought he was on henbane. He slew two of my men before we pulled away."

"How did you know it was my hut?" I ask. I find it hard to reconcile his description with the man I know as my father.

"Give me some credit." He gives me a wounded look, and I'm reminded he's the man in whose captivity I now find myself, not the other way around. "We didn't just charge into that village blindly, without surveying it first. I knew we couldn't defeat Aeric's guards, but I hoped we could get away with a few precious hostages."

I find nothing to say to that. Haesta hisses, pricking himself on the sharp point of the arrowhead and throws the missile into the grass.

"You don't believe me," he says.

"It just doesn't sound like him at all."

He sighs and sits lazily back. "You're fortunate to even know him," he says. "My father died at Aelle's Ford. Defending *your* father, when Aeric — *Ash* — was still a child. If he had lived, Hengist wouldn't have dared to treat me so poorly…"

I don't know much about Haesta's relations with the previous *Drihten*, or his family, and I don't much care. "Your men killed my mother," I remind him.

His lips narrow. He stands up and starts to walk away back to the campfire.

"Even if you force my father out, I doubt the *witan* would look kindly upon a man who sells our secrets!" I shout after him.

He turns around. "What are you talking about?"

"The henbane," I say. "You gave the recipe to Odowakr."

"What kind of fool do you take me for?" he scoffs. "I may have my disagreements with Aeric, but I'm still a Iute. If I am to rule the tribe one day, I'm not going to give away our greatest weapon."

"I've seen those bear-shirts that fought with the Saxons. You're the only one who could've given it to them."

"I brought a barrel-worth of dried herbs with me from Britannia, and I shared it with the Saxons. They'll be running out of it soon. But I never told them what it was made of. Those bear-shirts normally eat some mixture of wild mushrooms to achieve a similar effect, but it only gives them the madness, not power — and they're sick for days afterwards."

"So they can't brew any more if they run out?"

He opens his mouth, then closes, realising he's told me too much already. One of his men appears on the glade, runs up to Haesta and whispers something in his ear. Haesta scowls.

"Get him out of here," he says, nodding at me. The warrior cuts the binds at my legs and pulls me up. With a knife pressed at my back, he leads me to my pony, tied to another ash tree on the edge of the glade. Haesta picks up Basina's bow off the ground; his hand hovers over the leather bag with the siege engine plans, but he decides he doesn't need the burden and hobbles in haste to his horse.

One of the camp guards leaps out onto the glade, stumbles and falls face-down, with a short feathered metal shaft sticking out of his back. As I'm forced to run past his body, I notice it's a *plumbata* dart.

James Calbraith

At least I'm finally in Trever.

Trever prison, to be precise. A proper prison, a *carcer* — not a reused bath house, like the one my father was kept at in Londin. I must be somewhere in the bowels of Trever's *Praetorium*. I hear other prisoners moaning and cursing around me. To my right are the petty criminals, awaiting trial or execution. Life in a city this size, even under siege, must continue, and so the thieves, burglars and black marketers must still be punished.

To my left are a few of Haesta's mercenaries, captured with me in the attack on the camp. Fleeing the Roman soldiers, the group of riders with which I was forced to run away, split off from Haesta as we entered the wooded foothills east of the river. In the chaos, I tried to get away from my captors — but I only managed to ride a few hundred paces through the sparse heath before stumbling upon the pursuing Roman troops. With my hands still tied, I was unable to defend myself — and the Romans were not interested in my protestations. To them, I was just another barbarian warrior. With the stroke of a lance butt, I was thrown off the pony and hit the dirt. Exhausted and in pain, still wet, still cold, still tired after a night of running away from one foe to another, I drifted in and out of consciousness as the Roman patrol carried me back to Trever. I remember almost nothing of the city itself — passing through the great gate, riding down a broad avenue, reaching the *Praetorium* — and being thrown into a cell locked with iron bars. At least my hands were free now, so I could take off my wet clothes; though I soon grew to regret it in the cold, damp cell.

The Blood of the Iutes

I was grateful for a bowl of hot soup and some woollen rags that the guard brought me. Too weak to speak, I only managed to utter a thank you. He raised an eye, hearing my Imperial Latin, but said nothing.

One by one, the captive mercenaries are taken away — for interrogation, I guess, though none of them returns. At length, after a couple of days, the guard comes for me. He helps me up. I see pity in his eyes; I may be a barbarian warrior, but right now I'm just a shivering boy, no more of a threat that a street beggar.

He leads me out into the atrium and waits for my eyes to adjust to the light; we enter a small, cramped room to the left. Once, it was some clerk's office, now it's stacked with supplies, as are, I imagine, all the rooms in the *Praetorium* — dried meat, grain, jars of preserved vegetables, sacks of lime, *amphorae* with wine and oil, anything that city magistrates might need to survive a long siege in relative comfort.

The clerk's desk is still here, squeezed between the barrels and crates; a grumpy, bald man sits on its other side. He grunts at the guard. The guard sits me down on a three-legged stool. The bald man looks up in surprise at the gentle manner with which the guard treats me.

"*Namo?*" he asks.

"I'm sorry?" I reply in Imperial.

He frowns. "I asked, what is your name? Don't you speak Frankish?"

"I'm a Iute," I say. "Octa, son of Aeric, *Rex Iutae*."

He waves his hand. "Iutes." He takes a note. "Another chief of some heathen tribe I've never heard of, thinking himself a king. Where did Odowakr find you all? Some northern wasteland, no doubt," he adds, pointing at my hair with the tip of the stylus.

"I did not come with Odowakr," I reply wearily. "I was his prisoner when your men caught me."

"A likely story."

"There are men in this city who can confirm this," I say. "Find *Comes* Pinnosa, he's my friend."

He laughs. "*Comes* Pinnosa! Why not *Dux* Arbogast, while we're at it! I wouldn't bother Pinnosa with your allegations even if he *were* still alive…"

"*Comes* Pinnosa is dead?" I ask in shock.

"Shouldn't a friend of his know this?"

"How was I supposed to know?" I reply. "I haven't seen him since the bridge fell. How did he die?"

"I'll be asking the questions," the bald man replies grumpily. "Where is Odowakr's camp?"

"I've never seen him," I say. "I was with Haesta."

"Haesta." He looks at his notes. "He was the leader of your band of mercenaries."

"Not *my* band. I told you…"

"Yes, yes." He waves impatiently. "Something was odd about that Haesta. He's a Saxon, right? From Britannia?"

"Wrong. He's from Britannia, but he's a Iute, like I am."

"Ah." He smiles. "So you *were* together, after all. A band of *Iutes*." He makes another note.

"I wasn't…" I sigh and cough. I'm cold again, though it's much warmer here in the clerk's room than in the cells below. My gaze falls on the *amphorae* stacked in a row behind the bald man, stamped with grape marks.

"Is that the Mosella wine?" I ask.

He stares at me, dumbfounded with my question, but quickly returns to his gruff demeanour. "Of course it is."

"Can I have some? I'm so thirsty — and I haven't had any wine since Coln…"

"If you ask the guard nicely, I'm sure he'll give you some slop water." He pauses and checks on his notes. He taps the stylus on the desk. "Do all… *Iutes* speak good Latin and have taste for fine wine?"

"Only the sons of kings," I reply. I notice I have finally caught his attention and lean forward. "Look, isn't there anyone here who could vouch for me? What about other refugees from Coln — is Rav Asher still alive? How about *Praetor* Paulus of Ake?"

His face twitches when I say the names, but I can't tell which one of the two produced the reaction. He puts the stylus down and calls for the guard.

"Take him back…" He pauses. "Put him in the dry cell. I might have a few more questions for him later."

I didn't expect anything more to happen for at least a couple of days — but the gentle guard comes back for me before the day's done. He takes me past the atrium this time, into a corridor with red walls, where we meet the bald man again.

"Put this on," the clerk tells me, giving me fresh clothes. It's a drab tunic and plaid, woollen breeches, grimy and stained, but they're dry and warm, and that's all that matters to me right now. Once I'm done, he leads me further down the corridors of the *Praetorium*, until we reach an elegant room with a large window coming out onto a garden. From what I can glimpse, most of the once-lush garden has been turned into vegetable patches.

A table and two heavy chairs of dark oak stand in the middle of the room. On the table, I see a small marble statue of a goddess, a platter with bread and pickled olives and a goblet of rock crystal, filled with wine.

"I heard you like Mosellan."

The Blood of the Iutes

The man who speaks these words stands by the window, holding the other crystal glass. He's tall, red-haired — though it's a pale, dull hue, rather than my mother's fiery crimson — and green-eyed, with a long, straight nose and ruddy cheeks; he's wearing a purple-lined robe and a golden chain around his neck.

I sit down, take a bite of the bread and gulp some of the wine before answering. It's cool, sweet and fresh, even better than the one Pinnosa served me in Coln.

I share my observation with the man at the window. He chuckles.

"A man of taste. Fascinating."

He takes the seat opposite, puts down the goblet and steeples his hands.

"Severus tells me you claim to be a friend of poor Pinnosa."

"I may have exaggerated." A faint smile appears on his lips. "I met him just before the fall of Coln; we've been travelling and fighting ever since. We got separated at the battle of the bridge."

"Unfortunately, *Comes* Pinnosa died a week ago during a sally, so he can't confirm your tale."

"I'm… sorry to hear that."

The man nods sadly. "It was a great loss. It was he who convinced me of the value of these sallies — and they proved his undoing. Personally, I was hoping we could just sit this one out, as usual."

"Usually the barbarians don't come with siege engines," I note.

"Ah, yes." He comes up to a cabinet by the wall and takes out a pile of papers. He throws them on the table. "We found these in a bag at the mercenary camp. Do you know anything about them?"

"My men and I took it from one of Odowakr's engineers."

"Your *men*, is it? How many of you are there?"

I take another sip of wine. "Am I still being interrogated?"

"Maybe. Or maybe it's just a conversation among *friends*."

"I don't even know who I'm speaking to. I assume you're a *Comes* of this province?"

"Where are my manners?" He grins. "I am Arbogast, *Dux* of Belgica Prima. And Germania Prima, for that matter, ever since we lost Argentorate."

"I am Octa, son of Aeric, *Rex* of the Iutes," I reply with a bow. "And I am *not* your enemy. I came here with my men to assist *Comes* Pinnosa, not for mercenary pay, but out of respect and friendship. If you ask any of his men, they will tell you how we fought with them side by side at Tolbiac."

"I already have. It's the only reason I'm talking to you. They agreed that there *was* an Octa among the barbarians accompanying Pinnosa. But most of them are still out on watch, so I couldn't get any of them here to confirm it's really you. I'm sure you understand, we can't risk having a spy in our midst."

"Of course, *Dux*."

He taps the table's edge with his fingers, then looks me over again. "I don't think you belong in that cell," he says. "But I would like you to stay here as my guest for a couple of days."

"I have nowhere else to go."

"I'm having a small event tomorrow with a few officials," he continues. "Nothing grand — we are under siege, after all. But whoever you are, I'm certain you'll make a great diversion for my guests. A heathen boy who speaks pure Imperial and knows his wine! You have no idea how boring it gets here."

"I'm a prince of the Iutes, not a performing dwarf," I reply, indignant. "But I will gladly come to your feast. Perhaps one of your guests will recognise me."

"Splendid. I'll send you some better clothes — and a barber," he adds, rubbing his smooth chin.

"Some food wouldn't go amiss," I say. I don't know when it happened, but the plate before me has been cleared of all the bread and olives.

"Yes, of course. It's late, but I'll have the kitchen prepare something warm."

He watches me intently as I rise from the chair. I wobble as blood runs from my head, then stand straight again. The guard returns to lead me to my new room.

"Those siege engines…" I say, turning back on the threshold. "Will they be as troublesome for you as I fear?"

He rustles the papers. "I shouldn't tell you this, in case you *do* prove Odowakr's spy, but…" He sighs. "If we let them finish even one of these machines, the city is as good as doomed."

The guard takes me down the broad corridors of the palace, through the atrium, to another corridor, which comes out onto a grand balcony, with three sides open, overlooking a large, flat, oval space, bound by several rows of seats. As I stare at it, I realise with surprise that it must be the *circus* I saw from the cliffs above the city — a chariot-racing stadium. I've never seen one up close before; I've only read about them in the ancient chronicles. To my even greater astonishment, there are preparations for an actual chariot race going on at the starting line, with two competing crews making last checks on the horses and their single-axle vehicles, one dressed in red, the other in green. I pause to reflect how even after the centuries of barbarian raids, plagues and civil wars, even this far North, the ancient customs of Rome are being preserved here, albeit in a reduced manner — while in Britannia, they'd been all but forgotten within a generation. For the first time on this journey, I feel I am truly within the borders of the fabled Empire.

The stadium itself, the stands, the balcony, as well as the arena, are in such a bad shape that at first I take the damage for the result of the ongoing siege — before I remember that the city was already razed by Attila's Huns, years before Odowakr's arrival. Black soot stains peer from under the hastily applied white plaster all over the walls. Brighter rectangles mark spaces where rich tapestries once hung. The beams once supporting the cloth canopies hanging over the top row of seats are charred and burnt-down to half their original size. Remnants of mosaics adorn the floor of the entrance corridor, shattered and plundered of all precious stones beyond recognition. The only remaining decoration is a great map of Gaul, drawn in charcoal on calf-skin, hanging on the wall over the *Dux*'s carved oak seat.

There is plenty of food on the several small tables set up around the stands, but it is not what one would expect at a *Dux*'s feast. Scraps of salted meat thrown over groats, some boiled roots, cabbage, rounds of fresh goat cheese, and a small bowl of pepper for seasoning, to share between everyone — this is all more suitable for a dinner at a merchant's house, and one that's not very well off. But then, the city is in the second month of siege, and though there are still plenty of essential supplies left, the luxuries must now be in short supply…

I enter the balcony with apprehension, not sure what to expect of the guests and the purpose of Arbogast's invitation. But the fear turns into relief as soon as I hear a familiar, hoarse voice.

"Young Octa! It is you! Lord be praised!"

Rav Asher, in his resplendent robes and with the beard finely combed, sits at the far end of the balcony, a bit to the back, on account of his prominent belly. I rush to him, but I'm stopped by a guard's spear. Arbogast nods to let me through. I glance at the rest of the gathered — at first, I don't recognise anyone else, but then, to my shock, I spot a man I haven't seen in months, sitting at Arbogast's left hand. He's talking to some magistrate when he notices me enter.

"*Aetheling*. We meet again — what an auspicious day."

So much has happened since we last spoke — so many new faces and names to remember — that it takes me a moment to dig up his name from the depths of my memory.

"Legate Aegidius," I say at last. "What are *you* doing here?"

"I could ask you the same question."

Arbogast laughs out loud and claps his hands with glee. He's acting more like a heathen chieftain than a Roman magistrate — and perhaps that's exactly what he is; now I see how different he looks to a full-blooded Roman like Aegidius, with his dark curly hair, dark eyes and aquiline nose in a sun-bronzed face. There must be barbarian blood flowing in

The Blood of the Iutes

Arbogast's veins, perhaps even that of the Franks? Quite a few other officials at the table look more Frankish than Gaul or Roman. I'm guessing there must have been plenty of mixing the bloods in this frontier territory over the generations, even among the nobles.

The *Dux* invites me to take a seat at the foot of his chair and, as he starts nibbling on what looks like a roasted mouse, invites Aegidius to explain his presence in the city.

It was the legate who arrived in the gold-trimmed carriage, after a long drive from Mettis, on the day the bridge gate closed. For that brief moment, when Ursula, Odilia and I watched the commotion caused by the arrival of the new Saxon warband, we were only a few hundred feet apart…

Ursula and Odilia. Seeing Rav Asher and the legate is a pleasant surprise, but it only reminds me that my friends, if they live, are likely still somewhere in the city. I need to find out where, exactly, as soon as I'm allowed to leave the palace.

"We drove right into that Saxon warband, and had to retreat to Biliac," Aegidius recounts. The others nod, having heard this story before. "My carriage almost fell into the river through a hole in the bridge, but we got through just in time."

"Didn't you know the barbarians were coming to besiege Trever?" I ask.

"We had no idea," Aegidius replies, shaking his head. "I came here to request *Dux* Arbogast's assistance in our fight. Now I'm stuck here, waiting for the siege to end, one way or another." He chuckles. "I don't even know how the war with the Burgundians is going."

"There's a war against Burgundians now?" I ask.

A fanfare of single trumpet announces the start of the race. A roar of a few dozen throats echoes throughout the *circus*, and I notice there are some townsfolk scattered around the auditorium, sitting in small groups or alone, watching the chariots perform a trial lap around the circuit. I express my amazement that a city in siege can afford to organise an event like this.

"People need their spirits sustained, as well as their bodies," the *Dux* explains. "It's the least we can do. I already had to ban theatre plays. How do you do things in Britannia?"

"There is nothing like this in Londin anymore. The theatre was quarried for stone; the amphitheatre is a crumbling ruin... I don't even know if there ever was a *circus* — I suppose there must have been, but any trace of it was lost long ago."

"Enjoy the spectacle, then, young *Iute*."

The race starts in earnest. The small crowd of spectators erupts in applause, cheering their favourites and jeering at the opposition. After four laps, the green-clad charioteers move far ahead of the reds. Arbogast winces and loses interest in the race. He leans back in the seat. "The Greens lost their best driver in the siege," he says. "They haven't been the same since."

The Blood of the Iutes

With more wine poured into our cups, we start picking at the meat and groats. The *Dux* picks up the story told by Aegidius, with news the legate brought to the city.

"Imperator Maiorianus should have been here months ago," he says, "but he got delayed fighting off another invasion of the Vandals and Alemanns on Italia. At long last —" He points behind his head, at the map on the wall. A slave puts a pin with an eagle's badge into it, somewhere in Italia between the long arch of the Alps and the sea. "— he is setting off for Gaul. In response, *Magister* Agrippinus declared himself an Imperator and called on his barbarian allies: the Goths, the Alans and the Burgundians. He gave Arelate to the Goths, Aurelianum to the Alans, and barricaded himself at Lugdunum with those he trusted the most, the Burgundians."

I look at the map hanging above his head to make some sense of his words. The city of Arelate is the only one I'm familiar with; it lies to the south, near the coast, at the gates of Italia — it's where the poet Rutilius started his journey across Italia, and it's where I hoped my friends and I would have landed with Aegidius had we not tried to free the Iute slaves. I'm struck by the inevitability of destiny; if we had kept following Aegidius, we would still have ended in the besieged Trever… Nothing would have changed, no matter what we would have chosen to do — except, maybe, poor Gille would still be alive.

Lugdunum lies on the main highway between us and Maiorianus's army, on the crossroad of several main highways. It's easy to grasp its strategic importance, and the difficult position in which the Imperator found himself through the cunning of his enemies. If he wants to march on Arelate first, he will expose his right flank to the Burgundians at Lugdunum. If he chooses Lugdunum, the Goths from Arelate will be free to strike at his rear. Judging by Aegidius's mission to Trever, the Imperator decided on the latter direction for his campaign — choosing to deal with the Usurper first, before turning on the Goths.

All of this is a moot point as long as the siege lasts. I can see now why no relief has come for Trever; Aegidius and his entourage may have reached the city via minor roads, but any greater number of troops would need to go past the enemy-held Lugdunum.

"What use would Trever's garrison be in this war, anyway?" I ask. "I've read about the Empire's civil wars — thousands of soldiers on either side."

"It's true," says Arbogast with a nod. "I have less than a thousand men here — still less after a month's siege… Wouldn't make much of a dent in Agrippinus's force. But there are other garrisons in this part of Gaul — in Mettis, in Remi, in Tricas… And they all know, if Trever falls, they will be next. So they're sitting, waiting, not risking marching out while the barbarian horde is still out in force."

"How do you know they would join Maiorianus instead of this usurper?"

"We don't," replies Aegidius with a wry smile. "Not all of them. The *Comes* of Mettis probably would — he's my friend. But the others are waiting not just for the end of the siege, but for the *Dux* of Trever to make up his mind. They will follow Arbogast's lead in this conflict," he adds, pointing at the *Dux* with his thumb. "Whatever he decides."

"And you haven't decided yet?" I ask. I reach for the cloth to wipe my hands before picking an old, wrinkled apple up from a bowl of other old, wrinkled fruit.

"I have had a few more important matters on my mind recently," says Arbogast. He stands up and raises a goblet as the red chariot passes the finish line, waits for the applause to subdue, then turns back to us. I note Aegidius roll his eyes — he must know the speech the *Dux* is about to make. Rav Asher, in the corner, focuses on the dish of salted fish before him. He gives me a polite smile.

"How well versed are you in the history of your island, prince of the Iutes?" Arbogast asks. "Do you remember Magnus Maximus?"

"Of course," I reply. "The Briton Usurper. Every educated child in Britannia knows about him."

In truth, I know more about the Briton Usurper than most educated children. Seventy years ago, Magnus Maximus was proclaimed the Imperator by the Legions in Britannia and Gaul — not unlike Agrippinus now. When he left the island to fight for Rome, he left a child behind, a baby daughter; that daughter was Sevira: Wortigern's wife, and mother of Wortimer. It was Maximus's cursed offspring who waged war on the Iutes and destroyed my home village.

"It's an old family history," says Arbogast. For a moment, I'm startled, thinking he has somehow read my mind. "My grandfather, after whom I am named, stood faithfully by the side of the rightful Imperator, defending against Maximus. He was the *magister militum* in Gaul and in Iberia. He was sent to kill Maximus's son — after the war ended — here in Trever, in this very palace. After the war ended, he grew to be the most powerful man in the Empire, second only to the Imperator himself… But he could never wield this power in his own name."

"Because he was a barbarian," says Aegidius. "He knew the law."

"He was a citizen of the Empire!" says Arbogast. His fists clench on the sculpted ledge surrounding the balcony from three sides. "He sent thousands of his men to death in the Imperator's name. But because he was born a barbarian, he would never have a rank himself. He had to use the pretence of acting on behalf of the Imperator's son."

"What happened?" I ask, though I can guess where this old story is going. I've heard it so many times already in my travel through Gaul. A barbarian's allegiance to the Empire, rewarded with some kind of betrayal of trust… If there was one trait all the Roman Imperators shared it was their pragmatism. When it came to the Empire's interests, they held no loyalties to anyone, especially to barbarians. And now, it seemed, all the old grudges were coming to bite Rome back…

"There was a disagreement. The Imperator's son died. Some claimed he was murdered; my grandfather said the boy killed himself, not wishing to be a barbarian's puppet any longer. The Imperator marched on Gaul, like Maiorianus marches now, and defeated my grandfather in battle…" He shrugs and turns back. "This is what life is like in Rome. When you aim high, you'd better be prepared to fall hard," he continues. "I hold no grudge. The Imperator let my father live, and then his grandson made me a *Dux* here, where my grandfather did such great service to his family. But, knowing what I just told you, would you blame me for hesitating in choosing one Imperator over another?"

My head is spinning. There are too many names and places for me to grasp all at once, even with the help of the map. I'm beginning to wonder why the *Dux* needed my presence at the race at all — he seems to be providing all the necessary entertainment himself.

"Maiorianus was crowned in Rome," says Aegidius. "And accepted by the Imperator in Constantinople."

"Constantinople is far away from here. Agrippinus is my…" Arbogast hesitates. "…not *friend*, exactly, but I've known him for years, and I respect him as a politician. I know little of this Maiorianus, except that I've heard he's a skilled commander."

"He would've taken Aetius's place if not for the palace intrigues," says Aegidius. "He defeated the Vandals and the Alemanns, and he will defeat the Goths and the Burgundians, of that you may be certain."

"Then he may not need my help after all," replies Arbogast, with a smile that tells me the two of them have been through this argument several times before. "And there have been plenty talented commanders before him. Now, maybe if Ricimer was an Imperator…"

"You know very well why he isn't," says Aegidius grumpily. "The laws haven't changed much since your grandfather's days. Ricimer is as likely to be an Imperator as Odowakr — or young *aetheling*." He nods to me.

"Perhaps there is the solution to your dilemma," Rav Asher speaks from his corner, chuckling. "A third Imperator." He's making an obvious joke, but the others are not laughing. It seems Rav Asher touched a nerve. The matter is too serious for everyone involved to turn it into a simple jest.

Arbogast sits back down and runs fingers through his hair. He looks to me. "We are boring our guest with these old tales," he says. "I would rather listen to a new story — for example, how did a prince of the Iutes find himself in my palace, hundreds of miles away from home, during a Saxon siege…"

So this is why he invited me here — to use me as a distraction if the discussion didn't go his way… It's fine, I don't mind. I'm in a good mood. Thanks to Arbogast's generosity, I have slept in a comfortable bed and eaten food someone else made for me, for the first time in weeks. I can indulge him and his guests with a story of my adventure.

The fanfare rings out again; another couple of battered old chariots lines up at the start. The servants bring in freshly baked sweet buns and honey cakes. I salivate at the smell. I

The Blood of the Iutes

pick one up from a tray and start my tale with how I met Legate Aegidius in Londin…

CHAPTER XV
THE LAY OF HUDA

The feast ended, I return, sated and lethargic, to my room. In the corridor, I meet Rav Asher, heading back home — or, rather, to the house he's renting somewhere in the city.

"Come meet me, boy," he says. "As soon as Arbogast lets you move around."

"Of course."

"I mean it," he adds, with some insistence. "Find me in the *insula* south of the city baths."

"What is so urgent?" I ask when I meet him the next day in front of the *insula*. The baths behind me, though half burnt-down and plundered of anything valuable by the Huns, remain an imposing, extraordinary structure. The size of a small fortress surrounded by a *portico* on all four sides, their rear rises in great arches like a mountain in the far end of the eastern part of the city. The aqueduct linking the baths with the distant hills runs dry now, either cut off by the besieging army or simply fallen into disrepair. The city planners who devised the compound must have intended for it to be a centrepiece of some new development, for the street grid continues further east and disappears into the wheat fields, a mere vision of what could have been.

The Blood of the Iutes

"I wanted you to see them before they were sent out on another patrol," Rav Asher tells me.

"See whom?"

He takes me to the apartment upstairs; it's a tiny place compared to his library in Coln, made even tinier by all the books stacked in precarious cliffs everywhere along the walls. His wife greets me with a brief, warm embrace, and then they show me to the next room, which is even more crowded, this time with four people, waiting for my arrival.

"Octa!"

Ursula leaps at me and gives me a tight hug. I hug her back and look over her shoulder to see Audulf and *Praefect* Paulus. Audulf bears a fresh scar, running from ear to chin. Paulus's face is covered in bruises; their wide grins have some new gaps in them.

The fourth man is Aegidius. He's wearing drab clothes of a commoner and a hooded cloak; I instantly sense a conspiracy brewing: here's a man who didn't want to be seen on the streets. This isn't just a meeting of friends. Inadvertently, my muscles tighten as if expecting a fight.

Rav Asher squeezes past us and pushes away enough books to reach a small window. He opens it wide, but it doesn't do much to rid the room of the stale, musty air. He sneezes and coughs, raising a cloud of dust from the books. The dust makes my eyes water.

"Did anyone else make it into the city?" I ask when we all stop coughing. "Was Nodhbert with you?"

"He was, but he succumbed to his wounds after a short time," says Audulf. "A small handful of Hildrik's men made it through — and most of Pinnosa's. We've been riding with them on patrols ever since Arbogast agreed to let us out."

"How are you doing this? Aren't Odowakr's warriors guarding all the gates?"

"This city is well prepared for a siege," says Ursula. She, too, bears some fresh marks of some recent skirmish. "There are hidden sally gates and tunnels all over the perimeter of the walls, and in the fields outside. Whenever the Saxons find one, we jump out of another. They don't have enough men to guard them all."

"The one place we can't get to is the other side of the river," says Paulus. "You're the first visitor from there we've had since the siege started."

"And how have *you* been doing?" asks Ursula. "Rav Asher told us only a little bit of what you recounted yesterday. What happened to Hildrik?"

"Hildrik returned home," I reply, and tell them about the letter from Meroweg. The news is met with dismay, but no surprise. "I've built a small force from the survivors of the battle of the bridge, and we've been taking the fight to Odowakr these past few weeks," I continue. "We took out one of his engineers and disrupted the building of the siege machines, but I don't know how much we've delayed him, really."

We talk a bit more for a while, exchanging stories of fighting Odowakr's warriors; I discover the circumstances of Pinnosa's tragic death — he was shot through with a bolt from a *manuballista*, a small siege weapon Odowakr's engineers have built to test their designs, brought over to the eastern side of the river; I learn that Audulf's and Ursula's injuries came from a raid on that weapon; and that the command of Coln soldiers and their allies fell to *Praetor* Paulus, now a senior officer in the city's guard. But I soon grow weary of talking. My injuries still hurt, my fever is still lingering; I'm grateful to see my friends again, but I'm growing increasingly conscious of the shadowy presence of Legate Aegidius, sitting silently in a corner that has been made out of copies of Tacitus and some tattered volumes written in Greek.

"You're not here to listen to our tales of battle," I tell him. "You heard it all yesterday. Why are you here?"

Aegidius smiles. He glances to Rav Asher, standing in the door with his arms crossed on his chest.

"We are all newcomers to Trever," he says. "As such, we are not bound by the ties of loyalty as is everyone else in the city."

"I knew it." I lower my voice. "You're conspiring against Arbogast."

He raises his hand to indicate I should talk even quieter.

"But why?" I ask. "Is he not commanding the siege well?"

"No, he is a skilled commander. Perhaps too skilled. Therein lies our problem."

"A few days ago, when out on patrol, we intercepted a messenger," says Paulus. "It was most fortunate that it was our soldier who found him, and not one of Arbogast's."

"A messenger — from Odowakr?"

"*From* Arbogast," says Ursula. "To Odowakr."

I look at her in surprise. We've all changed so much since leaving Britannia; poor Gille died; I found myself commanding a unit of Roman soldiers… but in perhaps the most bewildering change, Ursula and Audulf, my childhood friends, a son of a Frankish guard and a daughter of a minor magistrate from a backwater town, got themselves somehow embroiled in a conspiracy at the highest levels of Imperial power. And all it took was for us to step outside the borders of our small, remote home country — to enter the Empire.

I'm struck by a vision of Rome, not as a wounded animal devouring its victims, like my father described it, but as an enormous machine, of pulleys and gears, swallowing people great and small, individuals and entire nations, and churning them out the other way. Some are diminished, others made greater, but none emerge unchanged.

"It was a response," says Aegidius. "We don't know what that earlier letter, or letters, said exactly, but we could guess from the reply. Odowakr was proposing to support Arbogast's bid for independence."

"Independence — from the Empire?"

Aegidius nods. "It's not as preposterous as it sounds. In times of chaos, Gaul was always bursting with usurpers and petty kings. With Trever as his seat, with the garrisons of Belgica at his command, and with Odowakr at his side, Arbogast could feasibly reach for the crown."

"Then there would be three Imperators in Gaul," says Paulus.

"It happened before," says Rav Asher, shrugging. "It didn't end well. This time, it might well mean the end of the Empire."

"What was the *Dux*'s response?" I ask.

"Non-committal," replies Aegidius. "But it wasn't an outright refusal, which is the only response a loyal *Dux* should make in this situation."

"Maybe he didn't want to anger Odowakr."

Aegidius tilts his head. "Maybe. But we can't risk the fate of the Empire on guesswork."

"I get it," I say. "You want us to help you kill the *Dux*."

"What?" He guffaws, genuinely surprised. "No, good Lord, no!"

"Then, what?"

"Arbogast is a decent man — and a good Roman, considering what the Empire did to his family," says Rav Asher. "He often visited Coln, and I would sometimes accompany Pinnosa to Trever, so I got to know him well. His loyalty to the Empire is paramount."

"But he holds an even greater loyalty to his city," adds Aegidius. "And the longer this siege takes, the greater the strain on these two loyalties."

"We need to end it soon," says Paulus. "Before Arbogast makes up his mind."

"And I assume you have an idea how to do it…" I pause. Something still doesn't add up. "One that you don't want to involve the *Dux* in. But why? Surely, he too would wish for the siege to end."

Aegidius clears his throat. "Not like this."

"As much as it pains me to say," says Paulus, "we need help from the River Franks."

"Hildebert?" I exclaim, before remembering we're supposed to be quiet. "*Hildebert?*" I repeat in a whisper. "Why would you want him to help you? And why would he even agree?"

"The River Franks were never fond of Saxons," says Rav Asher, smoothing his beard. "I'm aware this time they had some kind of… agreement… but these arrangements never last long among the barbarians."

"Nor among the Romans," I say. "I've heard more about the promises broken by the *wealas* than by our own kin."

"Yes… And we have been reaping what we have sown for a long time," admits Aegidius with a weary nod.

"You'll need more than contrition to convince Hildebert to help you."

"We would recognise his rule over all of Germania Secunda," says Aegidius. "Grant him the title of a *Comes*, with everything this entails. He would be free to rule as he pleased and gather the taxes and customs for himself."

"He already can do all of that," notes Audulf. "He's conquered Coln."

"But *only* Coln."

"Ah," I say. "I see why you'd be avoiding Arbogast. You want to give the River Franks some of his land. And power."

Their silence suffices for an answer. How much are they willing to trade, I wonder? Does the deal include the city itself?

"What does this have to do with me?" I ask. "With *us*?"

"We need someone the Franks would trust," says Aegidius. "You said it yourself, the Romans have a history of broken promises… Besides, you're the only one who's managed to cross the river since the siege started."

"It was just a stroke of fortune."

"The Lord works through such strokes of fortune," says Rav Asher, raising his eyes to the sky and folding his hands in prayer. "You have been blessed once already. Maybe you will be again."

"It's a long way back to Coln, even if we did get across the river," I say. "How much time do we have?"

"Judging by those machine plans you recovered," says Aegidius, handing me the papers I got from the engineers, "they'll be ready in some three weeks. Maybe more. Plenty of time to get there and back."

"Let's do this, Octa," says Ursula, her cheeks bright red with excitement. "I've been suffocating within these walls. I need to get out. There's just too much stone here, and not enough trees!"

The trap door opens and the first squadron rides out, torches blazing, into the night. We wait for them to vanish out of sight before venturing carefully outside ourselves — only me, Ursula and Audulf.

Once we're out, Audulf closes the trap door and covers it with the vines. If I didn't know it was there, it would be impossible to notice the entrance to the tunnel, painted over and disguised as an outcrop of the red rock. The tunnel, big enough to fit a war horse without a rider, took us from the catacombs by the city's Cathedral and into the thicket of yews a few hundred feet outside the city walls. According to Paulus, this is the last tunnel not yet discovered by Odowakr's men — and ours might be the last sally the city could afford to send out.

As we passed the catacombs, Ursula bade us stop and pointed to a new monument, hastily hewn in local red stone, set up at a prominent place in the middle of the graveyard. In tall, noble Roman letters, the stone-carver inscribed the names of Iutes and Franks fallen in the battles between — with Odilia's name at the top of the list.

Ursula kept her promise, and made sure Odilia had a lavish, if Christian, burial in the city's catacombs; everyone in the city knew her name now. But knowing that did little to ease the pangs of guilt I felt looking at her name on the stone.

"She'd have lived a long life at her farm if she hadn't come with us," I said.

"She wouldn't know what life was," replied Ursula. "She had the heart of a warrior, not a farmer."

I shook my head. "She was too young to know. Her father filled her head with old stories that she wanted to play out."

"You didn't force any of us to come here. We all made this choice. And so did Odilia. The best way you can honour her memory is to finish what we've started."

The three of us head out towards the river at an unhurried trot. A leather satchel bumps at my thigh — and for a moment, I'm reminded of another leather satchel, bumping at my thigh what seems like a lifetime ago, on the way to the Isle of Tanet… The bag contains the missives from Aegidius to Hildebert, copies of the Hunnic siege engine plans — to deliver to the Romans in case the city falls — and, most importantly, a scroll marked with Imperator Maiorianus's seal, to confirm my credentials and the seriousness of the proposal. To our north, the bright dots mark the position of the first squadron, led by Paulus. Unlike us, they are not making a secret out of their passing through the dark fields. Indeed, they're making more noise of it than would be normally necessary. The commotion soon yields the expected results.

"Look, by that ridge," says Ursula, pointing.

A new line of bright dots appears over a shadow of a hillside, heading towards Paulus's men. A couple of minutes later, another group, fewer in number, approaches from the riverside.

"Now."

I spur the pony to a gallop. By some fortunate accident, my mount was returned to me with no harm except to its dignity — for the few days of my captivity it was being used to draw the city's grain mill; as we approach the river crossing, it begins to buckle under me.

"I know you don't want to do it," I whisper. "Neither do I. But we have to."

The Blood of the Iutes

The night is warmer than the last time I swam across Mosella, but I expect the water to be just as cold and horrid as it was then. The pony can't be too keen on repeating the experience, either. At least this time, my wounds should not flare up again, since they've been expertly taken care of by Rav Asher.

"I hope they'll all be fine," says Ursula, glancing towards Paulus's squadron. All the clusters of lights now meet on the hill, directly to the east of where I believe the old bridge to be — I haven't quite had the chance to map out the river since the last time I was here. Paulus's men are only supposed to provide a distraction to our crossing; I can only hope they'll be able to disentangle themselves from their engagement before suffering too many casualties.

"These are the islands," I say, nodding at the shadows in the water. The moonlight shimmers in the current around them. "The bridge will be somewhere past the last one."

"I will go first," says Audulf. "My horse is stronger. If something goes wrong, I should manage to get across."

Audulf is not riding a moor pony anymore — he lost that one on an early patrol and replaced it with a Gaulish war horse from the *Dux*'s stables. It fits him better — he's a true Frankish warrior now, with a brand-new great axe slung over his back. Ursula, riding behind me, also wasted no time in Trever to arm herself to the teeth — she's got a cavalry lance holstered at her saddle, a *spatha* hangs at her left side, and a *seax*, a spoil of some skirmish with the Saxons, at her right.

I chose not to burden myself with any armour, other than a Legionnaire's helmet, remembering how difficult the crossing was when I wore a shirt of mail. My only new piece of armament is an ancient Roman *spatha* with a grip of ivory and gold wire, a parting gift from Arbogast, to replace the sword stolen from me by Haesta — the blade once belonged to the *Dux*'s father, when he was an officer in the *equites*. Arbogast doesn't know the true purpose of my mission: Aegidius told him we were going to try to reach Imperator Maiorianus at Lugdunum with the siege engine plans and one last urgent plea to send help to the besieged city.

"I see it," says Audulf. "Two rows of poles, just below the water."

"Wait." I stop him. "We may get separated in the current. If you end up alone, hide in the forest until morning. If we're still not there, go back to the city."

"I understand."

"Same goes for you, Ursula."

"We'll be fine," she says. I can't see her smile, but I can hear it in her voice. "You go second. I'll hold the rear."

I emerge on the other side, spluttering and spitting, but otherwise unharmed. Going the other way, I passed the strong current first before the pony grew too tired, and held on to the course for long enough not to drift too far away;

when I reach the western shore, the piers of the old bridge are less than a hundred feet away.

Ursula's pony climbs out next to me, but Audulf is nowhere to be seen. I lost sight of him before we reached the second island, but I hoped to catch up to him when the current grew weaker.

"You don't think he…" Ursula says.

"He could just have landed further downstream," I reply.

Somebody approaches — on foot, not on horseback. I reach for my sword — but leave it unsheathed when I notice it's Audulf.

"Get down!" he whispers urgently.

We dismount and hit the ground next to him. Our ponies are well trained and stay quiet in the reeds, even as a mounted patrol rides past us along the riverside road. From the way they're acting I can see this isn't a random guard: they're looking for something, or someone.

"How do they know we're here?" whispers Ursula.

"They don't," I whisper back. "Or they'd have noticed us already. They're hunting for someone else."

"Good," says Audulf. "Then we let them pass and go on our way."

"No," I say. "They may be after some of our men. I promised I'd get back for them. I'm not leaving them here."

There are four riders in the patrol, moving slowly upstream, towards the black wall of the forest looming in the distance. I gesture at Audulf and Ursula to follow on foot. Running along the shore, we soon find ourselves behind their backs. I order my friends to hide in the rushes; I stand in the middle of the road and call at the riders, my sword drawn in a defensive stance.

The Saxons turn in place. Confused, at first they can't see me in the dark. One of them tells the others to stay, and approaches me carefully to investigate, his lance lowered.

"Who in *Hel* are you?" he asks. There's a tremble in his voice. He's my age; I imagine patrolling the dark riverside hunting for some elusive enemy was not his idea of spending a summer night. "What are you doing here?"

"Careful, Deora," one of the other three calls. "It may be a trap."

"Deora?" I ask. That's a Iute name. "Are you Haesta's men?"

"What if we are?"

I lower my sword. "Haesta told me to tell you to get back to the camp," I speak in Iutish. "It's all sorted out."

"You found them?" Deora asks with relief. He lifts the lance.

The Blood of the Iutes

"Yes," I say. "It's all good now."

Deora repeats the good news to his comrades. Two of them raise a quiet cheer. But the third one, the same who suspected an ambush, remains unconvinced.

"Wait," he says. "I've never seen you around. And where's your horse? Have you run the whole mile from the camp?"

I pause too long to think of an answer. Deora leans down to take a closer look at my face. As the grimace of confusion turns into one of surprise, I grab him by the tunic and yank him down from the saddle. At that signal, Ursula leaps out of the reeds and, with a great cry, pierces the second rider's back with her lance. Audulf runs out from the other side, waving his great axe, and strikes at the third rider's leg, slicing it off at the thigh.

Within seconds, only the fourth rider remains on his horse. He turns about and launches into a panicked gallop, soon disappearing out of our sight — then, in a distance, I hear a familiar thwack of a javelin hitting flesh.

Ursula and Audulf finish off their enemies with swift blows, while I wrestle a moment with mine — until I manage to draw a knife and press it to his neck. This quietens him down at last.

"Look out," Audulf says, bloodied axe still in his hands, "someone's coming."

"Are there more of you?" I ask Deora. He shakes his head.

Four riders on ponies appear out of the shadows. I recognise the first one as soon as he emerges into the moonlight.

"Seawine!"

I pick the mercenary from the ground, the blade still at his neck, and hand him over to Audulf, who promptly disarms him. I greet Seawine and the other two Iutes.

"What fortune to find you here!" I say.

"It's no fortune," says Seawine. "We've been coming here every night, hoping to find you coming back."

"Is that why they were here?" I ask, nodding at Haesta's dead men. "Looking for you?"

"Yes. They got us two nights ago, captured half the men. We're all that's left."

"What about Wirtus?"

"Never saw him after you had gone," he says. "Only a few soldiers returned from the attack on your camp. They're recovering at the cherry farm." He looks around, and just now notices Audulf and Ursula. His face brightens. "You're all back! We can now start fighting Odowakr again!"

"We're not," I say. "I'm not here to fight, but…" I rub my chin. "You said Haesta's got the rest of the men?"

"That's right. We're all that's left."

"We need to get them back," I tell Ursula and Audulf. "I'm not leaving my warriors to Haesta's mercy."

"We don't have time," says Ursula.

"We have three weeks, maybe more. One night will not make a difference."

I grab Deora by the throat. "You. Where's your camp? How many of you are there?"

"I'm not telling you anything," he says.

I roll my eyes and punch him with the pommel of my knife. "Mercenaries have no loyalty. I don't care whether you live or die. We'll find Haesta sooner or later — I already know it's a mile away from here. Help us, be quick about it, and you'll live to find another master."

He spits blood, looks at his dead comrades on the ground, then back at me with a murderous stare. Then nods to the west.

"There's a ruin of an old watchtower on the hillside, half a mile from the road," he says.

"I know the place," says Seawine.

"How many men does Haesta have?" I ask again. There can't be many left of the original warband. Haesta's mercenaries were at the forefront of fighting against the sallies launched from Trever, and lost men in every skirmish.

The mercenary shrugs. "Ten, maybe a dozen. If you hurry, some of them will be still on patrol."

"Will Haesta be there?" asks Seawine. His voice is vengeful — the wounds from the encounter with Haesta must still be fresh.

"At this time of night?" Deora scoffs. "He'll be fast asleep, drunk on Mosellan wine."

I look into his eyes and see no more defiance in them. I let him go.

"Get out of here," I tell him, nodding at the horse.

"You're letting him ride?" asks Ursula, wide-eyed.

"He told us everything we wanted to know," I say. "And he *is* a Iute. Don't dare come back," I tell the mercenary. "I *will* kill you if I see you again."

"At least leave me a knife."

"Don't push it." I hit the rear of his horse with the flat of my sword. The beast and the rider vanish into the night.

"Search the bodies," I order the men. "Take anything valuable, and throw them and their weapons into the ri —"

The Blood of the Iutes

I lose my breath at that last word. As the excitement of the fight recedes, I realise I'm cold and weary again; the cold reminds me we have just swum across the Mosella. I have the right to be tired. I have the right to rest until morning.

But I don't have the time. If we dawdle too long, Haesta will realise something's gone wrong with his patrol, and either strengthen the guard, or move the camp somewhere we won't be able to find him.

"Can you fight any more tonight?" I ask Ursula and Audulf, after the three bodies splash quietly into the current. They each took a bronze armband from the fallen, and some coins from their purses. Ursula replaces her lance, damaged in the attack, with one taken from Deora's saddle holster.

"Of course," says Audulf, shaking his axe. "I'm just getting warmed up."

A part of me — the tired, cold part — was hoping he wouldn't say it. Or that Ursula would admit to being weary after the swim and the brawl… But no, their eyes gleam in the moonlight with such bright anticipation that they turn into stars. I'm reminded that they spent the past few weeks gaining experience and strength as part of Trever's bloodied cavalry, and that to them, this must be little more than a combat exercise.

I sigh, take a deep breath and sheathe my sword.

"Let's get our mounts," I say. "Looks like our destiny is to keep freeing these Iutes from captivity…"

There's time for planning, and then there's time for action.

As we ride towards the watchtower, for a while I entertain several schemes of complex attack. A diversion by setting the nearby forest on fire? But the dew is already out; it would take hours for the fire to grow big enough for anyone to notice. A precise sneak attack, without attracting too much attention? We would need to spend a long time to research the enemy's camp, and there'd be a risk of the guards spotting us. Besides, I'm not a strategist; maybe someone like my father or *Comes* Pinnosa would have been able to devise a plan of sufficient complexity in the short time available — but I'm neither of them and all I have on my side is the element of surprise.

"There is no plan," I tell the others when the camp appears in sight. The tower itself rises like a dark, crooked finger, lit up with a lantern hanging from a beam of what once would have been the second-floor look-out balcony. Crumbled remains of a low stone wall surround it on three sides; to the east, in the direction of the river, it's replaced by an earthen bank, eroded by rains and feet into little more than a ripple in the hillside. I see only five large tents, which means the mercenary was right — there can't be much more than a dozen men in the camp.

"We ride in, get the prisoners, load them onto the horses —" We're bringing with us the three mounts captured on the mercenaries. "— and ride out."

"What if they're hidden somewhere?" asks Seawine.

"Then we just ride out. Can't risk taking too long; there might be reinforcements nearby. Keep riding, in circle if you have to, just like Odo taught us. Don't get yourselves slowed down."

A hundred paces from the wall, I form us into two wedges, and spur the mounts to a charge. Audulf and Ursula lower their lances. The guards spot us, but they're too slow to react. One is pierced with Ursula's blade; the other leaps away from Audulf. I leap over the wall and turnabout in place, surveying the camp. The remaining guards run our way, raising alarm; some faces appear in the tent doors, then disappear, only to re-emerge with swords in their hands.

I spot the four Iutes by the wall of the watchtower, tied up; of course, Haesta wouldn't waste a shelter on his captives. The guard watching them flees as I get closer. I point them out to Audulf and Seawine, and as they leap down to cut the binds, I lead the remaining riders in a circle around the camp, trampling the tents under the hooves of our ponies.

Haesta leaps out of his tent, grabs a long spear from a stand and thrusts it at the nearest rider, throwing him down. I charge at him and strike with the sword; he parries and thrusts, inches from my stomach. I ride past him, stomping all over his tent, and draw a tight arc back. He throws the spear like a javelin, hitting another horse in the flank, leaving a bloody streak; then dives into the trampled remains of the tent in search of another weapon.

Tempting as it is to stay and fight him, I have no time for this. I reach Audulf and Seawine. They have got three of the captives on the horses already and are loading the fourth one

— this one's beaten-up and barely conscious; he slips from the saddle.

"Take him with you," I tell Audulf. "Seawine, get the other three out. Don't stop until you reach the river, then ride north, as far as you can."

I glance to Haesta — he's gathered most of his men around him by now, into a hedgehog bristling with blades; my Iutes are circling them at spear-length. Ursula picks up the warrior wounded by Haesta's spear from the ground and looks to me for orders.

"Get out!" I cry over the din of battle. She reads my lips, rather than hears my cry, and rears her pony to do a turnabout.

Audulf finally throws the last captive over the back of his war horse, leaps on top and spurs to a gallop, following Ursula and Seawine. He glances over his shoulder and notices me hesitating.

"What are you waiting for? Come on!"

But I just spotted something. In the middle of the circle of his men, Haesta stands with the weapons he took from his tent: a *seax* in his hand — and Basina's bow slung over his shoulder.

"Go," I cry. "Get everyone else out before more are wounded."

"What about you?"

The Blood of the Iutes

"I'll join you by the ruined bridge. Just give me a second."

"Don't do anything foolish," he says, before kicking his horse's sides again.

My heart racing, my breath short, I wait until all the Iutes turn tail and ride off downhill. Haesta's men rush for their mounts to start a pursuit — Haesta himself joins them at first, then turns slowly towards me, noticing I still haven't left the camp.

I launch into a charge with both hands on the reins, aiming past him; he wavers: he could get out of my way and lose a chance to strike at me — or risk getting trampled under my pony's hooves, if his attack fails. He chooses the latter, assuming a battle stance with the sword over his head. Just as I come near him, I tug on the reins and push with my rear; the pony slides in the sand and stops, suddenly. Haesta strikes a blow, but he misses by a good foot, misjudging my position. I lean down from the saddle, holding to the reins with one hand, and grab Basina's bow from his shoulder. The string tenses for a brief moment — then snaps, sending Haesta flying to the ground.

With the string-less bow in my hand, I dodge another mercenary springing before me, his axe swinging past me, climb up the earthen bank and leap down the other side. I look back: several of Haesta's men have already mounted up. Haesta scrambles from the ground and yells at them to go after me.

I holster the bow and swerve northwards, into the woods. I can't let them chase after the others — on the paved road, their war horses are bound to catch up to the moor ponies, even in the darkness. In the forest, I may have a chance to lose them.

An arrow flies past my ear. One of Haesta's men is riding and shooting after me, Hunnish style. I lower my head and kick the pony's flanks, but the poor beast is, like myself, too weary after the long night to make any more effort. Foam flies from its mouth, I can hear it wheezing desperately.

"Over here, lord!" I hear a call from somewhere to my right — a call in the Vulgar tongue, not Iutish. I turn towards the voice. Somehow, in the darkness my pony senses a ditch and leaps over it, but the leap costs it its last reserve of strength. The pony stumbles, whinnies, and falls under me.

I roll off it into the scrub. The man who called me appears with a small oil lamp — it's one of the woodsmen who was with us on the night of Odowakr's attack. I stir away, remembering the betrayal — but he puts his hand on my mouth and pulls me down to the ground. He covers us both with a cloak, with leaves and branches sewn into the cloth, until we resemble an overgrown boulder.

Haesta's men thunder past just a few feet away, noticing neither us nor the poor pony, lying motionless in the heather.

"You need to silence the beast," the woodsman whispers. The pony stirs and starts to snort and whinny again. "Before the others come." He nods at the approaching second wave of Haesta's riders, this one led by Haesta himself. Deep down, I know he's right, but the decision breaks my heart. I crawl up to the pony, cover its eyes with one hand and, with the other, I draw a knife across its neck. The woodsman pulls me away as the pony kicks its legs in silent agony.

"Come."

He drags me deeper into the ferns and heather and, again, we drop to the ground. Haesta and more of his men ride past: he slows down, sensing something's amiss; but by now, the pony has fallen silent. I hold my breath; we are invisible and noiseless. Haesta tuts and rides on with the rest of his men in tow.

"I need to get down to the river," I whisper. "Quickly."

"I know the way. Follow me."

"Wait." I grab his arm. "How do I know I can trust you? You could be taking me into another trap."

"That was all Kila's doing, lord," the woodsman explains apologetically. "Please, there's no time…" He pauses and notices I'm still not convinced. He makes a quick sign of the cross. "I swear by the Almighty God and all his Saints, I mean you no harm."

I may not believe in the Roman God myself — but I know a believer when I see one. These Christian peasants would never take their God's name in vain like that — not even when threatened by an entire heathen horde.

"Fine," I say. "Lead the way. But if you try anything, not even God and his Saints will save you from my wrath."

"At last!" Audulf exclaims, emerging from the tall reeds into the slowly creeping light of dawn. "We've been waiting for an hour. We thought they got you."

"I got held up."

"Who's that?" he asks, nodding at the woodsman.

"He's one of the serfs who betrayed us to the Saxons," says Seawine, approaching the woodsman with an axe drawn. "Step back, Octa, I'll deal with him."

I stand between them. "It's alright, Seawine. He saved me from Haesta."

Along the way, while avoiding the riders searching the flood plain between the forest and the riverside, the woodsman explained how Kila convinced them to give us away to Odowakr with the promise of gold — and freedom from the gruelling work on the siege machines.

"But we got no gold," he said. "And they forced us to fell another ancient oak the next day. These are sacred trees, they should not be cut down," he added, making a sign warding off an evil spirit, and thus betraying the traces of heathenry still running deep among the people of the forest, despite there having been a Bishop at Trever for more than a century.

"We ran away when your men attacked again," he said, "and when the four warriors got captured, we watched the camp, hoping to find a way to help them. But we were too few. We are not warriors."

"You did well enough."

"Where's your pony?" Ursula asks me.

"I… lost it. I will need to ride with one of you."

"You can have Huda's," says Seawine grimly. I follow his gaze — one of the four captives, the one most beaten-up, is hanging limply from the saddle. "He didn't make it."

"We should bury him," I say. "We can't carry him all the way to…"

"There's no time," says Audulf. "Haesta's men will find us any moment now. They already passed us once. They won't miss us again," he says, nodding towards the rising sun.

"We will take care of your fallen," says the woodsman. "It's the least we can do."

"Are you sure? You've already risked enough to get me here."

"We will give him a proper burial," he insists.

"He wasn't a Christian."

"It matters not in God's eyes."

I help him take poor Huda from the pony and mount up myself. I look to the South.

"We need to find another way than this road," I say. "By now it will be brimming with patrols, looking for us."

"If you're going west, you can cut through the hills, along the Kelb River," says the woodsman. "There's no road, but there's a good shore path the charcoal burners use. Your ponies should have no problem." He looks at Audulf's war horse. "Might be a bit tight for this one."

"Slippy will manage just fine," says Audulf, patting his mount's mane.

"*Slippy?*" I raise my eyebrow and chuckle. Ursula looks at us, not understanding the joke among the heathens. "You named your horse after Wodan's steed?"

"He proved he's worth it."

The Iutes mount up in a hurry. I bid farewell to the woodsman, burdened with Huda's corpse. Ursula rides up to me and studies the string-less bow, holstered at the saddle.

"Is this what you went back for?" she asks.

My cheeks burn. "Yes."

She laughs. "I'm sure Basina will be… suitably impressed."

The Blood of the Iutes

    I spur the pony to a gallop, towards the dark line of the hills.

CHAPTER XVI
THE LAY OF BETULA

After four days of marching — and riding, where possible — along the winding, wooded banks of the Kelb, we run out of the dry bread and salted pork we brought from Trever in our saddlebags. We have no time to forage or hunt — I want to reach the Roman-held territory as fast as possible. All the villages we pass are long abandoned, the villagers having fled in the same direction we're heading now.

On the fifth day, tired, hungry and saddle-sore, we reach the Roman road again, right by the border fortress of Icorig. The town is heaving. There seems to be even more people here than when we left. We make our way to the town's largest inn, and the innkeeper, seeing the state we're in, and hearing we've come from Trever, lets us all stay for free — in the stable, turned into one large dormitory; most of the horses are gone, and I dread to think what fate befell them in the town that, squeezed between Hildebert's Franks on one side and Odowakr's Saxons on the other, is as much under siege as Trever.

I sleep until late that night. The sun is high up already when Ursula wakes me.

"There's a messenger downstairs," she says. "From the *Praetor*."

I groan and rise from the straw. "I feared this would happen. We must be the first visitors from the South they've had in weeks. Tell him I'll be right over."

She throws me the tunic and breeches and leaves me to wash myself. I'm in no hurry to see the *Praetor*. My head hurts, my stomach grinds and growls after days of sitting in the saddle and eating nothing but oatcakes and salted meat. Still, I remind myself, I need to speak to him too, to see if he has any news from the North, before we enter the land of the River Franks.

"Where did all these people come from?" I ask, after recounting the situation in Trever.

"Tolbiac," the *Praetor* replies. He calls himself Falco — but I can't tell if it's his real name, or just a nickname based on the falcon-beak shape of his nose.

"Did the Franks take it?"

"Not yet — and I don't think they're planning to, not until the siege of Trever ends, one way or another. This Hildebert is too shrewd to try another city battle so soon after Coln. But he moved his camps closer, as a show of force; too close for some. They lost their nerve and fled here."

"You must be running out of supplies yourself. I've seen the stables…"

He winces. "It hasn't been easy. But we're not giving up. Even if Trever falls, even if the Saxons and the Franks ally against us, we will not go down without a fight. I'm not giving my town away like Pinnosa."

"You are a soldier," I say, nodding. I sense resentment in his voice. "In command of a fortress. Pinnosa was a *Comes*, leading a city full of civilians. He did what he had to do."

"I know, I know." He sits back with a sigh. "I would be the last to deny him valour. I remember him standing against the Huns when all the other towns fell. If he decided Coln was no longer defensible, he must have been right. His death is a great loss to us all."

He wraps his hand over his head and twiddles his thumbs. "What orders from Trever, then?" he asks. "Do they want us to come to their aid? Is a rescue effort mounting?"

"I have no orders from Trever," I say. "Not for you, anyway." I look around the room — the *Praetor*'s simple office in the corner of the barracks; its raw stone walls, unadorned with as much as a single painting or tapestry, once plastered white, are now grey with soot of the fireplace. It's a far cry from the opulent *Praetorium* halls of Coln or Trever, but I know that in such offices, in such barracks, was decided the fate of the Empire. That it was up to the commanders of the border fortresses, like the man sitting before me, to defend Rome's frontier.

He looks at me suspiciously. "Then why are you here? We are the last outpost of the Legions on this road."

I don't know how much I'm allowed to tell him. If Hildebert accepts the pact proposed to him by *legatus*

Aegidius, Icorig would be one of the places given up to the Franks without a fight. How would the *Praetor* and his men react to this? If I was in their place, I would deem it a gross betrayal. They are ready to fight to the death to defend the fortress and the pass, to give their lives for men like Aegidius — but for the legate and his likes, they are mere markers to move around the map as the interests of the Empire dictate.

He slams the table. "They have sent you to do some deal with the barbarians, haven't they? I always knew this half-Frank could not be trusted."

"Trever will not last a month," I reply. "And I was sent on the Imperator's orders, not Arbogast's."

"Imperator — which one?"

"You know about the Usurper in Lugdunum?"

"We are not completely cut off from the world, yet," he replies. "I see they told you to call him a Usurper — but I know Agrippinus well and trust him better than some general from Italia. He would never consider making deals with the River Franks."

"He made a deal with the Burgundians — and the Goths."

"And who told you that?"

"His enemies," I admit. I am not prepared to argue with him about the politics of the Empire. "I'm only a messenger,"

I say. "I'm not even from around here. I want to go back home to Britannia as soon as all this is over."

Falco rubs his cheeks, then points at me. "If I hold you here, you will never get to Hildebert."

"Then Trever will fall. And you with it."

"Better to die fighting than to give the fortress to the heathens without a javelin thrown."

"You sound like a heathen yourself," I say with a smile. "Wodan would gladly welcome you to his Mead Hall."

"You heathens are not the only ones who appreciate a warrior's death," he says, then adds: "All of us here have some Frankish or Alemannic blood in our veins. Maybe we are more alike than either of us think."

He picks up a stylus and doodles a few random lines on a tablet in thought.

"If Pinnosa had lived, he would never have agreed to this deal," he says. "It's one thing to give up a city that's already doomed to fall — and save its soul in exchange… But to surrender like this, when there are still men willing to fight…" He points the stylus at me. "There is something else going on," he says. "If they're willing to give up Icorig, then they must be ready to give up Trever as well. They know we're all that stands between the Franks and the city… This means that Imperator of theirs is afraid of something other than the Saxon warband."

I remain silent. If Aegidius wanted his courier to argue his cause with fellow Romans, he should have sent someone more eloquent and familiar with the Empire's politics.

Praetor Falco shrugs and puts down the stylus. "I'm just a soldier. And you're just a courier. This is all above both our heads. In the end, we are all just doing what we are ordered. If I keep you here, they will send someone else in your place. And you don't deserve the punishment for someone else's sins — not after what you and your men have been through."

"I appreciate your clemency."

"You will have no trouble finding the Franks. They have their camps scattered everywhere between Tolbiac and Ake."

"They didn't take Ake, either?"

"Maybe Hildebert bit more than he could chew with Coln. It is a *lot* of a city for a barbarian to rule over."

"If he can't control Coln, he might be in trouble having to rule an entire province," I blurt out before realising. I put my hand to my mouth, but it's too late.

"So that's what they're promising," Falco says and chuckles. "Fine." He waves his hand. "Go, do your politics. After all, you're a foreigner in a foreign land, none of this concerns you. Maybe that's why Aegidius chose you for his messenger."

"The fate of the Empire concerns me. That is why I came here in the first place."

"Then you better pray to your pagan gods that the men who sent you are doing the right thing. Because I can't see how giving any more of our land to those barbarians helps the Empire continue. But what do I know, I'm just a simple soldier?"

He gives me a nasty glance, and I know he counts me among the "barbarians" threatening Rome's survival. Iutes, Franks, Saxons — it makes no difference to him. To men like him, it never did.

"We are not all the same," I murmur, but too quiet for him to hear. I bid him farewell. He says nothing; as I leave, I hear him call the servant to bring him a bottle of the strongest Frankish mead.

Tolbiac is, indeed, half-empty when we reach it: a desolate shell of a town, with only those too infirm or too stubborn to leave still roaming its now too-wide streets. We don't stay there long, and I refuse a summons to meet with its magistrates, not wanting another futile conversation in which I would be required to answer the questions meant for Aegidius and, ultimately, the Imperator himself.

I don't have such choice when it comes to an invite from the Franks. A clan of them set up camp just outside the town's outskirts, between the road to Coln and a small, shadowed brook. His men intercept us on the highway and escort us to the sprawling tent of their chieftain. I recognise some of them along the way; and I recognise their chief, Weldelf.

"You've lost some men," he says, eyeing our group.

"I'm surprised you remember, chieftain."

"A dozen was an easy number to remember." We're now down to seven Iute riders — Audulf, Ursula and I round it up to a ten. "The *walhas* girl survived," Weldelf grins at Ursula. "I am glad."

"I'm glad, too," says Ursula. She dismounts, walks up to a guard drinking some ale, grabs it from his hand and downs it in one. She wipes her mouth and belches. "Finally, some good drink!" she says. "I've had enough wine for the rest of my life."

The Franks around her laugh. "There's more of it inside," says Weldelf, inviting us to his tent.

"We can't stay long," I say as we settle down on the bearskins scattered on the floor. The shieldmaidens roll in a barrel of ale and crack it open. Ursula is the first to plunge her mug into it. "We took too long to get here as it is."

"Where are you going in such a hurry?"

"We're on our way to see your *Drohten*. I can't say any more."

"I will give you an escort. It will make things easier. There are still some *walhas* soldiers in these woods who haven't given up the fight — they might mistake you for one of our patrols."

I can't help but smile. So the Romans have been following here the same Fabian tactics as we did in the Trever hills.

"Shouldn't you be chasing after them?"

"Hildebert hasn't ordered us to do anything yet. We just wait and watch. We're safe in our camps — and we're in no hurry."

"And where's Hildebert now?"

"Over in Coln," he says, nodding to the North. "Still figuring out what to do with it."

"I would have thought you'd be there as well. Don't you want to partake in the plunder?"

I notice he's got a new, wide band of bronze around his arm. It's roughly cut from some larger piece, and oddly sculpted. I realise it must have been hewn from some statue or decoration. I look around, noticing more disturbing details. There's a stack of such carved pieces of bronze lying in the corner, ready to be distributed among Weldelf's warriors — bits of arms and legs, half of a head of some Imperator. Weldelf's woman wears a chain bracelet with a small silver cross, taken from the neck of some acolyte. A pile of charred papers is thrown on the hearth as fuel, the spider web of black ink letters still visible on the corners, slowly consumed by the flames, the words lost to the world forever.

I say nothing about any of this to Weldelf, but he notices my gaze. He downs half a mug of ale and breathes out. "I

The Blood of the Iutes

don't care for the *walhas* cities or their treasure," he says. "I don't like being hemmed in by walls. None of us do. I prefer the woods, the rivers, the fields. I'd rather sit on a cliff and watch the mighty Rhenum flow past and pray to Aigir that he let me see the water nymphs, than live in a house of stone, among all the noise and stench."

"Then what did you need Coln for?"

"The *walhas* garrison was always a thorn in our side. We would have been satisfied with just the woods and the fields, but they could never just let us be. Now that they're gone…" He shrugs. "The *Drohten* will think of something to do with Coln. Maybe he'll let the *walhas* rule it in his name, as long as they give him a share of their gold."

I scratch my nose in thought.

"Then you wouldn't care much if the *walhas* offered you even more towns?"

He laughs. "And why would they grant us such a gift after we beat them so thoroughly? Has their god finally taken their minds?"

"Never mind the reasons," I say. "What would you do with the towns if you did take them over?"

"Nothing," he says. "If there was any gold and silver worth taking there, we would have taken it already — there are no soldiers left to stop us. All the food and ale we need is out here," he adds, spreading his hands. "There is nothing

[416]

but more stone there — and more *walhas* who hate us, just like the ones in Coln, or the ones hiding in the woods."

"Is this why you still haven't taken Tolbiac?"

"Tolbiac is like a man dying of plague — still shuffling around the village, but the flies are already around him, and the crows circle above him. Who would want to have anything to do with something like this?"

"You may as well be describing Rome itself," I ponder.

"I wouldn't know." He shakes his head. "I've never been anywhere beyond this country. When I first saw Coln, as a child, I thought *that* was Rome. I could not imagine there being a greater gathering of men than this."

"It's much smaller than Londin, where I grew up," I tell him. "And Rome is greater still."

"So I've heard. But I also heard Rome was taken by the Vandals a few years ago."

"They didn't stay long once they took all there was to take."

"See?" He raises both hands. "I say, let the *walhas* keep their cold, bare stones."

We both laugh and raise our mugs. The barrel soon ends, and Weldelf calls for another, but I insist we must leave.

"The day is still young," I tell him. "We can get halfway to Coln by dusk."

"What about that escort I promised —?"

"We'll be fine, I'm sure. We carry the Imperator's seal; that should keep the *walhas* at bay."

"As you wish."

I pick Ursula up from the ground — she's had one cup of ale too many; once outside, I tell Audulf to pour a bucket of well water on her head to sober her up.

"I thought we were staying the night here," says Audulf, surprised. He had already untied his saddlebags and started to unpack his belongings.

"There's no time. We'll set up camp on the road."

"Wha-ss the rush?" slurs Ursula.

"Just follow me, and don't ask questions. Trust me."

We mount up, bid farewell to Weldelf, and ride out towards Coln. Once the camp disappears out of sight, I turn away from the road into the fields. The others follow me in silence, but I can sense their questioning stares on my back. We ride in a wide westward arc around Tolbiac, until we reach another Roman road.

"This isn't the way to Coln," notes Audulf.

"No, it's not," I reply. "It's the road to Tornac."

"Tornac —" Ursula tilts her head, then grins. "Oh, I see. You want to take back the bow to its mistress."

"This has nothing to do with Basina," I say, red-cheeked, and kick the pony's sides.

There is an army at Tornac. A warband, at least a thousand warriors strong, gathered in a great camp sprawling all around the walls. The field smithies and campfires spew black smoke in a cloud so thick and tall that from a distance we take it at first for the smouldering of a burnt-down town. The camp is like a second town in its own right; we move through it slowly, passing warriors in training, merchants hawking cheap goods, women of pleasure seeking custom; the air is filled with the grinding of whetstones, clucking of hens being slaughtered for food and for auguries, clinking of hammers against anvils and thuds of wooden swords against wooden spears.

The guard at the top of the gatehouse refuses to let us in at first.

"We've had enough of your sort," he says enigmatically. "There's no place inside for any more mercenaries."

"We're not mercenaries," I cry back. "We are messengers. Let your *Herr* Hildrik know Octa is back from Trever."

"Trever?" This gets the guard's attention. He leans over the battlement. "You've come a long way."

"We have — and we are weary."

"Has the city fallen, then?"

"Not yet. But I will only bring my news to the ears of your masters."

He mulls my answer, then nods at the guard at the door to wave us through.

I can see why he was reluctant to let us in; there isn't a foot of grass inside the fort that isn't covered by a tent, a weapons rack, or a pile of supplies.

"Looks like we've arrived just in time," I say. "They're all ready to march out."

"You still haven't told us *why* we came here," says Audulf. "It was a long detour — I thought we were in a hurry."

"We are. Now doubly more so." We pass the door of the guesthouse where we stayed the last time — it's barred now, with a sign saying "no rooms".

"Look," Seawine says, pointing to the stables, "aren't these… moor ponies?"

"They sure look like them," says Ursula. She swerves nearer the stables to take a closer look. "They must be ours," she reports back. "I'm certain of it."

"Maybe my father sent another shipment to Meroweg," I say with a frown.

We reach the mead hall. Another grumpy guard tells us to wait, longer this time. Audulf grows impatient. "I'll go find us some lodgings," he says. "There must be *some* rooms in the town."

"Maybe those kindred of yours can take us in for a few nights," says Ursula. "We're not going to be staying here long, are we?" she asks me.

"No, I don't think so," I reply. "But then, by the looks of it, neither will anyone else."

A good hour passes before we're allowed into the hall. We enter in the middle of some heated debate between Meroweg and his counsellors. There have been some changes since our last visit. The long table is gone, replaced by what looks like a mosaic of hides and furs on the floor. As I look closer, I recognise it as an ingeniously devised rough map of northern Gaul, with rivers and roads marked in stripes of ox leather, and forest and hill ranges in swathes of different coloured fur. Tokens carved in horn and bone mark towns and fortresses.

"*Rex* Meroweg," I announce with a bow. "I see you're in the middle of a war council."

He lifts his head and stares at me for a long while with narrowed eyes.

"You're that young Iute," he says eventually. "The one who went with my son to hunt the Saxons."

"That's me. Octa, son of *Rex* Aeric."

"I thought you stayed at Trever."

"I did — until about a week ago. But I came here to bring you important —"

He stops me and waves at the servants. "Sit down, please," he says, pointing to a bench in the aisle to the side. There's a small desk there, with a bunch of papers which a servant rolls up and takes away to make place for pitchers and mugs. "You must be tired after the journey. I will speak to you presently. For now, have some warm ale. Or maybe you'd prefer wine?"

"Ale is good," says Ursula eagerly.

Meroweg adjusts the diadem on his head and sits back on the carved magisterial seat.

"Now then, remind me again, *Herr* Richomer," he addresses one of the counsellors, "how many *alae* of horse archers do the Alans have around Aurelianum?"

"I came as soon as I heard. I'm glad to see you alive."

Hildrik reaches out to embrace me and pats me on the back. When he moves to greet Ursula and Audulf, Basina steps in his place. Hildrik's embrace was brief, perfunctory, a greeting of warriors. Basina's is warm, long, her hands roaming on my back, her breath in my ear.

"I saw your pony outside," she whispers. "I see you took good care of my bow."

"Pity about the string."

"Don't worry about it. The string is not important. It's the… *shaft* that's irreplaceable. I missed it," she says, and I hear *I missed you* in her voice. Hildrik glances at us, and Basina pulls away from the embrace to tap Ursula on the shoulders.

"Where have you been all this time?" Hildrik asks when we sit back down at the small desk. He nods at Meroweg, still arguing with his men at the far end of the hall. "Don't tell me you stayed in those woods around Trever all this time."

"Some of it, yes," I say. "And then in Trever itself. We're here with a message from the *walhas* lords."

"Have you spoken to Father about it?"

"I have not had the chance yet," I reply.

He rolls his eyes and stands back up. He strides across the hall, trampling the hides, stepping on the carved tokens and pushing the elders out of his way.

"Father!" he speaks in a voice that makes the timber walls shudder. "Octa rode here across half of Gaul with his message for you! Why haven't you heard him out yet?"

Meroweg wearily looks up from the map.

"And what news could he bring me from Trever that I would not already know?" he says.

"You only know what Odowakr tells you. Octa came from *inside* the city."

Meroweg turns his attention towards me. "Why don't you talk to him, then? He's your friend. Find out what he knows."

Hildrik throws his hands in the air and comes back. "I'm sorry for my father. He's busy, as you can see. We're almost ready to march out."

"It's alright," I say. "It looks like it will be better if I talk to you anyway."

"What did you mean about Odowakr?" asks Ursula. "You're getting messengers from him?"

Hildrik glances around. "I think it might be better if we discuss this somewhere more private. Go to the guesthouse, I'll meet you there."

"The guesthouse is full."

"I know." He smiles. "My men are staying there." He summons one of his warriors and whispers something in his ear. "Berhtwalda will go with you. He'll find you a room."

Berhtwalda bangs on the gate of the guesthouse. I hear several locks and padlocks crack open. A head of white hair appears in the door.

"What do you want, Berht — *Aetheling*?" she exclaims.

"Betula? What in the — is it really you? What are *you* doing here?"

"Come inside! The others will be so happy to see you!"

"The *others*? The *Hiréd* is here?"

"I told you those were our moor ponies," says Ursula with a grin.

"The first news we got was from the merchant, Ingomer," says Betula. Just as Hildrik promised, his men clear three rooms for our use, on the guesthouse's second floor; as Seawine and his Iutes set themselves up there, my friends and I come down to the dining hall and sit at a large, round table, around a great plate heaped tall with local sausages and sour cabbage.

"Your father was losing his mind with worry. All we knew was what Bana told us — that you stowed away on that Roman ship… But we didn't know where he took you, or why."

"My father, worried?" I chuckle nervously.

"I've never seen him like that — not even when your mother died."

"I find that hard to believe."

"*Aetheling*… Octa —" She puts her hand on mine. "I know he doesn't know how to show this — he wasn't there when you grew up — but he loves you dearly. You're all he's got left. Of course he's worried about you."

"Was that why he sent you here?" asks Ursula. "To find us?"

"Not at first," says Betula. "When Ingomer told us you reached Meroweg's capital safely, we all breathed out in relief. Aeric was even glad to hear you set out on a raid with Hildrik. We both thought you could use an adventure like that. After all, when he was your age…"

"Yes, yes," I interrupt her impatiently. "We all know the heroic deeds my father performed in his youth. Why are you here, then? What changed his mind?"

"A second messenger arrived a month ago — from someone called Paulus of Ake."

"*Praetor* Paulus! He's kept his word, after all!"

"The news of Haesta and his mercenaries fighting on the side of the Saxons greatly disturbed your father," she says. "It's one thing to have him harass our borders in Britannia, and work with Aelle against us — but to transport this conflict to the Continent, where it might involve Franks and maybe even Rome… He was especially incensed when he learned Haesta shared the secret of henbane with the enemy."

"That — that isn't quite what happened," I say. "The Saxons still do not know how to brew henbane."

"Nevertheless — having the Saxons from the Old Country at Haesta's side could change the entire balance of power in Britannia. This is something your father could not abide."

"Then he did not send you here to find me and help me — but to fight Haesta and Aelle," I say. My voice comes out grumpier than I wanted. "So much for him worrying about me."

"You are not a child anymore, Octa," says Betula. "You are a Iute warrior. Your father may be worrying about you, but he understands you are free to make your own choices — even if it means you get hurt or die." She picks up a link of sausage and tears at it with her teeth. "But you're wrong. We were ordered to find *you* first, and then start looking for Haesta and his men."

"You haven't done either, I notice."

"We've only been here a couple of weeks; we're still getting our bearings. It's a strange land. This is the furthest anyone of us has ever been," she says, and I stifle a snigger. We've just been marching for days to get back *to* Tornac, a place that seems almost like home compared to the vastness of Gaul beyond…

"When Hildrik returned from Trever, he told us what happened there. We were supposed to follow after you, but we cannot move without Meroweg's permission — and he does not want anyone leaving the town, not until his *fyrd* marches out, at least."

"And where is he sending his *fyrd*?"

"You'll have to ask him about that yourself."

"Hildrik will know," says Ursula. "He's supposed to be here soon."

I reach for the meat; my hand hovers above the plate. "Now that you found me, what are you going to do?"

"Whatever you order us to do."

"*Me?*"

"You *are* the *aetheling*. The *Hiréd* is yours to command. Your father told us to obey you — within reason." She grins.

I scratch my head a few times. "But I... I'm not a commander," I say. "I'm barely even a warrior."

"That's not true. You've already led men," says Audulf. "To victory."

"A handful of farmers and sailors, a few lost Legionnaires," I say with a scoff. "You can't compare them to a *Hiréd*. And we were only accompanying Hildrik's warband. By the time he was my age, my father had already fought at Saffron Valley and Crei. He must think everyone —"

Betula bursts out laughing.

"What's so funny?"

"I'm sorry." She wipes a tear. "It's just — do you really think you're still living in Aeric's shadow?"

"He *is* a king."

"He is now, yes. And a *Gesith* before that, and Londin Councillor before that. But when he fought at Crei, he was a nobody. A green warrior, running errands for his brother. I was there, too, you know — a young shieldmaiden, fighting in the front line." She lifts her tunic up to show off an old scar under the stump of her arm. "A *wealh* spear, on the shores of Crei," she says. "I hadn't even heard about him then. Indeed, I didn't hear about him until I met him in Londin."

"What are you getting at?"

"At your age, his world — *our* world — was confined to Wortigern's realm. Cantiaca, Londin, maybe New Port if there was a reason to get there. By the time Hengist ceded the diadem to him, the furthest your father went was to Wecta and the land of Ikens. Even as a *Rex*, he's only been abroad twice — both times here, to see Meroweg." She waves her hand around the hall.

"Yes, he often complained about this. He called it *the shrinking of the world*," I remember. "He said things are slightly better now than when he was a youth — when one village only knew or cared about what happened at the nearest village — but not by much."

"And now, look at yourself —" she says. "You've sailed to Gaul on your own. You've been to all those strange, wonderful places we've only heard of: names we've only seen on maps. Trever — I don't even know where that is!"

"And Coln," adds Ursula.

"And you carry messages in the name of the Imperator," says Audulf.

"*Imperator?*" Betula's eyes widen. "What do you mean? You've met the Imperator?"

"No," I laugh. "Only his *legatus*, Aegidius — the same who visited my father at Robriwis. But I do carry the Imperator's seal…"

"*Only* the Imperator's *legatus*." Betula shakes her head. "Listen to yourself. You're only eighteen, by Lord's wounds. At this rate, by the time you're forty, you'll be the Imperator yourself!"

"I — I don't think that's possible."

"By the time he's forty, there may not *be* an Imperator anymore," says Hildrik.

I turn around — it's him and Basina, and a retinue of three Franks, each carrying an axe the size of a small tree.

"I thought you wanted to meet somewhere private," I say.

"This *is* private." Hildrik snaps his fingers, and his warriors clear the guesthouse from the patrons and staff. A minute later, we're all alone in the dining hall — not much smaller than Meroweg's mead hall, now that it's empty, except for the three axemen standing guard at the door and windows.

"How much have you heard?" I ask.

"I heard you mention something about the Imperator's seal," replies Hildrik.

I reach into the satchel and take out the parchment scroll from its tube. The seal is stamped with a stylised portrait of Maiorianus under a mark of a cross, and inscribed with his name and title, unreadable now in the wax. I hold it in my hands for a moment before showing it to the others.

"It's a letter from the Imperial Legate, Aegidius. I wanted to present it to your father, but I fear it might be too late. Would I be right thinking his *fyrd* is about to march on Trever?"

"Not on Trever, no." Hildrik shakes his head. "But there is a great swathe of land between Camarac and Aurelianum that's free for the taking. We could expand on Clodio's conquests now, while the *walhas* and barbarians are busy fighting each other and the promised Roman fleet is nowhere to be seen."

"The Roman fleet?"

"Have you forgotten how this entire thing started?" asks Betula. "Your father agreed to house the Roman ships at Leman, but we haven't seen any yet."

"The Empire's war plans have changed since then," I say. "The fighting moved south, to Lugdunum, so I imagine the harbour in Britannia is no longer a priority."

"So I gathered." Hildrik nods. "It matches the news we've been receiving from Odowakr."

"And what is Odowakr's role in this?"

"They agreed to share the North between them — Odowakr would take Belgica Prima, my father Belgica Secunda; and they would help each other defending from any Roman response."

"This would mean the end of Roman Gaul," I say. By now, I don't need to look at maps to remember the shape of the province and its internal divisions. "The South is already split between Goths and Burgundians. Even if Maiorianus wins against Agrippinus, it might be impossible to reconquer it all back again."

"I'm afraid you might be right," says Hildrik with a sad nod. "And without Gaul, who knows how long before Rome itself falls, and for good this time?"

"And you're fine with this?" I ask. "After everything we talked about?"

"Wouldn't you have done the same in my father's place? Between us and the Sequana River there are only a few small city garrisons. The Legions are far away, facing each other. It's a ripe fruit, ready for picking."

"What was in the message?" asks Basina.

I hand her the scroll. She breaks the seal and as she reads it, her wide brow furrows ever deeper. She gives it to Hildrik.

"I think you gave us the wrong missive," she says. "This is addressed to Hildebert, *Drohten* of the River Franks."

"Yes," I reply. "The legate sent me to him. But I didn't think Hildebert was the right man for this task."

Basina smiles. "So you've decided you're a better diplomat than the Imperial Legate."

"I…" I stutter. She struck right at my uncertainty; what right did I have to decide by myself what I did with the message? What if, through my arrogance, I just signed off a death warrant for the city of Trever and everyone in it — what if I sealed the fate of Gaul, the fate of Rome itself?

"I just didn't think Aegidius and Maiorianus were familiar enough with the situation in the North."

"Hmm… no, I'm pretty sure they are more than familiar with what's going on here," says Hildrik. "I told you, Maiorianus served on the Frankish frontier in his youth. And Aegidius fought at his side."

My cheeks burn. I rip the letter from his hands. "It's not too late yet for me to return to Coln."

"Hold on," says Hildrik. "Let's not be too hasty about it."

"What *did* Aegidius promise the River Franks, anyway?" asks Basina.

"Recognition of his rule in the entire province. A title of a *Comes*. Control over taxes and customs. Garrisons removed from border forts."

Hildrik and Basina look to each other. "They're really afraid," says Basina. "I didn't know it was that bad."

"There's nothing here that would interest Meroweg," says Hildrik. "Not when he can take it with his own hands."

"And waste time and men capturing all those fortified towns I saw on the map?" I say.

"All the more glory for his warriors," he replies, rubbing his chin. I can see it in his eyes and hear it in his voice: if it was up to him, he would take the deal.

"Your father gambles on Rome being a spent force," I say. "But what if he's wrong — what if this new Imperator is as good a commander as the *walhas* claim? You yourself told me he could be the new Aetius. He's defeated you once before. There'd be a bloody war — and all your father's conquests could be for naught."

"And even if we win, there will be widespread devastation," says Hildrik. "The land has barely recovered after the Huns. It will not survive another war."

"Then stop your father and convince him to take Aegidius's offer."

He shakes his head. "Nothing will convince him to trust the *walhas*. He would just dismiss it as another trick. And maybe he'd be right — what guarantees can they offer on this deal? They fear us now — if we help chase Odowakr away, what leverage will that leave us?"

I look to Basina pleadingly. She's the only one here who can help me change Hildrik's mind.

I'm not sure why I insist so much on convincing the Salians to march to Trever's help. Part of it must be unwilling to accept I've made a mistake; but that's not all of it. I don't know this Hildebert — I haven't even met him — but from what I've seen of the River Franks, I believe Hildrik, if not his father, is far more suited to play the role of the saviour of Gaul. The River Franks seem to me true "barbarians", almost caricatures of the kind described by the ancient Roman writers; living in camps and villages, rather than walled towns, not caring for the value of art and culture they inherit from the people they conquered, interested only in glory and plunder…

"It must be nice to be able to make such important decisions on your own," says Basina. "Without always checking with your father…"

"Oh, I'm sure my father —" I start, but Ursula squeezes my hand under the table to stop me from talking.

"My father is the king of the Salians," says Hildrik. "The tribe is his to command."

"And are *you* his to command, too?" asks Basina. "I did not choose to marry a man who takes orders from someone else."

"I doubt Octa could do what he does without his father's permission," snarls Hildrik.

"Actually, my father and I have always had an understanding about these things," I say, releasing my hand from Ursula's grip. "He promised he would never order me to do anything against my will."

"Nonsense," scoffs Hildrik. "He's been indulging you. It's not like you can take the Iute *fyrd* and march them on Londin."

"No, but he can command *us* to march with him wherever he wants," says Betula, guessing what I'm getting at with my argument. "Don't you have a warband of your own?"

[436]

"What about those men who went with us to Trever?" asks Audulf.

"Look, I don't know how they do things in Britannia, but I was banished once already. Eight years among the Thuringians is a long time — even if I did find my beloved there." He tries a smile at Basina, but she's having none of it. "I don't want to end up like your Haesta, running a mercenary band, looking for coin on the outskirts of the Empire."

"You mean you're scared to stand against Meroweg," murmurs Basina.

Hildrik stands up, overturning his stool. Red-faced, he slams his hands on the table. "I am *not* scared of anyone — not even you, Basina! As long as my father is alive, he is in charge of everything and everyone around here. What do you want me to do? *Kill* him?"

A silence falls on the table. I glance nervously to the door — the guards don't budge, and don't change the bland expressions on their faces.

"That *would* make you the king of Franks," says Basina quietly. She licks her lips in excitement. "I haven't slept with a king since my first husband."

"I am not going to kill my own father." He sits back down and rests his head on his hands.

"Wait," I say. "Nobody said anything about any kingslaying."

"Oh, but we have," says Basina. She turns back to Hildrik. "We talked about this before, didn't we, my love?"

"You — you thought about murdering your own father?" I gasp.

"Hildrik has no love for Meroweg," Basina explains. "He barely even knows him. He was just a child when he was sent to Thuringia."

"This isn't how I imagined my return to Frankia," says Hildrik, so quietly I can't hear him at first, staring into the table. "I thought Father would make me his second in command. Give me an army of my own. Give me a seat at his Council. But I was just an errand boy. When we returned from Trever, he took the warband from me. He called the *fyrd* against Rome without asking for my opinion."

"You've always disagreed with the way he led the tribe," says Basina.

"Betrayal at Maurica poisoned his mind," says Hildrik. "And he's jealous of Hildebert's successes. He would rather see all the Franks perish than seek peace with Rome."

"Then somebody must stop him," I whisper. I can't believe I'm saying this. It could be *my* father we're talking about. How different is what we're discussing from what Haesta did? He, too, believed my father, and Hengist before him, were wrong in how they led the tribe. He, too, had grievances that he felt were justified and went unaddressed. Is this why my father never fully committed to destroying him and his band of mercenaries?

"I — I don't think I should be involved," says Audulf, leaning away from the table. "I have relatives here. What if they somehow end up connected to this?"

"Calm down, Audulf," I say. "Nobody's getting involved in anything. We're just talking, right? Right?" I plead with Hildrik.

He stares at his hands for a long time. "If my Franks and I came to Trever's help instead of Hildebert, do you think Aegidius would honour the deal? Do you think the Empire would make me a *Comes*?"

"I… I don't think he would have much choice," I say, my lips suddenly dry. "They are desperate over there. If we don't bring reinforcements in…" I count in my head, "two weeks, at most, it's all over, one way or another."

"What do you mean, one way or another?"

"There is something else I haven't told you about yet," I say. I glance at Ursula. She nods. "Odowakr proposed to declare Arbogast *Dux* of Trever, an Imperator, and support his claim, in exchange for surrender."

Hildrik breathes out aloud. "A third Imperator! As if we didn't have enough trouble. It's all become tangled like a knot on a ship's rope." He taps on the table. "Odowakr said nothing of the sort to my father. Maybe if Meroweg finds out about it, he might change his…"

"No," Basina interrupts him. "It's too late for that. Two weeks is barely enough to reach Trever with the entire *fyrd* if we march out tomorrow. You need to take over. You need to cut that knot. And do it fast."

Hildrik reaches for the last sausage left on the plate. He munches on it in silence, then turns to me.

"I will need your help with this, Octa."

"Me? No — I will have no part in —"

"Yes, Octa," says Basina, her stare drilling into the back of my head, seductive and insistent. "*We* will need your help with this."

CHAPTER XVII
THE LAY OF MEROWEG

In the middle of a fallow field, several miles outside of town, on the other side of the river, rises a great mound of earth, taller than the tallest tree. Bound by a rim of weathered drystone, surrounded by ancient tombs popping out of the grass, it spreads the same air of piety and mystery as the old barrow mounds I know from the hills of Britannia. Somehow, even in the middle of the summer day, its base is shrouded in thick mist, rising from the marshes around it.

In a land that's been inhabited by Roman citizens for centuries, this is one of the few, and the most conspicuous, remnants of the ancient heathens who lived here before Rome's conquest. When the Franks moved to Tornac, they took the tombs to have belonged to the ancestors of some of their tribes, and so they chose to venerate it as their own; they started burying their own dead around it and built an altar to their gods on its top.

It is by this altar that we watch Meroweg and his retinue arrive in an ox-driven cart along the riverside road. The cart stops at the bottom of the mound. Meroweg leaps out and climbs hurriedly to the top, followed by half a dozen guards.

"Make it quick," he snaps. "I don't have all day."

"Yes, of course, *Rex*," I say with a bow. "Once again, we are most grateful you've agreed to this ceremony."

The Blood of the Iutes

"Yes, yes." He waves his hand. "And you're sure your folk will be fine with that? I wouldn't want to risk my good relations with Aeric over some youths' tryst."

"No, we have been betrothed for years," says Ursula. "Everything is arranged for us back home — it's just…"

"I understand, you want to be wedded before the coming war." Meroweg nods. "Clodeswinthe and I did the same before her father had us march against Aetius."

The ruse was a simple one. I did not think it would work, at first, but Hildrik knew his father well, and thought carefully about the plan's every detail. In Tornac, the conditions of the settlement did not allow for heathen priests — this was still a Christian town, albeit with only one church left, and only a handful of the congregation still living with its walls. In their absence, it was up to Meroweg to conduct the few important rites for his subjects — including prominent weddings, such as that of the son of an allied king and his Briton betrothed.

Ursula embraced the idea with surprising enthusiasm; it was she who eventually convinced a reluctant Meroweg of our impatience. We were about to join Meroweg in his march on Gaul — Betula, her *Hiréd*, and my remaining Iutes; after our experiences at Trever, we feared the upcoming war with the *walhas*. We both wanted to be wedded before our death. First in the pagan way, before the gods of my people, then at the town's small church, in a Christian manner. Back in Britannia, we claimed, our marriage would have united the houses of Iutish kings and Briton city magistrates; here, it was just an expression of our great love. The story impressed the king enough to agree to our request — and Hildrik slyly

[442]

suggested the great barrow mound as the only place fit to celebrate our union.

Meroweg, in a white, ceremonial robe thrown over his tunic, marches down a short avenue between two rows of Iutes — my riders on one side, six of Betula's *Hiréd* on the other. Together with the three axemen guarding Hildrik and Basina, the forces of the conspirators easily outnumber Meroweg's retinue; he suspects nothing. Even if he doesn't trust me and the other Iutes, he's certain his own son and his men would defend him if this wedding was to turn out to be some kind of Iutish trap...

The *Rex* reaches the altar, a great flat stone, carved with red runes and scattered over with sprigs of oak and mistletoe. Hildrik helps him light up a small charcoal brazier. Meroweg nods at me and Ursula to come closer and throws more herbs and sprigs on the brazier. The humid air stifles the flames; the brazier belches black smoke. Meroweg mumbles an invocation to the divine couple, Wodan — whom he calls Wuotan — and Frige, whom he calls Frouwa.

Ursula squeezes my arm, grinning. She's been oddly excited about the ceremony all day, even though for her it is doubly fake — after all, she does not believe in the heathen gods. As for me, I'm still not sure what to make of it all. I take a deep breath; the thick smoke enters my nostrils, making me dizzy. My father never instilled in me piety for any gods — neither Roman nor Iutish — even though he himself often played the role performed by Meroweg today, that of the high priest, when the custom called for it. But does my lack of piety mean the wedding is any less real? Meroweg is not a fake priest; he might be in a hurry, but I can see he's taking his duty seriously, more seriously than my father ever did. The ritual he performs, the names he invokes, are real enough. What if I really *am* marrying Ursula today?

I realise that even this pretend wedding is yet another event in my life that my father never got to experience. His beloved Rhedwyn was abducted by Wortimer on the day of their betrothal, and she died in Wortimer's thrall; he never married my mother. And here I am, aged eighteen, being wedded to my best friend as a mere ruse for regicide.

What is happening to my life?

"Have you the gifts?" asks Meroweg.

"*Ja*, we do," says Hildrik. He and Basina step up, each holding a bundle of cloth. Basina unravels hers first: it is a small, round shield, to be presented to me by Ursula as symbol of protection. Then Hildrik shows the gift that I am to give to Ursula: a brand-new *seax*, to show I am ready to fight for her and our family. It is the only weapon allowed on the hallowed top of the mound; all the guards were required to leave their swords and axes by the ox cart at the foot of the barrow. Though ceremonial, with a finely carved handle, the blade is still sharp.

It is now time to finish the ceremony. Meroweg moves from behind the altar and comes up to us with a length of white linen embroidered with runes and those strange bee symbols that are so ubiquitous in Tornac.

"Your hands," he says.

Ursula and I reach out. I glance at Hildrik nervously. With the fasting of hands, my marriage to Ursula will be bound in the eyes of the gods, even if this *is* all just a trap…

Meroweg wraps the linen around our extended hands and begins another chant. Hildrik nods. Ursula and I grab Meroweg's hands in ours. He looks up, surprised.

"This is not how —" he starts.

Hildrik whirls the *seax* in his grip and thrusts it under his father's ribs with a grunt. Blood splatters the white robe and the white linen cloth. Meroweg cries out and pulls back, grasping at Hildrik's wrist. They struggle for a while, before Basina bashes Meroweg on the head with the round shield. Blood and brain spurt from the crushed skull and onto my robe, but Meroweg, miraculously, still stands.

"I… am… the king… of Franks!" he grunts. He pushes Basina away, tears the *seax* from his side and turns it against Hildrik. He lunges forward, missing his son by an inch. The blade goes past me. I grab his wrist and twist; the sword falls to the floor. Ursula stoops to pick it up and throws it back to Hildrik. He grabs his father by the hair and slices his throat.

I step back, feeling sick. I look around; Hildrik's guards and the Iutes draw hidden blades from under their robes and make short work of Meroweg's unarmed retinue. The last of the Franks tries to run away down the hill, to the weapons cart; Basina picks up a knife from the ground. The blade lands in the Frank's back, as true as if it was an arrow shot from her Hunnish bow.

The Blood of the Iutes

I drop to my knees, heaving. I look at my hands — they're stained with royal blood. It really happened. In the presence of the gods, before Wodan and Frige, we have just killed a king.

Hildrik kneels down by his father and, with a sharp slash of the knife, cuts off his long locks. He then looks up to me. His face is grey. He's breathing heavily.

"It is done," he says. "There's no turning back now. Thank you for your help, *aetheling*."

"You are welcome…" I bow deeply. Everyone around us kneels, even Basina. "…*Rex* Hildrik."

The water in the bowl is as clear now as it was when I drew it from the well; my hands are clean, too, they must be, even if I can't tell by the dim light of the oil lamp, but still I can't stop scrubbing them.

Meroweg was just a man. A powerful man of his tribe to call himself a *Rex*, but still, just a man; if I met him in battle as an enemy, I would have no qualms about slaying him. But this wasn't a battle, and he wasn't *my* enemy. He was my father's friend, an ally to the Iutes; he freed Iutish captives and welcomed me to his household. And then I helped his son slaughter him like a sacrificial bull… because of politics, because of diplomacy.

Maybe I am so shattered by what I've done because Meroweg reminded me so much of my own father, another

Drihten turned *Rex*, another ruler of a heathen tribe living on Roman soil; I, too, grew up not knowing my father; I, too, disagree with his politics, with the way he rules the tribe. What if, through some twist of cruel fates, I would one day be forced to do to my father what Hildrik has done to his? Would I be able to do it as easily?

Somebody knocks. Thinking it must be Ursula, returning from a night of drinking with Audulf, I open the door — only to see Basina, wearing the same tight, thin tunic she wore on the night before we first left Tornac.

She lets herself in before I can say anything and sits down on my bed.

"I have never seen a funeral so quick," she says. "Certainly not of someone so important."

I detect a tinge of regret in her voice, maybe even shame?

"You didn't seem so fond of Meroweg yesterday when you bashed in his skull."

"A king deserves ceremony," she replies, shaking her head. "I know we're in a hurry, but Hildrik could have at least let his father burn before putting him in the ground."

To properly dispose of Meroweg's body, would have taken a great pyre and at least three days of burning, followed by a prescribed period of mourning. But Hildrik did not want to give the Franks — and the king's surviving wife, Queen Clodeswinthe — too much time to wonder what happened to their monarch when he and his retinue perished on the way to the barrow mound; or how a troop of River Franks found itself so near the Salian capital.

This was the official explanation, and it fell on fertile ground. The Salians never trusted their eastern brethren; they knew Hildebert was growing in strength, expanding his army and territory — at the cost of the *walhas* at first, true, but now that he had Coln and all the land around it, was it so unexpected that he'd want to strike West? Wodan knew the Salians would do the same in his place... And what better way to sow chaos in the enemy ranks than to kill their *Rex* on the eve of a campaign?

And now, like a weathervane changing direction upon the evening breeze, the mood switched in an instant. Instead of marching south, against the Roman garrisons in Gaul, the *fyrd* was clamouring to march east — against the River Franks, and their ally, Odowakr. This last piece of information was new to everyone, including Meroweg's advisors, but they had no reason to disbelieve the king's son — and myself.

"That was the news I was bringing from Trever," I told them, when we brought Meroweg's body back from the barrow mound. "I knew Odowakr and Hildebert were plotting something against you and your *Rex*, but I had no idea they would be so bold..."

So far, Hildrik's plan was working out perfectly. Nobody, not even the royal widow, suspected anything, or if they did, they were keeping quiet. Hildrik was the only rightful heir, and without a *witan*, there wasn't anyone to object to his quick ascension to the throne, or the way he handled the succession.

"It makes me worried about tomorrow," says Basina. "I didn't want our special day to be some hasty ritual in the middle of a war camp that's being dismantled."

"Tomorrow?" I ask. "What do you mean, 'special day'?"

"You haven't heard?" She looks up. "A king needs his queen."

"You're getting married? Who's conducting the ceremony?"

"Queen Clodeswinthe. It's the last official duty she'll perform before Hildrik takes over the rule of the tribe." She laughs, seeing the expression on my face. "Don't look so sad," she says. She puts her hand on my cheek. "Hildrik is the king of the Franks now. You are still only a king's son. I have made my choice."

"I… I understand." I move away, but she grabs my tunic and pulls me back to her.

"I am not his wife yet," she whispers and leans to kiss me. I give in for a moment, then push her away, gasping for breath.

"What are you —"

She grins. "You deserve a reward for everything you've done," she says. She unties her tunic and takes it off. It's the first time I have seen her like this; her naked body is as perfect as her face. She smells of smoke and soap. My breath quickens. My manhood stretches my breeches to bursting.

The Blood of the Iutes

"You brought back my bow," she says, and I think of how her lips resemble that Hunnish weapon. She takes my hand and puts it on her breast. "Ursula told me what you did to get it back." I caress her; she inhales sharply and lets out a quiet moan. "And then you convinced my betrothed to make that one final step to become the most powerful man in Gaul."

We kiss again. I push her gently down onto the bed. "He's only a *Rex* of Salians," I say between kisses.

"For now," she says. "But a man who's willing to kill his own father and lie to his mother and the entire tribe to get what he wants is destined for greatness."

I let her nipple out of my mouth.

"What's wrong?" she asks.

"He sliced his father's throat in cold blood just because he disagreed with his politics," I say. "What's he going to do if he finds out what we did?"

With a laugh, she unfastens her breeches and kicks them off to the floor.

"Hildrik knows," she says. "He, too, thinks you deserve a reward for what you did for him."

She grabs my head and pulls me down between her powerful thighs. Somewhere at the back of my head, a nagging voice tells me she's only doing this to distract me from wondering if I did the right thing; to ensure my loyalty to her and her husband. But all rational thought disappears as soon as I breathe in her moist lust and lose my mind inside her.

We crawl through the undergrowth, javelins in hand, in a long, spread-out line. Six feet to my right, Ursula and my Iute riders — six feet to my left, Betula and her *Hiréd*; we are the centre of the wide crescent, the arms of which, disappearing deeper into the wood, are formed of the Frankish hunters, more experienced in this wood.

One last hunt before we march out. My heart's not in it — it's another unnecessary delay; but the woodsmen of Charcoal Forest brought news of a great herd of deer appearing suddenly on the western outskirts, led by a magnificent old stag; the Frankish augurs interpreted it as Donar's blessing for the campaign, and for Hildrik's succession, a well-needed signal that Meroweg's death did not anger the gods — quite the opposite. Hildrik had no choice but to announce the hunt for the stag and its hinds. There is a practical side to it — if we gather enough fresh meat today, we will have less need for forage along the way, so the Franks will be able to march faster towards Trever. And so will we — if I decide we should do so…

I can't think of a good enough reason for us to accompany the Salian *fyrd*, for me to risk the lives not just of the handful of Iute riders, but of the entire Iutish *Hiréd* on some expedition that has nothing to do with the fate of my father's kingdom. Do I really care so much about the fate of Trever — a city the existence of which I wasn't even aware of just a few months ago? Do I care *this* much about Gaul, about the Empire? Surely, I've already done more to help the Empire than anyone could expect of a boy from faraway Britannia. Is it because of that elusive quality I've heard so much about since I came here — *warrior's honour*? I must have been spending too long in the company of Hildrik and his men. The only explanation of my continuing presence here must be that I still feel bound by duty to do so; we promised to help Hildrik defeat the Saxon warband, back when he was still just a king's son, and when the warband was supposed to be just another raiding party; but the circumstances have changed so dramatically since then — does that not absolve me of my duty?

I notice that, as we creep forth, Betula is shortening the distance between us. It can't be an accident — she wants something from me.

"How many warriors did Aelle send to Odowakr's help?" she asks when she's close enough for a whisper.

"A large *ceol*, at least," I reply. "That's what the captive told me at Ake."

"Fifty men," Betula grunts.

"Is it a lot?"

"It's plenty. More than Aeric ever sent to help the Franks."

"Does it matter? I thought my father was worried about Haesta, not Aelle."

"That's because we didn't know everything. Haesta is a local threat. A nuisance on the border. Aelle is our real enemy. Since you've been gone, his war of words has only intensified. It's as if he's feeling stronger now than he's ever been in the past three years… No doubt because of these new alliances."

"And now his ally is looking to raise an Imperator of his own," I note.

"You know more about these politics than I do," she replies. "But I can only imagine how much more powerful Aelle would grow if it turns out he's bet on the right chariot. A friend of an Imperator, one with a seat so close, in Gaul… He might even reach for the *Dux*'s circlet."

We pause. There's a rustle in the ferns ahead; it's just a fox — a red streak runs across the path. The pause gives me a moment to gather my thoughts.

"Then we have no choice," I say. "We *have* to go with Hildrik and try to save Trever from falling. It's as my father feared — the tribes of Britannia got themselves entangled in the great politics of the Empire, whether we wanted to or not."

"I thought you'd already decided that we were going?" Betula asks, surprised.

"I wasn't sure." I share my doubts with her.

She smiles. "You're starting to think like a leader who cares for his men, not just for himself. It took your father years to get there."

I wasn't looking for her praise, but I feel pleasantly tickled by it. I open my mouth to respond, but another rustle in the bushes interrupts me. It's a small roe deer — not from the herd we're after, running not from us but across our way, leaping over an overturned oak in panic.

"What's going on with these animals?" asks Betula with a frown. "Something else than us is scaring them."

The earth under my feet trembles. Some great animal is heading our way — if it's the stag, or a wild boar, it'll be the heaviest I've ever seen. Betula calls at me and Ursula to the gnarled oak.

"Climb!" she cries. I've never seen her like this — almost as if she's *scared*, but what could possibly scare the valiant *Gesith*?

I order Ursula to go first, then climb after her. I reach down to Betula just as a giant brown bear storms out of the bushes. I grab her hand and pull up at the last moment — the bear's paw swipes inches from her rear.

It's easy to see why the bear is so furious — half of a broken javelin sticks out of its side, leaving a bloody trail. The beast stands on its hind legs and leans against the oak's trunk, sniffing. It's blinded in one eye by a fresh scar; other, shallow wounds pock its hide. Somewhere in the forest, it must have fought a terrible battle with the Frankish hunters, who would have stumbled upon it by accident deep in the wilderness. The bear's presence explains the arrival of the deer herd in this part of the woods — but where did the bear itself come from?

"Hold me," says Betula, nodding at her waist. I grab her and hold on as tight as I can. She leans forward over the bear, aims her javelin carefully and throws. The narrow blade hits the animal's head just an inch over the healthy eye. It adds another terrible scar to the collection but fails to penetrate the skull. The bear drops back to its feet and shakes its head with an angry grunt.

"Next tree," says Betula. "Quickly."

The three of us move over the branches to a tall beech. Betula, despite having only one arm, climbs the fastest. I glance over my shoulder — the bear now starts to climb the oak we just left; if we had stayed there, it would have already reached us…

"Ursula, your turn," Betula orders.

Ursula nods. She throws without aiming — the target, now facing us with its flank, is big enough. The javelin strikes near the heart, wobbles, and falls off; a spurt of bright blood means the wound is serious. The bear groans and falls off the tree. Its fall shakes the forest.

Before it manages to stand back up, I leap back, from branch to branch, drawing my long knife. "*Aetheling*, no!" Betula cries, but she can't let go of the tree to stop me or she'd fall herself. I reach the oak, descend to the lowest branch — and jump down on the beast's back. I grasp at its fur as it rears and roars, trying to throw me off. I stab it repeatedly in the neck and sides, bathing in the beast's blood as if in a baptismal fountain. The stench of the beast's anger and fear are overpowering; I lose myself in it just as I lost

The Blood of the Iutes

myself in Basina's smell. At last, the bear succeeds, and I land in the ferns; but by now, it's too weak to go after me — and by now, we're no longer alone.

Hildrik and Basina ride out onto the glade. Basina pierces the bear's healthy eye with an arrow, and Hildrik throws a deft javelin straight into its heart. With a final mighty groan, the bear stands on its rear legs, waves its front paws futilely in the air, and falls on its side.

Betula leaps down from the tree and helps me up from the ferns.

"Are you alright, *aetheling*?"

I'm covered in blood, but none of it is my own.

"You're just as mad as your father," she says. "One swipe of that paw could've torn you in half!"

"What a hunt!" Hildrik cries, excitedly, riding up to us. He dismounts; his face is flushed red. "A bear! In these woods! This is an even better augury than the stag."

"How so?" I ask, rubbing my aching back.

"The bear is the messenger of the gods," he replies. "Sacred among the tribes beyond Rhenum that form Odowakr's army," he replies. "The Saxons, the Alemanns, the Longbeards... It is why their best warriors wear bearskin shirts. And we slayed it together, Iutes and Franks, side by side. This must be a message from the gods!"

He shakes me by the shoulders and I raise a weak cheer. *Bearskin shirts.* As I look at the blood-splattered fur of the fallen bear, and the strange awe I felt in its presence recedes, I feel an inkling of an idea appear in my mind.

"I'm starting to get sick of the sight of this place," I say, looking at the walls of Tolbiac, looming in a thin dark line on the flat horizon. "I'm now as familiar with it as with Robriwis."

"It's all new to me," says Betula. "I can't wait to see it. I can't wait to see Trever."

Everything in Gaul makes her excited like a little child — and makes me seem like a seasoned traveller, though I've only been here a few months. Some of her enthusiasm is rubbing off on me; we talked at length about the harbours of Gaul, of the great roads criss-crossing the land, we admired the mysterious darkness of the Charcoal Forest, and marvelled at the ruined *villas* and palaces of the countryside.

"I wish I could show all this to Croha," Betula adds. "She always wants to see new things."

"Don't expect too much," says Ursula. "Tolbiac's no bigger than Dorowern — and just as empty."

"And I don't think we'll have much time for admiring its wonders, such as they are," says Audulf. "We're late as it is."

The Blood of the Iutes

Somewhere between us and the town sprawls Weldelf's camp — hidden from sight by a fold of terrain. They're waiting for us. We have not concealed our arrival — it would have been impossible to hide a thousand-strong *fyrd* on the march — but Weldelf and his men are still not aware of the true purpose of our arrival.

Neither, for that matter are we. I'm still not certain what Hildrik's plans are. We've managed to avoid a fight until now, bypassing the villages and campsites of the River Franks along the way. But the thousand Salians marching with us demand plunder and glory — and bloody vengeance for their king's death, and Hildrik will have to grant it to them before we can turn towards Trever. Weldelf's is the last clan left in our way. If we want to have a battle, it has to be here.

I'm hoping I can get some answers from him now — as Hildrik and Basina ride from the direction of Tolbiac.

"You were right," says the new *Rex* of the Franks. "It will be a short fight. But I want it to be as brief and painless as possible. I need to preserve my men for more important battles. And we need to keep Hildebert from finding out about why we're here. Any ideas?"

I wince and scratch the back of my head. "You want us to plan another subterfuge."

"That would be for the best. Meet me in my hut later," he says. We set up our camp at an abandoned farmstead, half a day's march away from Tolbiac.

As they ride off, Basina gives me the knowing, impish smile she's been giving me ever since the night before her wedding. My cheeks and ears burn as if branded with hot irons.

"He's more like Aeric than any barbarian chieftain," I say, staring into Basina's back, receding into the distance. Every dot and blemish on that back is etched forever in my memory. "It's all tricks and ruses with him. Most warlords would just use their numbers to wipe out Weldelf's camp."

"I can brew some henbane, if that helps," offers Betula.

"You know how to brew henbane?"

"Of course," she replies proudly. "I am the *Gesith*. The keeper of the secret. We found the herbs in the Charcoal Forest. Enough to make a barrel."

"That's… good to know," I say. "But I don't think we'll need it tomorrow."

"You already have something in mind?" she asks with a wry smile. "That's so like your father."

"We don't have many options," I reply. "It's a flat, open land, with no place to make an ambush — and a city full of civilians in the middle…" I raise my finger. "I think I've got it." I look to the sun and estimate we have some three, four hours until sundown, more than enough for a well-rested pony…

I turn back to Betula.

The Blood of the Iutes

"You said you wanted to see Tolbiac — you may get your wish sooner than you expected."

I don't know the size of armies Hildrik used to command in his exile in Thuringia, but a thousand warriors is a mass far beyond his control. Fortunately for him, Meroweg knew how to select and train good officers; a Iute *fyrd* this size would just be a multitude of clans, each with its own chieftain at its head, moving more or less in the general direction of the enemy, before engaging them in a mess of individual skirmishes all over the battlefield. Not so for the Salians; Meroweg must have used his experience from accompanying the Roman armies at Maurica when he devised the way his army was divided, not into clans, but into cohorts, each commanded by one of his trusted generals.

One of those generals turns out to be our old friend, Ingomer; at my request, we are assigned to his cohort, which is supposed to charge together with Hildrik's own unit in the centre. The dawn raid on Weldelf's camp is not going to be an epic battle — we outnumber the River Franks at least five to one — but it will be the first, and possibly only, test of how well Hildrik can command his father's army before we reach Trever.

At the break of dawn, we march out in silence and darkness. To our left, Hildrik leads the Salian *Hiréd*, his palace guards, and a hundred other warriors, all related to him — or rather, his father — by blood. This force alone would likely be enough to deal with Weldelf, especially if my ruse worked. To our right, vanishing into darkness, is a cohort led by

Meroweg's brother-in-law, Sigemer. I know nothing about this man, or his warriors; I can only hope the dead king did not choose him as general simply because of the blood ties. Of all of Meroweg's commanders, Sigemer struck me as the most hot-headed — and the most gullible. He was the quickest to believe the story of the River Franks' treachery, and it took considerable effort for Hildrik and his advisors to stop him from destroying every village and encampment we encountered as we travelled through Hildebert's territory.

"If this was a proper battle, I'd be worried about having him on our flank," says Ingomer, nodding towards Sigemer's vanguard. "He cares little for strategy. I'd bet you a solid he will be the first to reach the enemy."

"I wouldn't take that bet," I say. Sigemer's men are already far ahead of us; they're wasting their strength on this unnecessary race — we still have some way to go before Weldelf's camp is in charging range.

"Yet there is a place even for men like him on a battlefield," I note. "When Hannibal was at Cannae…"

"Who?" asks Ingomer.

"I'm sorry — a general from the ancient days of Rome —"

"I jest," Ingomer says, laughing. He slaps me on the shoulder. "I've spent enough time among the *walhas* to have heard of all their old wars and heroes. Aetius had us all read Livy before Maurica… Or rather, have his slaves read it to us. I didn't know Latin well enough yet back then."

The Blood of the Iutes

"You also fought at Maurica?"

"We were all there, boy... Every Frank who could carry a blade went to Maurica that year, to fight on one side or the other. So few returned..."

His eyes turn misty, and I remember that only a few nights ago, I helped this man's nephew kill his brother... Ingomer's reaction to the recent events was a mysterious one. He was away on some errand on the day of the assassination — and he has remained morosely silent on the matter since the funeral. If he suspected any foul play, he said nothing about it, seemingly content with Hildrik's quick ascension to the vacant throne. Maybe he, too, secretly disagreed with the direction of Meroweg's politics?

"Would you have led your cohort against Gaul, if so ordered?" I ask him.

He winces. "I would, but with no enthusiasm. Meroweg was my *Rex*. To defy his command would have been to defy the tribe itself. It was enough that I tried to talk with the *walhas* without his clear permission."

"Talk? Is that what you were doing?"

"The news of my brother's death reached me in Bagac, where I was trying to negotiate some kind of new settlement for the Franks south of the border, one that might placate Meroweg... But I doubt I would've managed it in time."

"Your services may be needed again," I say, "when Hildrik negotiates a deal with Aegidius."

He chuckles. "Let's not get ahead of ourselves. We've got a war to win first."

We reach the top of the ridge separating us from Weldelf's camp. The sound of Hildrik's war horn booms across the pale-rose sky. Ingomer takes his own horn and repeats the call, echoed throughout the frontline to our left and right — and far out in front, where Sigemer's cohort disappeared in the gloom. The Franks start into a run — and the Iutes trot before them. I take the lance out of the holster. The fires of the River Frank camp twinkle like stars on the plain before us… and like stars at dawn, they are going out, one by one.

"Sigemer must have reached them already," I say.

We have reached halfway towards Weldelf's camp when a warrior runs out of the gloom, screaming, flailing one arm — the other hangs limp at his side, spurting blood. Another one follows, makes a few staggering steps, then falls face-down in the grass.

"These are Sigemer's men!" cries Ingomer. "Something's gone wrong."

I call for the Iutes to gather around me as we charge down the gentle slope. More of Sigemer's warriors appear, running away from Weldelf's camp. As we move closer, I can see more clearly now what's happening. Sigemer's cohort, having pushed deep into the enemy camp, got itself surrounded by the River Franks, and are now being slowly butchered.

"What happened to the plan?" asks Betula. "It's as if they're waiting for us!"

"Obviously, the ruse has failed," I say grimly.

Hildrik's horn sounds again. Six hundred Salian throats rise in a war cry and charge at the camp from all sides. I grind my teeth and lower the lance. "Skirt the edges of the camp, and kill anyone trying to get away," I tell my Iutes. "You don't want to get tangled in *that*," I say, pointing at the slaughter in the middle with the tip of my blade.

"Ursula, Audulf, Seawine, Betula — with me!"

We form into what Betula calls "the boar's head", with a wedge of riders in the front and two tight fists of the *Hiréd* in the back. We thrust our way through the meagre defences to the centre of the camp. I glance once over my shoulder to see if Betula's warriors are following the order; many of them seemed reluctant at first to heed someone they still only remembered as the cowardly, bookish boy, not worthy to be called a warrior, and did not believe the stories they heard about my adventures in Gaul. They still look to Betula first, to see if she agrees with my command.

Most of the River Franks get out of our way — mounted and bunched up together, armoured and armed with lances and swords, we are a more difficult target than the massed ranks of Hildrik's footmen following in our wake, rushing into battle half-naked, waving spears, axes and long knives.

"Weldelf's tent," I point with the lance. A dozen River Frank guards form a tight line of shields and spears around the tent, not quite a wall — for there is no place for it — but enough to make us swerve aside and make place for Betula. Her *Hiréd* smash into the line. All their doubts perish in the face of the enemy. This is what they've been training for all their lives: a fierce battle against a tough opposition, not a bunch of forest bandits. Within moments, they make a break through and clear a gap several men wide. We turnabout for another charge before the gap closes in. Our ponies overturn the braziers and trample the campfires, and for a moment all is darkness and chaos.

Weldelf leaps out of nowhere with more guards — not from the tent, but from some hideout nearby I haven't noticed before. He's holding a great two-handed axe, of the sort Audulf is so fond of. I know what damage the weapon can do to a pony, and I'd rather not risk it; I ride up to him, holster the lance and dismount.

"You!" Weldelf gives me a confused look but doesn't take his grip off the axe. He glances at Audulf and Ursula, still mounted at my sides. "I knew it. You never went to Coln."

Around us, the overturned braziers and campfires set the tent cloths ablaze. Against this fiery background, Weldelf, with his great axe and long hair flowing in the wind, appears like a figure out of some legend.

"Give up, chieftain," I say. I shield my eyes from the flames. "Or all of you will be slaughtered. Hildrik can't let any of you survive to tell the tale of this battle."

"Too late for that," he scoffs. "I sent out riders to Hildebert long before your attack."

The Blood of the Iutes

"How did you know?"

"I saw right through that little scheme of Hildrik's."

"It was *my* scheme."

He laughs. "Then you need to learn to plot better, youngling. I told you I wasn't fond of hiding behind stone walls."

He wasn't supposed to be here. He was supposed to be in Tolbiac with his entire retinue, negotiating the handover of the town to the River Franks. That was the plan I agreed to with the Tolbiac magistrates the day before: an urgent, formal invitation to overnight talks.

It took some effort to convince the town's officials to trust me, even after I showed them the Imperial seal — and even more to make them trust that Hildrik and his Salians were not just another warband of barbarians coming to conquer them. At the least, I hoped the invitation would have resulted in Weldelf's clan not having a commander when we attacked. At best, there was a chance that their best warriors would get trapped behind Tolbiac's gates until we destroyed their brethren outside.

Not only has none of this happened, it seems my ruse warned Weldelf of an approaching attack. I thought too little of him. I thought he was just a primitive barbarian warlord — and scores of Salian warriors have paid the price.

"Drop that axe then, Weldelf," I say. My voice falters. The flames grow nearer; I can feel their heat on my face and hands. "Tell your men to surrender. If Hildebert knows about everything anyway, there's no more point to this carnage. We will let you go free."

"I am a Frank! Wuotan awaits me! I surrender to none!" He roars and charges at me. I try to leap back, but the flames bar my way. An arrow whizzes past my ear and strikes him on the shoulder. His arm jerks back, but he doesn't stop. He steps forward again and raises the axe to strike. I glance to my sides — Ursula, still on horseback, is too close to make good use of the lance. Audulf drops his lance and struggles to draw the big axe from his back; he is too far to help me. Basina, who shot the arrow, is momentarily distracted by another enemy approaching her. It's only me against Weldelf: a green boy against a battle-hardened clan chieftain.

I draw my sword just as Weldelf's axe falls. The blade grinds against blade; the impact makes my arms shudder. The flames lick my back. Sweat turns the grip slippery. I step aside, letting Weldelf's momentum propel him forward. He stops just before falling into the burning remains of a tent, recovers, and turns back. I spot a spear shaft on the ground, its tip in flames. I pick it up and wave it before me, keeping the chieftain at bay.

Another of Basina's arrows hits him in the back. The fine mail shirt holds the arrowhead, but the impact is enough to push Weldelf towards me. I raise the spear shaft and stab his chest with the burning tip. He cries out in pain and anger. I hear the sizzling flesh even over the din of battle, and the sickening smell of burned meat reaches my nostrils. He grabs the spear and wrestles it out of my hand, then raises the axe to one last strike. Between his left hand, still holding on to the burning shaft, and his right, raised high over his head, I spot an opening.

"*Aetheling!*"

Betula leaps through the flame to my help, just as I thrust forth and skewer Weldelf with my *spatha*. The old Roman blade eats through Frankish mail as if it was cloth. Weldelf's axe falls feebly on my head and bounces off my Legionnaire's helmet.

"They're all... using you... boy..." Weldelf says as he falls down.

I look up to see Basina notching a new arrow on her Hunnic bow. She nods at me with a grin and turns to find a new target. All around me, Weldelf's men are getting massacred as the ring of Hildrik's *fyrd* tightens on the centre of the camp. A few River Franks break through and try to run across the oat field; they're soon caught by my Iutes and destroyed. One of the enemy warriors runs out from the brawl straight at me, growling, and waving a *seax*. Betula fells him with her throwing axe.

"Get back on that pony," she says. "It's not yet safe here."

"Wait," I say. "There's one more thing I need to do. Come help me."

We storm into Weldelf's tent before it's engulfed by flames. To my relief, they're still there, just as I remembered: the bearskins, strewn on the tent's floor.

"Pick them up," I say. "As much as you can carry."

"What for?"

"No time to explain. Maybe it's nothing — or maybe it's the best idea I've yet had in this war."

The Blood of the Iutes

CHAPTER XVIII
THE LAY OF FALCO

"This did not quite go to plan," grunts Hildrik, looking at the pile of corpses heaped high over the River Franks' camp. Most of them are Weldelf's men, but there are at least fifty Salians among the dead; double that number is injured. For the second time in as many months, the priests and acolytes of Tolbiac have to take care of the Salian wounded.

A few new graves have been dug in the town's cemetery, in the corner dedicated to the heathen dead. These will be the resting places for Sigemer and a couple of his noble clansmen, slain in the first charge on the enemy camp. There's no space for the rest of our dead, and no time to bury them all. A thin layer of dirt and lime scattered over the mound of bodies must be all that will keep them from crows and wolves, at least until we return from Trever.

"I'm sorry you lost so many of your kin," I say.

Hildrik scowls. "More plunder to share for the rest of us — and I still have enough men left to deal with Odowakr."

"And *Herr* Sigemer?"

He lowers his voice. "This, I'm glad of. I never liked my uncle. With him alive, my mother could still wield some influence over the tribe. He insisted we march on Hildebert instead of Odowakr, and I feared he would eventually convince the others... *And* he was a terrible commander. The dead are his fault. Now I can put someone more suitable in charge of Camarac..."

"You sound almost as if you're glad our plan failed."

"Not at all." He looks to the North, along the road to Coln. "Hildebert knows. That means we will have to look over our shoulder all the time. I will need to leave a substantial rear guard to slow him down."

"Not necessarily," I say.

He glances back at me. "You have yet another idea?"

"The *walhas* are on our side as long as I have this," I say, drawing the legate's letter from my satchel. "And there are still some soldiers left between here and Trever."

"That little fortress on the pass," says Hildrik.

"Icorig," I nod. "I talked to their *Praetor* on the way here. I can talk to him again."

"This time, I'm coming with you."

Two days later, with the *fyrd* camped in the foothills of Arduenna, at enough distance from Icorig to not be considered an immediate threat, Hildrik and I ride up to the fortress's northern gate.

"Back so soon?" *Praetor* Falco asks, once we meet in his room in the barracks. He looks at Hildrik. "Weren't you supposed to bring back Hildebert and his army?"

"Change of plans," I say. "Hildebert's army… might still come — but not as friends."

The *Praetor*'s eyebrow rides high. "I'm not even going to ask. Am I to give my fort over to Salians now?"

"That will not be necessary," says Hildrik. "We come as allies, marching to relieve the siege of Trever."

"Out of goodness of your hearts, I suppose."

"I'd lie if I said we're not counting on some recognition for our efforts," Hildrik replies. "But I have enough gold for my needs right now — your towns and villages are safe."

Back at Tolbiac, Hildrik went to check on the pots of gold and silver, buried in a secret spot outside the town walls by Pinnosa, as payment for the escort to Trever; satisfied that the gold was still there, Hildrik left it in the ground. "No need to burden ourselves with it now," he told me, "we'll get it out on the way back."

"We would, however, like to make use of the walls of your fortress," I interject. "To protect our rear — and yours — as we move south. Temporarily, of course."

The *Praetor* laughs. "Haven't you seen what the place looks like? I have twice as many people to feed as this fort was built for. And you still want to add more?"

The Blood of the Iutes

"Not add," I say. "Replace."

He stops laughing abruptly and leans back to the table. "You want me to leave my fort to your barbarian horde? How is that different from just giving it to Hildebert?"

"I'm not Hildebert," says Hildrik. "We Salians did not conquer the land we live on — we accepted it as gift from Rome, and we've been your allies ever since. We know how to honour agreements — as long as you *walhas* honour yours."

"Our warriors are fresh, well-fed and rested," I add. "Yours are hungry, tired and no doubt bored of sitting here waiting for the enemy. Come with us instead. Help us save your kin in Trever."

He rubs his chin in thought. "I put little trust in the oaths of a barbarian warlord," he says. "You, I trust even less," he adds, pointing at me. "You carry the Imperator's seal, but you're a nobody, coming from nowhere. You say you're the son of some king from a distant land, but I only have your word for it. And on that word, you want me to give you the keys to my fortress?"

He scoffs and leans back. "But you're right about one thing. We *are* bored and tired. To our north and to our south, a war rages, and we're stuck in the middle with nothing to do but sharpen our swords, training muster, and milling grain for our potage. For years, we saw warbands and armies pass us by. We told ourselves that we were valiant and important, guarding this vital pass, but the truth is, we were just too insignificant and too far from anywhere for anyone to care about us."

"Then you'll agree to our proposition?" I ask eagerly.

"I'll think about it. First, I need to send a courier to Tolbiac, to see if there's any truth to what you're saying."

"Of course," Hildrik agrees. "You can take my Thuringian steed."

"Our Gaulish ones will do just fine," Falco replies with a scowl. "I still have some left. Now leave before I change my mind."

The *Praetor* is not one for wasting time. Soon after we leave the fortress, a courier gallops past us, leaving us in a thick cloud of dust.

"He'll do it," says Hildrik.

"How do you know?" I ask.

"I know a warrior itching for glory when I see one," he replies. "There's a fire in this *Praetor* that's been left smouldering for too long. He could almost be one of us."

"I told him the exact same thing last time. He's more like a Frank — or a Iute — than a Roman."

He smiles and pats me on the shoulder. "You know, I never understood why my father, and Clodio before him, insisted on an alliance with your people. I can see now what they saw in you."

"You look terrible," says Ursula.

"I'm just tired, that's all."

We all are. My bones ache. My shoulders burn. My backside is sore. We have been marching for the past few days at the brisk pace of a Legion. Hildrik was right — the soldiers from Icorig were all itching for a fight so badly we could barely keep up with them as they rushed towards Trever. The *fyrd* column spreads out for miles now. Last night, the slowest of the warriors camped so far from the front that we're now forced to wait for them to catch up to us before we can conquer the last stretch of the Arduenna highway, and climb the tall cliffs overlooking the Mosella valley.

"Are you sure that's all it is?" She reaches out to check my forehead for fever. "You're not burning — but you do seem ill."

"I'll be fine. It's just —"

"Yes?"

"It's not just my body that is tired. My whole mind is numb, too. I talked to *Praetor* Falco today, and I could barely string a sentence in Latin. In the end, we had to speak in broken Frankish."

"What did you talk about?"

"Nothing important," I say with a shrug. "Setting up patrols and trying to establish contact with Trever. But it was just one thing too many. These last few weeks have been a daze; plotting, conspiring, making decisions that could impact the fate of the Empire, or the Salian kingdom… It is all too much. I'm just a boy. How long has it been since we chased each other through the woods of Robriwis? Since we saw that *liburna* for the first time?"

"I…" She puts a hand to her head. "Lord's wounds, I can't even remember!" She laughs. "Three months? Four? It was just before Easter…"

"Something like that," I say. "But it feels like a lifetime. So much has happened."

"It was certainly… an adventure," she says. "And it's not over yet."

"It almost is. One way or another."

"What do you mean?"

"After Trever… We're going back home. I need rest. We all need rest."

She brushes her hair from her eyes — she hasn't cut it since we left Britannia, and now wears it loose, longer than I've ever seen. It suits her — she looks like a Frankish warlord.

"It wouldn't have anything to do with the fact that you've extracted all the possible favours from Hildrik's betrothed — I mean *wife*?"

"How did you —"

"Audulf and I came back early that night." She chuckles. "You mewed under her like a flayed cat. But now she's married, that's not going to happen ever again, is it?"

"We haven't even talked since," I admit. "But, no, that isn't why I want us to go back home."

"The war is not over yet — what about helping the Empire, what about the Goths and the Burgundians? We could still see so much more of Gaul, win so much more glory."

"What use is a handful of Iutes in the war between the Imperators?" I say. "The battles at Lugdunum and Arelate will involve tens of thousands of warriors — even Hildrik's *fyrd* will amount to little more than a mention in the chronicles, if that. Trever is the last place where we can make a difference. Besides, I can't keep the *Hiréd* away for so long. The longer Betula and her men are here, the more chance there is Aelle will try something — or have you forgotten there's a war brewing back home, too?"

"Sounds like you've made up your mind," she replies. "We *will* follow you wherever you go, as always."

"I wish you'd stop saying that," I say. "I wish I wasn't the one who needs to make all these decisions on my own."

"But you're not on your own." She leans over and gives me a warm, tight hug. "Audulf and I are always here for you. And so is Betula now. It's alright." She strokes my back. "We'll go home soon. I'm sorry — I should've noticed how much of a strain all of this was on you."

To my surprise, I sense tears running from my eyes — tears of exhaustion and relief.

"Horses," I say. "I hear horses."

Ursula pulls back and looks over my back in the direction of Trever. "It's Falco." She shields her eyes from the sun. "One horse is riderless."

I leap up, wipe my eyes and mount the pony to meet the returning Roman soldiers.

"What happened?" I ask Falco.

"Saxon foragers, a dozen of them," he replies. "We routed them, but lost Claudius."

Hildrik rides up to us. He's only wearing his breeches. "Did you get them all?"

He shakes his head. "A couple got away. Now they know we're here."

"Then there's no point wasting any more time," decides Hildrik. "We move out now, before Odowakr has a chance to strengthen his defences in the rear."

The Blood of the Iutes

"What about the others?" I ask wearily. I was hoping for at least an hour more of rest while our stragglers pulled up to the front.

"They'll have to catch up. Right now, speed is more important than numbers. Gather your Iutes, *aetheling*. We go to war!"

The rope snaps, the wooden spoke flies, released from tension, until it hits the cross-bar. A stone ball, black against the bright blue sky, soars through the air. It draws a slow, inevitable arc towards Trever's mighty walls. As it begins its descent, it accelerates until, at the end of the arc, it smashes into the stones with an earth-shattering crash. A plume of stone and brick dust shrouds the place of impact from sight for a few seconds. When the view clears, a new scar appears in the wall.

We're too late. Odowakr finished his engines sooner than I hoped. Two more machines release their loads. One, a giant *ballista*, shoots a bolt the size of a footman's pike. It hits the roof of one of the round towers, flies right through it, bursting broken tiles and wood shards up in the air, before vanishing somewhere over the city. The third machine is similar to the first one, but instead of a stone ball, it launches a basket filled with burning pitch and charcoal. The missile, leaving an arc of black smoke behind it, strikes the battlements, scattering the flaming debris all over the parapet. A defending soldier's clothes catch fire; he stumbles and falls to his death from the wall, a screaming, flailing torch.

The crews gather around the three machines, bringing them all back into place after recoil, arming them up, loading, aiming; the entire process takes ten, maybe fifteen minutes, before the missiles are released again. The barrage is slow but relentless; I can see cracks in the Trever walls forming already. Near the bridge gatehouse, where most of the missiles hit, the stone balls churned out a deep, rubble-filled fissure. There are few soldiers out on the battlements — the others must be hiding from the deadly bolts of the *ballista*. Their absence explains the other new flaw in the city's defences: the hole in the bridge is being filled in, with Odowakr's men working hard to throw great planks of oak wood over the gap. Soon, the only thing that will stand between the barbarian army and the city will be the half-ruined gatehouse. To make sure that it doesn't stand for long, a fourth siege machine is being constructed on the western side of the bridge, under the watchful eye of Odowakr's surviving engineers: a great battering ram, a beam of a mighty beech tree, bound with iron at the tip, suspended on ropes from a wheeled frame, shielded from arrows by a roof of wooden planks and animal hides.

Beyond the wall, the city burns. The flaming missiles have taken a dreadful toll, spreading the fires all over Trever, from the vaulted roofs of the bath house, to the lofty dome of the *Praetorium*. I see no *vigiles* trying to put down the fires, and I guess that at long last, the city must have run out of water — and soldiers. I imagine this, more than anything else the machines have done, has finally brought terror of the siege into the minds of the city folk. They can no longer hope to just wait it out; now, they all need to start fighting for survival — or give up the city.

The Blood of the Iutes

Most of the Saxon army is now gathered on the western side of the river, waiting either for the siege engines to make a breach in the walls, or for the ram to smash through the gate, whichever comes sooner. They are settled in several large camps along the river's edge, in a concentric crescent, with the machines in the middle of it all, surrounded by a rectangle of raised earth and a primitive stockade. The fortification is far from finished. It's unlikely Odowakr would have felt the need to defend himself from the threat of an attack from Trever — he must have started it when the news of our march from the North reached him.

Unfinished or not, the earthen wall and the stockade, the concentric lines of camps, all mean Hildrik will need to come up with something more intricate than a simple head-on attack on the engines. But it is not all bad news; the great warband gathered on the shores of Mosella may look intimidating, but if the words of the foragers seized by Falco's men in the woods are to be believed, things are not looking great for Odowakr's worn-out army.

"We're out of food," the captive says. The fact that he shares this information with us willingly, without any coercion on our side, is proof enough how low the morale of the Saxons has deteriorated. "We have to go ever deeper into the woods, ever further out into the fields to gather supplies."

The Saxons have grown restless. It is still late summer here in northern Gaul; there is some fruit and game in the woods, but the grain has not yet grown tall enough for harvest. The men we caught were emaciated, their skin covered in lesions and blemishes of famine. One of them was coughing blood.

James Calbraith

"These engines are our last chance," they told us. "The clan chieftains are grumbling. If we can't breach the walls soon, we'll just have to pack up and go home."

Perhaps worst of all, there were rumours of the Romans finally mounting a relief effort for the beleaguered city, though not even our captives truly believed in them.

"Some of our raiding parties reached the outskirts of Mettis. We were pushed back by the garrison there, but nobody saw any trace of a gathering army. Yours are the first enemy troops we've seen in months."

There is still hope, then, for *Dux* Arbogast and his trapped soldiers — but how long this hope would last, we have no way of knowing. With the entire bank of Mosella occupied by the enemy camps, it's too risky for anyone to try to reach the city the usual way — an outpost of Alemannic axemen now guards the crossing at the old bridge. When I was leaving Trever, the *Dux* assured me that the city could hold for at least a month more; but with the stone balls pounding mercilessly at the walls, the *ballista* bolts skewering the defenders, the flaming baskets spreading flame and destruction throughout the districts, how much more of this assault can they really withstand?

The machines belch their loads again. With each shot, the missiles strike with more accuracy. Two stone balls hit the same spot on the parapet wall; the second one crushes a segment of the battlement, and anyone who was unfortunate or foolish enough to hide behind it.

"I don't know much about walls and sieges," says Audulf. "But that weakened fissure can't hold for more than a couple of days, if they keep hitting it like this."

"You may be right," I say, although I'm no more of an expert in these matters.

"Don't these machines look shoddy to you?" says Ursula. "It wouldn't take much to destroy them, if we could somehow get past all those guards."

She's right; the siege engines, though devastating in their impact on the city's walls, don't appear to have been built with resilience in mind. After each shot, the crews take longer to refasten the ropes, tighten the screws, patch up the splintered wood. I consult the plans I took from Trever; I can't make out much of the engineers' strange symbols and Hunnic runes, but the drawings are clear enough. The engineers, running out of time and supplies, sacrificed quality over speed. They built their machines to last just long enough to make one breach. A single breach that would be enough for the barbarian army to pour into Trever and slay everyone inside — or force Arbogast to surrender.

"One strike of my axe and I would snap that crossbeam like a twig," boasts Audulf.

"If we *could* destroy them, it would save Hildrik having to fight his way through Odowakr's entire army," I say. "We would end this siege in one stroke."

"It's impossible," says Audulf. "Look at how many of them there are. And those fortifications…"

"It's difficult," I say. "But not *impossible*…"

"You have an idea," says Ursula, grinning. "I thought you said you were too weary to think of any more plans."

"Fortunately, I had this idea *before* my mind went numb," I reply. "I just didn't know when and how to use it — until now."

A noise coming from the direction of the *Hiréd*'s tents interrupts my final speech to the Iutes.

"What is going on there?" I ask, annoyed.

"Sounds like women arguing," notes Seawine with a lewd grin.

I listen closer — he's right. One of the voices is Betula. The other…

"Basina? What is *she* doing here?"

Hildrik's army is on the other side of the camp, getting ready to march out to face Odowakr in the final reckoning between the two warlords. Basina should be at her betrothed's — *husband's*, I correct myself — side, not here with the handful of Iutes. I walk up to see what's happening.

"Out of the question," says Betula firmly. "I don't know you or your men. I don't know how they fare in battle, or how well will they listen to my orders."

"My husband's warriors are the scourge of Gaul!" Basina protests. "I'm certain they're better fighters than some backwater chieftain's farm guards!"

"What's wrong?" I ask.

"She wants to join our mission," says Betula. "With some warriors she got from Hildrik."

"Why? Shouldn't you be by your husband's side, at the frontline, where the real fighting is?"

"We both know the real fighting will be where *you're* going," she says. "I don't want to take part in another ruse or feint. I want to be where the danger is."

I sigh and scratch my forehead. I look to Betula — she seems adamant in her resistance. I don't blame her. To accommodate Basina's sudden request, we'd have to rethink the entire plan — and it's complex enough already.

On the other hand… I miss Basina's presence. We have barely spoken since her wedding with Hildrik. All through the march, she rode in front of the Frankish column, while our small Iutish contingent was relegated to guard the rear. Having her beside me even if for just the few miles doesn't sound like such a bad idea. It might be the last time ever — if after Trever Hildrik and I part our ways…

"Our success depends on small numbers," I say. "How many men have you got?"

"A dozen, no more."

"I know where I could use a dozen men."

"Fine." Basina raises her hands. "As long as there's chance for some glory."

"Gather your warriors and meet us at the crossroad. We're moving out shortly."

Betula stares at me with an odd look as Basina walks away.

"What is it?" I ask.

"Are you sure you're not just letting your cock make your decisions for you?"

"I hope not," I reply.

"Do you really know how to use Basina and her Franks?"

"No, I don't," I admit. "I'm hoping I'll figure something out by the time we get there."

She chuckles. "I can see how hard it must be to refuse a woman like her. And why would you? The queen of the Franks would rather fight at your side than at her husband's!"

"It's only because of the plan…"

"The plan that *you* devised."

"I also devised a plan to defeat Weldelf and look how that ended."

"Not every plan will work. It's also a lesson a leader must learn." She shakes her head. "But I don't think you need any more lessons in leadership. I wish I could've been here these past few months, to see what turned a child who ran naked from a flaming hut into a battle-hardened commander."

I feel my face burn. "I'd rather you didn't remind me of that... misadventure."

"I assure you, nobody else will ever mention it again when you're back home. You have nothing in common with that boy from Hrothwulf's farm. Aeric will have to start sending more of our young to Frankia. This place changes people."

"This place *kills* people," I say. "I have lost six men since I first set out from Tornac. I buried friends. And today, if the fates turn against us, we can all end up in Wodan's Hall. This is the only thing that concerns me right now."

"It's a warrior's fate to face death each day," Betula replies, and makes the sign of a cross — reminding me she's a Christian and doesn't believe in Wodan and his flying riders. "And it's a commander's duty to worry about his warriors." She pats me on the shoulder. "You'll do fine. Go back to your men and finish that speech."

"How long do we have to wait?" Ursula whispers.

"I don't know. Ask her," I reply, nodding at Betula. "The idea may be mine, but the execution is all hers."

There's a relief, a compelling comfort — in being able to depend on someone as experienced as Betula for once. Now that she and the *Hiréd* are with us, I no longer need to be the one making all the decisions in battle. Ever since we left Tornac, I've been deferring to her in everything, from tactics to weapons maintenance. She might claim I've become a war chief, but to me, it feels like I'm once again the boy in training, back in Cantia, asking *Hlaefdige* Betula for advice on how to hold a spear or how to flank an enemy on a hill.

Ursula rolls her eyes. "You don't need to hold on to her tunic all the time, you know," she says. "You've achieved so much since we came to Gaul. You can decide for yourself."

"Maybe I don't want to," I reply with a weak smile. "Besides, she's much more experienced in these matters than I am — why not make use of this knowledge?"

"My knowledge tells me to be quiet," Betula snaps from her hiding place. "The whole forest can hear your prattling."

"I'm just wondering…" starts Ursula.

"Be patient. The battle is miles away. It would be suspicious for the bear-shirts to return so soon." Betula looks up. It's hard to see the sun through the dense canopy; the diffused light moves slowly over the thick layer of leaves. "Not long now," she says. She reaches for the clay pot at her side, takes out the wooden stopper and hands it to us.

I reach inside and, fighting back nausea, plunge my fingers in the viscous, iron-smelling goo. In the pot is the congealed blood of the bullock sacrificed before the battle. I

The Blood of the Iutes

smear it all over my face and arms. Warmed up on contact with my body, the blood soon runs down my brow and eyes. The world turns bright red.

For many of the Iutes under my and Betula's joint command, this ritual has a powerful, pious meaning; the way they treat the blood of the bullock reminds me of the Christians revering the blood of their desert God. But to me and Ursula, it is nothing more than a part of our disguise, hiding our true faces under the coating of bloody sludge.

Ursula finishes applying the morbid make-up and hands the jar over to the next Iute behind her. She scratches her shoulder, wincing.

"These bearskins stink," she says, wrinkling her nose. "Why would anyone wear them willingly?"

"We did pick them up from the floor of a tent," I remind her. "If we had time, we could hunt for them, and boil them out — though I don't know where in these woods we would find so many bears."

"Couldn't we have at least washed them?"

"Will you two shut up!" snarls Betula. I can barely see her now; hidden under the ferns, covered in blood and mud, she really looks like a bear, lying in wait for its prey. I should be worried that she, a battle-hardened veteran, is so anxious about the coming fight. But I have faced death too many times in these past few months and am too weary to feel anything but numbness. I wish this whole thing was over soon, so that we can all go back home.

Perhaps what makes her so anxious is the fact that our salvation lies in the hands of a band of warriors she's not familiar with, and whom she doesn't trust. Hiding deeper in the forest, with our ponies and a relief troop formed of her Franks and the few Iutes for whom there weren't enough disguises, is Basina. A lot depends on her and her men, a lot more than I at first conceived, and I, too, am worried if they're up to the task; I know how well Basina can fight — but I don't know what sort of warriors Hildrik spared for her little adventure. After all, they are our only way back to safety — if any of us survives that long…

Several miles to our north, where the highway from Coln descends onto the river plain, the real battle should already be well on the way. A few hours ago we watched from our hideout as the Saxons departed from their camps to face Hildrik and his *fyrd* at the familiar narrowing of the road, before the Salians could spread their lines. It would be a bloody and difficult battle at the best of times. The two armies are well matched in size, considering Odowakr had to leave a substantial garrison in place to defend from a potential sally from Trever; but the Saxons have two distinct advantages: they're defending from an attack in advantageous terrain and they didn't just march a hundred miles through wooded hills. I trust Hildrik would find a way to eventually prevail over the war-weary Saxons, but it would cost him dearly if he insisted on breaking through and destroying the enemy army through sheer force of arms. A victory here might mean a sound defeat later, if he indeed decides to continue the campaign in aid of the Roman army… Or even if he resolves to return and face the pursuing River Franks. He claimed to be aware of the danger when we parted — but is that enough? Can he hold his men back from throwing themselves on the Saxon spears? And if he does — can he keep the ruse up long enough for Odowakr not to suspect that the battle is nothing more than a costly diversion?

"Can you see Haesta anywhere?" I ask Betula. She looks down; our friend the woodsman led us to this place, a secret hideout from which we can clearly observe the entire fortified enclosure surrounding the siege machines. She studies it for a while and shakes her head.

"Isn't this good news?" asks Ursula.

"I don't know," I reply. "I doubt he'd go fighting in the main battle. What's left of his mercenaries would be of little use there as our riders. Keeping him in reserve would make much more sense."

"Maybe he's guarding the crossing, like last time."

"Maybe."

"I wouldn't mind getting my hands on him," says Betula through clenched teeth, and I remember her long history with the rebel chieftain; she was there when his men killed my mother on the Isle of Wecta.

"We don't have time to fight him today," I remind her. "And we don't even have the ponies."

"I don't need a pony to kill him," she says. "But you're right. We mustn't get distracted." She looks to the sky again. "We've waited long enough. Check your weapons."

James Calbraith

I slide the sword in and out of its sheath, tighten the strap around my ankle that holds a throwing knife in place, and thrust the small axe — another element of the disguise, rather than a weapon I'm planning to use — into my belt.

Betula does the same, then she reaches for the water skin at her side. She uncorks it, gives it a sniff and, satisfied, plugs it back again.

"Are you sure you're not going to let me try it?" I ask one last time. "Even if I ordered you to?"

"Not unless things get really desperate," she replies. "Without proper training, you'd only get in everyone's way. Besides, your father would never forgive me — and that, I'm afraid, overrides any order of yours, *aetheling*."

The guard — a lean Saxon spearman with sunken cheeks and hollow eyes — moves to stop us, but one look at my grim, blood-soaked face, hidden under the hood of a bear's head, is enough to make him step away in silence. Just as I thought, the bear-shirts are as feared by their own men as by their enemies. For all the poor guard knows, the madness of the henbane and mushrooms might still be coursing in my veins and those of the men following me; one wrong move, and I could snap and tear him apart with my bare hands, just as I have, no doubt, torn apart the enemy warriors not long ago.

It makes sense for us to be the first to return from the battlefield; from what the captives told us — and from what Ursula and Audulf saw when they took part in the fighting around Trever — the bear-shirts were used by Odowakr as assault troops, breaking through the enemy's shield walls and wreaking havoc behind the lines, until, bloodied, exhausted and confused by the effects of their poisonous brew, they would be pulled back to rest, replaced with regulars pouring through the gaps they made.

The men we pass move out of our way and raise quiet cheers at our sight. There's no point asking us how the battle is going; that "we" still live means Odowakr's army is still fighting strong, but as the first line of attack we wouldn't know anything beyond our own role in the greater strategy.

We reach the siege engine enclosure undisturbed. One of the two men at the gate is not a Saxon — he looks Hunnish. There's no fear in his almond-shaped eyes.

"What are you doing here?" he asks in a harsh accent. "This is no place for you, *adiglek*. Only engineers and the crew are allowed."

I hold back retching. The bearskins may stink badly enough from the outside, but inside the hollowed-out skull that forms the hood of the garment the stench is unbearable. "Out of my way, Easterling," I grunt. I try to push him away, but he grabs my hand. His other hand reaches for the axe at his waist.

"I don't know you, or what you —" he starts.

With an ear-piercing shriek, Betula runs past me and throws herself at the Hun. Doing her best imitation of the henbane madness, she throws him to the ground and starts clawing at his face with her one hand. I draw my small axe and point it at the other guard, while two of Betula's men move to "drag her" from the Hun — but not before she slits his throat with a hidden dagger. By the time they lift her up, it looks like she tore the man's throat with her fingernails.

"Odowakr's orders," I tell the terrified second guard. "We're to replace you all — and you're supposed to take our place in battle."

The guard stares at his companion, gurgling and thrashing at his feet, and nods.

"Go get the others," I urge him. "Make haste."

He nods again and runs off, leaving us free to enter the compound beyond the stockade. I cross the threshold of the gate and take in the view. The three machines are still firing missiles — just because there's a battle going on a few miles away, doesn't mean the siege is paused. There's a crew of ten working at each engine, a dozen guards, and a few more men serving the others with food and water. Altogether maybe some fifty men to our twenty — but only a few are true warriors.

"The ones in fur caps must be engineers," I say, pointing out the three men under heavy guard ordering the engine crews around. "Don't take them too lightly — they know how to fight. If we get them, the Saxons will never be able to rebuild the machines."

Betula nods. She barks orders at her warriors, and they scatter throughout the compound, seeking targets.

The Blood of the Iutes

"Audulf, Seawine." I turn to the men remaining with me and point to the nearest machine: the catapult shooting the great stone balls. "Have fun with this one. Ursula, and the rest, with me."

Audulf grins and reaches for the great axe on his back. We split into two groups. I lead mine to the third siege engine, launching the flaming missiles; I leave the *ballista* for last — the bolts may be a menace to Trever's soldiers, but they can't threaten the walls like the other two.

We roar and howl wildly to make ourselves appear stricken with the blood rage. The guards notice something's amiss but are not yet certain how to react to the strange behaviour of their best, if erratic, warriors — until Ursula pierces the first one with her sword. We dispatch four of them before they manage to even realise what's happening. The fifth one makes a brave stand, but he shakes so much in fear of the dreaded bear-shirts that I strike the axe out of his hand and cut him across the chest with little effort.

The crew of the machine flees before us, even though they outnumber us easily. Ursula and the others want to pursue, but I stop them:

"There's no time. They're no warriors — not worth blunting the blade."

I cut through the ropes on the machine. The spoke flies one last time; its load lands harmlessly in the river. I grab the next prepared missile, a heavy basket of burning matter, and drag it onto the engine's frame, covering it in flaming pitch and oil. I pick up a barrel of pitch and pour it onto the flames.

The machine takes a moment to catch ablaze, even as Ursula and I throw more fuel, until suddenly one of the narrow crossbeams snaps, cracks open and showers me and everything around me in sparks.

I take no notice of the heat, just throw off the bearskin, now covered in burning embers, and continue to pour oil and pitch on the machine until all containers around me are empty. A couple of Iutes come at the engine with axes, hacking away where the fires let them, while Ursula and I turn to face the approaching guards.

There aren't any; while I struggled to destroy the machine, Betula and the *Hiréd* have killed most of the warriors and put the rest to flight. The surprise is total, and the slaughter in the enclosure is nearly complete. Audulf and Seawine stand by the remains of the first machine — using the knowledge we gained from studying the plans of the machines, they knew just which beams and ropes to cut through to render the flying arm silent forever. I notice the third machine, the *ballista*, is aimed straight at them, with the bolt still in its bed — but the brave crew who tried to make their last stand around the machine is no more, and the *ballista*'s ropes hang limp and impotent.

At the far end of the enclosure, the *Hiréd* are fighting their way through the last of the guards, to get at the three engineers cowering behind a sparse wall of shields. The Saxons are trapped in the corner of the stockade, but refuse to surrender, still hoping to be rescued. Their hopes are not all futile — there are at least a hundred men in the camp outside; but we've managed to deal with the enemy inside so fast they're all likely still confused about what's truly going on.

The Blood of the Iutes

The last thing anyone outside the stockade saw was twenty bear-shirts, marching inside on Odowakr's orders. Even if some of the crewmen escaped, their story must not be making much sense — and who would want to face twenty fierce, mushroom-maddened warriors in the tight space of the enclosure?

"They'll be waiting for us outside," I say to Ursula. "Go tell Audulf and Seawine to prepare for a breakout."

I take the couple of Iutes who helped us destroy the catapult and help Betula clear out the remaining guards in the corner. I glance at the *Hiréd* — a few are gravely wounded, but it looks like we haven't lost a single man in the assault.

"One of them decided to take a stand," says Betula, pointing at a body in a fur hat, lying at her feet. "The other two surrendered. What do you want with them?"

"We don't have time for prisoners," I say. We may have been quicker to subdue the enclosure than I expected, but the siege engines have been silent for almost half an hour, and by now Odowakr's men outside must have realised something's gone terribly wrong. "I fear —"

A cry, a sudden tumult and a clash of blades turn my attention back towards the gate. The wings burst open. A rider, in masked helmet, mounting a Thuringian war steed, thrusts his way through Seawine and his men, and tramples over Audulf, followed by four more horsemen, the tips of their lances already red with blood. Behind them, warriors on foot pour through the gate. I spot a few Alemann axemen in the crowd of Saxons, and other units I don't recognise.

Betula spits a globule of pink saliva, wipes her mouth and raises her sword over her head, with a weary hand.

"I'd recognise that horse anywhere," she says. "Come on, Haesta! Remember me?" she cries out a challenge. "Let's get this done once and for all!"

The Blood of the Iutes

[500]

CHAPTER XIX
THE LAY OF BASINA

I watch in stunned respect as Betula's men, without her even having to say a word, raise shields and lock them together in front of them in a perfect shield wall. Betula pushes me towards them; a shieldmaiden's hand drags me behind the wall, despite my loud protests.

"I let him kill your mother; I'm not going to let him kill you," says Betula. "Get back there and don't come out until you're the last man standing."

She hands me the henbane flask. This gesture says more than any orders; she expects us to die here.

Haesta's riders, wary of charging on the *Hiréd*'s pikes in the tight confines of the enclosure, draw a narrow turn at spear-range and ride towards Seawine's Iutes, clustered with Audulf next to the remains of the catapult. They pass the Saxon warriors, rushing at the shield wall with axes and spears. Seawine, taking cue from Betula's men, rounds his warriors up into a circle of shields, but without the *Hiréd*'s training it's only a poor imitation of a shield wall, and it gives Haesta only a moment's pause.

Audulf moves forward with his great axe. Ursula stands by him, poised behind a large Frankish shield. I can't see them well over the heads of the *Hiréd*. I feel a terror come over me — not for myself, but for my friends.

The Blood of the Iutes

"They'll get slaughtered if we don't help them!" I cry at Betula. She glances back angrily. Already, a trickle of blood runs down her brow from some stray stone or club thrown by an attacking Saxon.

"If we move to save them, *we'll* be slaughtered," she cries back, parrying a spear thrust. I can see in her bloodshot eyes that she's already drunk the henbane. In a few moments, she and all her warriors will turn into unflinching beasts, caring not for injuries and exhaustion. It will take all their training to hold the shield wall, even as the brew burns in their veins — lesser men would simply throw themselves into the brawl until either they or their enemies were all dead. The warriors grunt and heave under the Saxon onslaught, then, urged by Betula, start a shrieking war chant that freezes the blood in the veins of our foes, but still the Saxons come, launching wave after wave of attack on the unmoving wall of board and hide.

Stuck behind their backs, I have nothing to do except watch them die — and I grow furious. Despite Betula's words before the battle, she still does not see me as a warrior — rather, as a child who needs protection. I look around; there's a gap between the edge of the shield wall and the palisade where the bodies of the slain engineers and their guards are piled high enough to form a barrier for the enemy. I climb this gruesome ladder of bloody limbs and guts to the other side and rush to the aid of my Iutes.

I arrive unnoticed by either my men or the enemy — for a moment, surprise is on my side. Just as one of Haesta's riders aims his lance at Ursula's side, I leap and grab him by the waist. I try to pull him down, but he holds on to the reins;

James Calbraith

Ursula notices our struggle and, blocking a falling axe with her shield on one side, cuts the rider across the legs. He finally lets go and we both tumble into the blood-soaked mud. I reach for the long knife and stab him in the stomach before rolling aside from under the hooves of another horse.

I scramble up and look for another foe to fight. I notice one of my Iutes is lying in the dirt, bleeding but still moving; the others are being pushed into the corner of the enclosure opposite to where Betula and her *Hiréd* stand — and further away from the gate. I can't see a way out. We are outnumbered and outmatched — there must be at least fifty of Odowakr's warriors within the palisade — and though many have fallen already, many more are still pouring through the gate to replace them…

Until, there are no more. Shouts and cries of pain erupt at the gate, and as I plunge my sword in the chest of a small, squat Easterner — like all his kin, used more to shooting arrows from horseback, than fighting in a tight space — I glance in that direction, trying to see what's going on at the other side.

Just then, another small group of warriors bursts into the siege camp, screaming, shouting, yelling obscenities and waving weapons — and strikes at the side of the Saxon line. The last of the band to enter is Basina — riding her snow-white Thuringian mare, its belly now painted red with blood, and releasing arrow after arrow into the backs, chests, stomachs and heads of the enemy warriors.

It doesn't take much to turn what seemed like a victory into a rout; the Saxons, though they still outnumber us all, are already wearied by their relentless attacks on the grim shield wall. Their line wavers, then breaks; in their panic, they rush past Basina's band towards the salvation of the gate — and Basina's not stopping them, content with saving us from the immediate threat.

It is now Haesta's turn to react to the sudden change in circumstances. His men don't panic — but they are now alone in the enclosure, surrounded by enemy eager to avenge their fallen. Haesta calls retreat, and the horsemen leap, jump, gallop and push their way to the gate, through and over the Iutes, trampling everyone who dares stand in their way. Basina raises her bow one last time, but is too late, and her arrow hits a pole of the stockade a moment after Haesta vanishes out of our sight.

Basina dismounts, her cheeks bright red with excitement, her eyes wild and black. She kisses me passionately. "Now that's a battle!" she exclaims. "I must have killed a score of men getting here! Look — I'm almost out of arrows, each arrow a death!"

I wipe my mouth. The taste of her lips is mixed with the taste of blood, not all of it of the enemy's. I notice Basina's thigh and side are bleeding from what must be spear slashes, but she's shrugging the pain off as if she herself had drunk the henbane.

"We're not done fighting yet," I say. I see Betula's men drop their shields, some of them sway to the ground. This is a critical moment — they're weakened and vulnerable as the henbane brew stops its magic. For a few minutes, they're the ones needing our protection. I order the Iutes to gather the wounded and form a wedge. The Saxons may have dispersed in panic at Basina's arrival, but they're still out there, and they're still in great enough numbers to stop us fleeing, if they can gather their wits in time.

One last time, I raise my sword. It feels heavy in my numb hand. Audulf and Ursula stand beside me, both covered in blood. A great open gash runs along Audulf's left arm and side; Ursula is limping; she threw away the shield and holds her *spatha* tight with both hands. They're too weary to speak, but the stern resolve in their eyes is loud enough.

I nod at Basina. She leads her Franks out in the vanguard; we follow after them — and bringing up the rear, Betula and her *Hiréd* shuffle along, disoriented and dizzy, leaving their battered shields behind.

We run out, tired but ready to break through whoever's waiting for us outside — only to find nobody there.

A column of riders charges towards us with their lances down. They're neither Haesta's nor Odowakr's men — these are Romans, *equites*, wearing Arbogast's colours on their red capes. Basina raises her bow. I run past her, and stand before the approaching soldiers, waving my arms desperately.

"*Cessate!*" I cry in Latin. This makes the riders slow down to a trot, but they do not stop. I remember my satchel, still at my side; I pull the letter with the Imperial seal from it and raise it in the air. This finally makes them halt.

The Blood of the Iutes

"Who are you? Why do you have that seal?" the *Decurion* of the Roman riders asks.

"We came with the Frankish army to your aid. I know your *Dux*, Arbogast — he gave me this letter of passage." I spit the words out quickly before the officer loses his patience.

The *Decurion* looks around the enclosure and notices the damaged siege weapons and the piles of Odowakr's dead.

"Are you the ones who did this?" he asks.

"We are — and I gather you're the ones who cleared our way out?"

"We had no idea there was anyone here. We saw Odowakr march off somewhere with most of his army, so we sallied forth to try to destroy that battering ram on the bridge while there was still a chance," the officer replies. "Then the siege engines stopped, so we came here to investigate... I know you," the Roman says, noticing Ursula and Audulf. "You rode patrols with my men."

"We have, *Decurion*," replies Ursula. "We thank you for your help."

One of the Romans whispers something in the *Decurion*'s ear. The officer grimaces, annoyed.

"The Saxons are scattered, but not beaten yet — they're gathering to strike back," the *Decurion* says. "We have to go. I suggest you do the same. I'd offer to take you to the city, but I can't guarantee your safety on the way back."

"We'll be fine," I say. "Let your *Dux* know his city is safe — and if you see Legate Aegidius, tell him Octa fulfilled his part of the deal."

"*Octa*. I'll try to remember." The officer salutes me, then waves at his men to turn back. A small crowd of Odowakr's men gathers on the road, still wary of our combined force, but looking ready to strike as soon as the Romans depart. I can't see Haesta or his mercenaries anywhere — he must have realised that without the machines, the campaign is over and there's no more reason for him to stay with the Saxon army.

The *equites* turn around in a neat wedge formation and launch into a gallop back to Trever. The Saxons pull back to let them through — none are willing to face a Gaulish war horse in full charge.

"This is our chance," I tell Basina. "Now, run for the hills!"

The cold Mosella wine tastes sweeter and runs thicker than mead. I gulp an entire mug before Ursula manages to tear it out of my hand.

"Careful!" she says, laughing. "It's a precious bottle."

"I drank it before, you know," I say, wounded.

The Blood of the Iutes

"Not this one," says *Dux* Arbogast. "It's the last flask of the winter wine. I bet you've never tasted anything like it — and you probably never will."

"Winter wine?"

We are gathered in the dining room of his palace — just me, Ursula, the *Dux* and Rav Asher. A few rooms away, Audulf, and two more of my Iutes recuperate from their wounds; in the yard, Betula trains the *Hiréd*, not letting them rest even for the day of celebration. Outside, the city is almost empty; the people of Trever were cooped up inside the stone walls for too long, and now they have all left to wander the fields and forest, to stroll the shores of the river, to check what's left of their *villas* and farms, to breathe in fresh air, to swim in the cold waters of Mosella.

"From grapes cut by frost. Makes them sweeter than honey. Few remember how to make it — and fewer still knew how to keep such vines..." He sighs and looks at the dusty bottle in his hand. "And now, the barbarians trampled the last of the winter vineyards. Another wonder lost to the world forever."

"At least your city survived," I say.

"This time." He nods.

"But that's it, then, isn't it?" I ask. "The war is over."

"For now," Arbogast says. "Odowakr doesn't strike me as someone who gives up this easily. He's young, he still has most of his men with him — and most of our gold. It's only time that he ran out of."

"Gold?"

"We may have won the battle, but I still had to pay him off to make sure he doesn't return as soon as I march off to Maiorianus's help. We bought ourselves a year's respite. He will try again." He throws back his head and laughs. "Though next time, he might go straight for Rome instead, like the Goths and the Vandals before him. Gaul has become too complicated. Too many tribes, too many kings — too many Imperators! — to keep track of. *And* the weather in Italia is nicer!" He pours me the rest of the wine. "Drink up, hero. You deserve it. You saved us all."

"I didn't do anything," I protest. "It was Hildrik who led his army to your aid — and Betula and her *Hiréd* who destroyed the machines…"

He waves his hand. "Nonsense. I've heard the stories. I know how much the city owes you. Name your prize. My treasury is yours — what's left of it."

I shake my head and fall back into the chair.

"I don't need your gold," I say. "Give it to my men instead. I was promised a different reward."

"Of course," says Rav Asher, stroking his beard. "My books. Come to my house tomorrow. I will have everything ready. Is there anything particular that interests you?"

The Blood of the Iutes

"Anything you may have on the art of war," I say. "Especially, how to build those infernal machines."

Rav Asher and Arbogast look at each other nervously. I laugh.

"Don't worry — it's a long way to Britannia," I tell them. "You'd never see these engines here. My father could use a couple in his fight against the Saxons — our common enemy."

"Very well — a promise is a promise," says Rav Asher. "I'll see what I can find. Though I thought, as the heir to a young kingdom, you'd have been more interested in the writings on governance and statesmanship. I have a collection of Cicero's letters unparalleled north of the Alps…"

"Men —" scoffs Ursula. "Is war and politics all you can talk and read about? It's not the art of *war* that you need to learn about, Octa," she adds with an impish grin. My ears burn.

"What — what are you talking about?"

"You may have impressed Basina in the battlefield… But not where it really mattered." She stares at her fingers in feigned disinterest. "Women talk about these things, you know."

Rav Asher bursts in a fit of coughing, disguising laughter. "I'm — I'm sure Esther can find something among my books that will help you with that, as well."

Everyone laughs — except me. I sulk into embarrassment, and into memories of the last night with Basina.

She's gone now, taking her Hunnic bow and her strong white thighs with her. She's returning to Tornac, to recuperate from her wounds — the injuries proved so severe she had to be carried on a wagon, to her great annoyance — while Hildrik's *fyrd*, Falco's soldiers, and most of Arbogast's surviving garrison went south. The Imperial Legate, Aegidius, is with them, too, leading them towards Lugdunum, to help Imperator Maiorianus fight the Usurper. It's a long way to go, far longer even than the one we marched from Tornac, and time for campaigning is running short, so the combined armies left as soon as they were ready — and as soon as we made sure that Odowakr's men had indeed gone beyond the Rhenum.

"Tell me, *Dux*," I say, desperate to change the subject. "Would you have taken Odowakr's offer if we hadn't come?"

Everyone falls serious again. Arbogast studies the grain of the table.

"Only if it meant I would have saved the city," he says. "And, believe me, my heart would not have been in it. If I wanted to be an Imperator, I had plenty of chances to try it before the Saxons arrived."

"No need to dwell on what hasn't happened," Rav Asher says. "The Lord saw to it that we didn't have to make these difficult choices."

The Blood of the Iutes

"The war's not over yet," remarks Arbogast. "We may have to make difficult choices again, depending on what happens in Lugdunum."

Ursula leans back, lazily, and yawns. "I'll be glad to stay away from all these politics," she says quietly. "When we're finally back home."

"It's decided, then?" asks Arbogast. "You're going back to Britannia?"

I nod. "As soon as we're all healed and rested... Aelle's Saxons will be coming home, too, now that Odowakr's campaign is over — my father may need his household guard again."

"And his son, no doubt," remarks Rav Asher.

"I... don't know about that," I say. "If he had wanted me home, he'd have had Betula take me back."

"Come now, Octa," Ursula drapes her arm across the table to hold my hand. "You're returning a hero. You saved Trever — maybe even Rome itself. You have nothing left to prove."

"Lady Ursula is right," says Arbogast. "You've made your father proud — and your entire tribe. From now on, the Iutes will always be welcomed warmly in Gaul. Another toast for the hero of Trever?" He reaches under the table and takes out another grime-caked bottle.

"I thought you said that was the last one," I say.

"I lied." He grins. "But *this* one is." He opens the flask and takes a sniff. "And looks like this one's even better."

The entire length of the road from the river plain to the narrow pass is splattered with blood, scattered with hacked-off limbs, dented helmets, pieces of armour, scraps of mail and cloth, shards of broken weapons. Both sides have gathered their dead and wounded, so at least we don't have to wade through bodies, but it is still a gruesome sight.

We pass a few camps of stragglers, left by Hildrik to guard the road, bury the dead, and scavenge whatever useful items they could find on the battlefield that might be sent back to Tornac as spoils of the battle. The Franks give us friendly nods and wave as we trot past. Eventually we pass the last of them, and enter the empty, desolate, quiet stretch of the old Roman highway. It's hard to believe that just a few miles back, a couple of weeks ago, two great barbarian armies clashed in a flurry of hacked limbs and bloodied blades.

It's just the ten of us again — Ursula, Audulf and I on ponies, and the remaining Iute riders walking leisurely behind us, leading their beasts by the reins, enjoying the late summer sun. I told Betula to march back to Britannia as fast as she could, in case Aelle tries to use her absence and the return of his warriors from Trever to cause more chaos at Cantia's frontiers. She also took a wagon filled with gifts from Arbogast to King Aeric, and with books I took from Rav Asher's library. I'm not in as much of a hurry to return, and we no longer need Betula's protection; the road back should be safe from any danger, at least until Icorig.

The Blood of the Iutes

We're no more than a few miles from the walls of Icorig when I spot a handful of riders, approaching fast. Thinking they must be couriers from the fortress to Trever, I slow down and move aside to let them pass, not paying them much attention. When I realise who they are, it's too late.

Everything happens too fast for me to react. A mercenary's lance punches through Audulf's mail coat, raising him like meat on a skewer and throwing him off the pony. Two riders reach Ursula from both sides and grab her from the saddle. Two more pass me by and cut me off from Seawine's Iutes, who instinctively form into a defensive line along the road. The last one to come into view is Haesta: he raises his helmet's visor, draws his *seax* and approaches me, but is not poised for a fight.

"Safe passage!" he cries inexplicably. "Safe passage or we kill them!"

I glance to Audulf — he's alive but bleeding heavily from the new injury. A mercenary picks him up from the ground and throws him over the saddle. Behind us, Seawine is looking to me for orders, ready to strike — his men should have little trouble dispatching the two Haestingas and breaking through to help me, but I can't risk Audulf's and Ursula's safety.

"What are you talking about?" I ask, desperately trying to figure a way out of this new predicament. "Safe passage — from what?"

"Safe passage!" repeats Haesta. "Through Icorig! Those damn Franks are not letting me and my men go past the fort!"

One of the mercenaries grabs Ursula by the hair and puts a knife to her throat. She hisses and wriggles in his grasp. Audulf struggles in another rider's grip, until he, too, feels a cold blade on his neck.

"Fine," I say. "You're a coward without honour and will find no place at Wodan's table. Nobody deserves to die for your sake. You will have your safe passage, I swear it — but you'll have to take *me* instead."

"Don't be a fool, Octa!" cries Ursula, and hisses again as the knife draws a trickle of blood on her throat. "You're the *aetheling*, the future and hope of the tribe — we're just some worthless younglings!"

"You're not worthless to me," I say. "It's for the best. He's not going to hurt me — he's had plenty of chances to do so, if he wished. He knows how much I'm worth to my father."

"Works for me," says Haesta. "I see you're a more reasonable man than Aeric."

I drop my sword to the ground, dismount, and approach him with my hands raised. Haesta grabs me and forces me up onto his saddle in front of him.

Ursula and Audulf are still in their hands.

The Blood of the Iutes

"Let them go!" I cry.

"You may be reasonable, but you're naïve," says Haesta. "Three hostages are better than one!"

The guard at the Icorig gatehouse — one of Hildrik's men, left in place of Falco's soldiers who went with us to Trever — eyes us suspiciously.

"I fought you and your riders at Tolbiac," he tells Haesta. "And I have scars to show. I told you, you're not getting through this way. Come any closer, and I'll try my chance with the javelin."

"It's alright," I say, conscious of the knife point at my and Ursula's back. "They're my prisoners. I'm taking them to Tornac."

He gives me a doubtful grimace. There're only three of us against Haesta's four riders — Haesta ordered Seawine and the Iutes to stay a safe distance behind — and one of us is barely conscious, and bleeding. But the mercenaries are alone in a hostile territory, and it's just about possible they prefer being my captives, even if in this strange manner, rather than trying to make it through on their own…

At last, the gate opens. The Frankish guard is not letting us just pass through the fort — he dispatches an escort of three men to accompany us across the fort.

"How are we getting out of this?" says Ursula, quietly, as we reach the northern gate undisturbed.

"I don't know yet," I reply. "I'm thinking."

"Quiet." Haesta presses the knife deeper into my back. "One more word and the girl dies."

"Then you die, too."

"Are you willing to take that chance?"

I fall quiet. The Franks open the northern gate.

"Be careful," the guard tells me. "Hildebert's men are all over the road. Last night he overran Tolbiac."

Tolbiac! I look to Ursula. Are Betula and the *Hiréd* safe? Did Basina reach Tornac safely?

"We'll take care," I assure the guard. Haesta snaps the reins to ride through the gate; once we're on the other side, we'll be at his mercy — this is the last moment for me to think of a way for us to escape. But I can't think of anything. I glance around at the guards, at the wall, at the road, assess the distance between myself, Ursula and Audulf, twitch to test Haesta's reflexes… And my mind comes up empty.

"I always heard you were a fool and a coward, Iute!" cries a voice behind us, familiar, but coming as if from a dream. Can it really be her? She's supposed to be on a wagon heading for Tornac. I look over my shoulder. It *is* her.

The Blood of the Iutes

"You're a fool to show up here — and a coward to use captives in that manner! What kind of a warrior does that?"

Basina, swathed in bloodied cloths almost from head to toe, rides her white Thuringian mare with some effort — but has enough strength to draw her Hunnic bow and aim it at Haesta.

"What are you doing here?" I ask. I struggle to wriggle out of Haesta's grasp, but he puts the knife back to my throat, now dropping all pretence. The Frankish guards step back, raising their spears, confused.

"Shut up," he hisses.

"I was held up when the River Franks took Tolbiac," she replies. "I thought I'd ride out to see you to safety. Looks like I was right."

"And what were you planning to do?" Haesta asks mockingly. "One of you against the four of us?"

"I only need one arrow to kill you," Basina replies. "And I never miss. Not with this bow."

"She's right," I whisper to Haesta. "Let me go or we both die today."

In response, he draws the knife across my throat. Slowly. I feel the sting and the trickle of blood on my neck.

"If I can't get out of here, at least I'll take you with me."

"Go on, then, kill him," Basina goads him. "It'd be a warrior's death, unlike yours. Octa will gladly go to Tengri's Hall. You'd understand it if you were half the man he is."

"You — you fools!" Haesta exclaims, losing his patience. "All you talk about is honour and glory! Wodan's Hall! Death in battle! None of this matters! Look at Rome, it doesn't care about your honour — it lies and cheats its way through all the wars and disasters — and it survived longer than any of your tiny kingdoms ever will. In the end, only survivors win!"

"Survive this —!"

Basina releases the arrow. It flies faster than I can blink and hits Haesta on the right wrist, inches from my neck. He yelps and drops the knife. "You bitch —!" he cries. I elbow him in the stomach and tumble down from the saddle. As I hit the ground, Haesta spurs his mount to a mad dash. His men follow, taking Ursula and Audulf with them. Basina shoots again and hits one of the riders in the shoulder — he drops Audulf but keeps on riding. I scramble up just in time to see Haesta disappear up the bend.

Once again, he got away.

Basina rides up and helps me back up on the pony. "I'm sorry," she says. "If it wasn't for these damn wrappings, I'd have freed them both."

"Don't be a fool, Basina," I reply. "You saved us all. They're not going to go far — I'll catch up to them at the gates of Tolbiac. Take Audulf and go back to Seawine, tell

The Blood of the Iutes

them what happened here — you two are in no shape for a fight."

The cloths on her thigh and side are soaked through with blood. By now I'm familiar enough with battle medicine to know she needs to see the garrison's surgeon at once.

"I can still draw the bow, damn it," she replies with a weak grin. "We'll get your friend back and send that coward to the Depths of Tamag, where he belongs."

James Calbraith

Historical Note

The traditional dates of King Octa's reign place him in the beginning of the fifth century. The first historical king who follows him, Eormenric, is said to have ruled from the 540s onwards. However, the genealogies and timelines of the early kingdom of Kent are often muddled. Octa is at once a son and a father of a certain Oisc/Oeric. He's at once a son and a grandson of Hengist. Sometimes, he is Oisc's brother. Other times, he's not mentioned at all.

I chose to reconcile these differences, and my early chronology, by making Octa the son of Ash/Aeric, and giving him an heir before Eormenric, who in the chronicles is either omitted, or confused with their father and grandfather.

The years around 460 AD in Gaul are remembered for a mysterious sequence of events, the precise order and dating of which we can't be sure of. Meroweg, a semi-legendary king of the Salian Franks, dies of unknown causes, and is succeeded by his son, Childeric. Around the same time, the great city of Colonia, and the province around it, having withstood countless raids, sieges and sackings over the centuries, succumbs at last to the Ripuarians, though there's no mention of any great battle in the chronicles. And in the south of Gaul, Emperor Majorian successfully recaptures Lugdunum from the followers of his rival, Avitus, defeats Visigoths at Arelate, and places Aegidius as magister militum in Gaul — the last man to ever hold this title.

The Blood of the Iutes

I took some of the names for this story from the medieval legend of Saint Ursula of Coln and her 11,000 Virgins. Pinnosa, Ursula, Odilia are all mentioned in various versions of the confused legend of how the virgins saved the city from the barbarian invaders, as is, most curiously, a certain "Saint Octa".

TO BE CONTINUED IN THE SONG OF OCTA, BOOK TWO: THE WRATH OF THE IUTES

Printed in Great Britain
by Amazon